THE
M

SPUYTEN DUYVIL
NEW YORK CITY

with thanks to J-YM for his inspiration, his dedication to this story, and his research help; to Capt. David Durham (USMC Ret.), for his many informative and pleasurable consultations.

ISBN 978-1-941550-62-5

Library of Congress Cataloging-in-Publication Data

Nakell, Martin.
The lord of silence / Martin Nakell.
pages ; cm
ISBN 978-1-941550-62-5
I. Title.
PS3564.A5314L67 2016
813'.54--dc23
2015029814

for SUZANNE GOODMAN

for inspections. How they should be more organized. If his team found any problems, there might not be enough time to fix them before the delegation's arrival, and then they'd have to cancel the delegation's visit, and somebody high up somewhere wouldn't like that. But he did his job, and his team was good. The woman (he said) was the actual Chief Nuclear Inspector. She would sign off on everything. He himself was a bureaucrat, a manager from the Bureau of Internal Affairs, assigned to organize these operations. He had no knowledge of nuclear matters. He asked the guard if it made him nervous to work in a nuclear facility. The guard told him it didn't. He trusted the government wouldn't do anything dangerous.

He asked the guard if he knew anything about what they actually did here, just out of curiosity. No, the guard said, he just did his job, he just monitored the security of the compound from his bank of video monitors. At exactly 2245 by the clock on the wall an electronic bell rang. The guard picked up the phone, dialed a number, and said "Station 1 reporting in. 2245. All is well." Then he hung it up.

"Do you call like that on a regular schedule?" the man asked. "Sorry, am I being too nosy? I'm just naturally a curious type."

"Curiosity killed the cat."

"That's what they say. But it also saved another cat."

"Which one was that?"

"The cat who looked around the corner and saw the coyote searching for prey."

"That's pretty good," the guard said. "The cat who looked around the corner. I like it."

"So that's it? You call every fifteen minutes?"

"Are you the coyote, searching for prey, then?"

"Right. You're a clever guy. I'm the coyote hunting for prey."

"You inspectors, you're not all bad. At least you've got a sense of humor. Yeah, we call in every fifteen minutes."

The man took out a tin of mints, opened it, and offered one to the guard, who took it. Then the man took a mint for himself which had not come from the tin, but which he had pulled out of his pocket along with the tin. The guard began to suck on the mint. Within one minute he had slumped over on the desk. Had he not taken the mint, they would have had to kill him. The man was relieved. Things would be bad enough without killing one of their officials.

The man leaned over the desk. All the video monitors froze. In the bottom right corner of the screen each monitor recorded the frozen time: 2247.

At 2256 the three men and the woman re-appeared in the lobby.

"Done?" the man asked.

"Done," the woman said. "Let's go."

They drove out the front gate the same way they

had driven in, the Citroën first, then the van.

Down the road a quarter mile both vehicles pulled a short way up a small farm road. A green van pulled up. The driver of the Citroën got out and took the two French flags down and put them in the trunk. One of the men in the white van removed the NUCLEAR HAZARD magnetic panels from the truck's sides and put them in the Citroën's trunk. They all took off their hazardous materials outfits and put them in the trunk as well.

The man in the Citroën made a call on the mobile phone. "Phase One is a goner," he said. He turned off the phone and put it in the trash bag at his feet. He took it with him as he got out.

They all got into the green van.

"We better get going," the woman said.

"No," the man said, "we're all right here. It's ok. I've got to see this with my own eyes. This has been a long time coming."

The woman smiled at him.

"Yes," she said, "I'd love to see it too. We have no choice here but to pull it off."

The driver of the green van turned around in the front seat. "Smooth as silk?" he said.

"So far, as silk," the woman said. "Let's pray for our boys."

"Thank God," the driver said, then he turned out the headlights. The man and the woman got out, along with one of the men in the white van. They stood in the road in the moonless night.

At 23:02 exactly, the four men in dark black skin-tight slicks, with blackened faces, with heads covered with black skin-caps, who had waited motionless at the wire for exactly 94 seconds, began to cut. They carried with them only the wire cutters, plastic explosives in small pouches attached to belts, and one pistol each. The explosives pouches lay in the small of each man's back. Only the Leader wore a watch. Because they were communications silent they could receive no indication of whether Phase One had gone off. They had to assume it, which meant gambling that cutting the wires now would not set off sirens or electronic signals, that all that had been disarmed.

Ahead of them sat three large, shed-like, corrugated metal buildings, A, B, and C. They had to cross open space, then bypass buildings B and C to arrive at the building housing the nuclear reactor core itself, Building A, where two guards stood, 24/7, at the entrance. The only light came from a bulb hung over the door of Building A. If Phase One had not disarmed the barbed wire perimeter, cutting the wires would not only set off sirens, it would trigger 40 floodlights.

Having cut the wires, and without hesitation, the four men, snaking in through the opening, entered the quiet, dark compound from its northeastern border. The Leader set off on his belly across the 40 meters of grassy land between himself and Building C. Number 2 man followed him, Number 3 behind Number 2, Number 4 behind Number 3, crawling across the landscape like one long creature. They were head to toe. Each man ignored the dirt kicked in his face by the man ahead of him. They moved at a pace so practiced that none of them had to question or adjust it. The Leader alone guided the direction, although each one felt its familiar course. They knew what 40 meters felt like. They knew how long it would take.

No lights searched for them. No sirens. No dogs. No sound but the huff of each one's own breath, the breath of the others, and the slight noise of dirt dug up and slugged off.

They came against the northern wall of Building C, squatting down one after the other. They each checked each other. The group was intact and whole. The Leader, at the far end of the group, edged his way along the 12-meter wall, followed closely by each man in turn. At the further edge of Building C, they each hit the ground again, for a 4.5-meter crawl to the target, Building A. Once behind the northern wall of Building A they sat waiting out the one minute flex time, keeping their breathing low and smooth. After sixty seconds the two men of Team A walked the length of that wall to its edge. The Team A men stopped for 5 seconds at the far edge of the wall, then each team set out crawling along the east and west walls of Building A, toward its front entrance. They moved at a pace so well trained that all four men reached the edge of the front wall of Building A at the same moment. The front man in each Team dug a handful of earth, flinging it forward but slightly outward. The two clods of earth hit the ground almost simultaneously.

The two French guards at the entrance to Building A looked out into the night, looked at each other, shrugged. But when they heard the same sounds again, they took up their assault rifles to prowl out in opposite directions. Now in the darkness, as they passed the edge of Building A, a man attacked each guard from behind. Each guard found his neck in an arm-grip so tight he couldn't twist his head, had his wind cut off. Each guard took a punch to the solar plexus, lost consciousness, then lay on the ground. Before the Teams wrapped tape around each guard's mouth, they force-fed each one a small green pill, massaging their necks until the pill went down. They bound each guard's hands with plastic handcuffs, each guard's feet with plastic foot cuffs. They carried the unconscious guards to either side of the building and left them where their bodies wouldn't be noticed.

At the front door to Building A, the two Teams again became one, checking each other for any irregularities, while one man worked away at the Schlage model B800/UL437 lock, then opened it. All four men entered the building, closed the door behind them, split off in individual directions throughout the building.

Over the next 4 minutes and 26 seconds they planted 12 plastic explosives, 8 on the body of the nuclear core reactor. No matter what happened to them, Building A and the nuclear core reactor it contained, were history.

Leaving Building A, the same man who had opened the lock closed it. Splitting into two Teams again, each Team carried one of the still unconscious French guards along the back corridor of buildings to the shelter of the far side of Building D. Following the Leader, they then set out to return along the path they had come. They had no trouble crossing along the rear of Building A, no trouble crawling to Building C, no trouble crossing the rear of Building C. They followed their own trench again the 40 meters to the perimeter fence, crawled through the cut wires, left the wire cutters where they lay. The Leader checked his watch. 2351. They mounted the 4 dirt bikes which had brought them from the highway, rode back to the highway, dropped the bikes, jumped into the back of the covered truck which had just pulled up, and, as the truck pulled away, changed into street clothes.

They dumped their "blacks" into a plastic bag. The Leader took a mobile phone which had been in the truck, dialed a number, then said, "Phase Two is a goner." He threw the phone into the plastic bag. As the truck came to a stop, one of the men took the plastic bag, opened the back door, and handed it out to a man who waited for him. The truck took off again toward a countryside safe house. Tomorrow they would go back to Paris.

By the side of the road a quarter-mile from the nuclear warehouse compound, the man from the black Citroën checked his watch. 2409.

"Yes," he said to the woman and man standing with him. "Yes. I believe we can. Because we must, we can."

An explosion rocked the landscape. A red glow lit up the black sky. Farmers and villagers awakened. Farm animals, dogs, deer and boar bayed and howled. Light exploded inside every house. Some thought it was a bombing, even a nuclear bombing. Some old soldiers from the war had flashbacks. Sirens alarmed. Searchlights came on. Guard dogs in their pens yelped. Soldiers in the compound ran toward the explosion. Two fire trucks and an ambulance roared out of the compound's own fire department, while fire trucks from the next town, Seine-Sur-Mer, sped toward the explosion.

On the side road a quarter mile away, Col. Yossi Ben Luria screamed in the covering din of the explosion. "Yes!" he yelled to the red sky. He hugged the woman, Hannah Ben-Eliyahu, embraced Itzhak. The others got into the green van. Col. Ben Luria, standing alone in the lighted darkness, closed his eyes in thanks to the night itself, to all the powers that be. If only his four boys were all right. As his emotions overwhelmed him, he jumped into the van. The van pulled away, leaving behind the black Citroën and the white van. A local fire truck passed them, its red lights flashing, the seesaw wail of its siren blaring. The green van headed toward the same countryside safe house to meet up with their comrades.

Somewhere in the vicinity someone dialed a telephone number, said, "Phase Three is a goner," then hung up.

ONE

Col. Yossi Ben Luria drove from Jerusalem to Tel Aviv, made a stop in Tel Aviv, then drove home to Safed. On the passenger seat next to him three major international newspapers ran headlines of the Israeli attack in France. The *Times* of London called it an international crime deserving of U.N. sanctions. *Building that nuclear reactor core for the Iraqis was a French crime. When we had to do it, we did it without one loss of life - Israeli or French. We're not the criminals here.*

Ben Luria always felt grounded to whatever landscape he was in, the space around him becoming the space of his thought. The car in fourth gear, the driver's window rolled down, his arm on the windowsill, Ben Luria cruised homeward. The sea was beside him to the west, the land to the east.

At the Security Cabinet meeting that afternoon in Jerusalem, Ben Luria had stood behind Prime Minister Begin. As Aide-to-the-Prime Minister, Ben Luria never spoke at these meetings. But this afternoon, when Arie Solen, Managing Director of Mossad, had heaped praise on Ben Luria for the execution of *Operation Night Plastique,* Ben Luria had responded: "A red sky on a black night, sir. That was our reward. We saw the whole thing go up in flames."

But this morning the French have already voted $14 million to rebuild the reactor core for the Iraqis. Ben Luria turned off the radio. *The newspapers are wrong. We didn't violate the territory of the great and sovereign nation of France. We saved them from themselves. We saved them from Saddam Hussein.*

Yaakov Vulf was right this afternoon at the meeting. Ben Luria drove on. *He's the smartest of the bunch. Saddam would use that nuclear bomb against us. Thousands would fill the streets of the Arab world raising high Saddam's picture, screaming his glory, Saddam firing off that pistol of his from the balcony of his palace. And the world would have a nuclear madman on the loose. We saved the French, we saved ourselves, we even saved the Arab world. We bought ourselves some time. Now what? Roll into Iraq? Tanks? Troop carriers? Air drops? It's suicide. Doing nothing is suicide.*

Ben Luria calmed his racing thoughts. Prime Minister Begin's parting words to the Security Cabinet came back to him. "Think of every option, military, diplomatic, the expected and the unexpected," Begin had said. "Calm will be the mother of our genius."

Prime Minister Begin pushed back his chair, stood, and left. The American satellite photographs of Osiraq still lay at his place on the table.

What more could one ask for but just driving alone like this at night between Tel Aviv and home. Like the Americans, Ben Luria remembered from his

14

time in the States, driving along the coast of California, around Oceanside or San Clemente, where the road tracks right along the edge of the Pacific ocean. Where Ben Luria had done training years ago with the American Marines. *We'll never have that kind of security the Americans have. We'll never relax that much. This is good, smelling the sea, but always ready for a shelling from the north, a suicide bomber slipping the border near here, some Palestinian secret boat floating toward shore filled with the armaments to destroy us. This is fate. You meet your fate. You just meet it. This isn't California. This is the road from Tel Aviv. The wind in my face off the sea, and to the other side, Jewish villages, Arab villages. And out there on the plains, the Bedouin in their tents with their sheep roaming, with their satelite TVs hooked up. And the kibbutzim and the farms and the factories. This darkened silence. My country is a miracle. I'm no more than five miles from my enemy. Up ahead I'll be just three miles from the enemy. Then I'll be home.*

Ben Luria's wife, Tamar, was awake, waiting. They embraced, held each other, Tamar resting her head in Ben Luria's shoulder. They smiled with one another.

In the kitchen, Yossi stood at the stove, waiting for the tea-water to come to a boil. Behind him, Tamar sat at the kitchen table. When the water boiled, Yossi turned off the flame. Turning to Tamar, he asked her: "Tea?"

"No, sweetheart. You go ahead."

Yossi took one cup from the cupboard, put a tea-bag into it, then poured hot water into the cup. Swirling the tea-bag with a spoon, he stood at the end of the table.

"You're all right?" Tamar asked, looking him over. "No bruises, no broken bones, no concussion?"

"Completely fine."

Yossi pulled out the chair opposite Tamar, sat down, took out the tea-bag, placing it on a napkin, then blew lightly on his tea before sipping it.

"Have you been worried?"

"Of course."

"Are you relieved now?

"More than you know."

"I do know."

Yossi put his hand, plam flat down, on the table in a familiar gesture. Tamar lay her hand on top of his.

"And Samia?" Tamar asked.

"Samia?"

"Oh, Yossi! Samia Halevy." She patted the back of Yossi's hand.

Yossi laughed. "What makes you think Samia Halevy was with me?"

Tamar laughed in return. "It's ok. It's not for that. I don't care."

"Don't be crazy. I'm not in love with Samia Halevy. I never was."

"I don't care. I just want to know how she is."

"You think she's still in love with me. I know that."

Tamar smiled at him. She tapped the back of his hand, then took her hand back.

"Samia's brother called me yesterday, Yossi. Is she ok?"

"How do you even know I was on Mission? Maybe I had meetings in Jerusalem."

"Right," Tamar said. "Secret meetings in Jerusalm all day and all night for ten days – locked in your room with no phone.

"Strange he should call here. I haven't seen Samia in a long time. Six, seven years."

Tamar leaned over the table, Yossi did the same, and they kissed. They sat back.

"I told him nothing," Tamar reassured him. "Don't tell me. You know I don't want you to tell me. I'll read it tomorrow in the papers. Then I'll get really scared."

"Just for you, not for her brother, Samia wasn't with us."

"I'm not worried."

"I know."

"Is everyone ok?"

"Yes. Everyone is ok." Yossi took a few sips of tea, put the cup on the table. "Everyone is ok."

Reaching across the table, Tamar took Yossi's face in her hand. He placed his hand on hers.

"Are you tired?" Yossi asked.

"I'm beat," Tamar said. "I'll go up to bed. Come

soon. Finish your tea. I won't fall asleep. I'll wait for you. Promise."

"Yes, one minute," Yossi said. "A minute and a half to catch my breath."

Ben Luria dialed the Prime Minister's bedside telephone.

"It's me, sir, Yossi."

"Are you all right?"

"Yes. I got home no problem. It was a wonderful night out. Warm and soft."

"And how is Safed?"

"Quiet. It's good to be home. It's been 10 days."

--

--

"What is it, Yossi?"

"Mr. Prime Minister....."

"Yes...."

"There's going to be a way. There has to be. Something. Something crazy even."

"God willing we'll find it, Yossi."

"Mr. Prime Minister....."

"Yes, Yossi...?"

"Our country is a miracle, Mr. Prime Minister. You can't annihilate a miracle."

"A complicated, complex, difficult miracle."

"Aren't all miracles complicated, complex, difficult?"

"Of course, Yossi. But I'm supposed to be the wise one."

"No argument."

"Then here's my wisdom of the moment; We'll survive again."

"Good night. I'm sorry to have disturbed you."

"You haven't disturbed me, Yossi. As always, you've inspired me. I see your face in my mind and I have even more confidence. Have a good rest. I'll need you."

"Of course. Good night."

"Good night, Yossi. *Laila tov*. You know, I love you like a son."

"Thank you. Good night."

"Give my love to Tamar. To the children. Stay with them for a couple of days. I'll see you on Sunday."

Ben Luria hung up the phone. He stood in the kitchen, the only lighted room in the house.

"*Mr. Prime Minister,*" he said, continuing aloud by himself and to himself the conversation with the Primie Minister, "*if I go to sleep I am abandoning us all. I have to stay awake. To keep watch.*"

He smiled to himself, then continued, still speaking aloud.

"*But, on the other hand, if I don't go to sleep I'll just be tired and useless. So it's off to bed with you, Col. Yossi Ben Luria. Admit to yourself that you're worried beyond belief and take your anxiety to bed with you and get some sleep.*"

Ben Luria sat down with paper and a pencil at the kitchen table. He drew a crude map of the Middle East. To attack Osiraq. A ground invasion? Never. Naval shelling? No way. To attack it from the air the Israelis would have to fly 2000 kilometers through enemy air space. How? They'd need fast-moving, long-range, low-delivery fighter planes with heavy bomb capacity. Those are mutually exclusive capabilites. No such thing exists.

Ben Luria drew a line on his map starting from *Etzion Air Force Base* in the Sinai desert, Israel's largest. The line turned south, then east northeast, then east, and on to a point just south of Baghdad: Osiraq, the nuclear power plant at Al Tuwaitha. There, Ben Luria drew a jumble of short lines: an explosion. Then he drew a line from there back to *Etzion Air Force Base*.

"And home," Ben Luria said. "And impossible."

Ben Luria made another phone call, this one to his friend Maj. Ilan Hamal, Israeli Air Force.

Hamal grabbed the phone on the first ring.

"What's up?"

"Did I wake you, Ilan?"

Hearing Ben Luria's voice with no urgency in it, Hamal relaxed. "Yes, Yossi. You woke me. What do you think? It's the middle of the night. You also woke up Rachel, and now Rebecca's crying."

Hamal's wife, Rachel, went to take care of their daughter, Rebecca.

"Can you drive here tomorrow, Ilan, to Safed?" Ben Luria asked.

"Tomorrow? You mean today. It's 2 a.m. Yossi."

"All right. Today. I need you, Ilan. Come up in the morning."

"It's important?"

"Yes, Ilan. It's important. When will you come?"

"By 1100. I have something for you anyway."

"1100." Without any of their usual chit-chat, Ben Luria hung up. He scotch-taped the map he had drawn to the kitchen wall. He sat, staring at it. He stood up, went closer to the map.

Those squiggly lines, he stared at the map, *at Osiraq....it could be us, not them. Some Iraqi General right now must have a map where those squiggly lines of complete devastation, destruction, annihilation are us, not them. Get to them before they get to us, Yossi,"* he told himself.

He turned off the light, went to bed.

TWO

Maj. Ilan Hamal put his briefcase on the patio table, opened it, took out a 1:100 model of an airplane, held it up, airborne.

"This," he said, "is an F-16. The fastest fighter plane ever made. The sleekest." He put it on the table in front of Ben Luria. "Have you ever seen anything like it?"

"Small," Ben Luria said.

"And quick," Hamal snapped his fingers once. "You can't believe what it can do."

"What's the range?"

"It has whatever we need."

"You have no idea what we need, Ilan. We need range and speed and weight-bearing capacity."

"How far? How fast? How heavy?"

"Do you know about Osiraq, the Iraqi nuclear plant at Al Tuwaitha? Just south of Baghdad. Thirteen kilometers southeast, give or take."

"I know about it," Hamal said. "I know we hit the reactor core in France. I know the French are working on it with the Iraqis. That's all I know. What I read in the papers."

"I want to annihilate Osiraq from the air," Ben Luria said. "Fire, smoke, and ashes."

Hamal got up from the table, walked to the back of
Ben Luria's garden, took a lemon where it had fallen
beneath the lemon tree, inhaled to take in its acrid
summer aroma, tossed it from one hand to the other.

"So this morning you come to me with news of the
F-16. Is it coincidence, Ilan? Hell of a coincidence."

"Slow down," Hamal said. "You're not hitting Osiraq with an F-16."

"No way?" Ben Luria asked.

Hamal tossed the lemon to the ground, came back
to the patio table, sat facing Ben Luria.

"First of all, Yossi, we don't have any F-16s. I
brought you this model because the Americans just
formally cancelled the sale of six of these babies to
Iran. They've been sitting at Midnight Air Force Base
in the Utah desert for a year. Mossad found out about
it first. Arie Solen got the intelligence on them to Gen.
Dror, Gen. Dror came to me. We want them for defense, Yossie, but I want them for dogfights and airspace, dominance of the northern and southern borders."

"No more '73?"

"Air dominance so tight we're impenetrable and we
can go where we need to go. I want your help in con-
vincing the Security Cabinet to buy these planes."

"The Security Cabinet!" Ben Luria laughed. "Ilan,
what do you think I am? Who do you think I am?"

"You're Aide-to-the-Prime Minister. You whisper in
everyone's ear."

Ben Luria pulled out from his shirt pocket the crude map of the Middle East he had drawn the night before. Putting it down on the table between himself and his longtime friend, Ilan Hamal, he straightened it out with the edge of his hand.

"This is my dream," he said. "You're one of my oldest friends, Ilan."

Hamal stared at the map. He pointed a finger to the jangle of scribbled-up lines.

"This is Osiraq?" Hamal asked.

"Yes."

"This is no dream, Yossi. This is fantasy."

"You know what Rafi Stone said at the Security Cabinet meeting yesterday? He was screaming, 'This is Armaggedon!'"

"Rafi Stone is crazy," Hamal said. "He's a crazy, half-Jewish, half-Christian, half pagan mystic."

"Yes, he's crazy," Ben Luria said, "but why do you think he was hysterical at the meeting, screaming about Armaggedon? Because we're talking a nuclear bomb in Saddam Hussein's hands. Have you read the dossiers on Hussein?"

"I don't need dossiers to know what this means, Yossi."

"The F-16?"

"Neither the F-16 nor any other plane we have nor any other plane on earth could accomplish this mission. Bombers could never fly that far that fast undetected over enemy territory..."

"But..."

"Listen to me. Fighter planes could never carry the bomb load. A fighter plane has limits. A bomber has limits. You can't do this with bombers, and there's no way you could do it with a fighter plane, an F-16, an A-4, a MiG, a Mirage, anything. Get yourself another fantasy, Yossi. Naval bombardments. Ground troops. Mossad inside with explosives. Anything."

Ben Luria sat silently for a moment. Then he got up, walked slowly into the house, came back with two plates of huge slices of ice-cold watermelon, a knife and a fork for each. He put the plates on the table. He cut a piece from his own slice, savored the taste and the juice of it, spit out the seeds onto his plate.

Two Israeli jets thurdered the air above them, headed northward. Ben Luria and Hamal watched them for the several seconds they were visible.

"I will help you in whatever way I can to get the F-16s. I don't think it will be all that hard. It will be incredibly expensive. We can get credits. Somehow we can do it. Does the Prime Minister know about these planes?"

"Not yet. Gen. Dror asked me to talk to you first."

"Get me the specs."

Hamal opened the briefcase, took out a booklet of specifications on the F-16, handed it over to Ben Luria. Ben Luria leafed through it. He took the model plane off the table, flew it in a straight line toward

Hamal, then around in swirling formations. He landed the plane on top of Hamal's closed briefcase.

"Forget bombing Osiraq, Yossi." Hamal opened his briefcase, put the model into it, closed and locked it. "Find another way."

"It's this way or no way."

"What can Solen do?" Hamal asked. "Hasn't he got some plan? He always does."

"Blow up a nuclear power plant from inside?" Ben Luria asked. "With a few guys? Even Mossad has its limits. Its parameters, Ilan."

"Has anyone ever blown up a nuclear plant before?"

"Not yet."

"Right, it's a dangerous business. You'd ignite a nuclear explosion. I don't know anything about these things."

"Neither do I," Ben Luria said. "We have some very hard work to do. Do you know any nuclear scientists?"

"No," Hamal laughed. "Not personally. Not an uncle or a cousin or a schoolmate. Do you?"

"I imagine I will soon."

Ilan Hamal drove back to Jerusalem in the heat of the afternoon after a long swim in the pool at the YMHA. He kept the air conditioning on, listening to tapes of Dave Brubeck, Miles Davis, Thelonious Monk, Glen Gould playing Bach variations. The music carried his mood up and down, but his thoughts didn't stray from his talk with Ben Luria. He had gotten Ben Luria's help on buying the F-16s, but Ben Luria had bitten him with the Osiraq bug that now plagued him.

When he got home, he went upstairs to the attic where he kept his music room. He took up his tenor sax and played the first full jazz song he'd ever learned: "A-train." He played it through with his own improvisations for about half an hour. Uplifted, lightened in spirit, he drove in to his office.

THREE

A gentleman in a dark blue suit, a white shirt, a blue and gold tie met Ms. Samia Sa'ad at Gate 6 of Saddam Airport, where her flight on Iraqi Air deplaned. That flight had come from London, where Ms. Sa'ad changed planes after her flight from New York. Searching the deplaning passengers' faces, the gentleman recognized Ms. Sa'ad at once. As it happened, Ms. Sa'ad also wore a dark blue skirt, a white blouse, and a black, gold-edged scarf with which she had covered her head.

As Ms. Sa'ad walked past him, the man quietly called her.

"Ms. Samia Sa'ad?"

"Yes?" she turned.

"May I help you? I am Hikmat Sidqui. I'll take care of you."

"Thank you."

Sidqui called for his driver, who took the small bag of personal items Samia carried with her. She kept the thin, hard-shelled briefcase that she carried in her right hand.

"You have a beautiful scarf," Sidqui felt the gold and black material between his thumb and forefinger, as they walked the long wide airport hallways toward the baggage claim. "But bringing silk to Baghdad is like carrying coals to Newcastle."

Samia smiled. She fingered the scarf.

"Actually it's Italian," she said. "Am I unpatriotic wearing it here?"

Sidqui laughed.

"No, of course not," he said, "patriotism is deeper than a foreign silk garment in a country with the finest silks. Tell me about Rome."

"I've never been there," she said, "but my mother was there in '76. As a tourist."

"Your father, Mr. Khalid Sa'ad, he didn't go with her?"

"Unfortunately not. He couldn't get away."

"So your mother traveled alone, Ms. Sa'ad? That's unusual."

"Certainly not. She traveled with an aunt who also lives in New York."

Sidqui's driver gave Ms. Sa'ad's hand luggage to the porter who also took her suitcases from the baggage claim. The driver hurried outside to get the waiting Mercedes Benz loaded with the luggage and ready to go by the time Sidqui arrived with Ms. Sa'ad. The driver opened the rear passenger door for Samia, then rushed over to open the door on the other side for Sidqui, who slid in beside Ms. Sa'ad.

"To the Al Rashid Hotel," Sidqui told the driver.

"Could we stop to have a look at the Tigris River?" Samia asked.

"You want to see the River?" Sidqui asked.

"All my life I've dreamt of it," Ms. Sa'ad said. "Since my childhood."

"But you grew up in New York. All your life you had the Hudson River."

"Yes," Samia said, "but the Tigris and Euphrates are the Mesopotamian rivers, the very origins of civilization."

"It's too bad, Ms. Sa'ad, that you haven't been to Iraq until now,. You have a passion for it."

"It is a shame," Samia said, "but I'm here now."

The car crossed on a bridge over the Tigris.

"Slow down," Sidqui said. "Give Ms. Sa'ad a chance for a good first look at the Tigris."

Using the control panel on his side of the car, Sidqui opened Samia's window.

"It looks low," Samia observed. "And it looks dark. Murky."

"President Saddam has developed more advanced methods of transportation for Iraq. We're not a nation of barges, Ms. Sa'ad," Sidqui laughed. "We're the most modern power in the Arab world – we're a power again in the world."

Sidqui clicked his tongue, and the driver continued on across the bridge.

"I'm lucky to be here. I can't believe it. So much

greatness. So much history, human progress."

"And so many catastrophes," Sidqui added. "Do you prefer English or Arabic, Ms. Sa'ad? I can switch to English if you prefer."

"Oh, no, Arabic," Samia said.

"You don't have an accent at all," Sidqui said.

"No," she said. "Thanks to my parents."

The car entered central Baghdad. Samia watched a city of golden mosques and rising minarets in the modern downtown.

The car dropped Ms. Sa'ad at the Al Rashid Hotel, where Sidqui left her in the hands of the doorman and porter. As Sidqui pulled away in the Mercedes Benz, he made a call on the car phone.

"So far," he said, "all is more or less well and in order."

Alone in her room, Samia picked up a phone message from Dr. Yahia El Meshad, the Egyptian-born scientist leading the development of the nuclear reactor at Osiraq. Meshad asked if Ms. Sa'ad might have dinner with him at the hotel restaurant, a "very fine one," he said. She dialed the number he had left to confirm. They would dine at 9:30. She would have time to unpack her things, shower, go over some drawings and figures, dress, and still be at the dining room comfortably by 9:30. Good. Business begins.

Samia opened the closet, found the small jewelry safe locked, tapped in the appropriate code. She took the pistol inside, examined it, checked the ammunition, checked the silencer, then returned it to the safe. She took out the cyanide capsule, held it between her thumb and forefinger, then returned it to the safe. Taking out the lipstick case which could fire one .32-caliber bullet, she kept it to put in the left pocket of her purse. She closed the safe, reprogrammed the combination to the month before her mother's birth date, then closed it again.

After her shower, Samia laid out some drawings on the table. They were sketches she had made of Osiraq from her knowledge of what it must look like. She hadn't seen anything official yet.

She had brought three books with her. Two of them, *Nuclear Safety* and *Structural Properties of Nuclear Construction with Tables* lay on the desk. She put a well-worn Arabic copy of *The Thousand and One Nights* on the nightstand by her bed.

At 9:30, Samia entered the dining room with its crystal chandeliers, the white linen tablecloths, the single-stem centerpiece on each table holding one white rose in a silver vase, and three portraits of Saddam Hussein. In one, he wore a military uniform and held a raised rifle in the air. In another, he wore an elegant suit. In a third, he sat surrounded by his family.

Meshad rose. The Maitre d' escorted her to his table.

"I didn't expect such a charming woman," said Meshad. Samia detected immediately the formal manner she had been told to expect from Meshad, that she had already heard in recordings of his voice.

"You're a gentleman to say so, Dr. El Meshad," Samia answered him. She took the seat the Maitre d' had pulled back for her.

"It's perhaps Egyptian courtesy," Meshad said, "which taught me to be a gentleman. But it requires someone special to evoke it."

"Thank you," Samia said. "I accept your compliment, but, given your reputation, I have to take it with a grain of salt."

"My reputation?" Meshad asked her.

"I'm afraid so," Samia smiled at him. "I'm told that you're very much of a lady's man. I can see why, Dr. El Meshad. But I've never thought of myself as someone to attract a lady's man."

"You've complemented me as well, Ms. Sa'ad. Others might not consider it a worthy complement: 'a lady's man.' But let me assure you, you're an attractive woman to any man."

"Do you miss Egypt, Dr. El Meshad?"

"One always misses one's homeland. But without leaving it one would even more miss the larger world. I hope you won't be too homesick for New York."

"But I'm excited to be here in Baghdad. This is the country of my ancestors."

"Then there's much for you to see. It won't be all work for you. That's as it should be."

The waiter brought a wine list, from which Meshad ordered a Côtes du Rhone. An assistant waiter placed bread on Samia's and Meshad's plates. The waiter brought them each a small cup of lobster bisque.

"Do you know who Al Rashid was, Ms. Sa'ad, the namesake of your hotel?"

"Oh, yes, I do," she said.

"It will be my pleasure to show you Baghdad, if you'll allow me."

"Thank you," she said, "I promised my fiancé I'd write often describing what I've seen. He'll be glad to hear I'm in capable hands."

"I should have known," Meshad said, "that you'd be spoken for. I'm pleased for you. You must tell me about him."

The dinner came in exquisite courses, with lamb at its center.

Samia kept Meshad focused on Osiraq, its design problems, its safety issues. Retrieving a notepad from her purse, Samia took notes.

For a time they talked about Harun Al Rashid, namesake of the hotel. The fifth Caliph of the Abbasid Dynasty, a poet and scholar of the 8th Century, Al Rashid is immortalized in the *Thousand and One Nights*. He liked to disguise himself to wander among his subjects in the streets of Baghdad.

They talked about Samia's years at Stanford; they talked briefly about Saddam Hussein, but Meshad said that he wasn't much interested in politics, that he was interested in science and in life itself, the good living of it, and that if Saddam Hussein wants to unite the Arab world, that would be a great thing.

They finished dinner, they finished the bottle of Côtes du Rhone. Meshad ordered another, but when Samia protested fatigue, he asked for brandy. Through the brandy they continued talking, now mostly of the sites in Baghdad that Meshad would take Samia to see, "if your fiancé would permit." Samia showed interest, but pressed him for more information about Osiraq.

She asked him how long the project would take. When would the French finish rebuilding the new re-actor core? How soon would she need to finish her work? How far along were they with construction of the actual reactor building itself?

"I understand," Meshad said, "that you're anxious to make a good impression on the Iraqis. You're a dedicated scientist. But you have to enjoy life. Let me take you on a short walk along the banks of the Tigris. Then I'll see you back to your hotel."

"Of course, Dr. El Meshad. You're right. I would love to do that."

It was a clear night, warm. Meshad's car left them off along a promenade. The night seemed full of secret memories of Baghdad, both ancient and modern. As they walked and talked of Baghdad, Samia sensed the age of Mesopotamia, the rise of western civilization, knowledge and learning, warfare, court intrigue, betrayal, citizen uprisings, conquering and being conquered, the development of Islam.

"Are there Christians now in Baghdad?" she asked.

"Yes," Meshad answered, "a few, not many. And no Jews. Well, some. But most Jews have left for Israel or America. Good riddance. They've mostly left Egypt as well."

Samia sensed the presence of Baghdad's Jews. Their Quarter. Their trade. Their torture. Their murder. Their exile. She could almost smell and see and hear the layers of history, the spice trade, the silk trade, and now the oil trade. All of this surrounded by a modern city. High-rises in the night. Her own hotel. A modern luxury apartmentbuilding.

"Coming from a Christian country, from America," Samia said, "where Muslims are the minority, it's fascinating to be in my own country, where we're the majority. It relaxes you. It excites you. I'd like to walk here everyday, by this river, to absorb my own history."

"And you have not only Christians, but many Jews in New York," Meshad said. "Even among the Jews in New York, you're a minority."

"Yes," she said, "New York has everyone. We have to contend with them all. And so, it often feels to me, it has no one."

Sipping, Samia let silence fall between them.

"When do you think the French might finish the new reactor core?" she asked.

"You shouldn't be all science and business, Ms. Sa'ad."

"No, I'm enjoying my brandy very much. As it relaxes me I seem to contemplate the things that matter most."

"Of course. You're not only a scientist, but a philosopher. You impress me, Ms. Sa'ad. I look forward to working with you."

"You put me at ease," she said.

As they turned the corner of Al-Zaariyah street, Samia pointed to a café — *The Vizier's Daughter* — where she might have coffee in the morning.

"As far as I know," Meshad said, "it's a fine place."

When the hotel doorman opened her car door, Samia gestured for Meshad to stay seated, but he got out on his side, then came around under the hotel canopy.

"I had a charming evening," Meshad said. "If your fiancé is ever foolish enough to abandon you, you have to come first of all to me."

In her room, after making a few cryptic and distilled notes, changing into her nightclothes, washing her face and brushing her teeth, Samia Halevy lay down on the bed, on top of the covers. Taking the hotel's welcome-brochure from the nightstand, she opened it, reading:

- • -

I shall erect this capital and live in it all my life. It will be the residence of my descendants; it will certainly be the most prosperous city in the world.

Abu Ja`far al-Mansur

Second Abbasid Caliphate, Founder of Baghdad, 762

Baghdad is the center of the world. According to the unanimous opinion of the astronomers exposed in the writing of the ancient sages, it is located in the fourth climate. The terrain is excellent, the water is sweet, the trees flourish, the fruit is of perfect quality, the harvests are magnificent, good things abound.

The inhabitants are of a happy disposition, their countenances are bright, and their intelligence is of an open nature. The people excel through their knowledge, their understanding, their good education, their perspicacity, their distinction, their commercial, industrial, and business sense, their ingenuousness in all controversy, their competence in all trades, and their ability in all industry.

No one is better educated than their scholars, more supple than their singers, more expert than their physicians, clearer than their logicians, more zealous than their ascetics, better jurists than their magistrates, more eloquent than their preachers, more artistic than their poets, or more voluptuous than their gay blades.

al-Ya'qubi

Arab Historian, d. 897

- • -

She laid the pamphlet back on the nightstand. Her mind could wander. Dr. El Meshad would be no problem. The man who picked her up at the airport, Hikmat Sidqui, required caution. He didn't like her. As she stood outside the hotel while Meshad said goodnight, she had noticed a blue Peugeot parked 20 meters up the street, on the opposite side. They would be the night watch. And now, Samia Halevy, Israeli Jew, spy in the country where spying first began, you are Samia Sa'ad, she told herself. I am Samia Sa'ad. Let them watch me day and night. They'll never find me out. They'll never penetrate the twists and turns of my personal story, my cover story, the story of Samia Sa'ad that I'll tell them so well they'll want to know more and more. While I'll find out everything from them no matter how long it takes no matter how much it costs me personally.

FOUR

Samia sat at a sidewalk table close to the front door of the café, *The Vizier's Daughter*. When she left the Al Rashid that morning, the Peugeot down the block rolled away. The waiter, a tall Iraqi with a Saddam Hussein mustache, came to take her order.

"A cappuccino and a croissant, please."

"A plain croissant, a cheese croissant, a date croissant, or a jam croissant?" the waiter asked her.

"Nothing else, just plain," she said.

As Samia finished her coffee, she felt under the saucer to find the hollow nail the waiter had placed on the table with her cup. She curled her hand around the nail, just like a carpenter's nail, but hollow. It seemed, for the moment, that no one was watching her. Samia got up to leave, leaned over to pick up her purse, slid the nail into a slit in the side of her shoe.

At first, Samia didn't like the waiter. He was awkward. He wouldn't look her in the eye. He had asked the proper question about the croissant in the proper order – plain, cheese, date, jam – he seemed to understand when she responded with the exact words of the code —"nothing else, just plain"— he had brought the nail out inconspicuously. Yet, his awkwardness. As though he were afraid of her. As though he might have something to hide. But, she told herself, you're in the Field now. You operate according to plan with the people you've been given until something certain reveals itself. Who knows? Maybe he's never done something this dangerous before. Or maybe he has. First impressions can't be fixed, but they shouldn't be ignored.

The Mercedes Benz stopped for her at the curb. Samia left the table.

The waiter took up the saucer, noting that the nail was gone, that she had taken it, that the system of communications was in order. The following morning, Samia would carry the nail into the café, then leave it under the saucer for the waiter to retrieve. It would be empty. Their test run would be complete. On the third morning, the waiter would again leave her an empty nail. This time she would keep it until she had some microfiche to roll up into the hollow of the nail, or a message to send. Then she would leave it under her coffee saucer, where the waiter would pick it up. The waiter would leave the nail at a drop, where, later, another agent would pick up the nail, cover the open end of it with a nail head, nail it into a small box, which would go in a diplomatic pouch from a foreign embassy to another embassy in London, and thence to Jerusalem. It would all take 36 hours.

Hikmat Sidqui's driver held the car door open for Samia. "Good morning," Hikmat Sidqui said. "I'll accompany you every day to Osiraq, and I'll accompany you every evening back to your hotel. You can dine every evening, as you like, in the hotel. If there's anything I can do for you, President Saddam Hussein himself has put me at your service."

Samia leaned back in her seat toward the car door, away from Sidqui.

At Osiraq, Meshad greeted Samia at the gate. He gave her a tour, escorted her to her office. She saw rows of offices, she saw Meshad's office, but didn't go into it. She saw the ring where the French-built reactor core, the heart of the nuclear reactor, would eventually go. She looked up. The dome above the reactor core ring hadn't been completed. The Iraqis had already made several construction mistakes which would require demolition and reconstruction. Her job was not just to acquire information, but to stall. To sabotage with an undetectable subtlety. To find fault, then to insist that the fault be corrected. Her job was to resist pressure from the government, from Saddam Hussein directly, to get this thing going, to build a nuclear bomb.

"In the future," Meshad told her, "our plant will supply power to Baghdad and the entire region. That's the Iraq Plan."

Samia didn't ask Meshad if he really believed that. He couldn't possibly believe it. He must certainly know about the plans for bomb building. Yes, the French said that the plant was for civil nuclear development.

Yes, that's what they told the International Atomic Energy Commission. That's what some politicians perhaps believed somewhere in Geneva or New York. But Meshad must certainly know better. Someday, she would get to know Meshad enough that she would ask him everything he knew, and he would tell her. They continued on their tour of the plant. All around hung portraits of Saddam Hussein, in military dress, in civilian dress, beside a monument, with a child, at the ground-breaking for Osiraq.

All the essential offices, with the computers Samia would need to break into, were up on the third floor, in a corridor away from where she'd work. She'd have no legitimate reason to be there. They'd be hard to get to unnoticed, but once she got to one computer she'd be in the neighborhood of them all. It would just take time. It would just take ingenuity, it would just take cunning.

Samia's office was on the ground floor, for her convenience, Meshad told her. Her computer was in place, the drafting table was there, her phone was working, and there was a directory of phone numbers, including his, should she need him. He would get her for lunch at about one o'clock. They'd have lunch in the cafeteria, joined by the Project Director, Heraclium Al Hira. In the meantime, Ms. Sa'ad could settle in, orient herself, get used to her office.

The telephone linked her to no one. The computer could take her outside of the Field, but to use it that way would be suicide. *I am Samia Sa'ad. More and more as each hour passes Samia Halevy recedes into the background. Even my memory becomes the memory of Samia Sa'ad, who not only remembers her cover story, but has a real memory now, a walk with Meshad last night on the banks of the Tigris, a dinner at the Al Rashid, an ordinary cappuccino and croissant at a café, The Vizier's Daughter. Samia Halevy becomes a secret even to myself. This is how I'll succeed. I'll unpack my briefcase. I'll put my drafting tools on the drafting table. I'll put* Nuclear Safety *and* Structural Properties of Nuclear Construction with Tables *on my desk. I'll take out my sketches of Osiraq. I'll make notations on it from my tour this morning. I'll work all morning on this, until lunch. I'm an engineer. I'm a specialist in nuclear safety.*

FIVE

It wasn't hard for Samia to sneak out of the Al Rashid just before dawn. The lobby was full of men sitting in oversized chairs, most with beads in their hands. But they were there to watch others come and go, foreign businessmen, foreign press. Most dozed lightly. The two men in the Peugeot had fallen blissfully asleep. Samia walked in the opposite direction of their car, toward *The Vizier's Daughter*. She passed the empty, shuttered café, then kept going down al-Zaariyah Boulevard for several blocks, past empty shops, a few apartment buildings. By the time she reached Ghani Street she had picked up a tail. She crossed to the other side of al-Zaariyah Boulevard. The tail walked on a bit, then crossed over behind her. Samia went on 40 meters, crossed back again. The tail crossed back. Samia picked up her pace. So did the tail. She turned right at the corner of a small street, turned left at the next corner, left at the next corner, then, having made a complete circuit, right again onto al-Zaariyah. Dawn had come slowly. Light washed this city of the ancient world carrying on within a burgeoning modernity. The high-pitched cries of the muezzins rose into the air, calling the faithful to morning prayer from the towers and rooftops of the mosques. Light warmed the streets, warmed Samia. She slowed her pace. The tail, behind her, slowed. Obviously, he knew she knew. He knew she knew how to expose a tail. Perhaps it had been a mistake to expose him. Perhaps not. Catching sight of a small, dead-end street, Samia turned into it. The tail didn't follow, but kept going down al-Zaariyah Boulevard. Had that been all they wanted to know about her, that she knew how to expose a tail? Or had they actually worried about where she might go? Did they know nothing about her? Did they buy her cover story? Or did they know everything? Know her real story? Were they just probing?

On the south side of the cul-de-sac, Samia discovered a heavy shop door slightly open. She tested it. It creaked. Inside, a thin, elderly, mustached man welcomed her.

"Come," the man said in a small voice.

Large, painted portraits of Saddam Hussein leaned up against one another along the walls of the narrow, dingy shop.

"I'm a painter," the man said.

"I'm sorry...?" Samia hadn't made out what the man said in his dim voice.

"I'm a painter," he straightened his usually bent frame to announce himself.

"So I see," Samia said.

"A follower of Jewad Salim."

The man shuffled his feet along the floor into the shop. Samia followed him.

"I'm sorry...?" Samia said.

"Jewad Salim," the man raised his voice again.

"No, I'm sorry, I heard you. I don't know who Jewad Salim is."

"Mmmmm," the man muttered, looking up at Samia, looking her over.

"I've gone further than most in my dedication to the Master. I'm exceptional in my devotion."

He gestured toward his canvases, at the same time as he huddled his arms into himself.

"I can see that you are," Samia said.

"Yes," the man said, "I think you can see."

"And who, may I ask, is Jewad Salim?"

The man muttered, "Spiritual Master. Highest Spiritual Master Painter. Jewad Salim." He bowed at his own mention of the name.

"My name is al-Khalil," the man said a bit more clearly. "Khalid al-Khalil. A euphonious name, yes?" He giggled. "Do you like the way it rhymes, the way it rolls off the tongue: Khalid al-Khalil. It's very pretty, and that's because Allah has sent me to do his work. Khalid al-Khalil," he repeated, listening to it himself. "Yes, that's right," he said, "Khalid al-Khalil."

"Yes, certainly. It's a very pretty name."

"It's a name with a great meaning to it. I'm destined for the ashes of eternity, but my work, dedicated to the greatness of Iraqi eternity, will live on. Don't you see?"

"I think I do, yes."

al-Khalil walked over to one of his paintings of Saddam, rubbing his palm very lightly over its surface. "I paint not for today," he spoke hurridly, breathlessly, but still in a small voice, "but for timeless time. Let me show you."

Samia had followed the foot-shuffling, hunched-over al-Khalil to the back of his shop. There, in the murkiness, a stack of ten tall paintings leaned up against the wall.

"These," al-Khalil said, "these," his thin body trembled, "are my most precious work."

"Are you all right?" Samia asked. "Would you like a chair?"

Khalil, ignoring her, pulled off the top painting. Underneath it lay a second painting, similar to the first.

"These are portraits I have done of Saddam Hussein with my own blood." He turned toward Samia, his eyes wide, his brows raised, his voice even smaller, his one hand holding the Saddam portrait, his other spread out toward Samia. "I," he said, "Khalil al-Khalil, the humble man, with the grace of the blessings of Jewad Salim, have painted the image of The Leader in the blood of the Iraqi artist. Collected from my own body. From the sacred flow of the river of a terrible truth which flows in my own poor veins. May

I please offer one of them for sale to you?"

The painting which al-Khalil held up dropped back against the stack. He put his hand up against the wall to brace himself, and rested.

Samia took in the shop, the smell of dust, oil, possibly urine, yes, something sharp, acrid, the walls which hadn't been washed since the eternity the man spoke of. The hundreds of Baghdad years. The untold shops which had inhabited what amounted to a cave more than a store.

"Maybe if I come back to see them again, another time," Samia said.

"I would like you to have one. Please, please," al-Khalil pleaded. His hands lifted, palms together in supplication to Samia. "I could make you a special offer. You're a special person. I can tell." He walked toward Samia. She backed away, back toward the shop entrance.

"I'm just an ordinary woman," Samia said.

"I have an infallible sense about people. I can feel them. I can feel..." al-Khalil held up his hand to display that invisible thing he felt. "I can feel their potency, their authority. You look Iraqi, yes, you speak Arabic, but you have a foreign aura about you, something from an old time. The ancient times."

"All Iraqis come from ancient times," Samia said. "You, too..."

But the man interrupted her.

"Perhaps your people migrated here along a trade route, from China, the Urals, Vandals, the Germanics..."

"My people are pure Iraqi," Samia said.

"Please," al-Khalil begged, "I want you to own one of these magnificent artifacts of the rise of Iraq, the absolute faith of Iraq."

"I'm sure that your greatness..."

But again the man urgently interrupted her.

"Through someone like you that greatness will flow back into antiquity and forwards into the new glory." He smiled.

Samia stepped backward to step away from the man, to stand back into the light coming from the street, but no such light came into the shop.

"I have to go now," she said. "Another time perhaps."

"No," the man implored, "don't go. Please don't go. I'll make you tea. I'll lay out all the blood-portraits for you."

"I'm afraid..."

"Don't be afraid."

"No, I'm afraid I don't...."

"You'll contemplate them, all twelve of them, carefully, slowly, one by one. You'll know which one is yours. Then you'll take it."

"I can't..."

"Pay me when you can. You and I, we're of the same knowledge."

"Not...."

"You understand my paintings. I'll deliver it myself, no runners."

"I have an important meeting now," Samia said. "You're right. I better wait until I have time to absorb each painting until I know which one is mine. I'll come back."

"Soon?" the man said. "Soon, I hope."

"Yes," Samia promised him, "soon."

Samia walked quickly down the boulevard. Did these blood-portraits actually hang in each of Saddam's palaces? Samia thought of the legendary tortures of Saddam's police state, and the blood of those portraits....but, no. Pushing the image of those tortures away, she kept walking.

A broad-shouldered, well-dressed, mustached man blocked her way.

"Ms. Samia Sa'ad?"

"Yes?" she said.

The man stepped aside, but Samia didn't walk on.

"I apologize for startling you," the man smiled. "I recognized you from your passport photograph."

"And how is it that you've seen my passport photograph?" Samia demanded, coming face to face for the first time with Mohammed Azziz — the Director of Mukhabarat, Secret Internal Security — whose life she'd studied thoroughly.

"I'm sorry," he said. "I'm Mohammed Azziz." He made a slight bow. "From the State Department."

"And what do you do at the State Department, if I might ask?"

"I review special requests for entrance into Iraq, like the one Osiraq made on your behalf. I find your portfolio intriguing, Ms. Sa'ad. You're a fascinating woman, with your background, your education, your excellence in your field of engineering. How did you find Stanford? As a place to live. Was it charming? Kind of Edenic?"

Samia laughed.

"This is where the Garden of Eden was, Mr. Azziz," Samia said, "here in Iraq, between the Tigris and Euphrates."

Azziz laughed. "You're a clever woman, Ms. Sa'ad. I'm glad that you work on our side."

"I'm sorry, Mr. Azziz, what do you mean by 'our' side?"

"Perhaps you're not geopolitically so sophisticated, Ms. Sa'ad. Your studies must keep you occupied."

Far from being intimidated by this kind of verbal chess strategy, Samia reveled in it. For this she was made. To let him fool himself.

"Very much concentrated on my work," she said. "But not entirely. I did enjoy Stanford, San Francisco, the California coast. Stanford is idyllic. The coastline is dramatic. A great combination."

"May I offer you a coffee, Ms. Sa'ad, at my favorite café?"

———

When Samia didn't show up at the café, *The Vizier's Daughter*, by 8:00, the waiter, Samir al-Wahab, moved a potted plant from the right side of the doorway to the left. Beyond that, he had no further instructions. He swept up the sidewalk from where he had moved the potted palm. At 10:30 he would move it back, then sweep up from under it again.

———

Over coffee, Azziz continued their conversation.

"Would you like to go back to California, Ms. Sa'ad, to live someday?"

"It depends." Samia became thoughtful, then answered. "I prefer New York to California. Maybe in the end I'll prefer Baghdad. I already find it pretty wonderful."

"Wonderful in the literal sense," Azziz said, "full of wonders, don't you think?"

"There's nothing like this in America. Nowhere this feeling of an ancient tradition, an ancient faith."

"What is your faith, Ms. Sa'ad?"

"Muslim, of course, Mr. Azziz."

"Of course. But Baghdad is a cosmopolitan city. Not all of our women cover themselves, not all of our men have a deep faith."

"Do you have a deep faith, Mr. Azziz?"

Azziz laughed. "Aha," he said. "You turn the questions back on me. I have a deep faith in Arab unity, in the fate of the Arab people. In the Arab past, which will become the truth of the Arab future."

"Do you think," Samia asked, "that the Arab future depends on the Arab past?"

"We're destined as Iraqis to create that Arab future." Azziz became serious. "It all began right here, Ms. Sa'ad. Arab glory."

"You have an ambitious vision, Mr. Azziz."

"To accomplish our vision," Azziz said, "we exploit the ingenious tools of our culture. We go beyond the restrictions of mediocre men. Common nations. I have a deep faith in bringing people like you to contribute to our future."

"I appreciate your honesty," Samia said. "The fire in your voice."

"I have to tell you, Ms. Sa'ad, that you'll come to learn the sun itself has copied fire from the light of our convictions."

"What you say, Mr. Azziz, it's what I came here to hear. Why I've come to work. To dedicate my talents."

"Let me ask you a very practical question, Ms. Sa'ad."

"Of course."

"Your fiancé, would he come here to marry you, to stay with you here?"

Samia became thoughtful again, wistful even, troubled.

"I would hope so. He's just started his career in America."

"What's his work?"

"I thought you'd know. From my dossier."

"Of course. It slipped my mind." Azziz smiled at Samia.

"He's an environmental attorney. He loves the environment around New York."

"He has a cause."

"Yes."

"He's a fortunate man," Azziz said, "a cause frees you. You do whatever it takes to pursue your cause. That liberates a man. And...." He nodded toward Samia, "a woman."

Samia blushed.

"Yes," she said, "thank you. I'd like to think that my contribution to the cause of Iraq might equal my fiancé's contribution to his cause."

"If you were to decide to stay.....if we asked you to stay.....what about your fiancé's career? Could he leave America for a desert?"

"He's thrown himself into the cause of that landscape he loves."

"I assure you, Ms. Sa'ad, that your cause surpasses every cause," Azziz said.

"Yes," Samia said, "I've begun to understand that."

"Good," Azziz said, "soon you'll have joined that cause with all your heart."

Samia smiled, nodded her head in affirmation. "Yes," she said, "I may find that within myself."

"And so," Azziz asked, "you think your fiancé would not come here for you?"

"To be honest," she said, "I don't think he could."

"And.....?"

"I don't know, Mr. Azziz. You ask me a difficult question. If he wouldn't come, would I stay without him? I'll only know the answer when that day comes."

"If I may be impertinent, Ms. Sa'ad. You grew a passion for him in your youth. Only youth can grow that passion. How could you abandon it?"

"Some of us do have the strength for that, Mr. Azziz. Do I? I don't know. Maybe I do."

"Perhaps you do, Ms. Sa'ad. Perhaps you don't."

"Yes. Of course. Perhaps I don't."

With that uncalculated response, Samia feigned and exposed a vulnerability.

After a moment of silence, Azziz spoke again.

"Let me ask you, Ms. Sa'ad, what do you feel of Iraq now, in your very short time here?"

"I feel hope," Samia said. "President Saddam is our next Nasser."

"Saddam Hussein is the first Saddam. He is not the next of anything," Azziz warned Samia. "Saddam is not the next Nebuchadnezzar. Or the next Saladin.

He's a genius of the first order rarely known on earth. He's the first Saddam."

"But like Nebuchadnezzar, he'll destroy the Jews?"

"We'll turn the Zionist state into a cinder," Azziz snapped.

"And the Palestinians?"

Azziz looked at Samia for a moment.

"Ms. Sa'ad, I'm giving you a lesson in the realities of your homeland. Let me assure you, despite whatever propaganda you've heard, the Palestinians are sheep, weak, ignorant. They're as a cipher, a zero. They've invented nothing, created nothing, developed nothing."

"I thought...."

"I know what you thought. You're an Iraqi Arab living in America who reads the New York Times. You thought these Palestinians were noble fighters for freedom. They're thieves, back-stabbing liars. They've failed in their fight with the Zionists. We'll find a place for them."

"But President Saddam himself...."

"Of course. Let me explain the language of the international struggle. We have to be true to our cause, and we have to be clever in pursuit of it. When President Saddam speaks to the world, he indicts the Israelis of their crimes against the Palestinians, yes. The Zionists are monsters. But the Palestinians, they're the stupid cousins we have to invite to the party. We just have to make sure they don't embarrass us."

Azziz laughed with such abandon that no one could tell if he had in fact let himself go in front of Samia, or if, behind his laughter, he watched her. "The Palestinians!" he huffed. "The Palestinians!" and he laughed again.

"I'm a scientist, Mr. Azziz, who should stick to science." Samia smiled at Azziz.

"Perhaps, yes, perhaps." Azziz was still laughing. "That's your contribution."

Azziz paused for a moment, then, serious again, he continued. "That man you met this morning, on your adventurous walk, the painter, al-Khalil. He's a man of an extreme. But you can see in his extreme the extreme that our people will go to in their love of Saddam. You'll understand the passion which drives him to extremes. Take him for a symbol of the people, which proclaims the extreme devotion of the average man for the extreme genius of their leader."

"But....Mr. Azziz, how do you know about the man I visited this morning?"

"Tell me, Ms. Sa'ad, were you pleased with yourself this morning when you evaded your tracker?"

"My tracker?"

"The man following you."

"Yes. There was a man. How did you know? I thought he was dangerous. A stalker. Yes. I was pleased with myself. Tricks my mother taught me. In New York."

"A dangerous city, New York. Corrupt with Jews, with the West. It's filthy with crime. They don't have the will power to stop crime. Or the moral courage. We have no crime in Baghdad, Ms. Sa'ad. We respect our women. Walk anywhere you like."

SIX

As dawn rendered visible the skies over Osiraq, the high-pitched air raid siren blasted the air. The military personnel ran to their stations; the civilian workers hadn't yet arrived. The anti-aircraft guns around Osiraq's perimeter, already turned eastward, swiveled on turrets to gain their targets. Two Iranian bombers flew high toward the plant. Both released bombs, most of them falling outside of Osiraq's grounds, but two hitting hard inside, one near the barracks, another near an administration building. The AA unleashed thousands of rounds unable to reach the high-flying Iranian bombers as Iraqi soldiers rushed to prepare their surface-to-air missiles for firing. The two bombers, alone in the sky, circled to come in this time from a northward position. As they came within 500 yards of Osiraq, they descended, seeking a closer run within visual range of their target. Both planes charged forward and downward as if in a sudden fit of enraged madness they would hurl their huge planes right into the dome of the building their bombs couldn't hit. One pilot released two bombs well in advance of his target. The planes wobbled. As they came within range, the AA fire ripped into their hulls, through the windows of their cockpits, into the engines, tore holes in their wings. Both planes spun out, hitting the ground 20 yards from the Osiraq compound. No one could see the planes at all, just the smoke and the flames.

Two hours later in Jerusalem, Arie Solen paced in the ante-room of the Prime Minister's office. The Prime Minister's Secretary picked up the phone, told him that Solen had arrived, listened for a moment, then told Solen he could go in.

"Sorry, Arie," Prime Minister Begin said. "I was on the phone. To my son."

"Two things at once," Solen bypassed the small talk.

Solen sat down in the chair facing the Prime Minister.

"The Iranians sent two bombers out to destroy Osiraq," Solen said.

"When?"

"This morning."

"In the morning? They went in the morning?"

"They lost both planes. Iraqi AA tore them to pieces. Shredded them. Gunner practice."

"Two bombers?" the Prime Minister said. "That's it? Bombers?"

"That's it," Solen said.

"Good God," said the Prime Minister, "they wasted their advantage."

"Yes," Solen replied, "surprise and range. The close

range that I only wish we had. It was our fault. Our failure."

"No, Arie," the Prime Minister got angry with Solen. "Not your failure. You convinced them to attack Osiraq without them ever knowing it was our plan. What? We should have trained their pilots for them?" The Prime Minister got even angrier, both at Solen's bad habit of taking the blame and at the Iranians for bungling the job. "We gave them the plans," he argued, his voice full of his anger and his anguish, "we told them what planes to use. Did we have to show them how to release their bombs, how to turn their planes to the right, to the left, up and down?"

"Yes," Solen agreed. "We gave them great plans. Down to the minute. Down to the second. They didn't follow them and they failed. They sent out two bombers alone."

"What a carnage it must have been," Prime Minister Begin slammed his fist on his desk. "What a sick sight. What a waste of a beautiful chance! And what's worse now...."

"What's worse now," Arie Solen jumped in to finish the Prime Minister's thought, "the Iraqis will defend Osiraq better. They'll put a hundred and fifty percent into it."

"Defended from the sky, yes." The Prime Minister pointed a finger at Solen, "but not from the ground!"

Solen, standing up, now paced the Prime Minister's

office. With his right hand he rubbed the stub of his missing left hand. Begin, leaning forward on his desk, waited for Solen's answer.

"General Slomovic…." Solen began.

"I *know* what Gen. Slomovic thinks," Begin said, "what do *you* think about what Gen. Slomovic thinks?"

"Can't be done," Solen said.

"Give me a formal Mossad report on it," Begin said. "Slomovic is pushing hard for a surgical ground assault. 2000 troops, 20 tanks. He says we can do it."

"What do you think?" Solen asked.

"That we can do it," the Prime Minister said. "Slomovic's plan is very smart, very strong. Review it for me."

"Send it over."

"Here," the Prime Minister shoved over a report marked *Top Secret* and titled *Osiraq Ground Battle Assault Plan.* "Quick strikes. In and out. Forty-two hours."

"Casualty projections?" Solen asked.

"Yes, Arie, they're in there. You think they'll be heavy?"

"You like it?"

"Give me a better way."

"If there is no better way?"

"Then we'll do it," the Prime Minister said, "Slomovic's way."

"You didn't answer my first question," Solen pressed the Prime Minister. "Do you like it?"

"I hate it," he said.

Solen sat again. He said, after a reflective moment, "It wouldn't be the first thing you've done that you hated to do."

Prime Minister Begin, thinking, tapped his finger loudly on the desk. "Of course," he said, "I'm perfectly capable of doing things I hate to do." He stopped tapping his finger, which accentuated the silence. "But," he said, "I've never been sorry that I did them. Only sorry that I had to. Was your agent there this morning?"

"At Osiraq?"

"I didn't give her advance notice. Tried to. Couldn't."

"And....? She's all right?"

"Yes," Solen snapped. "She's all right. What should I have done? Tell her to take the day off?"

"Arie!" the Prime Minister snapped back at him. "It wouldn't have been your fault."

"No, there's never any fault," Solen said. "Nobody's fault."

"And the second thing, Arie? You said there were two things."

Solen leaned back in his chair. "The Americans," he said, "have eight F-16s sitting at Midnight Air Force Base in Utah. They sold them to the Iranians under the Shah, but hadn't shipped them when the Ayatollah came in. The Americans just formally cancelled the deal four days ago. They've been sitting on those planes for a long time."

Solen put the folder he held in his good hand on the Prime Minister's desk. Leaning over, he opened it. "These are the stats," he said.

"Let's get them," the Prime Minister said.

"These are them," Solen repeated, "the stats, the photos, the costs."

"The planes, Arie, let's get the planes."

Solen leaned away from the desk, smiling, and said slowly, "someone already got to you?"

"Let's say," the Prime Minister answered, "yes, someone got to me."

"He's quick."

"Yes, he's quick."

Solen got up, shoved the two files – the F-16 file and the *Operation Opera* file under his right arm, leaving his right hand free to turn the door handle. "Deal done," he said. "Eight F-16s. Dror will be very happy."

"*I'm* very happy about it, Arie," the Prime Minister said.

SEVEN

"No," Maj. Ilan Hamal said to Gen. Dror, "don't tell the Prime Minister who designed it. Present the plan to him wholly as your own."

"But it's your plan, Yossi," Gen. Dror addressed Ben Luria. "Without you I wouldn't have done it. I didn't believe in it. I would never have done the research you did. I'd have said it was impossible. I told you it was impossible months ago. Take credit for what you've done."

"It's all right," Yossi said. "I want victory more than I need credit."

"The Prime Minister will listen to you," Dror said.

"No," Arie Solen said, "Hamal is right. Yossi's right. The Prime Minister will listen to you long before he'd listen to Yossi. It's natural. You're senior, Dror. You've got rank and experience and clout. Listen to me. I know Begin a little, too."

"Begin thinks of Yossi as a son," Hamal said. "It's nice. But you don't trust your son with the fate of your country."

"It's true," Yossi agreed. "I don't mind."

"More wine? Tea?" Yossi asked the group, which included Yossi Ben Luria; Israeli Air Force Gen. Jonathon Dror; Israeli Air Force Maj. Ilan Hamal; and Director General of Mossad, Arie Solen.

"Tea would be great, Yossi. Thank you," Dror said.

Ben Luria left the garden, went into the kitchen, prepared tea and sweets for all. He returned to the table with a tray of tea and teacups, then went back to the kitchen for pastries.

"The damn thing is," Dror said, just as Ben Luria came back with the sweets, "that if I present it as my own, I have to take responsibility for the plan." He laughed.

"And?" Solen asked. "Do you believe in it now?"

"I believe in it and I don't believe in it," Dror said.

"Wait!" Solen stopped him. "Tamar..?" he said.

"Thank you," Tamar said. "Don't want to hear, don't want to know."

"But…" Dror began.

"But," Tamar cut him off. "I am no longer active. Not for a long time."

"But…" Dror began again.

"And it was Col. Solen who taught me, 'They can't make you tell what you don't know.'"

"She's right," Solen said. "She's by the book."

They waited for Tamar to get inside.

"It's Yossi's game," Dror went on. "It's very risky.

"I never said it wasn't," Yossi said.

Dror got up from the table. He walked over to a lemon tree in the Ben Luria's garden, picked a ripe lemon, tossed it from hand to hand.

"The plan is your idea, Yossi," Dror said. "If I present it to the Security Cabinet, to the Prime Minister, then it becomes my plan. I don't care. I'll take the responsibility. But I have to have faith in it."

"And?" Solen said. "Yossi has faith in it. Maj. Hamal does, and he'll be the one who flies it. I have faith in it."

"You have faith in it," Dror said to Solen, "because you're desperate."

"Is that wrong?" Solen asked.

"No." Dror tossed the lemon back under the tree, then retrieved it. "Sorry," he said, as he handed the lemon to Ben Luria, "they're good lemons." Ben Luria took the lemon, put it on the table as a paper weight to hold down the original map of the proposed attack which he had drawn late that night when he sat alone in the kitchen. Ben Luria picked up another lemon off the grass, tossed it to Dror, who tossed it back. They played catch with it.

"Let me ask you one last question, Yossi," Dror said.

"Shoot."

"It's a question you've already answered, but it's important to ask one last time. We've gone over and over this plan. It's a crazy plan. Everyone will see that right away. Do you believe in it? Really believe in it?"

"I believe," Yossi said, tossing the lemon back, "that we can do it. What it will cost us in lives and money and matériel no one will ever answer until it's over."

"And the political cost and the international diplomatic cost," Solen added.

"Yes," Yossi said, "those too."

"And you, Hamal?" Dror said to his own IAF man, "you'll have to lead this mission. Are you sure enough to fly it?"

"I am," Hamal said. "I'm sure that we have to do it."

"We've been wrong before," Dror said.

"We?" Yossi asked.

"Israel," Dror said. "Military, strategic, diplomatic errors. We pay a very heavy price for each one of them."

"He's right," Solen said. "It's because we're small. Each error of judgment hurts us all the more."

"How sure are you, Yossi, that this plan is the right way? That it'll work? That it'll destroy Osiraq?" Dror asked.

"I'm sure," Ilan Hamal said, "that it's our very best shot."

"You mean that it's all we've got," Dror said.

"It's all we've got," Hamal answered.

"Then," Dror said. "It's up to me. To IAF. I accept." Ben Luria and Dror tossed the lemon back and forth for another minute, Ben Luria to Dror, Dror to Ben Luria, until they tired of it.

The group accepted Tamar Ben Luria's invitation to stay for dinner on the condition that Tamar let them help. She agreed, knowing that they wouldn't.

"It's a done deal," Dror said when Tamar had gone back into the house. "No backing out. I'm going to the Prime Minister with it tomorrow."

"Good luck," Solen said.

"We'll do it," Hamal said. "I look forward to it."

"Don't be too crazy," Dror admonished him. "I'm IAF," Hamal said. "I'm crazy. I'm cautious crazy." Dror, laughing, patted Hamal on the shoulder.

Col. Ben Luria and Gen. Dror shook hands on the deal. Ben Luria folded up the original map he had drawn, then gave it to Dror.

"A little good luck charm for you," Ben Luria said. "We have big problems now to solve."

"We have a history of solving the unsolvable," Dror said. "By the skin of our teeth. We'll do it again."

They ate on the back patio, where earlier they had held their meeting. The Ben Luria kids joined them for dinner, Reuven, 6, Dina, 4, Danny, 2 1/2. By 11:00 the kids were long asleep and everyone was tired. Tamar offered them all to stay for the night, but Dror, who lived in Jerusalem, Hamal, who lived in Tel Aviv, and Solen, who lived in Jerusalem, all insisted on going home. Dror had a driver, and the drive would relax him. He would listen to Verdi all the way home. Hamal and Solen would drive themselves. After some persuasion, Tamar convinced Solen to stay the night. He had the longest drive, alone. Solen called his wife to say he'd stay the night with Yossi and Tamar Ben Luria. He'd go straight to the office in the morning and call her from there.

At the front door, as they said good-bye, Tamar asked Ilan Hamal about Meirav, Hamal's wife. Tamar and Meirav knew each other well, but in the midst of busy lives hadn't spoken for a couple of weeks. Meirav had just gone back to school to finish her degree in archeology.

"It isn't easy with the kids," Hamal said. "But, one class a semester. She loves it. And I'm not such a bad husband, I help out a little."

"Hey! I know you," Tamar said, "you help out a lot. Meirav tells me."

"She doesn't tell me," Hamal laughed.

"Stop," Tamar said, "I'm sure she tells you all the time."

"Yes," Hamal grinned, "once in a while."

Yossi alread lay in bed as Tamar joined him.

"I think you're going to be gone a lot now."

"I'm afraid you're right."

"It's the way it is," Tamar said. "No choice."

Yossi put his arm under her, she lay her head on his chest.

"You have no choice," she said.

"We have no choice," Yossi answered her.

"We have to be quiet," Tamar said. "The kids."

"And Solen," Yossi laughed lightly. "You want Solen to hear us?"

And they made love.

Side-by-side, turned and facing in opposite directions but connected in that particular awareness that follows lovemaking, Yossi and Tamar lay still, thoughts floating in their minds.

"Something big is up," Tamar whispered. "Something difficult, I think. It'll work out, Yossi. Whatever it is. I have a good feeling about it. I don't know why." Tamar fell asleep.

Turning onto his back, Yossi watched the dark ceiling. Ilan Hamal's voice came back to him again, as it had been at their meeting. "I'm ready to go," Ilan had said. "I look forward to it." Was Ilan putting up a good front? Courage? Ilan would lead the armada to Osiraq, not Yossi. *Who knows where I'll be? Lying in bed with my wife, while they go off to a fate I planned out for them? The pilots on this mission cramped up in their tight cockpits, flying through enemy airspace with little but their own guts or their own fear or their own valor to keep them up there. I wrote the plan. Every plan I ever wrote I executed myself. Now I'm becoming a senior member of the military. That's the way it happens. One day, you take your place. I won't send you out there into hell, Ilan. Only into victory. I hope. I hope.* Ben Luria fell asleep.

EIGHT

United States Air Force Maj. David Durham stood
before the group of eight Israeli Air Force pilots.
He spoke to them with the hint of his Alabama accent. Behind him, a slick, head-on color photograph
of the F-16 mid-flight filled the wall of the meeting
room. It was the sleekest fighter plane the Israelis had
ever seen. The most efficient, the most beautiful. At
47.5 ft. long, just under 17 yards, it was not big, especially with its narrow, aerodynamic body. Its wings
engineered for maximum wingspan-to-fuselage lift. Its
nose cone narrowed to a fine point. It was built to be
swift, agile, instantaneously responsive, not big. It was
just past 0600.

"The F-16 fighter aircraft is an awesome thing,"
Maj. Durham began in a voice softer than one might
expect from such a man. "That's a truth. Simple.
You've often heard this said of many a fighter plane:
that plane is an awesome thing, almost unreal. But
watch yourselves."

Maj. Durham stopped for a moment. He looked
around the room at each man in turn. He had trained
scores of pilots. When he saw them for the first time,
he couldn't help but wonder who would survive

training, who would survive combat. He knew the statistics, knew they varied for each war, each battle, all depending on many things like skill, training, personality of the pilot, quality of the aircraft, even the weather. He also knew about the mystique of warfare, about the unpredictable events which overtake everything. He knew about probability, statistics. He accepted these men now into the community of those hard statistics where they would each play out their numbers. He would make every one of them a winner; the impersonal calculations of war would decide the rest. No man could take Durham's job — to make these men as invulnerable as possible, then send them off to war — without suffering some degree of self-doubt. Am I good enough? Have I done enough? Gone the extra mile? The extra five miles? No one could take his job without the ability to live with those doubts. He looked around the room, from one pilot to the next:

Maj. Ilan Hamal. Wing Leader. Born - 1954 - and raised in Tel Aviv. His father immigrated to Israel from Poland in 1922. His mother and maternal grand-mother both survived Auschwitz. His father fought in the 1948 War of Independence, and in the 1967 Six Day War. Maj. Hamal has one brother and one sister, both of whom did their military service, then returned to civilian life. Maj. Hamal maintains a close friendship with his university schoolmate, Col. Yossi Ben Luria, an Aide to Prime Minister Menachem Begin, and, purportedly, a member of Mossad. Maj. Hamal is married to Meirav Hamal (nee Ginz), with whom he has two children, Benjamin, 3 years old, and Rebecca, 1 year old. His family, which for a time lived in Beer-sheba, has moved back to Tel Aviv.

Capt. Reuven Samy. Wingman to the Wing Leader. Born - 1954 - on a kibbutz near Tel Aviv. His father was born in British Mandate Palestine, his mother immigrated to British Palestine from Morocco. His father and mother both fought in the 1948 War of Liberation. His father fought in the 1952 Suez campaign, in the 1973 Yom Kippur war. Capt. Samy first saw battle in 1973. His uncle on his father's side, and his brother Shaul, were killed in '73. Capt. Samy has three remaining siblings, two sisters and one brother, all of whom did their military service, then returned to civilian life. Capt. Samy is married to Mara Samy (nèe Beshart). They have a daughter, Yaffa, 3 years old.

Capt. Rai Atari. Rai Atari was born of Yemenite parents in 1947 in Sanaa, Yemen. His parents, Moshe and Gila Atari, immigrated in Operation Magic Carpet, the Israeli airlift of over 50,000 Yemenite Jews following the 1947 Aden pogrom, in which Arab Muslim rioters killed 82 Jews, destroyed hundreds of Jewish homes, Jewish stores, and Jewish businesses. Moshe Atari served in the IDF in a non-combatant role in the 1967 war. Following high school, Rai Atari was the first Yemenite Jew accepted into the pilot training program of the IAF. He flew on the Egyptian front in the 1973 war, flew missions on the northern front during the war in Lebanon. He was chosen for this mission because of his outstanding courage, his cool head in a crisis, and his ability to learn new equipment. While dark-skinned Yemenite Jews did face discrimination in Israel, Rai Atari earned the respect of his colleagues and his superiors.

Capt. Zev Nussbaum. Wingman to the 2nd Section Leader. Born - 1956 - Michigan, USA. Immigrated to Israel with his parents in 1958. His father worked as a construction engineer on an industrial kibbutz, where his mother worked as a teacher. Capt. Nussbaum's father saw service in the 1967 and 1973 wars, but in 1973 lost his right leg above the knee when an anti-tank shell hit his tank in the desert. He returned to the kibbutz thereafter to assume the job he had left. Capt. Nussbaum's older brother, Ravi, was killed in the '73 war. Another older brother, Rami, served in the operation tracking down and killing the three escaped Black September Palestinians who had kidnapped and murdered Israeli athletes at the 1972 Summer Olympics in Munich. Capt. Nussbaum was married in 1974

to Ziva Nussbaum (nee Moshat), who had recently
immigrated from Yemen. They have two children, a
son, Zev, 7 years old, and a daughter, Golda, 5 years
old. They divorced in 1980. Capt. Nussbaum has not
remarried.

Capt. Alexander Davidov. 2nd Division Section
Leader. Born - 1952 - Moscow. Arguing constantly
with his parents, Capt. Davidov fled, immigrating by
himself to Israel in 1968. Lying about his age, Capt.
Davidov joined the Israeli Air Force at 16. He flew in
the Yom Kippur War in 1973, and flew subsequent
missions over southern Lebanon. His parents remain
in Soviet Russia. He married Isvelta Gutman (nee Po-
dolsky) in 1974. They have one child, Reuven, 4 years
old.

Capt. Schmuel Halevy. 2nd Division Section Leader. Born — 1954 — British Mandate Jerusalem. His
Grandfather and Grandmother, early Zionists, immigrated to Ottoman Palestine from Morocco in 1907.
His father and mother were both born in Jerusalem.
His father is a roofer and tinner, his mother is a restor-
er of ancient books. Capt. Halevy has one sister, who
served her military duty, then retired to civilian life,
studying medicine at Hebrew University, becoming a
pediatrician. Capt. Halevy has a cousin by marriage,
Samia Halevy, an Iraqi immigrant, who graduated in

electrical engineering from Stanford University; Capt. Halevy suspects that his cousin joined Mossad, the Israeli Secret Service, and that she might be an ISS-1 Mossad agent, International Secret Service, with the license to kill. The family has not heard from Samia Halevy for two years. Her parents and her husband, Dov, substantiate rumors that she is working on a dam project in Australia. Capt. Halevy is married to Frieda Halevy (nee Shamat). They have one daughter, Ruth, 7 years old.

Capt. Mihael Klatzkin. Wingman to the 2nd Division Section Leader. Born - 1947 - in a displaced persons camp en route from Czechoslovakia to Israel. Once he arrived in Israel with his father (his mother died en route), Capt. Klatzkin's father settled in a kibbutz in the Galilee. Although Capt. Klatzkin's father remarried in 1953, Capt. Klatzkin remains an only child. Capt. Klatzkin's great-great-aunt, Eva Cohen, of Hamburg, attended the First Zionist Congress at Basle in 1897. Capt. Klatzkin is married to Suzanne Klatzkin (nee Paperno). They have two children, Eva, 8, and Guntar Gavrielle, 6.

Capt. David Rose. Wingman to the 2nd Division 2nd Section Leader (Trailing Plane). Born – 1948 – in Jerusalem. Parents smuggled into British Mandate Palestine from England. They were boyfriend and girlfriend. Father, Jacob Rose, fought under the British, in the Jewish Brigade, in WWII. After the war, his father took his military expertise into the underground Jewish Army in Palestine, the Palmach. He fought in the IDF in the War of Independence in 1948. He last fought in the '68 Six Day War. Capt. Rose's mother, Sylvia, suffered a nervous breakdown at the outset of the War of Independence. She recovered enough to leave the hospital, but struggles continously with anxiety and depression. Capt. Rose has one sister, Shira. He is unmarried, and without children.

"The F-16, the Fighting Falcon," Durham went on, "will never ask more of you than you can deliver. But if you lose contact with her and lose your delicate control of her, all the power of nature will destroy you. Gravity. G-force. Wing lift. All the natural sciences which built her and keep her flying trim and fighting hard will wipe you out like you never existed. If you control her with a touch sensitive enough to know her, secure enough to command her, you're invincible. Can you sustain that kind of presence of mind and clarity of spirit for an hour, two hours, four hours?

Durham looked at the men one-by-one.

"Israel believes you can," he said. "They tell me you're the best sticks in the air. So I'm going to put you in the driver's seat of these $24 million machines. I'll show you the monkey-skills and the headwork you need to vanquish your enemy."

Nine days later the eight pilots took off for the first time. They knew the plane upside down and inside out from the classroom, from charts, graphs, figures; they knew it from flight control trainers; from walking around it, sitting inside it. They knew it from practice touch controls and from actual controls.

Durham yelled over the din of the take-offs.

"Looks like some gods of fire hurling those things into the air."

"No gods of fire," the ground crew officer yelled back, "Pratt & Whitney single engines. Twenty-seven thousand pounds of jet engine gasoline burning thrust."

"I'm going up after them," Durham said. "See you later."

At 13,000 ft. and climbing, Maj. Ilan Hamal's voice came over the radios.

"Eagle Leader to Eagles. Boy! This baby loves to fly! Keep up with me kids."

"Eagle One to Eagles," Capt. Schmuel Halevy crackled back. "Love to fly? Knows no resistance. Kisses the air, slides on through."

"Eagle Leader to Eagles. Up to three five oh. Level off at one two six. Over."

All eight planes flew in succession up to 35,000 feet, where they leveled off, rolling into formation. From just ahead and just above them, in the blue sky Durham, in his F-16, came on the radio.

"Bravo One to Eagle Leader. How you doing, Hamal? How's your boys? Over."

"Eagle Leader to Bravo One. In line. Formation Delta. Over."

"Bravo One to Eagle Leader. Roll three oh degrees left. One after another. Come up in a Formation Epsilon at two two six at point seven five mach. Over."

"Eagle Leader to Bravo One. Roger. Eagle Leader to Eagles. Roll over 30 degrees left, come up at Formation Epsilon at two six oh at point seven five mach. Over."

They flew a few more seconds, the ground still visible, but all eyes were riveted on the sky. All hands held their sticks. Everyone's heart beat just a little harder, but everyone stayed steady. Light and steady. The fastest aircraft they had ever flown. The most nimble. You felt it in your hand. She would go anywhere you told her to go; you listened for her to tell you what she wanted. It felt like she would climb to the sun for you. The moon just there, off in the distance, above the eastern horizon. White moon and they flew straight toward her. In those 2 - 3 seconds they would travel 2511 feet, half a mile.

Hamal came on again. "Eagle Leader to Eagles. Execute." One by one following each other each plane rolled to the left, slid through the air, coming up in a new formation with Hamal's Eagle One above and slightly ahead of the others, Eagles Two, Three, and

Four in a horizontal row, Eagles Five, Six, and Seven below them in another horizontal row, but slightly behind them, and Eagle Eight between and slightly behind the other two rows.

Durham came on. "Bravo One to Eagle Leader. Smash it up. Mach One in formation."

Hamal repeated it to his crew. "Eagle Leader to Eagles. Mach One in formation. Hold on. Keep cool. Execute."

All eight planes simultaneously ratcheted up to Mach One, slipping into supersonic speed, 1116 ft/second; 66,960 ft./minute, 4,017,600 ft./hour, 761 miles per hour. A crack broke the air as they passed the sound barrier. Far below them, desert creatures felt it in their bodies.

Durham slowed to point 80 mach, dropped behind the formation, then down below them, then sped up to Mach One plus to keep up. He came back on the radio.

"Bravo One to Eagles. You're hot shots. How do you like Mach One?"

"Eagle Leader to Bravo One. It's the cat's meow, Major. Don't you say that in English? It's the damn cat's meow. Over."

"Bravo One to Eagle Leader. Raise the stakes. Take them straight through to Mach 2. Over."

"Roger. Eagle Leader to Eagles. Ease up to Mach 2. Over."

Each pilot kept his left hand on the throttle, right hand on the stick between his legs, pushing it up through Mach 1.1…1.3…1.5…1.6…1.8. At Mach 2, one thousand five hundred miles per hour, each pilot's craft soared through the air while the clouds whizzed by, the land a blur, and the pilots themselves lost in space and time and total concentration.

"Bravo One to Eagle Leader. Good. Up four five oh and hold. Over."

"Roger. Eagle Leader to Eagles. Climb to four five oh and hold."

The planes took off. They shot up like rockets. Who could catch them? No one.

"Bravo One to Eagles. Just about your limit. Kings of the skies. You have 5000 more feet above you. Only take it for life or death. Eagle Leader: take them home, Cat, Maj. Meow. Over."

Durham came into the briefing room. The pilots were drinking sodas and coffee, eating cookies, light sandwiches, laughing like a bunch of college guys. When he opened the door they called out in one voice:

"For he's a jolly good fellow, for he's a jolly good fellow, for he's a jolly good fellow, that took us for a ride. That took us for a ride. That gave us F-16. That took us for a ride....."

Durham raised his hands. They quieted down.

"If you guys flew in the kind of harmony you sing in we'd be out eight F-16s."

"Yeah!" they shouted, "Yeah!"

"But we're not out one nut, one bolt. You guys are terrific. I knew you could do it."

"But," Halevy said, "you had some fears. Confess."

"Damn right I had fears," Durham said, his southern drawl coming on hard, "a long sleepless night of fears if you want to know the truth. But you guys, you're all right. And your Major here, Maj. Cat, Maj. Meow, Maj. Ilan Hamal, he's the cat's meow, ain't he?"

Raising their drinks they sang out:

"For he's a jolly good fellow, for he's a jolly good fellow, for he's a jolly good fellow, what took us on a ride..."

"*Havarim*," Hamal said in Hebrew, "*todah rabah. Aval atem...atem hagiborim shelee.*"

"Hey!" Durham shouted. "Speak good American Southern English!"

"Ahhh," Capt. Klatzkin said, "Hamal just spouted some nonsense about how we're the good guys here."

"Heroes, I called them," Hamal said. "My heroes."

"All right," Durham called out, "sit down for a minute. I'm going to give you a little lesson. You ready?"

They took their seats. Durham took his usual place at the front of the room, in front of the photograph of the F-16. Durham turned, looked up at it. So big it could fly straight into that room.

"You guys. That's what I'll call you from now on, Capt. Meow and The Guys. You guys, you're a special group now. You've flown this sweet honey-come-by machine. You've taken her up, mached her out, brought her home. Mach One. Mach Two. Maybe you know this, but I'm going to remind you. The year One Thousand Six Hundred and Eighty Seven...1687....after Jesus Christ, of course. Sir Isaac Newton publishes the *Philosophiae Naturalis Principia Mathematica*. I have held that book in my hands, the original 1687 edition. The *Principia* as you may know it."

Halevy raised his hand, but spoke out before Durham called on him.

"No, sir," Halevy called out, "we know it as the *Philosophiae Naturalis Principia Mathematica*, even though that's not Hebrew, it's Latin."

They laughed.

"I should've known," Durham said, "you bunch of smart-asses. And did you know that in the *Principia,* Sir Isaac Newton, in Book II, Proposition 49, Newton for the first time in human history calculated the speed of sound."

"No, sir," Halevy said, "honestly, sir, I did not know that."

"But Newton never dreamed you'd bust it!" Durham said. "In an F-16! Now let's go over my notes. You need some details worked out. You're good, but you're not good enough. I want you perfect. Questions first. Any questions, problems, things you didn't expect?"

After a few questions, Durham dismissed the group.

"Now go on, get out of here, go drink yourselves

silly, but be back here sober as a stone, bright eyed and bushy tailed at 04:30. I want that morning air to rise up into. I want you all to bring up the sun tomorrow."

As they got up, Halevy walked over to Maj. Durham.

"Stone sober, ok. Bright eyed, ok," Halevy said, "but bushy-tailed?" Halevy wiggled his behind. "You say this in English?"

Durham laughed at Halevy, pushed him on the shoulder. "Yeah," Durham said, "you're damn right you Hebrew-speaking sonofabitch, 'bushy-tailed.' If you don't get it look it up in a Hebrew/English.....Hebrew/*American-Southern*-English dictionary."

"You know," Halevy said, "I think that your American Southern is as foreign around here in Utah as our Hebrew is."

"It is," Durham said, "but you and I, we speak the same language now. We speak F-16. You won't ever forget that language."

"No, sir," Halevy said. "I will not."

$\mathbf{M}$aj. Ilan Hamal drank from a mug of beer while he wrote to his wife. Above him a neon light tube sputtered in the nearly empty cafeteria. He wanted to write, "It's midnight here at Midnight Air Force Base," but he couldn't reveal his location. After staring at the notepad for a moment, he wrote:

Dear Meirav,
    I'm having the last beer of the day. Well, maybe one more. Won't you join me? We'd talk about nothing at all. And everything. Laugh a lot. I'm in the PX – 'slopshop' they call it here – so if you were here we'd have to go out to a nice bar. But then, if you were here and we were out at a nice bar, I wouldn't be drinking a beer. I'd be having a brandy. You see how my quality of life dimishes without you?

"May I?" Maj. Durham stood on the other side of the table. "If I'm not interrupting…"

"Sit. You're not interrupting." Hamal closed the cover of his notepad, laid the pen on top.

"It's ok," Durham said, "go back to your work."

"Letter to my wife," Hamal said. "Come on. Sit down."

"Can't sleep." Durham sat on the wooden bench across from Hamal.

"Let me get you a beer." Hamal got up. Durham reached in his pocket, but Hamal gestured for him to put his money away. Hamal came back with two cold mugs of beer.

"Just a second," Hamal sat down, opened the notepad, added to the letter:

Ok, one more beer, but with a friend now, so it's raised to the level of social drinking.

Smiling, Hamal closed the notepad. "You married?" he asked.

"Twelve years," Durham said. "Two kids. Wild boys. My wife – we call her Dixie – she's a teacher. Childhood sweethearts kind of thing."

"You flew in Vietnam, didn't you?" Hamal asked.

"Flew A-4s," said Durham. "Skyhawks." Durham took a long drink of his beer, set it on the table, wiped his mouth with the handkerchief he pulled from his back pocket. "Hate paper napkins," he explained. "Want to see the Skyhawk I flew in Vietnam?"

"It's here?"

"Dry dock," Durham said.

Durham and Hamal walked a good half-mile at a fast clip, not talking. At the back lot where Durham's A-4 Skyhawk sat parked, along with a few hundred other planes, Durham led Hamal in the darkness to his old craft.

"That's the one," Durham said as they stood beside the plane, "that's her. Five hundred twelve missions all over Southeast Asia."

Durham pulled a flask from his back pocket, unscrewed the top, handed it to Hamal. "Don't worry," Durham said, "it's first class Bourbon whiskey."

Hamal took a drink, puckered his cheeks at the harsh liquor, took a short breath, and said, "that's fire." He gave the flask back to Durham, who wiped the mouthpiece with his handkerchief, then drank.

"Look at that moon." Durham pointed up to the sky. "It's a killer beauty. Big and bright and round. I can fly by the stars, Hamal. Can you?"

Each man took another drink of Bourbon. Together they looked up at the moon.

As Durham still gazed up at the moon, Hamal walked over closer to the A-4 Skyhawk. He patted one of the A-4's struts. "She brought you home."

Durham laughed. "She brought me home," he said, "and I brought me home."

"And the rest of it doesn't matter, then," Hamal said.

"In Vietnam," Durham said, "we made up our own armpatch." He pointed to his right upper arm. "It said: *IDFMA*. Can you imagine?" he laughed a short, bitter laugh. "*IDFMA*," Durham said. "We were the only ones who knew what it meant. *It Doesn't Fucking Matter Any More*. I went to fly for my country and I came back *IDFMA*. I almost quit the Marines."

"And….?" Hamal asked.

"And I didn't," Durham said. "You can see that for yourself, can't you?"

"Sorry," Hamal apologized. "Hand me that flask." Durham took another drink.

"I'll tell you something, Jew-jockey." Durham passed the flask back to Hamal, who drank from it. "I've seen guys come back from Vietnam," Durham said, "and lose it – drunks – drugs – homeless – divorced. Some of the best guys. My good friends. Make it through the war, come home, and completely lose a grip."

"Sorry, Major," the MP's flashlight lit up Hamal and Durham. "This is a restricted area. I'll have to ask you to leave."

"You can ask me, Lieutenant whoever-you-are," Durham said, "whatever the hell you like."

"Sorry, sorry," Hamal jumped in, "we're just on our way." Hamal took Durham's arm, pulled him away, and the two walked back to the PX, where Durham bought them two more beers. They sat down with a Sergeant, and Durham introduced him to Hamal as Mike Healy, from Albany, New York.

Sgt. Healey stood, saluted the Major, then sat down again and shook hands with Hamal. "That's right, sir. Albany, New York. A hell of a place to come from. Whatever you haven't learned on the streets of Albany ain't much. For the rest, there's the Marine corps."

"I was just telling our friend here, Maj. Ilan Hamal," Durham's speech was now slurring, and his tone was too jolly, "about Vietnam. You were in Vietnam, weren't you, Sgt. Mike Healy from Albany, New York?"

"Yes, sir," Healy said. "Da Nang the whole damn dang time."

"And you came home, and you didn't lose it, did you?"

"Lose what, sir?"

"We better get to bed," Hamal interjected.

"Lose your marbles, Healy. Up here." Durham, getting louder, pointed his finger at Healy's forehead.

"I should never have…." Hamal began.

Durham cut him off. "You should have and you did have."

"He did what, sir?" Healy asked.

"He said you lost your marbles in Vietnam."

"Hey!" Hamal interjected. "Vietnam was a tough mess. I never said…."

"Yeah," Healy said, "Vietnam was a damn tough mess, but if you weren't there don't talk about it. All right?"

"Look," Hamal said, "I just meant…."

"Don't matter what you meant," said Healy. "The Major was there. I was there. You weren't."

"All right," Hamal said, backing off, "you were there, tell me about it then."

"Look!" Healy jumped up, yelling. "Drop it! I told you…."

Hamal got up too, but before he got to his feet, Healy swung at him, caught Hamal on the head, knocked him over.

"Stop!" Durham yelled, adrenelin-sobered in an instant.

Capt. David Rose and Capt. Rai Atari, who had just come into the PX, ran to the fight. They hauled Sgt. Healy out and faced him off. Three Americans in for a snack hurried to help Healy. Capt. Rose joined the fray, while Hamal and Durham both yelled out orders: "Everybody freeze!" "Stand off!"

The fight raged on scattering burgers, fries, cokes, tacos. Rose and Atari opened up with punches and kicks. They had one man down, three others still on the attack, two of them about to take Rose down. Rose crashed to the floor with two Americans on top of him, swinging, as Atari fought to pull the Americans off and away.

Durham joined the battle, kicking at one Ameican's belly. The American rolled over holding his stomach. Durham kicked at another American's shoulder. He rolled off. Durham stood back, yelled: "Up! Attention! Do it!"

The four Americans scrambled up, all at attention, all breathing hard. Durham yelled at them: "Form up! Over there!"

Sgt. Healy whirled around on Hamal, shoved his clenched fist toward him. "Watch your fucking back."

"Sit down!" Durham yelled. "Shut down! Listen up!"

Durham turned to the Israelis. Rose was up, steadying himself, brushing himself off. Atari stood beside him. Hamal stood closer to the table, on the other side.

Durham turned back to the four Americans. "Not one word out of you men. Sergeant!" Durham called out to the Mess Officer. "Seven hot black java, cream and sugar on the side, and one for me, hot and black. You got that?"

"Sir. Right up, sir."

The seven men sat in silence. When the coffee came, they mixed cream and sugar to their liking.

Durham spoke to the Americans. "If I've got a gripe with these guys," Durham gestured toward the Israelis, "I'll take care of it myself. I fight my own damn fights. Don't ever get in my way again. I could have you all up on charges. Court martial."

Durham walked back and forth in front of the Americans, eyeing each one. The men held their heads down. "When I look at you, you look back at me!" he yelled at them.

"Yes, sir!" the men sang in unison.

Durham looked at each man again, each one now looking back at him, Durham staring them down. Durham paced in front of the group. "Stand up, Marine!" he commanded one of the men. "Name, rank, serial number!"

"Corporal Mark Skeeter, sir! 1285762, sir!"

"Where you from, Skeeter?"

"Flint, Michigan, sir."

"Aren't you proud of that, Skeeter?" Durham yelled.

"Flint, Michigan, sir!" Skeeter yelled.

"You couldn't fight your way out of a wet paper bag, Skeeter, could you?" Durham asked.

Skeeter glanced at the Israelis.

"You're talking to me, Skeeter, not them!" Durham yelled.

"No, sir."

"No, sir, what sir?" Durham demanded.

"No, sir, I could not fight my way out of a paper bag, sir."

"Out of a *wet* paper bag, Skeeter. Listen to me when I talk to you. I said you couldn't fight your goddamn way out of a goddamn *wet* paper bag."

"Yes, sir. No, sir, I could not fight my goddamn way out of a goddamn wet paper bag, sir."

"That's better, Skeeter." Durham lowered his voice. "But that's a lie, isn't it, Skeeter?"

"Yes, sir," Skeeter snapped back, smiling. "It's a damn lie."

"Why'd you lie, Skeeter?"

"Because you told me to, sir."

"If I told you to piss your pants, Skeeter, would you piss your pants?"

"If I could sir, yes, sir."

"Would you, Skeeter?"

"Yes, sir. I would."

"What are you smiling at Skeeter?"

"Nothing, sir." Skeeter straightened himself up.

"Are you a United States Marine, Skeeter?" Durham barked out.

"One hundred percent, sir."

"How many?"

"One hundred fifty percent, sir."

"Sit down Skeeter. Now you guys all get yourselevs some food and get the hell on out of here. Go eat somewhere else. You want to fight, beat the crap out of each other."

While the Americans re-ordered and waited for their food, the three Israelis sat without speaking. Durham sat at the table next to them. When the Americans were gone, Durham spoke first.

"These guys are tough," Durham said. "I wouldn't mess with them."

"We take care of things," Capt. Rose said.

"You got the worst of it, Rose," said Durham. He sipped his coffee. "You all right?"

"I'll live," Rose said.

"It looks like it," Durham said. "Watch out. Some guys have a very short fuse on Vietnam."

"It's all right," Hamal said. "Shit happens, as you guys say."

"Up!" Durham yelled. "At attention."

Atari and Rose looked toward Hamal. After a second, Hamal stood, at attention. The other two followed.

"Don't tell me shit happens!" Durham yelled. "I know shit." Durham now paced in front of the three Israelis, Hamal, Atari, and Rose. "Whose turf you on now?" Durham asked them.

"Yours," Hamal alone answered.

"Act like it," Durham said.

"But...." Rose began.

"No goddamn 'buts', Rose." Durham came face to face with Rose. "Answer me!"

"OK," Rose said. "OK."

"OK, what, Rose?"

"OK, sir," Rose said.

"OK, sir, what, sir?" Durham demanded.

"OK," Rose yelled out as loud as he could, "sir! No goddamn buts, sir!"

"Better, Rose," Durham said, straight faced.

"Major...?" Hamal said.

"At ease!" Durham commanded. "What is it, *Major*?"

"I'd like all four of those Americans shipped out of here tomorrow."

Durham thought for a moment., looking straight at the Israelis. "You're not worried," he said slowly, "about a personal vendetta, are you, Hamal?"

"No" Hamal said. "I'm worried about the security

of our aircraft, about our training."

"And you're not thinking about the welfare of those four Americans, who may happen to like it here at Midnight?" Durham asked.

"I care about our mission."

"And what if I care about those Americans. They're my mission, too."

"Your choice," Hamal said. "Your authority."

"I'll do it," Durham said. "I'm turning in. Maybe I can sleep now."

Hamal caught up with Durham, walked with him outside.

"Goodnight," Hamal said, as Durham walked off. "Sorry if I started something."

Durham had walked about thirty yards, but stopped, looked back at Hamal where Hamal stood under the one lamp over the door of the PX.

"Don't take prisoners and don't apologize," Durham said loudly so his voice would carry clearly the thirty yards between them. "Vietnam was a goddamn dirty, stupid, son-of-a-bitching, long, drawn out, fucked up war run by a bunch of politicians who wouldn't let us win and couldn't let themselves lose. And furthermore," Durham finished in one breath, paused, added, "you've never heard me cuss so much before. You never will again. I'm a proper Southern Genleman, even if my great-great-grandfather was an escaped black slave and my great-great-grandmother was Cherokee Indian, and my great-grandfather got shot to death stealing a goddamn goat."

Hamal was laughing. "You look like a typical American white guy," he said.

I *am* America," Durham said. "I'm more American than George Washington – Thomas Jefferson – John F. Kennedy – Lyndon Johnson – Jimmy-the-peanut-Carter and Ronald Reagan all rolled up together. When I went on mission in Vietnam I used to climb aboard and say," Durham yelled out loud, "Look out, you bastards, America's flying here!" He raised his fist in the air.

"I do understand you on Vietnam," Hamal called out across the distance between them.

"I don't need your understanding," Durham said. "It's our thing."

"Don't ever call me 'Jew-jockey' again," Hamal said.

"In my country," Durham said more quietly, "that's love."

"In mine, it's not," Hamal persisted.

"No offense. Never again."

"If I can't trust you completely, in every way, then we're doomed here," Hamal said.

"Likewise," Durham said. "If I can't trust you completely, each one of the guys in every way, then we're doomed here."

"I'm in," Hamal said.

"I'm in." Durham turned, walked off. But then,

turning back, he walked quickly toward Hamal. When he stood close to Hamal, he grabbed Hamal by his shoulder, and said, through clenched teeth, "And don't ever go to war and do something you'll be ashamed of. Ever!"

He let go of Hamal's shoulder.

"Did you?" Hamal asked. "Did you?"

"No," Durham said. "I'm one of the lucky ones."

TEN

Hamal rejoined his pilots where they sat, in the otherwise empty PX, sipping coffee, talking in hushed tones.

"Do you trust him?" Capt. Rose said to Hamal.

"Trust who?"

"Durham. He's on their side."

Maj. Hamal, leaning into the table, spoke in a low, measured, firm voice. "You have one job here," he said. "We all have the same job. Train. Forget about Durham. Do I trust him? My instinct trusts him every turn of the way. They went through something we never will. Do you trust me, David?"

"Of course," Rose said.

"Then trust my trust of Durham. Durham's a hundred percent."

Everyone sat quietly. Hamal broke the silence with a question. "Are you with me?" he asked Rose.

"Of course," Rose said. "What a crazy question."

Hamal stared at Rose, challenging Rose to look back at him steadily and honestly. Hamal held out his hand. Rose grasped it, held it firmly.

"You don't trust Durham," Hamal said, holding on to Rose's grip, looking Rose right in the eye. "OK. I can't make you trust him. Just trust me, Rose." Hamal let go his grip. Hamal and Rose both relaxed.

"Ilan," Rose said, "give me your best guess on what we're up to here."

"If I knew," Hamal said, lying, "I'd tell you, David."

"We're not just training here cause we've got some new toys," Rose said. "We're doing this for a reason."

"So, David? For what reason?" Atari asked.

"Think about it."

Hamal took a bite of his burrito, a sip of his beer. "I don't know," he said, "things are never quiet in Israel."

"Lebanon?" Atari asked.

"Not Lebanon," Rose said.

"How do you know?" Atari asked. "You're so sure of yourself."

"Yes," Rose said, "I'm sure it's not Lebanon. But it's something specific. I feel it in my bones."

"Go put your bones to bed," Hamal told him.

"I'm serious." Rose persisted.

The other two looked at Rose. No one spoke for a few seconds, then Hamal said, "OK, David, you're serious. And if I believe you, then what? And if it's not Lebanon, then what? Syria? Perhaps. Egypt? No. Jordan? No. Iran? No. Iraq? No."

"Look," Rose said, "think about it. Syria, perhaps. Iraq, perhaps. Two possibilities. Think it over guys. Two very serious possibilities. Syria: do we push the Syrians out of Lebanon? Iraq: I don't know why I say

Iraq. I can eliminate everybody else. Egypt, Jordan, Iran. Not Syria and not Iraq."

"Why Iraq? Why now?" Atari said. "It doesn't make sense."

"Syria I can explain. Iraq I can't," Rose said. "Don't ask me."

Although they had the cafeteria to themselves, the four men huddled together. They spoke in lowered voices.

"If...." Atari began, "if....let's put Syria aside for a moment. If it's Iraq, it must be because Iraq plans an attack on us. But Iraq alone wouldn't try anything against us, not without Syria, probably not without Egypt. So if it's Iraq, it's Iraq *and* Syria. And if so, on the Iraqi front....this time we have to fight in......"

"Go ahead," Rose prompted him.

"We fight in....Iraq."

"Which means...." Rose pushed again.

"Which means to get to Iraq we'd overfly Jordan, Syria, Saudi Arabia. We'd overheat ourselves. We'd draw out the line, we'd go too far."

"We never go too far," Rose corrected. "You know that. We're IAF. We're invincible. We go anywhere."

"You're listening to too much IAF propaganda, David," Atari said. "Even we can go too far."

"Is it true, Ilan? Maj. Hamal? Can even we go too far? And come back?"

"Who ever said it was Iraq?" Hamal said.

"Right," Rose said. "Whoever said that? Just a dumb hunch I had. Right? Bedtime all."

All but Ilan Hamal went to bed. Hamal added to the letter to his wife: "Sorry. Got interrupted. More tomorrow." He signed the letter, put it in an envelope, then took his saxaphone out to a place he had found earlier, and played some improvised tunes by himself for an hour.

ELEVEN

At 0430 the dawn only suggested itself across the desert. A hint of whitish-blue increased minute by minute, mixing in with the night's darkness.

The pilots had all explored the desert. They knew how close the moon and stars look in the expanse of the desert sky. Even this morning, as they each heard only the rustle of their own flight suits, they heard that rustling inside the desert silence. Distinct from other silences, it is made up of the absence of sound and the vastness of space.

It is a desert space filled with white evening primrose, purple sand verbena, yellow, green, and dark purple cactus flowers. Filled with an unlimited expanse of the light brown, pock-marked skeletons of desiccated, decaying cholla cactus, the green of the tall suguaro cactus, the bright orange of wavering ocotillo spines, the fluffy white heads of teddy-bear cactus. Filled with the wildness of coyote who live without water but who survive only on meat and blood, of the gila monster, deer and javelina, sidewinder and desert bighorn and pronghorn. Filled with mountains, valleys, watering basins, oases, mirages, wind-worn and water-worn rock formations. And filled with the remnants of ancient, pre-historic human life: holes in granite rock made by pounding small seeds and mesquite beans into flour, petroglyphs of animals, dancing figures, geometric shapes carved and painted into reddish-brown rock.

Each pilot mounted his craft — each one with the help of his own Plane Captain — got strapped in, settled in, checked gauges, waited. Maj. Durham had wanted this dawn take-off partly for the excitement of the light at this time of day, partly for the experience of the aircraft taking off, then rising in this light air. As the planes took off, Durham watched their ascent from the cockpit of his own F-16.

Then Durham took off behind them, along the same runway, right-hand side of the white center-line. Airborne, Durham found the Israelis at 22,000 feet, ascending. At 30,000 feet he called them into Alpha formation. Then sent them off in pairs for practice combat. They dove, rolled, pulled, rose and spun in, around and at each other. They watched each other, keeping an eye on the target. They snuck around each other. They kept their stick easy, the parameters of their craft's possibilities within limits. They watched screens and laser beams. They weighed their options so fast that each instant's decision was gone before thought could catch up with it. They kept themselves within their own task-overload zone.

As they finished these exercises and went in for

landing, Hamal ordered his men into a trailing formation at 3000 feet. They descended to 500 feet. Flat hatting. A touch above the desert they flew just over canyons, briefly dove into a canyon and through it, made abrupt turns, turned back on their route to fly it another way, flew between narrow canyon walls, rolled over hilltops, followed each other by an instinct and a visual and manual acuity so sharp that the distance between the tail of one plane and the nose of the next hardly varied.

"What the hell are you doing, Hamal?" Durham said aloud, descending through 10,000 feet, but not over the radio. Just to himself. He watched the eight Israelis pilot their planes through low-flight high intensity maneuvers, curves and turns, following the terrain so closely they might be out hiking it. "Hamal, what kind of games are you playing?" Durham said aloud. "What are you doing to those planes?" He could watch no more.

"Bravo One to Eagle Leader. Hamal, back to base. Now. Over."

"Roger. Eagle One to Eagles, back to base. Over."

In the briefing room, the pilots waited for Durham to show up. They sipped coffee, ate toast, drank orange juice.

When Durham came in they all stood to attention, saluting, even Hamal. Durham said nothing, saluted back, then walked up to the front of the room.

"Sit down," Durham ordered. When the men sat, he continued:

"I've put you into $24 million machines. Israel has bought them. But don't forget where they come from. I've got a stake in these planes no matter who owns them. The people who designed them have a stake in them. The people who built them have a stake in them. If one of those planes goes down, everyone goes down. Don't hot-rod with my planes. That's how you come to die. You had your fun. All right? No more. Breakfast in twenty minutes. Back in the saddle at 0900. Ready to learn. Dismissed!"

On the way out of the room Durham grabbed Hamal by the arm, held him back from the others.

"You guys were up to something out there. You're not a bunch of jokers. There's not a stupid hot-roding bone in any one of your bodies. Something's going on. You pulled that low-flying stunt very much on purpose."

Hamal didn't answer, didn't move. He looked Durham in the eye with the look of a patient man.

"You're up to something, Hamal. You're not going to tell me what it is. I thought you guys were playing with me. But you're all work out there. Unfortunately I happened to be around. Is that right?"

Durham waited for an answer. None came.

"You're playing with disaster."

Hamal nodded his head, once.

"But you have no choice?" Durham asked.

Again, Hamal nodded his head once in the affir-mative.

"When you get these beauties back to Israel, you fly them however you like. While you're under my command you fly them like I tell you to. I won't have disasters on my watch."

Hamal took a breath, exhaled it.

"I would like to promise you that, Maj. Durham."

"But you won't?"

"I can't."

"You need this particular desert terrain to practice in?"

Hamal didn't answer.

"But you have plenty of desert in Israel."

Again, Hamal didn't answer.

"Any unapproved maneuvers you practice against my orders I'll record in the transmission tapes. I'll make a record in my own flight logs. I'll write them up in my reports."

"I understand."

"I'll cover my ass. I won't be responsible for your crashes. I like you guys. I even like you, Hamal. I don't want you on my conscience."

"I understand," Hamal said. "I would do the same."

"There's a difference between my Air Force and your IAF, isn't there?"

"Maybe so."

"In Vietnam our blood and guts were on the line. But Ho Chi Minh would never march up Pennsylvania Avenue. It's not that way with you."

Hamal stood silent. Durham watched him for a moment, reading him.

"You understand," Durham said, "that I won't file any reports of your flight violations until you guys leave here with your new merchandise."

"I understand," Hamal answered.

Capt. Rose caught up with Hamal on the way to the dining room. "What did Durham want from you just now?"

"I told you, David, trust Durham. Trust my trust of Durham. Leave him to me."

As they came to the dining room, Rose said, "Don't let him get in our way."

Hamal sanpped back, "Leave Durham to me, David. That's an order."

Later, in one of his regular phone conversations with Col. Yossi Ben Luria, Hamal reported on the success they had flying at super low altitudes. Ben Luria spoke to Gen. Dror the next morning, relaying that information. Dror would leave that night for Midnight Air Force Base. To keep in touch with the guys. Did Ben Luria want to join him?

"Just for a few days," Ben Luria said. "I can't stay away from home too long."

Dror and Ben Luria boarded a regular El Al commercial flight for New York. During the flight, Col. Ben Luria read, while Dror listened to famous opera arias on the airline's headphones. From there they took a United Airlines flight to Salt Lake City, where they rented a car, drove on to Midnight. They met Maj. Durham, then met with their eight Israeli pilots.

Dror and Ben Luria saw the F-16s. They sat in the cockpits. They held the controls. Dror, especially, took the feel of the plane, what it might feel like airborne. They watched their IAF pilots take off in them.

Hamal and Ben Luria took some time for themselves alone. They had dinner together off base. Ben Luria brought news of home, of his family, of Hamal's family, while Hamal reported in detail about the successes and difficulties of the F-16. Hamal and Ben Luria planned a hike together in the Utah landscape, but there was no time. Both were busy.

Landing back in Tel Aviv, Dror and Ben Luria agreed that it was good to be home, but bad to leave America, where they had a good time, where they felt a little relief from the strains of Israeli life. They promised each other that on the next trip they'd take time for themselves, go to Zion National Park, relax. They knew it was unlikely they would find time for all that.

Aviva Dror and Tamar Ben Luria met them at the airport.

TWELVE

After a 20-minute phone conversation with Ben Luria, Dror woke his wife, then sat beside her on the bed, talking for a few minutes as she came out of her morning drowsiness. Aviva went to wake the kids, their eldest daughter, Batya, who was studying at the University, their teen-age daughter, Rachel, and their teen-age son, Adam, both in high school.

Gen. Dror left home at 6:45 a.m. It was already warm. Dror wore a short-sleeve olive-green uniform shirt, and no jacket. From the Jerusalem hilltop where he lived, Dror's house looked out over the ancient walls of the Old City. The Drors lived next to an art center founded in 1907 by one of the Rothschilds. Smaller houses with courtyards and walkways stepped all the way down the hill. One concrete stairway from the top to the bottom of the hill connected all the houses.

From East Jerusalem, meuzzins called the Muslims to prayer. Pious Jews gathered in small synagogues for their early morning service. Jerusalem was already busy, filling with Jews, Muslims, Christians, Druze, Bedouin, Armenians, Turks, tourists.

From his hilltop home, Dror liked to watch the life of the Old City through binoculars: Arab women squatting at the Damascus gate, selling spices from the open burlap bags in front of them; the Western Wall, what remained of the Temple of Solomon; the Temple Mount, Al Aqsa in Arabic, the site sacred to Muslims from where Mohammed had risen to the heavens, and sacred to some Jews as the site of the original Temple of Solomon. Dror liked to take foreign visitors to this vantage point, to let them see that small piece of real estate containing both the Western Wall and the Temple Mount. "The same land to fight over, holy to everyone," he would tell his guests. "Why exactly the same small piece of land?"

Most mornings, at about this time, Dror would ride down the hill, past his cousins' house two doors down from his own, into the hub of the city, to the government buildings. Most days, as today, he would ride in his car, a new 1980 armored Mercedes Benz, with only his driver, David.

Two Shin Bet Internal Security cars made up Dror's entourage. One Shin Bet car went ahead of the General, the other Shin Bet car followed. The four Shin Bet men had been with the General for several years.

Dror had a funny habit of reading the Jerusalem Post in the morning, the English language newspaper, rather than the Hebrew newspapers. Those he saved for later, in his office.

They passed a car parked on the General's right. An older model from the early '70s, a maroon Toyota

Corolla. As they came beside it, the Toyota exploded with a deafening blast. Just feet from the General's car. Glass, metal, rubber, flames flew through the street. The blast incinerated a street-cat asleep under the Toyota. The explosion rocked the General's armored Mercedes Benz, lifting it and knocking it over a foot. David controlled the car, following the now speeding Shin Bet lead car. The trailing Shin Bet car stopped dead.

The two Shin Bet agents in the trailing car studied the area. Another car bomb went off, this time just as the lead Shin Bet car passed it. The exploding debris blew out two tires of the Shin Bet car, careening it into a line of parked cars.

The General's car stood dead stuck between the two Shin Bet cars. One agent in the trailing car was on the radio to headquarters. The two agents in the lead car jumped out with Uzis. The trailing car pulled up tight behind the General. The General had ducked to the floor in the back seat. He lay in that tight space, seeing nothing, only listening. He had his pistol out. He grabbed his briefcase off the back seat, then, by twisting his body he managed to shove it under the driver's seat. David stood outside the car, waving his pistol in every direction.

Then it came: a small black car stopped at the intersection just up the block. Three men in black ski masks jumped out, AK-47s blasting rounds. One lead

Shin Bet agent — Avi Katz — collapsed to the ground, gushing blood. The other lead-car agent returned fire from behind the armored door of his car. Both Shin Bet agents from the trailing car jumped onto the hood of their car. From that high ground they fired over the General's car, spraying the street with blasts of round after round after round of Uzi. Bullets banged off cars. Shattered windows. Shredded the bodies of the three PLO assassins. Dror aimed his pistol at the car's passenger window. If they would get him at least he would return fire. Had they attacked his house? Aviva? The kids? Quiet came. Dror lay still. He hadn't been hit. Were they all dead out there? He raised himself up, but David motioned for him to get down.

David and the three surviving Shin Bet agents waited a minute. They watched. Two minutes........ three minutes.......... four........

They relaxed their vigilance only when a chaos of helicopters flew overhead, sirens wailed in the streets, soldiers ran from both directions up and down the block. Six soldiers ran straight to the General's car, took him out, surrounded him. They walked him down the block, past the flaming car, past the trailing Shin Bet car, along this street of catastrophe to where an armored vehicle awaited him. The armored car sped off toward the hospital. Dror demanded that they take him straight to his meeting with the Prime Minister's Security Cabinet.

"I'm shaken," Dror said, "but this meeting will take place. I'll get a drink when I get there. A stiff whiskey. I'll be all right."

"I have firm orders, sir," the Lieutenant protested, "that I take you straight to the hospital."

"Call for amended instructions," Dror insisted. "I countermand your instructions myself."

The Lieutenant called in, got new orders, then sped off toward the government buildings. Dror arrived exactly 38 minutes late, given that he had set out exactly 15 minutes early.

When he entered the meeting room, Col. Yossi Ben Luria greeted him.

"Get me a drink, Yossi. Whiskey on the rocks."

"Yes, sir," Ben Luria left the room. When he came back with the whiskey, Arie Solen said,

"Yossi, damn it, get me one too."

"Sure," Ben Luria said, "don't worry. Mr. Prime Minister?"

"No!"

With a trembling hand, Dror raised the whiskey to his lips.

"Drink it, Jonathan," the Prime Minister demanded. "I need you now."

"I know it, damnit!" Dror said.

Col. Ben Luria came back with another whiskey for Arie Solen.

"Get a blanket for Dror," the Prime Minister ordered Ben Luria, "he may be in shock."

"I'm not in shock!"

"Even you, Dror. Get the blanket, Yossi."

For the third time, Ben Luria rushed out of the room, this time returning with an army issue blanket which he draped over Dror's shoulders. Dror's body shook.

"Who was it?" Solen asked.

"Arafat," Dror answered him. "Who the hell do you think it was!"

"Come on," Solen got angry, "of course it was Arafat, but who, do you know who?"

"Yes," Dror said, "it was PLO. Al Fatah. They're getting more organized, more sophisticated now to pull this off. But still not smart enough to execute it. If three more of them had come in from the rear, or the side alley, they would have killed us all." He sat up to finish his whiskey.

"Bring in the bottle, Yossi," the Prime Minister said.

"I should get a doctor," Ben Luria said.

"Yes," the Prime Minister said, "get a doctor."

Ben Luria dashed out of the room for the fourth time. He hurried back in with the bottle of whiskey.

"The doctor's on his way." He poured another drink for both Dror and Solen.

"Take one yourself, Yossi," the Prime Minister said.

"Thank you, sir. I'm fine. I need my wits about me."

"Have Moshé call a Cabinet meeting. In one hour.

Hurry," the Prime Minister ordered.

Again, Ben Luria rushed out of the room.

"Can you talk?" the Prime Minister asked Dror.

In one swift movement Dror threw off the blanket, jumped up, paced the room.

"The bastards!" Dror screamed. "The fucking bastards! On my own street! Where my family lives! Add more guards to my house! My wife. My kids, for God's sake! No. Forget it. I have enough goddamn guards for a fortress. I think they killed Avi Katz. He was in the lead car. I saw him down. They got Avi Katz! It was a fire fight. On my own street! They're fucking savages!"

Arie Solen took the General by the shoulders.

"Sit down," Solen said. "You may be in shock. Cover yourself. Stay warm. In fact, here, lie down on the couch. We have already fortified your house. We're watching your wife. The kids. Everyone's ok."

Solen got Dror to lie down on the couch, then covered him with the blanket.

"I'm all right," Dror said.

The doctor arrived, took Dror's temperature, his pulse, checked his breathing, his lungs, generally checked him out. He agreed with the General: he was not in shock, just shaken up. The whiskey and the blanket, the doctor said, were the best medicine. Dror got up from the couch with Arie Solen's helping hand, then sat down at the meeting table.

"Let's go," Dror said. "We've got much to do. And I

left my goddamn briefcase in my goddamn car."

The Prime Minister looked up at Ben Luria.

"I'll have Moshé send someone," Col. Ben Luria said.

"They're monsters." Dror was on the point of hysteria, of bursting into uncontrollable rage. He steadied himself.

"Take your time," Solen said.

"Yes, take your time," the Prime Minister said, "but don't forget that I need you now."

"I'll make them pay for this," Dror said.

"We will absolutely make them pay," the Prime Minister agreed. "Heavily."

"I have real news for you," Dror said. "I intend to report it. I have documents in my brief case, charts, drawings, photographs of the F-16 with our boys inside them. But I can tell you all of it."

"Go on," the Prime Minister said.

"The F-16," Dror continued, "is a fantastic aircraft. It can accomplish its mission once it gets to Osiraq. I have no doubt about that. It can annihilate Osiraq. Lay it in ruins."

"Then why attack on the ground?" the Prime Minister asked. "If we can do it from the air, then by all means, from the air."

"I'm ready," said Gen. Menasche Slomovic, Commander of the Army. "I'm ready for a two-day ground assault anytime. We can do it. Give me 2,000 men and

20 tanks. That's what I'll need. Put me on the ground near Tuwaitha"

"But let's do it from the air," Prime Minister Begin said. "Why not from the air?"

"I don't trust it," Slomovic said. "The F-16 can't make it to Osiraq and back. It doesn't have the range. It has to fly over miles and miles and miles of enemy air space. Vulnerable for hours on end."

"You're right," Dror said, "the F-16 can't make the mission to Osiraq as it is now. It's too far. Fully loaded, the F-16 can fly about 600 kilometers. The round trip to Osiraq is about 1,800 kilometers. On top of that the boys will have to do some fancy flying. That extends the total mileage. Plus the bombing dives. Then climbing out. That all cuts down on their range. Make it 2,000 kilometers altogether, there and back."

"They won't come back," Gen. Slomovic said.

"So," Dror continued, "what do we do?" He took a sip of whiskey. "Damn that is the right medicine." Shoulders shivering slightly, he went on. "I told my engineers: I *must* get that aircraft 2,000 kilometers at least. I have no options. What the engineers told me is this: We retrofit the F-16 with two extra external gas tanks."

"That's not so easy," Slomovic said.

"No, it's not so easy." He took another sip of whiskey. "We have to build a feeding system between the two extra tanks to keep them balanced in weight.

THE LORD OF SILENCE

Electronic sensors. We'll need new avionics. Recalibrations."

"You're trying to jerry-rig a highly specific aircraft."

"We can do that," Gen. Dror said. "We strip her canon. We take away her air-to-air missiles. We give her extra gasoline in return. She can carry two 90 kilo bombs per aircraft. Eight planes. Sixteen bombs. She can get to Osiraq, she can deliver her payload with unbelievable accuracy because we have unbelievable pilots, she can return home. But she cannot defend herself along the way."

"That's insane," Slomovic said.

"No, not mad. Brilliant. Think about it. Those boys will overfly Jordan, Saudi Arabia, then come all the way across Iraq. It's insane. But we can do it. They *will be* attacked.

"Yes!" Slomovic shouted. "They will be attacked."

"Our solution? An armada: we surround the F-16s with six F-15s. Those things are fighting tigers. We ask the F-16 pilots to accept the F-15s as their only protection. That's a lot to ask of a fighter pilot."

"What about the mission's success," Slomovic said. "If it fails, there's no second chance. Saddam gets the bomb. The Army can't fail."

"We already have the F-15s, we have the pilots," Dror went on. "I've put those guys on alert training. They're flying four, five hours a day now, they're doing maneuvers. This plan is sheer madness, yes, and that's why it *will* work. If it doesn't work, you're right, we're in deep trouble."

"How far can the F-15s go?" Slomovic asked.

"They're lighter," Gen. Dror answered. "They keep all their defenses."

"How will you overfly Saudi Arabia, Jordan, and most of Iraq?" Slomovic pursued his questioning. "Then drop a payload under air and ground fire, turn around, come back over the same sky? You'll have dogfights every millimeter of the way."

"Listen carefully," Dror said. "Once the F-16s get here from the States, I'll train those pilots in maneuvers no one has ever heard of. They'll fly under radar, they'll skim the deck at altitudes lower than anybody believes they can. They'll hide in the alleyways between desert walls, around natural formations."

"My God," Slomovic said, "you expect supermen. These guys are just mortal human pilots."

"No, I expect F-16s, F-15s, and *my* pilots. When they get back from the States, we retrofit those F-16s. I'll do test flights to prove we can do it. I'll document it all. Come out to the desert to watch. I promise you."

"We can succeed on the ground," Slomovic said. "No question. We go in. We do the job. We get out. Just give me the air support I need."

"How many troops would you lose on the ground?"

"And how many planes," Slomovic asked, "must we count on losing?"

"If we destroy Osiraq," Dror said, "then get one airplane home, would I count that a success? I would."

"Your plan is madness. Braggadocio," Slomovic said, "ill conceived. What if you destroy Osiraq and don't bring one plane home?"

"Mission accomplished."

"And if you send them out there and they don't destroy Osiraq?" Slomovic asked.

"Then," Dror said, "we fight our way in with your 2,000 men and your 20 tanks. Whatever the hell you want then."

"By then we've lost surprise. It's a possibility, Jonathan. You could lose every plane."

"Yes. I could. But it's also a possibility I could obliterate Osiraq."

"Can we attack unilaterally, pre-emptively?" Rafi Stone said.

"You leave diplomacy to me," the Prime Minister said. "I want this plan to go ahead. *This* is the plan I choose.

"We'll need our own engineers, our mechanics," Dror said. "We need to retrain our boys in those retrofitted machines. The planes will fly differently. Their mission will be different."

"Bring them home soon," the Prime Minister said. "I want everything ready. Then prove to me they can do it. How fast can the F-16 go?"

"Mach 2," Dror said.

"Not fast enough, but it'll do," the Prime Minister said.

"Mach 2!" Dror said. "What do you want, the speed of light?"

"Arrange a meeting for me with the F-16 pilots," the Prime Minister said. "I know what we're asking of them — to go out there unarmed. I want to see the F-15 boys, too. Make those meetings look like some ordinary event."

"When do we go?" Dror asked.

"I want everything ready, Jonathan. I decide when we go."

Dror stared at the Prime Minister.

"But Menahem," Dror said, "you'll decide when to go based on my advice."

"I'll take your advice as always I do," the Prime Minister said, "but I'll decide. I'll base my decision on factors you can't even imagine."

"I want to know everything. I won't send my boys out there without knowing everything."

Ben Luria stood behind the Prime Minister, laid his hand on the Prime Minister's shoulder.

"Jonathan," the Prime Minister began, "you have military problems to solve. I have military and political problems to solve. I have internal political problems and I have geopolitical problems. I'll have them all secured before I make my move."

"I want consultation on them all. I'll know every consequence of my orders."

"Things move fast. But things take time. I'll report to you on everything as I can. I promise you. I want your promise that you'll follow whatever orders I give you when I give them."

"That you have," Dror said. "Arie," Dror addressed Arie Solen, "I need to talk with you. Right away. Can you come to me this afternoon, at my house?"

"I'll be there. 3:00?"

"No. They'll need you here. Not until...say....5:30. Then stay for dinner."

"Of course," Solen said. "I'll be there. 5:30."

"Does anyone remember Avi Katz?" Dror asked the room.

No one answered.

"No one remembers Avi Katz? Shin Bet. You remember him, don't you, Arie?"

"No, Jonathan, I don't. Avi Katz?" Solen shook his head.

"Menahem?" Dror asked the Prime Minister. "You remember him? Avi Katz. A young guy. Thirty-five maybe. Shin Bet. Avi Katz. A really good kid. A joker."

"Sorry. No."

"Too bad," Dror said. "They killed him this morning."

Solen and Dror left the room, closing the door behind them, leaving the Prime Minister alone in the room with Ben Luria.

Yossi had walked over to the window, looked out at the city.

"Sit down, Yossi," the Prime Minister said.

"If you don't mind, sir, I'd rather stand. I don't mean to turn my back to you, but it calms me a bit. My city. Jerusalem."

"All right, Yossi, that's fine."

The Prime Minister took two ice cubes from the bucket Ben Luria had brought in. He clanked the two ice cubes into a clean glass, then poured himself a whiskey.

"Maj. Ilan Hamal, he's a good friend of yours?"

"Yes, sir," Ben Luria said. "We were at University together. Roommates. I was older. Because I'd stayed in the army."

"And you were close friends?"

"Yes," Ben Luria answered him, "very close friends."

"Where's he from?"

"Kibbutz. Gan Yosef."

"In the Galilee."

"Yes, sir."

"Do you know his family?"

"Yes, sir. A big family. His mother and father came from Poland around '20, '22, something like that. They both fought in '48."

"They both survived?"

"Yes. He's got two brothers, three sisters."

"All here, in Israel?"

"Yes."

"Do they all get along?"

"More or less. The little family squabbles, different

personalities, but they all get along, yes. They're all pretty close."

"But Maj. Ilan Hamal is the only one in the family still in the military?

"Yes."

"He will lead this mission. To Osiraq. Wing Leader."

Ben Luria looked still out the window, his hands behind his back.

"I've lost other friends, good friends," Ben Luria said.

"You won't lose your friend Maj. Ilan Hamal on this mission, Yossi."

"Yes, sir."

"I'd like to make that a promise to you, but I can't," the Prime Minister said.

"Thank you."

"We can't afford to lose him. Or the others. But especially him. Do you understand me?"

"Of course."

"A whiskey, Yossi?"

"Yes, sir."

Ben Luria sat next to the Prime Minister. The Prime Minister took ice from the bucket, then poured a glass of whiskey. He raised his glass in a toast, Ben Luria did the same.

"To your friend, then. To Maj. Ilan Hamal."

"To Ilan."

They clinked, and drank.

"Do you talk to Maj. Hamal?" the Prime Minister asked him.

"Not in a while. Not since he left for the States."

"So you know where he is?"

"I've figured it out. Not hard to tell. He's training on an F-16."

"I have political trouble, Yossi."

"Yes, sir. I know."

"My own party, my own Likud, has problems with my plan. And of course the entire Labor Party is against it. Right up the line, right up to the top. But Dror believes in it a hundred percent. And Solen believes in it a hundred percent. It's our best option. It's genius. Dror's genius. Very risky, dangerous, outlandish genius. We could lose some of those men. Calm will be the mother of our genius, I always say, and you know who said that to me?"

"No, sir."

"My mother," the Prime Minister laughed. "And she was calm, in every crisis."

"You have that calm yourself, sir. A stormy calm."

"Calm did give birth to this plan, Yossi. If we'd acted too quickly, a year ago, a year and a half, back in '79, we'd have done something foolish, defective. We could've lost. We might still lose, Yossi, but the genius in this plan convinces me we can't lose. Something this audacious won't fail us."

"I agree, sir. I believe in it a hundred percent."

"Who do you talk to about our plan, Yossi, besides

your wife? She's ok, she's got security clearance. But who else? Your mother? Your girlfriend? Your army buddy? Who?"

"I don't have a girlfriend, sir. I'm very happy with Tamar. If you want to provide me with one....a mistress...." Ben Luria laughed.

"So, who? You must talk to someone. Everyone must."

"Only my father."

The Prime Minister laughed heartily. "Very good. You amaze me again. So, you talk to your father. Of course. You're the genius, Yossi. Then how is your father?"

Yossi smiled. "He's fine, sir. He sends his regards."

"That's grand," the Prime Minister laughed, this time with a loud delight. "Give him my love."

Yossi laughed. "I will, sir. I talk to him all the time. It's a running conversation. All my life."

"Yes," the Prime Minister said, "I talk to my mother also. In my head. Ever since she died. I once heard Isaac Bashevis Singer give a lecture. He'd met his mother, who had been dead for five years at the time.... he met his deceased mother walking on Broadway in New York. He took her home for tea where they had a wonderful talk. He's such an imp, that Bashevis Singer. He told the whole story in Yiddish. I can see him. He was just fantasizing when he told that story, don't you think, Yossi? He doesn't believe he really met his long-dead mother on Broadway, does he? The man's not delusional."

"He's a writer," Yossi said.

The intercom buzzed.

"Yes," Begin answered.

"The Cabinet's waiting for you, sir."

"Just a minute. They can start arguing without me."

"Go on," the Prime Minister said.

"Isaac Singer is a writer, sir, so he must have a great imagination. Maybe he imagined it all so strongly that he sort of believed it happened, he felt as if it happened. And so, for him, it happened. He met his deceased mother walking on Broadway. He took her home. They had a nice tea together."

"Yes, Yossi, you put it well. When you talk to your father, do you believe that actually happens? That he actually speaks to you."

"I certainly do not disbelieve that he talks to me. I hear him loud and clear."

"Give your father a message. Tell him the war goes on. We haven't stopped fighting even one day since he died. But we continue to win. Tell him he didn't die in vain. To die the way he did. Tell him I'll never regret being there with him. Tell him I have the privilege of taking good care of his son." The Prime Minister smiled over at Ben Luria. "Let's go to the Cabinet meeting."

The intercom buzzed again.

"President Carter on the phone, sir. About the attack on Dror."

"I'll take it in my office," the Prime Minister said, then turned to Ben Luria. "What should I say to him, Yossi?"

THIRTEEN

At 5:15 that evening the street was still a catastrophe. Neither of the two fire-hose soaked cars had been removed. The coroner had removed the bodies of the three PLO would-be assassins in body bags, as well as the body of Avi Katz. Dror himself had gone to inform Katz's wife. He arranged for a car to take her to her parents' house in a quiet village off the Jerusalem Road. The street smelled of burnt rubber, scorched metal, spent gunpowder. Firemen had high-pressure hosed the blood off the street, but stains of it remained.

Rescue workers in red plastic vests went door-to-door. Army experts, Jerusalem police, independent investigators took measurements, photographs, drew diagrams, searched for relevant material. No neighborhood life remained of the street.

At the block's entrance, at the intersection where the PLO car had stopped, then sped away, an army Sergeant asked Arie Solen for his identity papers. The Sergeant checked Solen's name against a list he held on a clipboard. He asked Solen his destination.

"Gen. Dror's house. I'm expected."

"What time?"

"1730," Solen told him.

"Could you step out. We'll have to search you and the car."

"I have a gun."

"A pistol?"

"Yes."

"You'll have to leave it here with us," the sergeant said. "As you can see, the area's secure."

"Yes," Solen said, "now it is."

Dror met Solen at the door. Dror had showered and changed into non-military slacks and a short-sleeved white shirt. He ushered Solen into the study.

"Scotch, Arie? Bourbon? Gin?"

"Gin and tonic."

Dror made a gin and tonic, poured a whiskey for himself.

"You know Rafi Stone's stuff about Armageddon?" Solen asked as they sat down.

"Sure," Dror said. "His obsession."

"Stone really believes in his Armageddon stuff. He's been to Megiddo. The plains of Megiddo. He's stood there and stared out at it. He's told me about this trip. He thinks Osiraq is the beginning of Armageddon. But it looks like Armageddon to me right outside the door here."

"If only," Dror said, "this attack would be the final battle. Wouldn't that be something."

The two men sat in silence for just a moment.

"Are you all right?" Solen asked.

"Oh, yes, Arie. Aside from the fact that they're getting more sophisticated. That they bombed me and
attacked me on my own street where I live. That they
killed one of my men. Oh yes, I'm all right. I'm just
fine."

"Sorry, Jonathan," Solen said, "stupid question. I
just meant...."

"You have someone inside Osiraq, don't you?" Dror
asked.

"I don't know," Solen answered.

"I know you have. You must," Dror said.

"Perhaps," Solen answered.

"How long has he been there?" Dror asked.

"I don't know," Solen said. "If we had someone
there we would likely have put her there a year, a year
and a half ago. Probably not long after we blew up the
reactor core in France. *If* we had someone there. And
if I were in on it. That's probably when I would have
put them there."

"OK." Dror said. "What do you get from her?"

"Her?"

"You said 'her,' Arie, I'm afraid you said 'her.'"

Solen looked down at his lap, his right hand rested
in it. He lifted his left arm onto his lap, rubbed the
stump of it, where his left hand was missing.

"I can't afford those kinds of slips, Jonathan," Solen
said, still looking down. Then he looked up. "But even
I make them. How can I not? I'm human. You were
quick. You threw me off guard."

"What do you get from her?"

"If she were there...." Solen began. The two men smiled at each other. "If she were there, we'd probably get technical stuff. We'd want to know how far along they are. We'd ask her to stall the project as much as possible. So on and so forth. No overt sabotage."

"That's it?"

"From her, that's it."

"Do you have photographs?" Dror asked him.

"Only documents she's managed to get to. Computer printouts."

"No photographs of the site itself? External?" Dror asked him.

"She couldn't do that without getting caught."

"Of course."

"What are you getting at, Jonathan? You're after something."

"Yes. I am."

"I'm at your service, General."

"I need the location of every SAM missile battery and every anti-aircraft installation around Osiraq. The anti-aircraft will be stationary. I need cross-hairs co-ordinates."

"The kind a fighter pilot could hit?"

"That kind. Precise."

"My agent can't get that kind of information for you."

"All right, Arie, send in someone who can."

"You don't know what you're asking. This isn't some agent in New York, Cairo, Tehran, this is an agent in *Baghdad*. Do you know what Baghdad is like?"

"Of course I do."

"If they caught an agent there'd be no diplomatic wrangling. You know that."

"Yes, Arie. I do know that."

"They'd torture them so slowly.....I can't even tell you."

"Enough, Arie."

"You know about the '69 spy trials. Thirteen Iraqi Jews, 4 Muslims hung up to dangle in Liberation Plaza. All accused of spying for Israel."

"Of course I know."

"And if they caught an actual spy...."

"Arie, one of those Jews was my cousin."

"Your cousin?"

Dror had closed his eyes. Without opening them he responded.

"Yes, Arie. My father's brother's daughter."

"I'm sorry, Jonathan. I didn't know."

"Of course."

"Any agent I send in there is at risk of torture every day. I don't need to go into the details of their terrors, Jonathan, it would make you sick."

"I am sick, Arie. I'm sick of them, but I'm also sick of being threatened day by day right here in Jerusalem."

Now the men switched positions. Dror sat forward in his chair, Solen sat back, closing his eyes, taking a breath.

"And I'm sick," Solen said, "of worrying every night for the last year about my agent in Baghdad. A woman, Jonathan. They'd.....my God, you know what they'd do to her. She knows it."

"What's her name?" Dror asked.

"Never mind her name," Solen said, his eyes still closed.

"No," Dror said, "just her first name. So I can have a handle on her, personally."

Solen let out a sigh.

"I can't, Jonathan," he said.

"Send in one more, Arie," Dror pleaded. "A man. He won't stay long. Not a year. I promise you. All I need is that information, but I need it precisely."

Solen had gotten up, paced around the room. With his right hand he fingered books, ashtrays, the desktop.

"We ask a lot of you," Dror said, "When it becomes too much, step aside. You have to know your own limits."

"I know my limits," Solen said. "Every day I stretch them. Don't worry."

"I'm sorry," Dror said. "Forgive me for what I ask of you."

Solen sat down again, face to face with Dror.

"At first," Solen said, "when we began this project, it was the worst nightmare I had. Get an agent into Osiraq, keep her there for a prolonged time. It's an elaborate scheme. You can't imagine. You have no idea the number of people involved."

"I can imagine," Dror said.

"Make her cover. Mask her up. Get her into Osiraq. It's a miracle I found a match. Get transmissions in and out. Keep an eye on her. I can't protect her. I pretend I can. I have a scheme to extract her if necessary. But who knows if it would work? I've lost enough agents. You know that."

"Of course," Dror said.

"We're up against it," Solen said.

"Yes. We are."

The two men sat without talking. Dror gave Solen all the time Solen might need to accept Dror's request.

"All right, Jonathan," Solen gave in. "Of course. I'll find you someone. Give me two weeks. I'll get what you need."

"Bless you, Arie. I've never asked you for something like this. I know it. I do know what Baghdad is like."

At dinner they didn't talk about Osiraq, about the ISS-1 agent who was there or the ISS-1 agent they'd now have to send there.

Dror and his wife, Aviva, and Solen talked with the Dror's college-age daughter, Batya, with their teen-age daughter, Sarah, and their teen-age son, Adam, about the attack on Dror that morning. They talked about how the attack against Dror would change the lives of the whole family, how they would need to tighten security.

They talked about Solen's daughter, who was in the University with Dror's daughter, a year behind Batya, both studying English language and literature.

Aviva talked about her work in a laboratory doing medical research. Mostly, they returned to talk about the morning's attack, about the Israeli response. Border closures. Air strikes. Commando raids into the West Bank.

Dror's youngest, his son, Adam, complained about the Israeli presence in the West Bank.

"It's where I might have to serve," Adam said. "I don't want to serve in an immoral occupation."

"An 'immoral' occupation?" his mother asked him. "*They* attacked *us* in '67. We won that war. We took the land. Do you remember that, my moralist son?"

"I'm no simple moralist!" Adam shot back. "It's their fault anyway, all the crazy religious rabbis who are the moralists, the ones who want to keep the West Bank and to hell with the Palestinians."

"Don't talk like that about the rabbis," his eldest sister, Batya warned him. "You don't know anything about it. Rabbi Hillel. Rambam. Rabbi Adler. The great ones."

"I don't care even for the great ones, the ancient ones," Adam answered her. "let alone for the modern ones. They're ruining the country. They've got us in a stranglehold. It's not the Bible, you know, this is 1981, the Twentieth Century.

"The Twentieth Century is no different from the First Century," Batya argued, "when it comes to the rabbis."

"Religion died at least a hundred years ago. The rabbis haven't caught up yet," Adam said. "And listen," he leaned forward with his hands poised on the white linen tablecloth, "the rabbis have no monopoly on morality. I know, you're in college, I'm in high school. I don't know what I'm talking about. But I do know."

"You know nothing," Batya said. "Did you know that the Patriarch Isaac studied Mosaic Law — and Mosaic law didn't even exist until ten generations after Isaac. Explain *that* to me, wise guy."

"You and your miracles!" Adam said.

"Not miracles. Facts. And," Batya went on, "Isaac studied Mosaic law in the Academy of Shem, and Shem lived ten generations before Isaac. Isaac studied law which didn't yet exist in an Academy which was long out of existence. Don't let time fool you, Adam. All things occur in all times, backwards and forwards."

"Backwards and forwards," Adam mocked her.

That's why we've had to fight for a thousand years and we have to fight today."

"Time has made a fool of you, Batya, and so has college."

"Adam.....!" Aviva admonished.

"Let him go, Aviva," Dror appealed to his wife.

"He's attacking the whole of Jewish tradition," Aviva argued.

"Yes," Dror said, "Jewish tradition gives him the right to attack. Even to attack Jewish tradition."

"They tried to kill you this morning," Batya jumped in. "He doesn't know what he's talking about."

"No," Aviva agreed, "he doesn't. It was a war in '67. If you attack someone to destroy them and you lose, you lose your land. It's called war. They lost the West Bank."

"No. I agree," Dror said. "Adam doesn't know what he's talking about. He's dead wrong. But let him fight for what he believes."

"Sorry to intrude on family affairs," Solen interrupted, "but...."

"You *are* family," Aviva said.

"My friend the general here sounds like Solomon," Solen said. "If you were my son, Adam, I'd give you a good washing behind the ears. You don't choose where to fight in Israel. You don't even choose to fight or not to fight. You fight."

"They're right in what they say," Adam shot back at Solen. "You don't give a damn for the Palestinians, for what happens to them. You want to annex the whole thing."

"Don't talk to Arie that way," Aviva warned, "he's

our guest, your elder. Show him respect."

"Argument *is* respect," Dror said. "I want my kids to have strength, let them practice it now."

Adam hardly heard what anyone else said. "You do want to take the whole West Bank, don't you? You do mean to make it Israel. I'm for a Palestinian State. How can we expect them to have any satisfaction in life and leave us alone until they have their dignity, their own state."

"You get your dignity in your own life, Adam," Solen said, "let the Palestinians get theirs."

"Shut up," Batya yelled at Adam. "A Palestinian State!? So they can build an army in the open instead of in secret? Sure. Give them power, Adam. Put down your arms. Follow Jesus why don't you right through Jerusalem right through 'turn the other cheek.' Even Jesus was talking about the Romans, he would never say that about the Palestinians because they'd stab him in the back he turned to them."

"Hey!" Dror called out to the table. "At least leave poor Jesus out of this."

Batya jumped up, stalked out, stomped up the stairs one step at a time.

"Doesn't it hurt you, Jonathan," Solen asked, "to hear your own son talk like this? Be honest."

"It heartens me to hear Adam talk, Arie," Dror answered him. "Then it hurts me to hear what he says. They tried to kill me this morning and they came damn close. They killed Avi Katz. But let the kids think for themselves. Adam's 17 already. Let him fight for himself."

"I can't believe what I hear," Solen said. "The man who created the IAF from two little airplanes with his own two hands. You're like some saint, Jonathan, some patient Buddha or something."

Everyone had gotten up from the table. Dror and Solen had walked out to the front porch of the house. Soldiers stood guard.

"No saint, Arie," Dror said. "I'm practical. I'm not even a politician like you are."

"I'm no politician, Jonathan. I'm a soldier."

"I'm not even a soldier," Dror said. "All I ever wanted to do was to fly airplanes. You know that, Arie?"

"We're soldiers by now, Jonathan."

"I first saw them fly when I was a kid. Whoever dreamed a Jew would fly an airplane? In Egypt in those days! So look. I'm a Jew who commands an air force. I built an air force, like you say, from two old airplanes. I won that war in '67 with my airplanes. Let the kids have their say. Be more Talmudic, Arie, let each one argue from his own thoughts. They'll change. They'll grow up."

"How's Ben Luria?" Solen asked.

"Yossi?" Dror said. "Something wrong with Yossi?"

"No," Solen said. "He's under a lot of pressure, that's all."

"We all are," Gen. Dror said.

"We are," Solen agreed, "but, like you say, these are the wars of his generation. We sign off on them, but they're fighting them."

"Yossi can handle it," Dror said.

"I think so," Solen said. "But even Shamir cracked once. Even Shamir. We need Yossi now. He's at the heart of it all. And we're all human."

When he came to the dark street corner still guarded by the same Sergeant, Solen asked the Sergeant, had they had any success?

"Yes," the Sergeant said, "they've caught the driver of the PLO car. He's in custody."

"Tov m'ohd," Solen said. "Good work."

"It wasn't my work, sir. I've been standing guard here the whole night long. I wish it had been my work."

Solen smiled at the Sergeant.

"Yes," Solen said, "I know what you mean."

Solen would drive back that night on the Jerusalem Road to Tel Aviv. He never traveled with security, but always only alone. It was his particular style.

On the drive home he realized which agent he would send to Osiraq. Hannah Ben Eliyahu. The beautiful Hannah Ben Eliyahu would seduce the womanizer, Dr. Yahia El Meshad. It, too, would be an elaborate scheme, involving a woman again. You don't choose where to fight or how to fight.

When he arrived home, Solen talked with his own family about the morning's attack. He reported to them on the General's condition, that Dror was more or less all right, and on the Dror family. The Solens sat up late talking. After Mrs. Solen and their two sons had gone to bed, Solen stayed up late talking with his daughter.

Before going to bed, Solen called Ben Luria. Tamar answered.

"What are you doing still up?" Solen asked her.

"Worrying," Tamar said. "What else?"

"Is Yossi asleep?"

"An hour ago," Tamar said. "Do you need him?"

"Let him sleep," Solen said.

"What is it?" Tamar asked.

"Nothing," Solen said. "I'm having second thoughts about some things, that's all."

"I'm sure you both will," Tamar said. "Whatever it is you're working on. I'll have Yossi call you in the morning."

"Thanks, Tamar. Go to bed."

"You, too, Arie."

In Jerusalem, a little later that night, in a silk robe and black leather slippers, his cotton pajamas taken from the closet and laid neatly on the dressing counter, Dror stood before the bathroom mirror. Shaving at night, before bed, he found the solitude he required daily. In his mind, he spoke to himself. *"You almost died today, Jonathan Dror. The mirror almost died today."* The mirror's image looked back. *"This is the human condition. I am the human condition. To stare at yourself in a mirror thinking unspoken thoughts as though it were the most intimate of conversations with yourself. Here you are Jonathan Dror, again with your shaving brush and your shaving mug and your straight razor wishing you could think some profound or religious or eternal thought when in fact you take in and let out a deep breath which enlivens your mundane and ordinary thoughts, your memory of yourself as a young boy in a small Egyptian village on the banks of the Lower Nile. Because you were born in the first year of World War I, you feared you might yourself be an omen for war. When you saw that little plane fly along the Nile banks — the airmail plane to Cairo, you stared up at it, stock still, listening to the rattle of its single engine. You thought only of the thrill of it, to fly off up there, to fly away from your war-fate.*

"They could have taken you today, Jonathan Dror." He continued to think, as if talking to his mirror-image. "*Bullets tearing through your heart, lungs, brain, your guts, your spleen....all those parts of you....your stomach, kidneys, bowels, your sex, your legs.....*

Dror opened his bathrobe to see his body whole and undamaged. "*The 67 years of it, the births it had given birth to, the mystery of it, its wanderings and its building.*

....all those parts of your body that keep you alive. Could have been dozens and dozens of bullets."

He closed and tied his robe.

"Golda Meir was right, of course....1967. After the war. Golda. What she said: 'I will never forgive the Palestinians for making us kill their children.' So, right, Golda. And so much more I can never forgive them. Or their Iraqi buddies. Buddies? Bullshit. They all hate each other. Iraqis, Palestinians. They only hate us more."

After washing the shaving soap off his face, then savoring the astringent he slapped on, Dror stepped onto the scale, his nightly habit.

"My corporeal weight," he thought, but this time not to the mirror, away from which he had turned. *"My still living, breathing, corporeal body. 186 pounds. Two pounds too heavy. How much does the soul weigh.... had they gotten me today. Nothing."*

Dressed in clean pajamas, Dror turned out the light in the dressing room. In the dark there was no more mirror, yet it still seemed there was someone to listen to his unspoken thoughts. Now he had none. He rested into the darkness, was loathe to leave it, breathed as if breathing in a benevolent obscurity.

"Batya," he thought, *"and they begat Batya and Rachel and Adam. And my Palestinian friends, they too begit and begit and begit. Is Batya right? Are all things true at all times?"*

Then again his thoughts were quiet. The image came to him of his cousin, also born in Egypt, who had fled Egypt not to Palestine but to the Jewish community in Iraq, who was hanged by the Iraqi Ba'ath Party in Liberation Square, Baghdad, January 6, 1969. Saddam Hussein had then been Chief of Mukhabarat, the Iraqi secret police. *"Saddam Hussein hanged my cousin."*

"When our planes fly into Iraq," Dror thought, *"they'll come not to avenge, but as a natural consequence of terror. They'll answer terror with terror. In the end my cousin Sophia and the 12 other Iraqi Jews and the 4 innocent Iraqi Muslims hanged in a public square at a public spectacle will be avenged of that moment when they stood there blindfolded and terrorized."*

FOURTEEN

First thing in the morning, Maj. Durham stood before the Israeli pilots – 'The Guys' – in the briefing room.

"Questions? comments? complaints?" Durham asked them.

"We're stuck," Atari said. "We're doing it over and over the same way. We're stuck."

"You will get stuck," Durham said. "Anybody play a musical instrument?"

"I do," Hamal said from where he stood in the front of the room, beside Durham. "I play saxaphone."

"Ever get stuck in your progress?" Durham asked.

"Lots," Hamal said. "I'm always pushing myself up one step more."

"That's it!" Durham said. "One step more. Little by little. Inch on up. Frustrating? Get frustrated! Hold that frustration. That's how it goes. And you're not on saxaphones here. These are killer airplanes. Be safe, get great. Got it? Be safe, get great."

"You're not moving us up," Rose said. "You're holding us back. Challenge us."

Durham gave Hamal a look of concern. "You box?" Durham asked Rose.

"Box?" Rose said. "You mean box, like in the ring, boxing?"

"Like in the ring," Durham said.

"Some," Rose said.

"Let's go," Durham said, "you and me. Right now."

"You got it," Rose was ready. "Right now."

At the gym all the guys gathered around the ring as Durham and Rose changed into their workout clothes, put their leather helmets and their boxing gloves on. When they stepped into the ring, Durham laid down the house rules. Four rounds. "Hamal as referee. ok?"

Rose agreed.

"I'm gonna pound the shit out of you," Durham warned. "Then you'll believe in me." Durham danced and weaved. He fought a smart fight, reading Rose's moves all the way. Rose, younger and stronger, came on with all he had, looked for every punch he could throw and threw it, chased Durham around the ring. The guys cheered on the fight, all behind Rose.

In round one, Rose threw 33 punches, 8 of them landing solidly on Durham's midsection, 2 to the head. But Durham didn't flinch. He took each punch with ease, recovering instantly, dancing around, watching Rose, anticipating Rose, letting Rose exhaust himself with his 23 failed thrusts. Each man went to a corner. Atari stepped up to second for Rose, Nussbaum stepped up to second for Durham. Atari and Nussbaum wiped their man's sweat away, gave them encouragement, some water, checked them for any serious damage, while Rose and Durham each caught their breath.

In round two, both men fought the same fight, but Rose hit more, hit harder. Durham took some punishing punches, but looked for the opening following each of Rose's thrusts. Finding those openings, Durham landed six strong punches. Well placed. It was a vigorous round, fought closer, more hand-to-hand. It strained both Rose and Durham's resources. From his corner after the second round, Durham called out: "You're gonna get all I've got." Rose answered him: "It won't be half of enough!"

In the third round, Durham threw more feints and more offensive punches, forcing his own openings now. Rose caught Durham off-balance three times, and took quick advantage to land tough gut punches, shoulder jabs which threw Durham more off-balance. Rose got in some rounds to the head and neck. Durham recovered each time, danced backward pulling Rose toward him, then, when he felt Rose leaning into him, he let Rose have it. A cut opened up above Rose's right eye. Hamal stopped the action to examine the cut, but the guys and both boxers protested that the fight go on. The guys were yelling like crazy, as if they fought the fight. Hamal backed off from between the two fighters. The guys were yelling mostly for Rose, but they also yelled out their praise for

Durham's skill, his endurance, his guts. They urged Durham on into the fight. Toward the end of the third round, Durham went down from a head shot. Hamal counted only to two, when Durham got up. "Give me all you've got, you sonofabitch," Durham said when he got up. "You hold back on me and I'll hang you." Enraged, Rose swung wildly, then gained control again to aim his punches. The third round came to an end.

In the fourth round, each man came out worn down, but determined and inspired to win decisively. Rose tore a page from Durham's book, trying to step lightly and quickly. He wasn't as good at it as Durham was, but it was effective, drawing Durham to him, as Durham found more power behind his punches. Rose took all of Durham's spirit which came in those punches. Twice, Rose reeled, but kept moving enough to gain a moment's recovery, protecting his guard all the while. Once, Rose switched directions quickly, moved forward on the incoming Durham, catching Durham with a shot to the midsection that had all of Rose's formidable power plus Durham's own forward-rushing impact to it. Durham didn't flinch, didn't stop; he came on with a volley of shots, catching Rose on the head and in the chest. Hamal almost ran in between the men in fear for their safety, but held himself back as each man stood, backed off, faced off again.

Not five seconds of the whole fourth round went without a punch. Both men worked relentlessly. The guys thought for sure one or the other of them would fall. Hamal worried for the dedicated fury the fight had become. At the very end of the fourth round, Rose was punching away in a flurry on the inside while Durham threw a surprise roundhouse blow with his right that caught Rose dead on the ear. Rose stumbled back, hit the ropes, seemed utterly dazed, but within four seconds he was back on his agile feet, coming for Durham.

Hamal called the round. He was glad to see it over.

Both men backed into their respective corners for a clean up, water, and recuperation. It had been the furious fight that Durham had expected, a more ferocious fight than Hamal or the guys had expected. The guys stood hushed ringside.

Hamal stepped center ring.

"I take it upon myself," Hamal said, "to call this fight a tie. An absolute tie." He turned to Rose. "Can you accept that?" Rose, huffing for breath, nodded his acceptance of the call. Hamal turned to Durham. "Can you accept that?" Durham nodded his acceptance.

Hamal brought the two men center ring, where they shook gloved hands.

After showers, Durham left the gym walking with Atari.

Rose lingered outside the ring with his friends, talking about the fight, then went back to the locker room alone. As he went into the showers, he met Maj.

Durham coming out of the showers. Durham grabbed a towel off a hook and dried himself off.

"And," Rose called out from the hot shower, "what the hell did that prove?"

Durham stepped into the doorway of the shower room where Rose could see him. "Whatever the hell you think it proved," Durham said.

"And," Rose said, "if I think it didn't prove a damn thing?"

"It proved we can both fight our hearts out," Durham called into the showers.

"If I'm supposed to like you now...." Rose said.

"You can hate me," Durham said, "but now you trust me. End of discussion."

Durham went back to his locker, got dressed, and left the locker room.

Rose stood under the shower for a long time, soaping up, washing his hair, and just thinking through what felt to him like confusion.

Later that day, Maj. Hamal approached Rose about the fight.

"What do you think of Durham now?" Hamal asked Rose.

"Don't know," Rose said.

"Well," Hamal said, "that's a change, isn't it?"

FIFTEEN

Samia stopped at the café, *The Vizier's Daughter*, for an espresso. It was early evening, still light. She watched the streets for Meshad's car. She sat, as always, at the table by the front door, to the right of it. The waiter, Samir al-Wahab, brought her an espresso without asking, but then asked if she wanted something with it, a sweet?

"No," Samia said, "just the espresso. Thank you, Samir."

Samia read the morning paper, the *Forward*. Saddam Hussein had given a speech yesterday to a gathering of military leaders: "Prepare for the destruction of Israel, the liberation of Palestine. The Zionist entity has developed special weapons. We, too, are developing special weapons. We will obliterate the Zionist invaders who pollute the Arab world."

Samir glanced at the newspaper on Samia's table. "You know, Ms. Sa'ad," he said, "I never read the paper anymore. I find it so disturbing. Everywhere we're losing our ways, our culture, all that we fought for and so many died for. Everywhere we've become corrupt. Like the West. Everywhere money, greed, lack of faith, even divorce. How can we hold our country together if we can't hold our family together? It's the most painful thing for a man and a woman. Everywhere divorce."

Samir wiped off the table with the habitual action of a waiter. Then he left Samia alone. Why is Samir so angry this afternoon? Disparaged, disparaging? But… wait. There's no divorce in Iraq. That's crazy what he said. And another thing, Samir reads the paper every day, thoroughly. She sipped at her espresso. No sign yet of Meshad. Samir makes such a good espresso, dark, slightly bitter. It's because he taps it down tightly. She had watched him do it hundreds of times over the past year. He moved awkwardly with his body, filling the bowl with coffee, tapping it with a charmingly graceless strength. He did it well. Morning, afternoon, and evening. Then it dawned on Samia. Samir was telling her something clear and obvious. Samia's husband in Israel, Dov, had filed for divorce. No. She sat up straight. It can't be. But the message is obvious. Samia's breathing quickened. She became light headed. She wanted not to move a muscle. She listened to her short breaths forced through her nose. She lifted the espresso with a steady hand.

As Samir passed on the way to another customer, he looked at her, and nodded to her with a slight smile which confirmed everything. Samir was the one person she might talk to, had come to trust over many months of contacts, many passings of messages, yet without any open conversation, no acknowledgment of who the other was.

As Samir passed her again on the way back into the cafe his hand came to rest on her shoulder. But of course, no, that was an hallucination. No such thing could happen.

Meshad's car pulled up, he got out, walked over to her table, sat down facing her.

"Is something wrong, Ms. Sa'ad? You look pale."

"Nothing. I'm fine. Would you like an espresso before we go?"

"No, thank you," Meshad said. "But if you're not feeling well there's no point in going to a party. I'll have dinner sent up to your room. If you feel you can eat."

"No, really, that's kind of you. But I'm fine. I need to be out in fact, among people. A party's just the thing. At the Presidential Palace. This doesn't happen every day."

"The family knows about your work. They'd have you back another time. Believe me."

"Thank you, Dr. El Meshad, but we should go."

Samia got up to leave. Meshad followed her to the car. They made a stop along the way for Meshad to pick up some documents. As Meshad got out of the car, gunfire erupted into the still evening air. Meshad's driver jumped quickly out of the car, pistol drawn, but was shot down immediately. The shooting stopped, leaving only a silence. Samia looked around for Meshad. He'd disappeared. The street had cleared of people in seconds. Had Meshad dissolved into the running crowd? Had he been shot? Kidnapped? She sat in the car alone. The hard, short tone of her breath coming from her nose, her mouth closed. Her hands stiffened on the back seat of the car. The driver's body convulsed. Samia's breath slowed, but never came easily. Opening the side door, as if her slow caution would prevent anything else from happening, Samia slid from the car.

It was just on the other side of dusk now, the city more darkened than lighted, and darkening quickly. Samia walked without knowing what street, direction, or purpose she had. Walking itself was purpose enough. The movement of her body made sense in and of itself. Certainly they had not been after her. They were after Meshad. They were Iranians. She knew it the minute they opened fire. Iranian agents. But they were so inept.

After wandering for an untold time, half an hour? an hour? three hours? Samia stood in the dark in the midst of Liberation Plaza. People still lingered. Some crossed the Plaza using it as a transit passage. Others sat at the tea shops and cafés lining the edges of the Plaza, reading newspapers, smoking, talking.

And then, there they are before her. Hanging in Liberation Plaza twenty-five feet apart as Saddam Hussein had ordered them hung. The thirteen Iraqi Jews and the four Iraqi Muslims accused of spying for Israel. But that was in 1969. And this is 1981. *"Am I hal-*

lucinating? Quick, catch yourself before you lose clarity. Don't." Samia had fallen into delusion, her depleted, exhausted, and defeated body which had withstood the mounting pressure of a one-and-a-half year exile from life itself now passed its endurance, and caved in. For her, in her hallucination, those bodies from 1969 now hung there. Their bodies turned. Their daily clothes. Their necks broken with their heads yanked upwards. She saw them, not as solid as they would have been had they been real, had it been January 6, 1969. Now they were a shadowy, ghostly outline, but surely, certainly there. In a silence as certain as their presence. And with them, the thousands of people who had filled Liberation Plaza to witness their demise. The thousands who had actually walked around the hanging bodies placed far enough apart so that people could walk between them, brush up against them, feel their death, touch their fate. A message from Saddam.

Samia walked among the shadowy crowd. The real world, the men in the Plaza, in the cafés, were beyond the borders of her reality. Only January 6, 1969 in Liberation Plaza was real for her. The faces of the crowds were strange, glaring as she passed them, but with a stony glare, a look of amazement born of a fascination and a fear which turned them into humanoids rather than humans. They constituted a new citizenry. This night was a rite of passage into the new Iraq in which Saddam would move up and up and up.

This was nothing like the *Farhoud* of 1951 and '52 when Iraqis ran rampant through the Jewish Quarter raping, pillaging and kidnapping. No. The *Farhoud* were wild, driven by overindulged and exploding passions. Here only the bizarre prevailed. The clammy knowledge of death as arbitrary. The crowd all died, they were all dead that night. Their randomness, not their guilt, caused the effect Saddam wanted. Their innocence sent the message he reveled in. It could have been anyone; it was everyone. Tomorrow, you, or so-and-so's cousin, brother-in-law, mother. Bodies swayed. The crowds meandered. The people laughed their crazy laughter of 1969.

Samia, shoved by the crowd, stood beside one of the bodies. She reached up to touch the hem of the victim's pants. Frayed. Thin khaki. Cheap. Taking his foot by the shoe she stopped his slow spin. She looked up at his face, dropped and hidden in his chest. She looked longer, then was able to figure out his face, his eyes. She reached out to touch his calf. It was the shape and feel of an ordinary human leg.

Samia moved a few steps to her left, took hold of the pant-leg of the next victim. Held it for a moment. Then moved to the next, took the hem of her skirt, held it for a moment, then on to the next until she had touched each of the seventeen, Jews and Muslims. Each time she moved from one to the next, the crowd stood still. Then, as she took hold of the next victim, the crowd moved in that direction. By the end of her journey through these dead, Samia knew each one of them.

She walked through the crowd to the center of the actually empty Liberation Plaza. There, Samia collapsed.

Dressed in her evening gown, Samia awoke to a policeman squatting over her. A group of men looked down on her.

"Are you all right?" the policeman asked her. "Do you know your name? Do you know where you are?"

"Yes," Samia whispered. "I am Samia Sa'ad. I am in Liberation Plaza. Baghdad. I work for the government. Please take me to the Al Rashid Hotel."

SIXTEEN

The hot water beat down on Samia. She wouldn't think of Dov, of divorce. She must remember only her training, her job. *Should I go home? Tomorrow they'll leave a sign asking if I want to come in. Tomorrow morning. There'll be a single-stem rose vase on my table signifying I can have a meeting. I'll leave my purse at the table, then go to the car, then come back to get my purse. Then they'll give me a meeting. We had agreed, though: no meetings. No."*

Samia showered, dressed, then went out. Asking the doorman for a car, she directed the driver to the Presidential Palace. At the Palace gates, thirty-feet high, wrought iron, with matching engraved portraits of Saddam Hussein hung on either gate, she replied to the Gate Officer that she didn't have an invitation. Her companion, Dr. Yahia El Meshad, who had the invitation, had disappeared. She had her identification, which she produced, and if the Gate Officer would be so kind as to ask for the Chief of Palace Security they would admit her.

The Gate Officer apologized. He couldn't do that.

Samia insisted.

A car pulled up right behind Samia's car, honking

its horn, its headlights beaming into Samia's car. The Gate Officer yelled for Samia's driver to turn around, to get out of there.

The Gate Officer walked to the car behind them. Samia warned her driver to stay right where he was.

"But madam," the driver pleaded, "that Gate Officer would shoot me. He's got his hand on his pistol now. Look!"

Samia looked out through the rear window. The Gate Officer stooped down to the front window of the other car, his hand on his pistol grip.

The Gate Officer drew his pistol. Shots from the back seat of the car drove the Gate Officer across the lawn. Throwing open the far side back door of the car, a man jumped out already firing his assault weapon, taking out the two military guards who flanked the gates. The car jumped back, the shooter pulled himself inside the swinging door, as the car whirled around, sped off.

Guards ran from the main Palace road. They leveled an army of rifles at Samia's car.

Mohammed Azziz, running out from a different road inside the compound, broke through the crowd of soldiers. He approached Samia's car, his hand on his own pistol. He stood a few yards from the car.

"Get out!" Azziz yelled. "Everyone in that car. Out!" Azziz couldn't see inside the car, he saw only the glare of the spotlights covering it in a white light.

Samia stepped out onto the stone drive.

"Mr. Azziz," she cried out. "Thank God. You'll vouch for me."

Azziz looked back and forth over the car, at the body of the Gate Officer on the grass, he glanced over at the two bullet-riddled guards, one on the ground, the other caught in the wrought iron, he looked back to the car, shielding his eyes with his forearm.

"Come. Come," he said. "Hurry up."

Samia approached Azziz, while her driver stood in the dazzle of spotlights, his arms high.

"Search him," Azziz ordered, "get his papers."

"We were trying to get in....Dr. Yahia El Meshad...."

"I know," Azziz said, "Meshad has disappeared."

"You haven't found him?"

"No, Ms. Sa'ad, we haven't found him."

"A car pulled up...pulled up...."

"It's all right now, Ms. Sa'ad," Azziz tried to quiet her down, while keeping his eye on the scene at large for other threats, "tell me calmly."

"A car pulled up behind us," she said.

"Blocking you in?" Azziz asked her.

"Yes," Samia said. "The Gate Officer went to investigate. They...they shot him. Just right there."

"Do you have anything to do with this?"

"With....?"

"With this mess, Ms. Sa'ad. Please answer me directly."

"I just pulled up...."

"Do you have anything to do with any of this, Ms. Sa'ad? Answer the question."

"No, I do not."

"And did you have anything at all to do with the disappearance of Dr. El Meshad?"

"No. I did not."

"Come in," Azziz turned Samia by the arm toward the entrance gate, now opened. A soldier took her in. "Get the driver's information," Azziz ordered an assistant, "and send him home. He's to tell no one what he saw here. Not his wife. Not his mistress. Not his boy lover. He's probably screwing his daughter. Not even her. Or he'll have nothing left to screw with."

Azziz met Samia inside the gates.

"Let me get you a car," Azziz said. "It's a bit far to the Palace. No. Better you go rest up. You don't see these things everyday. I do."

"Yes," Samia said. They walked down a stone road lighted on either side by street lamps. "I am shaken. But a drink and the crowd might be better for me right now."

Azziz called for a car.

The Palace, built only in the last few years, wasn't a building of this century. It was a Palace of Nebuchadnezzar, of gold leaf and minarets, of arches and, inside, of halls with vaulted ceilings. Of deeply colored carpets on marble flooring, of intricate blue and ivory tile work, of portraits of Saddam Hussein on every wall.

They entered the celebration hall through heavy crimson drapery pulled back by a servant. Inside, at the head of the hall, a band played rock-and-roll standards while a singer sang them in Arabic. But that was hardly visible, for the hall was still at this late hour crowded with guests. White-gloved waiters in white jackets passed through the crowd bearing silver trays of hors d'ouevres. Dates on a mild white cheese, small pieces of lamb on a miniature skewer with a spicy dark sauce, shrimps with a thin mint sauce. Behind each waiter stood another white-jacketed, white-gloved servant with another silver tray, this one ready to receive the detritus of the h'ors d'oeuvre, the used miniature skewers — which Ms. Sa'ad had just noticed were gold — the paper h'ors d'oeuvre cups which held the shrimp, or the dates, or the small sections of orange in a pear liquor. In one part of the room a circle of tables was piled high with cheeses, fruits, nuts.

Azziz escorted Samia to an area of the room set off by a white tent, a sort of beach cabana. At the entrance to it guards acknowledged Azziz, patted him down, then respected his wish not to search his guest. From a couch inside, a teenager in a gray Armani suit, surrounded by men and women, arose to greet the guests. Azziz announced Samia.

"Ms. Samia Sa'ad," Azziz said, "May I present the eldest son of President Saddam Hussein, His Excellency Udai Saddam Hussein."

Samia very slightly curtsied, nodded her head. Udai Saddam Hussein had hardly begun to grow facial hair, yet he had the beginnings of a Saddam Hussein mustache. Lanky, like his father, he stood five feet ten.

"Your Excellency," Azziz said, "Ms. Samia Sa'ad, Nuclear Safety Construction Engineer at Osiraq."

Udai offered Samia a seat in one of the several surrounding lounge chairs. A servant appeared with a soda water and a small tray of arranged hors d'oeuvres.

"I hope you don't mind," Udai said, sipping at his glass of scotch, "we don't drink liquor inside this tent. Only outside of it. Not as a matter of purity," he said, "but as a matter of security." Udai laughed with his whole body, throwing back his head. The others in the tent joined him in laughter.

"But I know you, Ms. Sa'ad," Udai said. He spoke quickly, in jerks, with hesitations and pauses in the wrong places. He drank again from his scotch. "You've come to my attention. When someone comes to my attention they are either very lucky or very unlucky. You're lucky."

"Thank you," Samia nodded her head again.

"All these people here," Udai gestured toward the others, "they're my uncles, my cousins, my girlfriends, my friends. But they don't matter. They are as nothing. You have met Udai Saddam Hussein. No matter how long you stay here now, when you return to New York, you can say that you have met Udai Saddam Hussein.

When will you return to New York, Ms. Sa'ad?"

"Perhaps not at all," she answered. "I'm enamored of Iraq. Who could leave the Hanging Gardens, the Gate of Ishtar, the Presidential Palaces, the great mosques, the origins of the very science I practice as an engineer. The great rebirth of all that majesty now."

"Ms. Sa'ad!" Udai yelled. "Don't bullshit me! I have behind me thousands of years of greatness, and as many thousands of years of treachery and betrayal. I know how to tell the difference. You think that because I'm seventeen years old that I'm not sharp. My eyes see through everyone!"

"Your Excellency," Samia said, "New York has spiritually exhausted itself. I could live there with my family. But to build the future, that's a fate not to be thrown away lightly."

Udai looked Samia up and down. He called over a man sitting in one of the plush chairs, a military man.

"Taer Umeed," Udai addressed the man in barking orders. "You are a man of honor. Take out your pistol!"

The man obeyed.

"If Ms. Sa'ad is a spy, shoot her this instant. In the head. Between her eyes. Make it a good shot. If she is a friend of Hussein, shoot yourself and prove your loyalty!"

Without the slightest hesitation Taer Umeed made his decision. Putting his pistol to his head, he blew his brains out. Samia and others screamed out. Skull and brains flew everywhere, while Taer Umeed's body sprawled to the ground. The men all jumped up. Udai shrieked out orders to dismantle the tent, clean the area, move the entourage to a fresh tent, fresh drinks, fresh food! As the occupants of the tent left, the crowd of partygoers gaped at them. The band had stopped playing.

Udai walked beside Samia to the new tent being set up.

"Are you shocked, Ms. Sa'ad?" Udai said, "that we have Western rock-and-roll music here? I love that music. We take what we want from the West, and we make it worthwhile. But the singer sings in Arabic. Of course." Udai laughed again. "We have traditional music here, too, if you prefer. Do you prefer? You're my guest of honor."

"Yes," Samia managed to say, "I would prefer traditional music. It calms me."

"Yes, some of our music is very calming," Udai said, "isn't it? It's a music born over centuries in the desert. That time and that desert are woven into our traditional music. As you hear the music shifting you hear the desert, and you hear immense time. And that calms one. It haunts one."

SEVENTEEN

Maj. Durham put on power. From his already supersonic speed he took off yet faster into open sky. Maj. Hamal took the challenge. He pushed the throttle, punched up his machine, flew out after the quickly disappearing Durham. Durham broke to the left, Hamal broke after him, closing behind him. Durham shot up into the altitudes, then, just as Hamal shot almost straight up after him, Durham pulled a maneuver astonishing even to Hamal. Durham seemed to flip his aircraft head over tail to charge back toward where he'd come from. Hamal followed him. He *did* flip head over tail and kept right on Durham's own tail.

Durham broke right, then dove at the ground. Hamal followed. They descended quickly, 35,000, 22,000, 9,000 feet, and there, just under the 10,000 foot limit where, by all the rules, Durham should never have gone and Hamal should never have followed him, Durham pulled himself just up and just out of the dive, taking the g-forces of that maneuver well enough to still fly off at a hell of a speed toward the west.

Hamal's reaction was more than split second. He pulled his plane out from a dive it should have fatally spun into. Hamal climbed at the only angle climbing could achieve from that descent. He flew out hell-bent-for-hell after Durham, caught him from behind, locked radar steady on him, and then, pushing the pickle button, he scored. Hamal pulled up and flew right alongside Durham. He saw Durham eyeball-to-eyeball. Durham was laughing.

"You son-of-a-bitch," Durham came on the radio. "You are one hell of a pilot. I want every one of your damn boys to do it. Just like you did it."

"They'll each one of them do it better. You watch them!"

Hamal pulled ahead into a victory roll.

All afternoon they went through these games, each Israeli pilot required to catch Durham. Some caught him, some he eluded. All did well. All afternoon Durham never let up. He flew sharp in the late afternoon as he had flown sharp with Hamal, flying in the first glows of dawn.

After dinner, Durham and Hamal reviewed their notes from the day. Durham's only complaint concerned Capt. Atari.

"Tell me about Atari," Durham said. "What do you know about him?"

"What's up?" Hamal said. "Something wrong with his work?"

"Where's he from?"

"Jerusalem."

"Been in combat?"

"Fierce. He flew on the Egyptian border in the '73 war. We lost a lot of guys there."

"His friends?"

"Sure. He lost his brother then, too, on the Syrian front."

"How'd he lose his brother?"

"That war caught us by surprise. Off guard."

"I remember."

"Atari's brother, Shaul, was in the reserves. By the time he got news of the war, his unit had left. Some in their regular clothes just hustled to their stations. Shaul......"

"Yes.....?" Durham said.

"Shaul grabbed his gear, jumped into his old Fiat, picked up two of his buddies, and they headed for his unit. They found their unit, grabbed a jeep, headed for the battle. The Golan Pass."

"Yes....?"

"Their jeep hit a land mine. Tumbled them. They all survived. One of them got away. The Syrians got Shaul and the other guy. Nothing ever heard from them again. The Syrians never reported it. Nothing on prisoner of war lists. Nothing."

"Yes.....?"

"After the war the army called Atari to come get his brother's car. Can you imagine, going out alone to get that Fiat?"

"Yes....?"

"Think about what they did to Shaul and his bud-dy, fucking barbarians. Wouldn't even report it."

"Yes...." Durham said.

"You just keep saying '*Yes*.....'" Hamal complained. "Is that all you've got to say?"

"I want to hear," Durham said. "In your rambling I'll learn what I need to know about Atari."

"Nothing to know," Hamal said. "But I know what you saw today. I'm sure of it. You saw Atari's...insecu-rity."

"You hit it," Durham said. "He comes after you with a personal rage. Or fear. To overcome some personal fault. Some anxiety. That's not good. A guy who's been what he's gone through...."

"We've talked to him. IAF psychologists. But not everyone can take that kind of insecurity or fear or anger and turn it into brilliant flying."

"True..."

"I'm telling you: Atari — he can do it."

"You know he can do it?"

"Not that I like him or I don't like him. I don't care about like and don't like. I care about fly and can't fly. The man can fly," Hamal said.

"Once you see his fear," Durham said, "you feel it there all the time."

"How many great pilots can you find in a popula-tion of four and a half million people?"

"Not many."

"Does Atari's fear come from what he thinks they did to his brother? Who knows? He sees Shaul out there with Syrians rushing them. He imagines Shaul's terror. He imagines they tortured him. He's told me all that. Is that where his fear comes from? Who knows? I respect his insecurity. I don't like it. I see it in him."

"He's a Sabra." Durham said.

Hamal laughed. "How the hell do you know about Sabras?"

"I read up on you guys before you got here. My research," Durham said. "Israelis are like the Sabra cactus, they say. Tough on the outside, soft on the inside."

Hamal shook his head, smiling. "Tough on the inside, too."

They sat in silence for a moment. Then Hamal spoke:

"Have you ever had Jewish food, Major?"

"Pastrami? Bagels? That stuff?" Durham asked.

"No. I mean real Jewish food. I'm going to make you guys a meal. The whole crew. The mechanics, medics, cooks, everybody. A Jewish farewell feast."

"Sounds good to me."

"But real Jewish food. Middle Eastern food. Like my mother cooks. North African. Moroccan. Couscous. Harissa. Preserved lemons. Oh! Tagines, I need tagines. 10, 15 of them. Where am I going to get tagines in Utah?"

"Give me a list," Durham said, "just give me a list.

This is the United Marine Corps, boy. We'll get you what you need from any corner in the world."

Hamal thought a moment.

"Let's figure a meal for about 50 people, right?"

"About right."

"I'll give you the list, then we'll figure the amounts."

"Go give the cook a list," Durham said. "Don't worry. I'll get you what you want from wherever we can get it."

"Your damn marines can get anything anywhere, can't they?" Hamal asked.

EIGHTEEN

"I want a meeting with the Chief of Mossad," Yossi Ben Luria made his request. "Right away."

"You want....." Prime Minister Menahem Begin said, but Ben Luria interrupted him.

"I know what you'll say, Mr. Prime Minister," Ben Luria said, "but I want it. I know who they're planning to send into Iraq now. Hannah. I know it. Hannah Ben Eliyahu. And I know who's there now. How could I not have figured it out? I utter her name:...." Ben Luria hesitated. "OK, no, I don't utter her name. But I know damn well who it is. And you can't send Hannah Ben Eliyahu in there, too."

"A meeting with the Chief of Mossad? Have you lost your senses?" Begin said.

"Yes. Maybe I have. Too many sleepless nights. But I ask for it, sir."

"Are you having *personal qualms*?" the Prime Minister said. "If you are, Col. Yossi Ben Luria, I'll accept your resignation the sooner the better."

Ben Luria fell into a chair in the Prime Minister's office.

"I'll go to Iraq myself, sir, undercover. Don't send Hannah. Please."

"Listen to me carefully, Ben Luria," the Prime Minister began, "Yossi Ben Luria. In 1948..."

"I know all about 1948," Ben Luria said, then added, "Sir."

"And I'll tell you again," the Prime Minister raised himself from his chair, then sat again. "You need to hear it again. Listen to me. In 1948 we bought the ship, the *Altalena*. We loaded her with arms and men, we brought her from France to Israel. That alone was a miracle. And... Think about it. Money for a ship. Buying arms, ammunition. The men, barely trained."

"I know sir. I know sir. And my father was on board."

"Listen to me, Yossi. You need to hear it again. When we arrived in Israel — there was no Israel yet — Ben Gurion's Israeli Defense Force opened fire on us. Jews firing on Jews in 1948! Just after the holocaust. Can you imagine? But we were a renegade faction then. The Israeli Defense Force was already the official army. When we came in the *Altalena* we weren't heroes anymore. We threatened the existing military command. If the Israeli Defense Forces hadn't opened fire on us, we would have never unified, made one fighting force. I'm not an old man telling war stories. I hate war stories. I'm keeping something alive in you which it's almost impossible for any man to keep alive in himself. Jewish bullets from Jewish guns killed Jewish soldiers. Can you imagine the guts Ben Gurion had to do that?"

"Yes, I know, sir," Ben Luria spoke just above a whisper.

"Do you think Ben Gurion had *personal qualms* in '48? Was he right to open fire on Jews? He won, I lost. We united. Together we won Israel. Had we had personal qualms, had Ben Gurion had personal qualms, we would have lost Israel."

"Yes, sir."

"Any personal qualms about your friends going into danger, Col. Ben Luria?"

"No, sir."

"There's the election coming up, Yossi. If Labor wins that election they won't have the guts to carry the Osiraq mission through. I'll do it before the election. I'll have everything in order, including all the intelligence I need. We have to send the right people into severe danger to get that intelligence."

"Yes, sir."

"Do you want a meeting with the Chief of the Mossad?"

"No, sir."

"I'll try not to lose even one of your friends, Yossi. But I'll risk them all to the end of the precipice. You'll help me every step of the way."

"Yes, sir, I will," Ben Luria said, "of course I will, sir."

"And together, Yossi, you and I and the others, Slomovic, and Dror, and the others, we'll peer over the precipice into the void until this thing is over."

"Yes, sir."

"There, at the edge of the void, I'll pray to God. You won't, because you're not religious. Like your father. Secular. But you're a Jew. You'll look over the precipice into the void with us. As a Jew, you'll find a Jewish courage to do it day by day until we succeed."

"Yes, sir," Ben Luria said. "I will."

"There are madmen out there, Yossi, truly madmen. Ruling the world."

"Yes, sir. Of course. I know that."

"Saddam Hussein....he wants to be the next Saladin."

"He does. I know. I've read a lot of...."

"He wants to unite the whole Arab world. To ride some great white Arabian steed..."

"I know what you're saying."

"And what am I saying?"

"To destroy Israel is to rule the whole Arab world."

The Prime Minister nodded.

Ben Luria left. The Prime Minister called the Chief of Mossad. They agreed that Ben Luria was a great asset to the Prime Minister, and to Israel. A terrific soldier. And they agreed it was important to keep an eye on Ben Luria, that the pressures not get to him.

**

The following evening, Ben Luria met Hannah Ben Eliyahu at a café in Jerusalem. They sat out in

178

the night air, both having ordered a glass of Israeli red wine, from the Golan vineyards. Yossi told Hannah about yesterday's request of the Prime Minister, that Yossi wanted to meet with the Chief of Mossad. Of course, Yossi said, only the Prime Minister, the Director General of Mossad, and the Minister of Defense — in this case, Begin himself — even know who the Chief of Mossad is. I must have gone crazy to ask for that, Yossi said. I actually told the Prime Minister that I wanted a meeting with the Chief of Mossad! Can you imagine?

Hannah surprised Yossi with her answer.

"Yes," she told him, "I can imagine."

"Then you know already?" Yossi asked her.

"Know what?" Hannah said.

"Sorry," Yossi said, "I'm losing my cool these days. Wherever you're going, whatever you're doing…."

"I'm not going anywhere, Yossi. I'm assigned to the U.N. delegation. Agricultural section. Water rights. I'm off to New York. If you want me, write care of the Israeli delegation, New York, New York 10017. You know the address. That's it."

"I know you, Hannah," Yossi said. "You're a risk taker. Don't take unnecessary risks."

"In New York?" Hannah asked. "What risks? Too many movies? Too many good restaurants?"

NINETEEN

As Hannan Khatib entered the restaurant of the Plaza Athenée Hotel in Paris, she was noticed. Dark, but with blue eyes. Of medium height for a woman, her bearing gave her an appearance of tallness. She dressed in a narrow brown wool skirt reaching to below her knees and a silk satin blouse the color of mocha. She wore brown leather boots laced to the top.

The Maitre d' approached her.

"Dining alone, Ms. Khatib? The same table? I held it for you."

"Thank you."

The Maitre d' escorted Hannan to a table for two in the center of the busy dining room, held her chair back for her, took the linen napkin folded in thirds from the table, opened it with a twist of his wrist, then let it alight onto her lap.

As the Maitre d' walked back to his station, Dr. Yahia El Meshad stopped him.

"Please," Meshad asked, "present a bottle of Cristal champagne to the woman who has just been seated."

When the waiter told Hannan who had sent the champagne, Hannan looked over to Meshad at his table.

Meshad raised his wine glass toward Hannan, then getting up, he walked to join her.

"Allow me to introduce myself. I'm Dr. Yahia El Meshad. It's not often one sees such a beautiful woman. I sent the champagne to celebrate your presence. May I sit down?"

"I suppose you might," Hannan said. "Yes. It's very kind of you. Please. Do sit down."

The Maitre d' walked from his station, pulled back a chair for Meshad, then retrieved Meshad's dinner from his table.

"I recommend the rack of lamb," Meshad said, referring to his own choice. "But anything on the menu's good. I always stay here in Paris, and I eat in the restaurant when I can. It's excellent. The wines are terrific. Are you Parisian?"

"Well," Hannan hesitated.

"I'm not snooping," Meshad laughed. "You can make up a story entirely if you like. Tell me complete lies about yourself. One after another. I love to hear stories. Anyway, I'm just making small talk, looking for a way to begin a conversation with you."

Hannan ordered the rack of lamb, medium rare. Meshad ordered a 1971 Nuits St. George.

"That works perfectly with the lamb," the waiter said.

"As long as it's at least eight years old," Hannan said, "otherwise, it gives me a terrible headache."

"Then," Meshad said, "from now on I'll only drink wines with you from '73 backwards."

"To answer your question, Dr. El Mes...."

"Meshad," Meshad said.

"...Dr. El Meshad, I do live in Paris, but I was born in Lebanon."

"Lebanon! I knew you were Middle Eastern!" Meshad exclaimed. "You have the beautiful face of the Middle East. A face open, but hidden, with the mouth ready to speak, but reticent."

"Hidden only when there's something to hide," Hannan said, "reticent only when the moment requires silence."

"A woman should always have something to hide. To live fully, a woman must have moments in her life that require silence. You see?" Meshad said when Hannan smiled, "Your enigmatic smile expresses it all."

"And you?" Hannan asked, "Where are you from in the Middle East?"

"Cairo. I live now mostly in Baghdad. I work there as a physicist. Once a month I travel to Paris on business."

"On the business of physics?" Hannan teased.

Meshad laughed. "Yes," he said, "on the business of physics."

"I studied sciences at the Sorbonne," Hannan said. "I'm not a scientist. I couldn't claim that. But I do have a strong background. In chemistry. Biology. Even a little physics."

"Is that right?" said Meshad. "How fortunate. But you haven't even told me your name. And here we are, two scientists."

Hannan held out her hand. "I am Hannan Khatib," she said. "It's my pleasure to meet you, Dr. Yahia El Meshad."

"Yes, one never knows where a chance meeting will lead."

That night Meshad persuaded Hannan to go out with him after dinner. She recommended one of her favorite jazz clubs, the Duke D'Orleans. They ordered brandy and sat until 2 a.m. An exceptional American quartet played that night, with Shelly Berg on piano, John Herd on bass, Roy McCurdy on drums, and Sal Marquez on the saxophone. They sat side by side. Hannan talked about the music. The pianist was one of her favorites, she said. He doesn't just play one note, one chord after another. He glides along on the musicality of the entire piece, leaving himself lots more room for creativity. The drummer, she pointed out, builds entire ideas of rhythm.

"Tell me more," Meshad said. "I'm your enchanted student."

As the evening went on, Meshad became ever more physical with Hannan, touching her shoulder with some comment he made, then her hand on the table, which he kept, and held.

Meshad saw Hannan home in a taxi, made her promise to have dinner with him the following night, then went back to his room at the Hotel Athenée.

Before going to bed, Hannan called a Parisian friend, Jeannette Cenci. Hannan told Jeannette all about her evening. She had a wonderful time with an Egyptian physicist she had met at the Hotel Athenée. When they finished talking, Jeannette called Hannah Ben Eliyahu's Mossad Head of Station in Paris to tell him that all had gone as expected, that Hannah is as attractive as they always knew she was, that Dr. El Meshad is as much of a womanizer as they suspected. The Mossad Head of Station asked when Hannah would see Meshad again. Tomorrow night, Jeannette Cenci told him. Excellent, he said.

Meshad didn't wait for the next evening. He called Hannan in the morning, insisting they have lunch together. She agreed. They had a simple lunch in a wine bar near the Luxembourg gardens. A few cold meats with a green salad and a glass of red wine. Hannan said that she had put her obligations on hold, she was free to spend the day with Meshad.

After their lingering lunch, which extended into two glasses of wine and a plate of cheeses, they walked along the river. Walking far, they wound up in a dusty, chaotic bookstore on the left bank near Notre Dame. Meshad bought a boxed set of *The Alexandria Quartet*, four novels which take place in his native Cairo.

They walked over the bridge, stopping to gaze at the Notre Dame Cathedral. They talked about the Middle Ages, about Baroque architecture, which led to a talk about modern architecture in Paris. While they walked on, Hannan answered Meshad's questions about her life, drawing on her cover story, telling him about Beirut, once the "Paris of the Middle East," about her move to Paris to attend the Sorbonne, her first difficult year in Paris, her adjustments to the city, to the university, to rigorous studies, and then about her years after the Sorbonne, with small jobs in the chemical field, her dissatisfaction with those, and her current job as a design assistant with her friend, an architect.

Hannan got Meshad to talk about his childhood in Cairo: his family, his parents and two brothers, both younger, one an officer in the Egyptian Air Force, the other a musician, a pianist, about his years at Cambridge, his pursuit of his career. By the time they noticed where they were, they had walked all the way to the Marais district. Pleasant, comfortable chatter had kept them going, the overtones of intimacy had made time go astray.

Having talked about the modern architecture of Paris, they walked up Rue du Renard and there it was, the Centre Pompidou, the complex of modern art and culture. Meshad loved the building, pointing out to Hannan how the outside, with its mazes of colored pipes, ducts, and exposed surfaces, was announcing some playfulness within the rough life of the industrial world. They walked around the pond with its kinetic sculptures. They watched three street-dancers perform slow movements without music. Meshad put his arm around Hannan's shoulder.

The following morning, over coffee, Meshad told Hannan that he would return to Baghdad in two days. It was foolish of him to say this so quickly, after just two days and nights, after one night of intimacy, but he wanted her to come with him. He was, he said to her, completely enamored of her. Her beauty, her charm, her sophistication, her curiosity about the world. She could stay with him in Baghdad, free to leave whenever she liked. Stay for a day, a week, a month. Whatever you like. He would find her a position at Osiraq, not just something to pass the time, but some position where she could use her skills in chemistry and physics, a real job for her.

When Hannan accepted his offer, Meshad said her spontaneous response proved that she was a self-assured woman who knew herself, who acted on that knowledge. That was a good omen for their future.

TWENTY

When Hannan met Samia at Osiraq, the hostility between them surfaced immediately. Meshad tried to smooth things over. He praised each of them to the other.

Later that afternoon, Samia ran into Hannan in the hallway near Meshad's office. Hannan had just come out of the small staff kitchen with a cup of hot tea with milk and a piece of sweet halvah. Samia was headed for Meshad's office.

"I need the specifications on the housings for the aluminum uranium enrichment rods," Samia said. "I don't suppose you could find them for me?"

"I'll look for them."

"No," Samia said, "I didn't say that you should look for them. I said you should get them for me. Frankly, you'll slow things down here, not speed them up. It's obvious why you're here. Try not to get in the way."

"Are you jealous?" Hannan asked.

"You can have Meshad. He's a good friend. I have no other interest in him."

"I'm not good enough for your good friend?"

"Oh, no," Samia said. "You're fine. You're just what he likes. You won't last long."

"You're wearing your jealousy on your sleeve," Hannan said. "I'm here for the long term. I'm a scientist. I intend to do scientific work here. When I'm done fetching what you need, of course. What I do after work with Meshad is my business. And his business."

"I wish you all the happiness with Meshad," Samia said. "Don't worry. But, first and foremost, I'm a scientist. A dedicated scientist. I won't have our scientific work diverted by personal passions. Let's stay focused on the work, shall we?"

Hannan stared at Samia. Gathering her anger, then turning it into thought, then into resolve, she said, "If you try to turn Meshad against me, I'll destroy you. I promise."

"Take your tea," Samia said, "and your halvah into the office before your tea gets cold. Meshad loves halvah. I always see to it that he has some here."

"You're gracious to a fault. I'll get you the specifications you require. Don't wait. Please. I'll send them down to your office."

After dining alone that evening at the Al Rashid Hotel, Samia worked in her room to prepare a microfiche to send home to her HQ Mossad Case Officer. Decoded, it read:

Meshad brought back a lover from Paris, Lebanese, Hannan Khatib. She works at Osiraq. She may interfere with my efforts to get data from offices. I can eliminate her.

Samia rolled the microfiche into the courier-nail, then inserted it into the sheath in her shoe. She went to bed that night at about 11:00 p.m. Before falling asleep, she read from the *Thousand and One Nights*, the story of Shahrazad's "Eighth Night." Samia fell asleep pondering over the line she found in the story: *"I am one of the demons who believe in God."*

TWENTY-ONE

"Samia Sa'ad," Hikmat Sidqui said, "isn't legitimate. She's an Israeli spy."

"I hope you're sure of that," Mohammed Azziz said. They sat in Azziz's office at Mukhabarat Headquarters.

"I've known it from the minute I laid eyes on her. At Saddam airport. Now I have proof."

"We're in the business of suspicion. You want me to suspect Ms. Samia Sa'ad. But I warn you, Sidqui, I also suspect your accusation of Ms. Sa'ad. I'm a man of total suspicion."

"Every morning," Sidqui went on, "I pick up Ms. Sa'ad at the café, *The Vizier's Daughter*. Every morning something happens between Ms. Sa'ad and the waiter. They're in secret collusion. I'm sure of it. I see it with my own eyes."

"I hope that you see what you think you see. Some people see only what they want to see."

"You made me her daily escort for a reason. Because I'm the best that you have. She's a spy, Azziz. To be wrong in a case like this would have serious consequences for you. I know that. I've hated Ms. Sa'ad from the very beginning."

"Thank you for your protection," Azziz smiled. "You are so very thoughtful."

"I've hated that woman," Sidqui said, "from the beginning. I trust my feelings."

"Be careful," Azziz said. "You've come far in Mukhabarat. Don't let hatred ruin you."

"No," Sidqui stood up. Turning his back to Azziz, he spoke as he paced away. "Trust your own hatred, Azziz. Trust all of your own feelings. I watched her mercilessly." He turned back to face Azziz. "Now I've seen it. It's subtle. It took a long time. Something, every day, between her and the waiter at *The Vizier's Daughter*."

"You know that we've investigated Samia Sa'ad. She was indeed born in New York when she said she was. I have hospital records. She did graduate from Stanford in a special program of nuclear physics. I have all of her Stanford transcripts on file. I have the transcript of a telephone interview we did with one of her Stanford professors. We've observed her parents in New York. Will you quit pacing and sit down. Are you so nervous?"

Sidqui sat back again in the chair across from Azziz.

"Have you spoken with her parents?" Sidqui asked.

"Of course not," Azziz said. "How stupid to alert them. We can find out a hell of a lot more by observing them. You should know that, Sidqui."

"And the fiancé? Have you seen him?"

Azziz laughed, coughed on the cigar smoke he had inhaled, pounded on the desk as he coughed.

"Sidqui! How inept do you think I am?"

"You're not on the street any more, Azziz. You're locked up in your office."

"I know everything that you do, Sidqui," Azziz said, "and everything that anybody who means anything in Iraq does. I know what Saddam does before Saddam knows what he does. Do what I tell you."

"I'm your eyes. I've found the missing piece to this puzzle. I'm handing it to you. You better take it."

Azziz stared at Sidqui for a long moment, drew on his cigar again, blew out the smoke slowly, leaned back in his chair. "I wouldn't interrupt Ms. Sa'ad's work at Osiraq right now. But for your sake, Sidqui, I'll pick up the waiter. His interrogation will be rigorous. Give me his name."

"Samir al-Wahab."

Azziz wrote it down.

"You won't be sorry."

"I know you well. I know of your friendship with Udai Saddam Hussein. I know of the women he supplies for you, of your predilection for a certain kind of beauty. If Ms. Sa'ad were beautiful, I'd suspect you of jealousy, because you can't have her. But she's not beautiful. She's plain. A touch unattractive, a touch masculine. So I know you don't desire her. But," Azziz brought his large swivel desk chair upright. Opening his eyes wide, raising his eyebrows, Azziz smiled. "Perhaps you hate Samia Sa'ad for being plain. I've known men like that. Perhaps you hate her because she doesn't appeal to you. She dares to stand outside the sphere of your desires. In that way, she rejects you. And yet, she's important to Iraq. Think carefully." Azziz relaxed his focus on Sidqui. "She's a valuable asset to Osiraq. If you're wrong, you would be very embarrassed. Do you know what I mean by 'embarrassed'?"

"Bring in the waiter. Interrogate him. Destroy him. He'll talk."

"And should I also question our dear Egyptian brother, Dr. Yahia El Meshad? He discovered Samia Sa'ad. He brought her here."

"No!" Sidqui insisted. "No! Just the waiter first."

"Don't worry, my friend, I won't expose you to any more danger than necessary."

Hikmat Sidqui sat in a tall-backed red leather chair that faced Azziz's desk. On the wall behind Azziz hung a portrait of Saddam Hussein with his wife and their two sons.

Sidqui had been in this office many times. To his left hung another portrait of Saddam Hussein. It was a blood-portrait, done by the only artist in Iraq who did such portraits, Khalid al-Khalil.

Sidqui himself had arrested Khalid al-Khalil's wife eight years ago. She had complained in the marketplace about the government's system of food rations. And she publicly blamed Saddam Hussein — at that time Chief of Mukhabarat — for the disappearance of her brother.

Hikmat Sidqui himself had interrogated al-Khalil's wife. Sidqui himself had delivered color photographs of her interrogation to her husband, Khalid al-Khalil. After her interrogation, she never spoke again. When Sidqui was done with her, he sent her home to her husband, to her children, to her friends and family, to her neighborhood. People from the neighborhood would come to see her, to gaze at her bizarre behavior, the glazed-over terror in her eyes. She spent her days in a chair shivering as though very cold. She had to be led off to bed at night, where her shivering abated in her few hours of sleep.

"Whatever I do, I do for the Leader, for Iraq," Sidqui said.

"Yes," Azziz said, "Udai Saddam Hussein knows that. He rewards you for it. In the way of your desires. And he laughs about you. Yes. To me. He laughs about you. Don't ever try to get bigger than you are. You're small. Remain small, where you belong. I'll take care of you."

TWENTY-TWO

In the morning, Samia stopped at the café, *The Vizier's Daughter,* for her morning coffee. Putting her purse down, she drew out the courier-nail, with its message about Hannan Khatib, from the slot in her shoe. She held the nail curled in her hand as she put her hand on the table. When the waiter came, it was not Samir al-Wahab. She tightened her hand around the curled-up nail.

"He's gone," the waiter said.

"Where?"

"I don't know."

Time stopped for Samia. Samir al-Wahab gone. Arrested. What else could it be? They were closing in on her. Baghdad had stopped. Even though people around her kept moving, the waiter moving among his tables, the customers sipping their coffee, eating their morning's pastries, the pedestrians in the streets walking, the cars creeping along, even so the whole city had stopped dead still. The sun itself had stopped, dead still. Here she was, a solitary spy remote in a time warp. To whom could she signal? Only Samir al-Wahab. But whoever else watches her, some other agent, Israeli, or Iraqi working for Israel, would know that

Samir al-Wahab was gone. Mossad in Jerusalem. Arie Solen; they know it. They're moving into action. *I should just wait for them. I shouldn't make any moves. There's information I have to get now before it's altogether too late. Only Hannan Khatib stands between me and those computers now. Who is she? Iranian spy? CIA? I just don't know. I hold in my hand the microfiche about her, and I have no one to transmit it to. I'll take her out. Tonight. My God! Poor Samir al-Wahab! He'll reveal me. Under torture the poor man. Time stands still Baghdad stands still the air stands still and the sun stands still over Baghdad. My body doesn't move. Time doesn't move in my body. My mind. An emptiness. A terror. Don't think of tortures. You're Samia Sa'ad. You're a nuclear safety.....No! You're Samia Halevy. An Israeli spy. You'll get what you need, and fast. Today. No. Tomorrow. After I've taken care of Hannan.* Still wrapped in a timelessness, Samia jumped up, running to the bathroom, where she pulled the door shut behind her, locked it, squatted before the toilet to vomit. Her face was flushed, her head burned and pulsed. "Oh, Mama, I'm so sorry," she said, barely whispered.

Picking up the courier nail from where she had let it fall from her hand to the floor, Samia returned it to the sheath in her right shoe. She stood, washed her face, put on fresh makeup, straightened her clothes, opened the stall door. No one there. She left the bathroom. As she left, an Iraqi man crowded her in the narrow hallway. Without hardly moving his lips, brushing very close to her, he whispered quick words to her. Too quick. She didn't make them out. The man disappeared into the bathroom. As she walked back to her table, her coffee and croissant, the whispered message disentangled itself in Samia's mind. Indeed, it made perfect sense. "Cyanide," he had said. "Samir al-Wahab cyanide. No interrogation." That's what the man had whispered to her. In Arabic.

As she sat at her table without having taken a sip of her coffee or a bite of her croissant, the man from the bathroom hallway passed by without looking at her. A mustached man. Tall, young, maybe 30, 32 years old. In a business suit and tie. He walked back in the direction of the Hotel Al Rashid.

If only she had the decent luxury to cry in relief. If only she could shake someone, kill someone in vengeance for Samir al-Wahab. If only, right there, she could pray out loud for him. Say *Kaddish* for him. She wanted to thank him. Samir al-Wahab. *Hardly knew him. But the secret we shared. He knew me. Who knew anything about that lovely, awkward man? Had saved her life. Had even saved his own from their tortures.*

Only slowly did a sense of time return for Samia. That it was Tuesday. That her car would come soon. That she must finish her coffee and croissant and not raise any suspicion. That the courier-nail was still in her shoe. It must become an ordinary day of coffee and croissant. Crossing her legs, sipping her coffee, Samia leaned back like a woman relaxing a bit after sleep and before work, taking in the sight of the city and its pedestrians, its traffic.

The car arrived. The driver held the car door open for Samia, then he closed it after her.

"Good morning, Ms. Sa'ad," Sidqui said. "Well rested?"

"Thank you," Samia answered him.

Sidqui turned toward Samia, so that his right knee came up onto the car seat between them, and rested there. "Did you miss your waiter, Ms. Sa'ad?" Sidqui asked.

"I'm sorry?"

"Your regular waiter, Ms. Sa'ad. Did you miss him?" Sidqui moved his face closer to Samia's face. Samia turned her head to look right back at Sidqui.

"I'm sorry. My regular waiter?"

"Ms. Sa'ad." Sidqui leaned his body towards her, "at *The Vizier's Daughter* this morning. Did you miss your regular waiter?"

"I didn't notice. Do you know him? Is he sick?"

"Yes," Sidqui answered, "now I know him. And, no, he is not sick. Illness won't bother him."

"Good," Samia said, "then I expect I'll see him tomorrow again." Samia turned her head to face front, away from Sidqui.

"Yes, perhaps you will." Sidqui watched Samia for

a second, then turned to sit, facing forward in the car again, as they drove on to Osiraq.

oo

The Baghdad Mossad Illegal Officer reported to Samia's Case Officer in Jerusalem that the waiter, Samir al-Wahab, had been arrested. Samia's Jerusalem Case Officer reported al-Wahab's disappearance to Arie Solen. Solen took over supervision of the Samia Halevy case himself. He consulted first with Col. Yossi Ben Luria.

Ben Luria called his wife. He had to stay in Jerusalem. For a few nights. Tamar suggested they should move to Jerusalem. She could be happy there, she said.

Ben Luria said that yes, he was lonely for her, but they could never leave Safed. They loved Safed. Tamar agreed. Safed was a special place. They could never leave Safed.

Later that night, in Solen's office, Solen informed Ben Luria that the waiter, Samir al-Wahab, had taken cyanide.

"He saved himself from their torture," Ben Luria said. "But he saved our Samia Halevy's life. They would have taken him apart piece by piece."

"They would have flayed al-Wahab alive," Solen said. "One of Azziz's favorite techniques."

"Azziz himself must be in on this, although Azziz learned everything he knows from Saddam."

"Same thing," Solen said, "Azziz, Saddam."

"And what of our Samia? What of her now?"

"What do you say? I want your opinion."

"I say we wait for her. I assume she has a way to signal us."

"We leave a rose in a single-stem vase on her habitual table at the café, *The Vizier's Daughter*. She leaves her purse when she gets up, then goes back to get it just as Hikmat Sidqui opens the car door for her. Like, '*Ooops, I left my purse.*' Then we arrange a meeting for her."

"Then it's her call. We arrange a different courier route for her, but in the meantime, it's her call. If she wants to come in, we bring her in. If she doesn't, we don't. She'll let us know."

"She declined our last call for a meeting when her husband filed for divorce."

"Dov?" Ben Luria said. "He filed for divorce?"

"I'm afraid so," Solen said.

"But that's awful. While she's in Iraq…."

"We let her know. She could have come home."

"She chose to stay?"

"She declined our meeting," Solen repeated, "she chose to stay. You know her, don't you, Yossi?"

"I know her quite well. We dated for a while. In High School."

"We are such a small country." Solen smiled and shook his head. "Her cousin," Arie said, "Capt.

Schmuel Halevy, is training on the F-16's as we speak. Did you know that?"

"Yes, sir, I did. I met him in the States."

"Would you be able to sacrifice Samia," Solen asked, "if it came to that?"

"Would you?" Ben Luria asked.

"Yes," Solen said. "I would. I'd be willing. I'd be able."

Ben Luria hesitated for a moment.

"I'd be willing. I'd be able. But who among us knows his breaking point?"

Solen's office was small. Two windows gave it light and air and a view of the world outside. Pictures of his family were tacked up on the wall, an old news clipping of Solen as an amateur boxer, a large abstract painting in blues and greens by an Israeli artist, Yosef Shahan, a friend of Solen's. Solen sat behind his desk with his chair tilted back and his feet up on the desk. Ben Luria relaxed in a wooden desk-chair with his feet up on another similar chair.

"Do you know Ibrahim?" Solen asked.

"Ibrahim?" Col. Ben Luria said. "I suppose I know many Ibrahims. Arabs. Palestinians."

"And," Solen asked him, "Do you know an Ibrahim in Baghdad, at one time a Mujahadeen, fighting the Russians in Afghanistan? Ibrahim Ibrahim."

"And now......?"

"And now....as you've apparently guessed, Ibrahim Ibrahim is fighting Saddam Hussein in Iraq."

"And," Ben Luria finished the description, "working with us in the meantime?"

"After three years in an Iraqi prison. Abu Ghraib."

"That's the worst."

"He used to listen to the floor of the gallows drop all day, he told me."

"He got out....?"

"I don't know how. During the early days of the Mujahadeen…" Solen began as if to begin a long tale, but made it a short one, "I knew him in Afghanistan. I helped train him. I saved his life, actually."

"How so?" Ben Luria asked.

"I had a feeling one night that he and his men were in danger where they had camped. I grabbed a jeep, I drove three hours over pitted dirt roads in the dark to get to them, to get them the hell out of there. In the morning, their campsite was shelled to bits."

"And now Ibrahim thinks you're a military genius?"

"Let's not get carried away. Ibrahim's a rational man. He knows I have an instinct. And he loves me. And...."

"Yes, sir."

"And I love him."

"Yes, sir."

"Remember that he's there to help us. He can help us with Samia. He runs a bookstall in the Casbah. Have you eaten?"

"No, sir, I haven't. Not yet."

"Like to go out with me?"

"Actually, sir," Ben Luria said, "I'd like to head home. I'll be back at 0900. On the dot."

"You'll drive all night. You'll see your wife for half an hour."

"That's enough," Ben Luria said, "for now."

"OK," Solen said. "I'll see you in the morning. 0900. Right here. I've got you on loan from the Prime Minister for as long as I need you. You needn't report in to him."

"Yes, sir. He told me."

TWENTY-THREE

The knock on the door of Meshad's suite at the Hotel Baghdad came violently.

Meshad opened the door to Lt. Ha'ad Jazzar and two uniformed, machine-gun bearing Iraqi soldiers. Lt. Jazzar flashed a document.

"Orders from the Bureau of Internal Security," Jazzar barked out, stepping forward, pushing Meshad aside.

"Orders for what?" Meshad yelled back at him.

"Orders," the Lieutenant said, as the two other soldiers dispersed into the suite, "to search your living quarters. Don't give me a hard time, Doctor. I don't like a hard time."

The Lieutenant stood eye to eye with Meshad.

"This is preposterous," Meshad protested. "Do you know who I am?"

"You're Dr. Yahia El Meshad. You're 47 years old. You were born in Cairo on March 8, 1934. You're an Egyptian national. You're on a 16-B visa to work in Iraq. You've come here to work as a scientist. A physicist. Do you want any more information about yourself, Dr. El Meshad? Shall I tell you about your mother? Your brother? Do you still want trouble?"

"I didn't come here begging for work," Meshad defended himself, "the Iraqi government – *at the highest level* – begged me to come. I have more security clearance than an Iraqi general! Now get out of my apartment." Meshad motioned toward the front door. "Take your goons with you!"

One soldier had already encountered Hannan, dressed in a white negligee and slippers, in the bedroom. She was yelling at him.

Jazzar pushed Meshad aside, hard. Meshad, losing his footing, fell to the floor.

The Lieutenant headed for the bedroom, leaving Meshad on the floor.

"Shut up!" the Lieutenant yelled at Hannan. "Put on a robe. You're shameful! Dressed like a whore!" He rifled through the closet, found a robe, threw it at Hannan. "Here!" he yelled. "Put this on." The Lieutenant turned to the other soldier. "No rape tonight. Empty everything, closets, drawers, cabinets. Empty it all out. Her purse. Her other purses. Drop out every shoe! Open anything that opens, large and small. Do a good job."

Jazzar grabbed Hannan.

"Come on," he said, "let's go visit your boyfriend."

He pulled Hannan into the living room, told Meshad to sit on the couch, then pushed Hannan down next to Meshad.

"Go on," the Lieutenant said to Meshad, "comfort

her. Look. She looks frightened. Don't worry. When we're finished, we'll leave you alone. You can continue with your evening's activities. Just what were you doing?"

"You filth!" Meshad started up from the couch.

"Uh-uh," Jazzar cautioned him. "I have orders not to harm you. I don't like to disobey orders. It requires so much paperwork."

Meshad sat back on the couch.

"Just what are you looking for?" Meshad asked.

"Your secrets," the Lieutenant answered him. "Whatever they may be."

"I have no secrets," Meshad said. "You can tear out the walls if you like. You'll just find the bugs you planted here."

The Lieutenant, having a great laugh at that one, said, "Ah Iraq, my Iraq. The world's greatest consumer of electronic bugs, eh? We're proud of it, Dr. El Meshad. We even manufacture our own. We know what's going on in our country. You don't fear a bug if you have nothing to hide,."

It took the soldiers two-and-a-half hours. Hannan and Meshad endured. The soldiers left the suite in chaotic upheaval. Dishes thrown to the floor, drawers emptied, rare books flung from their shelves, paintings and photographs ripped off the walls. As they left, Meshad yelled after them, "You found nothing! Nothing!"

"We'll see!" Jazzar called back.

"I'm so very sorry." Meshad embraced Hannan. She collapsed into his arms.

"I'm exhausted," she said. "I'm sorry. I should be stronger. The stress of it. Those thugs. The place..... we'll have to get it cleaned up."

"No, no," Meshad insisted. "I'll get you a drink. Your favorite, your American drink. I'll make you a martini. Sit down. My poor, sweet dear. Lie down on the couch. Here."

Meshad rescued his liquor bottles, found two unbroken martini glasses, found ice in the freezer. As he mixed the drink, he muttered on.

"I've been here for five years. They know who I am. Why would they do this to me? I've never done anything to draw their suspicion. I've worked day and night for them. Believe me, my dear, I believe in their belief. They want to build a great modern country. They're not religious fanatics. They're not communist dupes. They're Arabs – modern, progressive, intelligent. They're for the people. Oh!" Meshad spilled the martini he was mixing. He started over again with the vermouth.

"Calm yourself. It's all right," Hannan said.

"Yes, yes," Meshad ranted on. "Saddam Hussein – I've met him – he's the calmest man alive. He's a great leader. A great leader. Arabs, they dream of the past, the great caliphate, before the conquests... the be-

trayals…the Ottoman, the French, the British. Saddam may see to the past but – believe me – he lives in
the present. He dreams of the present! A present of
honor. Dignity. Arab dignity. Arab progress. A modern
Muslim world. And a man like that – and his follow-
ers – they have furious enemies. Here, stay still. I'm
getting the drinks. I've almost got it. You don't know
what Saddam has already done for the people. It's incredible. The roads. Hospitals. The hope! If you knew
about Saddam. He grew up. A poor boy. In the village.
Betrayed. Beaten. Inspired. Visions. Annointed! Yes.
Annointed! How can you oppose a man whom Allah
has annointed! Why would you? Furious enemies!
The Iranians tried to assassinate me one night. I was
in a car. I disappeared into the streets. I eluded them.
I know Baghdad. I ran into a police station. For sure
they'd gun me down. I ducked, I swerved back and
forth I ran up the steps. Praise Allah – I got inside. The
police took me in. I'm telling you. They have powerful
enemies. I've been here over five years. It's intolera-
ble. My apartment! They would never do this to all
the French scientists working with us. Never! They're
racists!"

"Come, calm yourself, Meshad," Hannan called to
him.

Meshad brought the two martinis. Hannan com-
forted him. His body trembled, not outwardly, but in-
wardly, as she touched him, his muscles trembling and
twitching.

As they lay on the couch in a quiet daze, under the relieving influence of their martinis, a knock came again at the door. Gently this time. Meshad rose to open it; Hannan sat up, watching.

Standing in the hallway, a hotel clerk held an enormous flower arrangement. The kind that belonged more in the center of the hotel lobby than it did in Meshad's suite. Meshad stared at it.

"May I come in, sir? It's awfully heavy."

Meshad stood aside. The clerk came into the suite.

"My God, sir," the clerk said. "Look at what they've done to you!"

The clerk placed the flowers on the coffee table Meshad had set right side up, took the tip Meshad offered him, then left.

Downstairs, the clerk met Lt. Jazzar, reporting to him that both Dr. El Meshad and the woman were still in the suite, both looking haggard.

The note attached to the flower arrangement read:

"My Dear Ms. Hannan Khatib; My Dear Dr. Yahia El Meshad:

Humbly and sorrowfully do I present my apologies for what has befallen you this evening.
The audacious Lieutenant and his two underlings acted without authorization. Severe will be their punishment. With all the authority of my office, I assure you. Severe and swift. Even as you read this apology.
I have arranged for another room for you in the hotel for tonight. Please accept my insufficient offer.

Soon, two of my men will arrive to assist you.

In the morning, a small crew will restore your suite to its original comfort. Please direct them as you wish. Keep them as long as you need. Replace any losses at my expense.

With the blessings of Allah,
I remain in your service.

Mohammed Azziz
Chief, Mukhabarat, Internal Security

Later that night, Lt. Jazzar reported to his Commanding Officer that he had found nothing in the apartment which might compromise or indict Ms. Hannan Khatib. The Commanding Officer wrote a full report to Mukhabarat Chief Mohammed Azziz, noting that although nothing was found, Dr. Yahia El Meshad and his companion, Ms. Hannan Khatib, surely know that any misstep on their part will not go unnoticed.

TWENTY-FOUR

When the men and women of Midnight Air Force base came into the dining room, they found the tables set with standard plates and silverware, but a white cotton tablecloth covered each table. Bottles of white wine sat on the tables. A host of salads in big bowls were scattered throughout. The Air Force and the few Marines sat down quietly, talking in low voices among themselves. When they were all seated, Maj. Durham took the floor.

"Ladies and Gentlemen of the combined military forces of the United States of America," Durham spoke in the thickest southern accent he could muster, "y'all are present tonight at a rare occasion. Tonight, and tonight alone, you will not eat fried chicken, you will not eat tacos, you will not eat rice and red beans."

A cheer arose.

"But I have to confess," he went on, "that I don't know what the hell you will eat."

"When you join the Marine Corps," someone called from the back of the room, "you're ready to eat dirt."

"You won't eat dirt tonight," Durham answered him. "But like I said, I don't know what the hell you will eat. I do know that we have flown in, courtesy of the United States Air Force and the United States

Marine Corps, ingredients for this meal from parts of the United States you didn't ever know existed."

"Oh yeah," another voice called out, "like the South?!"

"You ain't good enough to eat the food of the South," Durham drawled. "Hear? You underdeveloped Yankee goat. Now shut up and listen up. Those ingredients we brought in, you haven't ever heard of either. You ever heard of *Hobz Belboula?*"

"*Hobs Bell-what*?" the same Marine called out. "I said I'd eat dirt, but I won't eat poison. What's that *Hobs* stuff? Fall out of a camel's ass?"

"Hey," Durham drawled, "keep it clean fellows. There are ladies present."

The Israeli pilots came out of the kitchen with trays full of *Hobz Belboula*, a Moroccan party specialty, barley bread with cumin. The assembled crowd applauded, whistled, cat-called.

"Barley bread with cumin!" Hamal yelled over the noise of the crowd.

Durham called out:

"Y'all know our Israeli buddies here. They're hosting us for the night. If you like the food, sign up to go there and get yourself into some real trouble. If you don't like it you're in real trouble right here 'cause it's all the kitchen's putting out tonight."

The Israelis served a meal of salads, lamb with cumin and preserved lemons, couscous, a cinnamon-orange sherbet dessert, and mint tea. The men and women of Midnight ate with gusto, some of them loving it, some calling for tacos.

All right, Chief," one young guy stood up. "I like the food. I'll volunteer for duty in the Middle East. So what if I have to stand in between the Jews and the Arabs while they all fire away at me. At least I won't eat tacos no more."

The room became quiet.

Another young soldier yelled out, "Don't be a sap. Let the bastards kill each other, not you!"

Durham sat still, his face blanched.

Halevy stood at the doorway to the kitchen. He grabbed a glass, filled it with wine, lifted it, and toasted into the uncomfortable silence:

"To peace," Halevy said, "to universal peace. To peace between the Arabs and the Jews, the Protestants and the Catholics, the blacks and the whites."

Durham stood up. "To universal peace."

Someone called out, "And short of peace, to victory."

"I'll drink to that," Halevy agreed, "short of peace, to victory."

Atari joined in, "Short of peace, to victory."

Durham stood with his glass raised.

"Hey! We have a new motto for Midnight Air Force Base. Stand up you guys. Everybody up. Up!"

All stood, pushing back their wooden benches, wine glasses in hand.

"To universal peace," Durham said, "and short of peace," their voices raised and they sang out: "to victory."

"To universal peace," the crowd intoned together, "and short of peace, to victory."

Hamal raised his glass, "Here's to Midnight Air Force Base. Thanks, all of you."

The crowd yelled back, hooting and hollering. Then the Americans grabbed all the Israelis, pushed them out the door, over to the swimming pool, and gave them a good dunking.

As the Israelis crawled out of the pool, soldiers handed them glasses of wine. Atari and Halevy dove back into the pool on their own, smashing walls of water at each other, diving under to tackle the other guy's legs, then racing each other back and forth along the pool. A couple of Airmen disrobed down to their skivvies, hopped in, and joined the races.

Groups of soldiers wandered off with bottles of wine and glasses to find spots around the compound to continue drinking all night. Atari found an isolated place where he spent the night with a female Air Force pilot. When they awoke, at about 0300, Atari snuck back into camp for a couple of blankets.

In the morning, squadron leaders wandered the Base, gathering up their men.

Durham gathered a clean-up crew for the disasters in the kitchen and the chow room.

The day after that, Durham saw the Israelis off on their way back to Israel. He wished them good-luck, bade them to wash their F-16s once in a while, polish them up. The Israelis gave Durham an Israeli flight jacket, along with an honorary membership in the IAF.

TWENTY-FIVE

At Etzion Israeli Air Force Base, Ilan Hamal awoke before dawn. Rather than jump out of bed, he lay still for a few moments. The Sinai desert of southern Israel is not like the desert of Utah. It's more barren. More vast. Over the five million years since the creation of the Negev and the Sinai deserts, winds have blown, churled, swirled the golden-hued sand into eddies, flatlands, rises, caverns. It is more worn down, more finely grained than the landscape of Utah. Little of the Sinai landscape is predictable or stable.

The Sinai desert separates Israel from Egypt.

To the East of the Sinai lies the Dead Sea.

Beyond the Dead Sea, to the east, lies Jordan, with whom Israel has an uneasy peace. Beyond that, come Israel's sworn enemies: Syria, Saudi Arabia, Iraq.

In a briefing room at Etzion, Gen. Dror stood together with Israeli Air Force Maj. Gen. Moshe Mitztan, Commander of *Etzion Air Force Base*. Dror spoke to the returning pilots. He stood at the front of the room, before a large wall map of the Middle East, a pointer in his hand.

"You guys will figure out your mission in a few days anyway, so I'm going to tell you now," Gen. Mitztan said. "No need to stress how top secret this is. During the next couple of days, the mechanics and the engineers are retrofitting your aircraft. You can study charts, walk around our mock-up, write letters, whatever you like.

"The Iraqis have been building a nuclear plant called Osiraq, at Al Tawaitha, south of Baghdad. Already they're sneaking enriched uranium out of the plant for a nuclear bomb."

Dror pointed at the location on the map.

"The French have been working very closely with them. The Russians too. The French built them the reactor core. The French call their nuclear program 'Osiris.' After the Egyptian Sun God. In Iraq, they call it Osiraq. We're going to bomb Osiraq into nothing but little tiny bits of useless steel and concrete rubble."

Hamal and Atari looked over at Rose, who shrugged his shoulders.

"Yes, is there something we need to know?" Gen. Mitztan asked.

"Rose," Atari said, "he guessed it while we were in the States. He said it could be Iraq."

"And why," Mitztan asked, "Capt. Rose, did you suspect Iraq? Did you have any tip-off?"

"No, sir," Rose said. "None, sir. Just a feeling I had in my bones."

"Smart bones," Mitztan said. "But think about it. I want to know about anything that might have tipped you off."

"Yes, sir," Rose said. "I'll think about it."

"Your Mission, *Operation Opera*, is ready when you're ready," Mitztan said.

"A silly question…" Halevy said.

"No questions are silly," Mitztan encouraged.

"Why *Operation Opera?*" Halevy asked.

"Good question," Dror laughed.

"Just that," Halevy added, "to me names are important, sir. A superstition maybe."

Dror stepped forward. "I chose this name. It's no frivolous choice, Halevy. Think about opera. A hundred parts working together – composer and librettist and conductor and musician and performer and audience and so on – all in precision. All together. Like your Mission. Opera takes different voices in different songs from different singers." Dror's hands waved about in front of him as if gathering things, "to weave them together toward some difficult, fantastic accomplishment." His arms fell to his sides. "That's you, guys. You're the voices of this *Operation Opera*." Dror waited a moment, then asked, "Question answered?"

"My God," Halevy said. "Yes, sir, question very much answered."

"Excuse me, sir," Klatzkin spoke up. "I don't know much about opera, but it's always tragic, isn't it?"

"No!" Dror pointed a finger at Klatzkin. "Exactly

the point. Opera *uses* tragedy to achieve beauty. We're turning tragedy into beauty here. Got it?"

"Yes," Klatzkin said. "Got it, sir."

Gen. Mitztan took over again

"Your F-16s," Mitztan said, "won't make it to Osiraq and back. They don't have the range for it. Today, we've started retrofitting them with two external gas tanks. But you've lost all your gunnery. All your guns, all your air-to-air missiles. All you will have will be your bombs. Two 2,000-pound bombs for each plane, port and starboard wings. Questions?"

The room sat silent. Until Atari spoke.

"Without gunnery. Without missiles. You don't mean to put us out there like that, sir. You can't."

"That's right, Captain. I can't, I don't mean to, and I won't. But I will ask you to go out there like that protected by six F-15s. All right?"

Again the room sat silent.

"You understand, sir," Halevy spoke out, "that we're fighter pilots. You're asking us to go out there in a fishbowl, over…I don't know, Jordan, Saudi Arabia, Iraq, and never be able to fire a shot. Just watch the battle rage and hope to God."

"Who the hell else you going to hope to?" Atari shot in.

"Then go on to Osiraq," Halevy went on, "run our bombs in low level bombing runs I assume, then haul ass home another… how many kilometers I don't even know… over all that same airspace again."

"That's what I'm saying, guys. That's it. Anyone wants to drop out, just fill out your request. No questions asked. I know what I'm asking from you. We all do. Day after tomorrow we're busing into Jerusalem because Prime Minister Begin himself wants to talk to you guys. Any dropouts, no questions. Drop on Request. DOR."

"Any dropouts, no questions," Dror stepped forward to emphasize the point, to lend his authority to it. "This raid on Osiraq – believe me, it's no crazy idea. It's an idea born, as Prime Minister Begin would say, from the genius of an acute, urgent calm. We're training the F-15 guys right now. Have been for a month. The whole plan took us over a year to work out. This is no quirk-of-the-moment operation. I'm on top of every detail myself. So is Gen. Mitztan."

"When might we go?" Hamal asked.

"In a month," Dror said. "Now listen. There's a trick to this mission."

The guys all laughed.

"Well, yes," Dror joined them, "the whole mission is a trick. But there's this trick added. Once you get to Osiraq, you've got a ten-minute window to drop your loads. Ten minutes. They have to go right down the tunnel. Eight planes, two bombs each. The whole thing rests on your sixteen bombs. Or we're looking at an Iraq with a nuclear bomb pointed right at us."

"What's this ten-minute window?" Halevy asked.

"You have to get in there *after* they've installed the reactor core." Dror explained. "Once they install it, they turn it on right away. To test it. Then they turn it off again. They look over all the dials and gauges, make sure everything went right on the test run. It sits like that – turned off – for exactly ten minutes. Cooling. Getting ready. While it's shut down, the computer reads all the test results. It calculates it all and tells them everything's ok. They can go. Then they turn it on again, forever. We can never bomb it again. Got it? Ten minutes."

"Got it," Atari said. "We get there just as they've installed the reactor core."

"Right," Dror said.

"They turn it on," Atari went on, "to test it. We don't drop."

"Right."

"They turn it off to read the test results. We go. We have to slide in there while it's off."

"Right."

"If we miss it, they turn the thing on again."

"Yes, Atari, that's it."

"If we're early…."

"If we're early we miss the reactor core."

"And if we're late?" Atari asked.

"We lose our chance," Dror said. "If we hit it too late, it's total nuclear meltdown disaster. Saddam Hussein put the damn thing near Baghdad for exactly that reason. So nobody could bomb it without taking out the whole city. But we're going to do it."

"Of course we're going to do it, we're IAF" Halevy said. "We do anything."

"I know," Dror said, "I know. It sounds crazy. It sounds tough. But look over the details, guys. We can do it. You can do it. When it's all over I'll see each one of you back here at Etzion. I don't send missions out to fail. Do I?"

"No, sir," some of the men said.

"How many planes do you figure we lose, Gen. Dror?" Atari asked.

Without answering right away, Dror stood before the men. He absorbed the question.

"I don't know," he said. "I appreciate your question, Atari. I don't know."

"Half?" Atari asked. "Two thirds?"

"I don't know," Dror said. "Anyone who wants out, drop out. I swear to you, this is not a suicide mission."

"We're flying....what? 2,000, 2,500 kilometers over enemy airspace. That's a hell of a lot of time to get us. And we're disarmed, in the F-16s."

"Actually," Dror said, "we figure it at 2,246 kilometers. You'll have to do a lot of crest jumping, hiding out in canyons, that kind of thing. Then there's the bombing runs. We hope to bring you home at 2,246 kilometers."

"You *hope* to bring us home," Atari said.

"Study the plans. Look it all over. Give us your thoughts. Everybody get home last week?"

"Yes, sir," they said.

"You?" the General asked Hamal.

"No, sir. But it's all right. I'm all right. One more month we can hack it."

"Sometime early in May," Dror said. "I think. Let me put it this way. Day after tomorrow we bus up to Jerusalem to see the Prime Minister. He can't come to the Base without drawing suspicion, or he would. Believe me. The bus drops you off at some neutral spot. You each make your own way separately to the King David Hotel. Anyone who's out, miss the bus. All right? No questions asked."

Two days later all fourteen pilots rode together to Jerusalem. Each one had a private room at the King David Hotel. That evening, Prime Minister Menahem Begin hosted a reception in the hotel to honor the violinist, Itzhak Perlman. After the pre-dinner speeches, toasts, introductions, Itzhak Perlman played a piece on a Stradivarius violin that had originally been brought to Jerusalem in 1901. Then the head waiter escorted the two tables of pilots to a private room. The Prime Minister shook hands with each man as he entered. Col. Yossi Ben Luria stood in front of the room, next to the Prime Minister.

"I'll be brief," the Prime Minister said. "We're asking you to save Israel from the next holocaust. Nothing less. The annihilation of Israel. We've drawn our plans carefully. It's immense. It's passionately conceived. I wanted to see each one of you before you left. Do it, and come back to me here in Jerusalem. I want to kiss every one of you a welcome home kiss. I won't stop thinking about you until you come home. On the day you go, I'll be watching your every move." The Prime Minister left the room. The pilots sat by themselves for a short time. They returned to the ballroom for dinner.

TWENTY-SIX

On Thursday, April 4, 1981, Hannan left the Hotel Baghdad with Dr. Yahia El Meshad at 7:15 a.m. The usual Mercedes Benz with the usual driver awaited them at the curb. Across the street, two Arab men sat in a lime green BMW. The man in the passenger seat wore a dark fedora. The driver smoked a cigar. "A lime-green BMW. A fedora and a cigar."

That evening, Hannan phoned Meshad from their hotel suite. He had stayed to work late at Osiraq. She left the hotel at 5:45, telling the doorman that she would go out for a stroll, that she and Meshad would dine in the hotel at 10:00. The doorman said he would take care of the restaurant reservation.

Leaving the hotel, Hannan turned right. Two blocks down, a red thumb-tack stuck into a telephone pole. Hannan turned left. Two more blocks down, a blue thumb tack stuck into a telephone pole. Hannan turned right. One more block down a red thumb tack stuck into a telephone pole. She turned right. Red-blue-red.

Halfway down the block, where a white cloth hung from an outside doorknob, Hannan entered an apartment building. A red thumb-tack stuck into the first door on her right. She knocked.

A short, Arab-looking man opened the door, but said in Hebrew, "Shalom."

Plain shades were drawn down over the windows. In the middle of the otherwise bare front room a card table held a lamp, two cups and saucers, a pot of hot tea, sugar packets, cream, an open package of sweet cookies. A folding chair sat on either side of the table.

The man sat opposite Hannan while she nibbled at a cookie, drinking the hot black tea.

"It's good to speak Hebrew," Hannan said.

"Welcome home to your language," the man said to her.

They smiled at each other.

"Your message comes from Col. Yossi Ben Luria," the man said.

"Who's that?"

Pulling out one half of an American silver dollar, the man put it on the wobbly card table. Taking the other half of the same silver dollar from her purse, Hannan fitted it against the half the man had just put down. She examined the fit.

"Send back my love to Col. Yossi Ben Luria," Hannan said, smiling. "That's a world away."

"Yes," the man said. "It is. A world away. The message is this: "We need time. Delay the project. We'll eliminate the lover.""

"Eliminate the lover?"

"Yes," the man said. "He gave me no name. Just, 'eliminate the lover'."

"I understand," Hannan said.

"Col. Ben Luria's message went on," the man said. "He said they'll do it. You just set him up. In Paris. You'll go to Paris with 'the lover.'"

"I sleep with the man," Hannan said. "I'm not inhuman. Yes, he's an anti-Semite. Big time. Yes, he knows exactly why Saddam is building Osiraq. For the bomb. But you tell Col. Yossi Ben Luria that life is more complex than he'll ever know. A certain tenderness grows. No one is immune. Even an ISS-1 woman. What am I saying? Have I lost my mind? Tell Ben Luria there are better targets. Let the lover go back to Egypt. Give him a warning in an alley one night. I know his body! I kiss his lips. I make love to that body. The man lays his arm around me when he sleeps at night. Oh God! Kill him. I don't give a damn. Get somebody else. I've got limits. Everyone does. Look," Hannan said, "I'm just human. First I have to make love to a man I hate. I do it. For three months now I've done it. I laugh with him. I drink with him. I know all about his family at home. He's a womanizer, ok, all right, but I'm somebody to him. I'm Hannan Khatib. You have to put your hatred aside. You come in a funny awful way to love the man. Now just kill him? Set him up? I'll kill anyone else they want me to. Samia Sa'ad. The Plant Director, Al Hira. That bastard Azziz. Now there's a target for you. Azziz. But the lover? Forget it. Get yourself another agent. You do it. Not me. That's the message. I don't love the man. Of course I don't love the man. But a certain tenderness grows. Not even that, but the body you've slept with, made love to. You would kill your own lovemaking. Your own body. What am I talking about? I'm sorry. I'm going on and on. I'm just babbling."

Two days later, at the Hotel Athenée in Paris, Hannan and Meshad dressed for dinner. While Hannan was in the shower the phone rang. Meshad took the call. A man on the other end said, "11 rue de la Gare."

"That's on the left bank," Meshad said. "Can't we make it closer? I'm busy tonight."

"I'm sorry," the man said, "someone in the lobby will bring you to the room. As usual."

"All right," Meshad said.

When Meshad and Hannan came downstairs, a woman in the Athenée lobby watched them as they passed into the dining room. Hannan wore a black dress.

Their dinner began quietly, made so by the service of the Maitre d' and the waiters. As they ate and drank wine and talked of the day, they began to engage each other, and to laugh. Meshad told Hannan about an error he made a couple of days ago, in arithmetic. They laughed that Meshad, for all his scientific wisdom, could sometimes not add one and one to get two.

"I can just see you as a child," Hannan said, "in Cairo, dazzling your teachers with scientific formulas they couldn't even understand, but then – poor Meshad – unable to make change to buy his lunch with."

"Not quite," Meshad said, "but a charming image."

"Tell me," Hannan said, "when I first came with you to Baghdad, were you nervous?"

"No," Meshad said, "I was excited. If you didn't like it, you would leave. If I didn't like it.....I would kick you out!"

They laughed, raising their glasses of dark red wine together, clinking them against the other.

"And," Meshad said, "does your mother know about me yet?"

"Oh, no!" Hannan exclaimed. "Don't tell me that now you're becoming formal?"

"Well, does she?"

"My mother is one of those crazy Arabs," Hannan said, "the kind who are thrilled that you go off to Baghdad because it's the birthplace of knowledge, but who also want you to go back to Paris to marry a Westerner."

"Then your mother and my mother should marry each other!" Meshad threw his head backward in laughter.

"My mother, too, would have me marry a Westerner," Meshad said, "a Parisian, even an American! And yet, she, too, is a devout Muslim. She begs me to write her letters about the center of Arab culture, all about Baghdad. And, she asks, when will you return to Paris, to find a wife? We are a schizophrenic people!"

"Yes," Hannan laughed, "you have the perfect idea! Let your mother marry my mother."

"I'm sorry, Mother," Meshad raised his newly re-filled glass yet again, "I haven't found a Westerner for you, but at least I haven't found a Negro or a Jew!"

"Yes!" Hannan said, "you haven't shamed your poor mother altogether!"

"Maybe someday you'll meet her," Meshad said. "She's quite a character, really. You would like each other, I think."

"Bring her to Baghdad," Hannan said.

"She'd never leave Cairo," Meshad said. "She went once on Hajj to Mecca, but that's it. She's made her holy journey, to make no others. She's a woman of Cairo who will stay in Cairo."

"Then you'll have to take me to Cairo," Hannan said.

"Oh no," Meshad said, "don't tell me now that *you* want to make our affair a formal thing?"

"Oh, never, never!" Hannan said. "We don't want to ruin our fun!"

They finished dinner. Meshad checked his watch, then apologized that he had to tear himself away for his very quick meeting.

"It's a little odd, though," Meshad said.

"How so?" she asked him.

"They want me to come to an odd address, on the Left Bank. They've never asked to go over to the Left Bank before. It just feels odd."

"Be careful," Hannan said. She took his hand in her own. "I'll go with you."

"No," Meshad insisted. "I would never do that."

"Tell me," Hannan still held on to Meshad's hand, "who are you meeting? Trust me. You know you can. Let me go with you. I'm tougher than you think I am."

"I'll just go," Meshad said. "Don't worry. I'm being silly. I've gone to dozens of these meetings."

"What kind of meeting? Why the secrets? Are you in danger? I'll go with you."

"I shouldn't have mentioned it. You go up to the room and freshen up. I'll be back in time for cognac. We still have a lovely night ahead of us. We'll hear jazz again until dawn."

Meshad got up from the table, took Hannan's hand to help her up, and led her to the elevators. The same woman in the lobby who had noticed them earlier saw them pass again. She stepped outside, turned right, and walked away.

When Dr. El Meshad left the Hotel Athenée, a taxi pulled up immediately, before the concierge could step into the street to hail one. Dr. El Meshad got in, gave the taxi-driver the address on the Left Bank, and the taxi rolled out onto the street.

Hannan waited in the room for an hour and a half. His clothes in the closet. His papers on the desk. His toiletries on the vanity in the bathroom. She turned on the TV. It irritated her. She turned it off. For a while, she stared out the window at Paris, then stepped out on to the balcony. She came back in. She tried to read

Paris Match. It, too, irritated her. She sat on the couch. She got up, went into the living room. Sitting at the desk, she scribbled on a notepad. Then she wrote: "sorry, Meshad." She crossed that out with heavy scratches. She said aloud, "I am not sorry." She went back into the bathroom. She took an emery board with her into the bedroom, sat on the bed. She filed her nails for a good twenty minutes. When she finished filing her nails, she pulled herself out of the trance she had fallen into. She reached for the telephone beside the bed, but stopped herself half-way. She got up and paced in the bedroom. She lay down on the bed. She got up. She lay down again, forcing herself to stay still, even to fall into a light sleep.

After an hour and a half she called the desk.

"Have you seen Dr. El Meshad?" she asked. "I've been expecting him."

By 2:00 a.m., the Hotel Manager insisted that they call the police.

Two days later, the police, who had already interrogated Hannan, informed her that Dr. Yahia El Meshad's body had been found in a hotel room on the left bank, Rue de la Gare. His throat had been slit. According to the coroner, the death took place two days ago, most likely shortly after Ms. Khatib had last seen Dr. El Meshad. Did she know why he might be in the Rue de la Gare? No, she said, she didn't.

Two days later, Hannan asked the Paris police for

permission to return to Baghdad, to resume her duties at Osiraq. They agreed.

Hannan returned to the apartment she had shared with Meshad in Baghdad. Lt. Jazzar delivered a note to her, asking if she would meet a gentleman by the name of Hikmat Sidqui. A routine affair of questioning on the fate of Dr. El Meshad. The Paris Police were working closely with the Baghdad authorities. Hannan protested that she had already undergone extensive interviews with the Paris Police. Lt. Jazzar apologized, but said he had no authority in the matter. Ms. Khatib would have to meet with Hikmat Sidqui.

TWENTY-SEVEN

"**O**siraq is Armageddon," Rafi Stone said. "It's the beginning of Armageddon."

Stone had finally cornered Col. Yossi Ben Luria. They spent the early afternoon in the conference room of the Prime Minister's suite, Ben Luria the captive of Rafi Stone.

"Prime Minister Begin called it a holocaust," Stone said. "We'll go in there we'll drop our bombs the whole place will go up in an inferno that won't stop." Rafi Stone waved his arms in a wide circle, the fire igniting in the sweep of his arms.

"Iraq is already aflame," Ben Luria said. "Only a few people outside of Iraq see it yet. It's a fire burning the whole country."

"You're a smart guy, Yossi. That's why I've grabbed you. To talk to you," Stone said.

"I'm smart enough to see what's in front of me," Ben Luria said.

"Our bombs will fuel the inflammation that's already begun in Iraq," Stone warned. "It's all part of the same conflagration: Armageddon. Who knows where it'll end?"

"It won't end with our bombing of Osiraq. But we've got to act now."

"Armageddon will take time. One battle begetting the next battle. It'll go on and on until it erupts into Armageddon. Believe me."

"No, Rafi. It'll go on until we destroy the nuclear threat from Baghdad."

"Until it reaches Armageddon," Stone said.

Ben Luria asked Stone where he got these ideas from which he talked about with such wild, breathless excitement. Stone protested. They were not wild ideas. They come from obscure books of Jewish learning, from the Christian Bible, from Christian mystics, from the Gnostic mystics of the 1st Century.

"You're a Jew," Ben Luria told him, "you're no Christian, and you're certainly no Gnostic."

"We take knowledge from everywhere to make a Jewish truth of it," Stone said, interlacing the fingers of his two hands to demonstrate. "The early Christians were all still Jews."

"True," Ben Luria said.

"It's ok, Yossi." Stone took Ben Luria by the shoulders. "Most of what I'm telling you comes from the Jewish mystics, from Kabbalah."

Ben Luria admitted he had only very slight knowledge of Kabbalah.

"How could *you*," Stone said, "Col. Yossi Ben Luria, not know the books of our great Jewish mystical tradition of Kabbalah? You're a direct descendant of Isaac Luria. Your very name: *Yossi Ben Luria,* means Yossi, son of Luria."

"I suppose I must be," Ben Luria admitted. "It's never been important to me."

"Isaac Luria," Stone repeated. He let go of Ben Luria's shoulders, but the passion in his voice didn't subside. "The 16th Century Kabbalah master. You live in Safed."

"And?"

"Safed, Yossi. The Medieval center of Kabbalah. Isaac Luria himself lived in Safed."

"Yes," Ben Luria acknowledged, "I know of Isaac Luria. I know Safed has some history like this. I don't know much about it."

"Look into your heritage," Stone urged Ben Luria. "You're old enough to understand it now. It's time for you to study the books of Kabbalah. You are ready to encounter the great tradition of the mystics – and the mystical path to god."

On his way home to Safed that afternoon, Ben Luria took a detour to the northern town of Tel Megiddo. He would have a look at Megiddo, the historical site of Armageddon.

Ben Luria parked his car in town, then wandered until, at dusk, he roamed the ruins of King Solomon's stables. Here, in the 10th Century BCE, Solomon had kept 450 military horses. Centuries of wind-blown soil had buried the stables, now uncovered. Ben Luria walked on the ground above the emptied stone stables, on the weeds and dirt and wild grasses. *That was the 10th Century BCE*, Ben Luria thought, *almost three thousand years ago. Solomon's empire spread to the Euphrates River. To the edge of Iraq. And three thousand years later, F-16s. My great friend. Soon, Ilan. It will fall on your shoulders.*

"Col. Yossi Ben Luria!" a voice yelled out.

Ben Luria stood stock still. It had darkened. In the bright moonlight and the star-filled sky one could still see. But Ben Luria couldn't see who had called to him. The voice called out again, closer.

"Col. Yossi Ben Luria! It's me. Avraham Bloch!"

A man approached from Ben Luria's left. Ben Luria stepped back.

"It's me. Avraham Bloch. You don't remember me? I fought with your father on the *Altalena*."

"I'm sorry....?"

"I saw you a few years ago. A reception at Rafi Stone's house. You don't remember me?"

The man came into view.

"Oh," Ben Luria said, "yes, yes I do. Mr. Bloch. Yes. I remember you. Your son went to university with me."

"Yes," Bloch said, "that's right. My son, Avraham. He's named after your father. But you know that. Your father was Lieutenant of my squadron. I was much older than your father, but he was the Lieutenant. Lieutenant! We hardly had an army let alone all those ranks. I know. I know. Jews don't name our children after the living. And I'm Avraham! And my son is Avraham. I didn't name my son after myself. I named

him after your father. It all works out. Three Avraha-
ms. Who first wandered out from the ancient city of
Ur? In Iraq. Abraham. So we're all named after the first
one, who came from the earth's first city. It all works
out."

Bloch didn't even take a breath. Ben Luria had to
interrupt him.

"I remember your son, Avraham. He did chemistry,
yes?"

"Yes!" Bloch said. "Yes! He's in the States now,
working for Monsanto. Or Dow. One of them. I can
never remember. He shifts around from one to the other. He lives in California. But how are you, how are
you?"

"I'm fine. You knew I was a Colonel?"

"I know everything in Israel. I'm a great gossip."

Avraham Bloch: mop of white hair. Fluffy, unruly
white eyebrows. The beginnings of a stoop. Thin.

"What are you doing here?" Bloch asked.

"What are *you* doing here?" Ben Luria turned
Bloch's question back on him.

"Here? Solomon's stables? I come here often. I sit
on the stable walls and I think. I smell the horses that
were here." Bloch pointed to various places around the
site. "I see the stable boys running around with feed,
saddles, curry combs. I feel the whole scurrying of
Solomon's empire. I think here. I meditate. Here I feel
the commingling of…" He stopped short.

"Yes?" Ben Luria asked.

"Do you have a moment?"

"A few," Ben Luria said.

"Sit with me on the wall. I'll tell you what I feel here. You'll…..I think you can…."

"Yes?"

"I think…..sit down, Colonel."

The two sat on a part of the ancient wall that had not yet been buried by millennia of shifting soil. They dangled their feet into the ruins of the stables below, which had been covered, now opened by archeological digs.

"Talking to you," Bloch said, "is like talking to your father, to the holes in my life left by those who have died."

"You can never replace those who are gone."

"No. They're gone. That's it. But when I see you, you remind me of your father, then I see things begin again. Time is a funny thing. Your father and I were going to be professors in the first Jewish university in Israel. That was our ambition together. He'd teach physics, I'd teach philosophy. We were young."

"Do you teach? Now?"

"Life intervenes, Yossi. I was practical. After independence I became a barber, like my father. In Jerusalem. I fought again in '67. By '73 I was too old to fight. But I'm really a philosopher. I always studied. I read all the philosophers, Jewish, European, Islamic, Asian.

Even the Americans."

"Who do you like best?" Ben Luria asked. "Who has the truth?"

"One philosophical problem always stumps me: Evil. How do we have enormous evil in a world which God created?"

Ben Luria didn't respond, either with enthusiasm for the problem, or with an answer to the question.

"Do you know what I mean, Colonel? How? Such enormous evil."

"You're the Philosopher-Barber of Jerusalem," Ben Luria said.

Bloch laughed with Ben Luria. "I like that. I used to cut hair and I would think of questions like this. I drove my customers crazy. They came back for more philosophy. We talked constantly in the barbershop. After the Holocaust, I had to think deeper. How? Does God not exist?"

"Is that your answer?" Ben Luria asked. "God doesn't exist? You wouldn't be the only one to think that after the Holocaust."

"God exists," Bloch said. Picking up a clump of dirt and weed, he held it out for Ben Luria to see. "Smell it. Take in the odor of it," he said. "It's the odor of the God who made it."

Ben Luria breathed in the odors of dry, mineral soil and wild plant life.

"I feel God everywhere," Bloch said. "I know God

every day. God exists. Yes. But tell me, Yossi, how does evil exist in a world God made?"

"I have no idea. I'm no philosopher. I'm a military man. A soldier."

"Here in Megiddo," Bloch said, "Armageddon will occur. According to the Christian Bible, to the legends. The battle between good and evil. I imagine good and evil coming together here. Becoming one." Bloch interlaced the fingers of his two hands together. "If I keep coming here to sit on these walls, if I think, if I wait, if my mind wanders, it'll come to me before I die: how is it that the world of God contains enormous, putrid evil."

"If good and evil become one," Ben Luria said, "they'll be the same thing. Neither good nor evil."

Bloch raised a finger in the air. "You're clever. Your father was clever."

"Evil exists. That's all there is to it. It exists."

"What about God? Why would God afflict his creation with horrifying evil?"

"I don't know about God," Ben Luria said. "Like my father. I don't know anything about God."

"But you," Bloch said, "you live in Safed. The old center of Kabbalah. You're a descendant of Isaac Luria himself. Even if you don't admit it to yourself. It's in your blood."

"Wait, what's going on here? Are you conspiring with Rafi Stone?"

"I conspire with everyone!" Bloch laughed a great laugh into the night.

"Rafi Stone," Ben Luria pressed on, "was lecturing me about Isaac Luria this afternoon, about Kabbalah. He sent you after me, didn't he?"

"Rafi Stone! What a character!" Bloch laughed again. "Isaac Luria. 'The Lion,' they called him. He was strong and swift and wise enough to hunt through the jungles of illusion for a fleeting truth. You're old enough to understand now. It's time for you to study the books of Kabbalah."

Ben Luria, rocking on the wall's edge, lost his balance, fell backward onto the ground.

"Wait a minute," Ben Luria called out from where he had fallen, leaned on his elbows, "you're repeating *exactly* Rafi Stone's words."

"The common language belongs to everyone."

"But it's just what Rafi Stone said."

"We all shuffle and reshuffle the same words. That's why the truth's so hard to see."

"For me, truth is pretty simple. I know what's true, what's not."

"At least look into Isaac Luria," Bloch said.

"He lived a long time ago. Things are different now."

"Time fools us. Three thousand years ago, right here in Megiddo, King Solomon defended his empire. In World War I, the British Gen. Sir Edmund Allenby defeated the Turks right here, in Meggido, at the Battle of Meggido, Sept. 18–21, 1918. Four hellish days and the end of the Ottoman Empire. Time goes on and it stays the same. History is the same over and over yet different each time it comes around. Isaac Luria lived only 400 years ago."

"Do you know much about Isaac Luria?" Ben Luria asked.

"Some," Bloch said. "Isaac Luria was a great mystic. Not everyone can follow where his footsteps lead."

"Then tell me some," Ben Luria asked.

"Come, sit on the wall. I'll tell you one thing."

Block offered his hand. Ben Luria took it, pulled himself up off the ground, sat on the wall beside Bloch. Bloch patted the dirt off Ben Luria's back. As they sat, they rubbed shoulders.

"Isaac Luria had a system for seeing God. This was in the 1500s mind you. If I could see God now…" Bloch raised a fist in the air."

"It frustrates you?" Ben Luria said.

"Yes," Bloch said. "If I could see God now I would understand how evil came into the world. I can't. Not yet."

"But you hope to see God?" Ben Luria said.

"Doesn't everyone?"

"No. I don't. I find evil in the world. I fight it. That's all."

"Isaac Luria's method for seeing God, for achieving understanding," Bloch continued, "tells us there are seven gates on the way to God. A hostile angel stands guard at each one of those gates."

"A hostile angel!" Ben Luria laughed. "How can you have a hostile angel?"

"Yes. A unique vision, hostile angels. A vision open only to those who have the courage to see it. To go through each of the seven gates on your way to God, you have to bring a certain potion with you to pacify the hostile angel of that particular gate."

"Quite a journey."

"Before you begin your journey, even to the very first gate, you have to fast. Then you have to acquire the essential potion. Then you begin your journey. There are dangers. You can be fooled. You could bring the wrong potion to the wrong angel."

"And," Ben Luria asked, "what would happen if you did?"

"Then," Bloch said, "when you gave that wrong potion to the hostile angel, the guardian of the first gate, you would die in a terrible fiery death."

The two men sat together in the night. Bloch's words had quieted them.

"I don't believe in God," Ben Luria said. "These are stories out of fairy tales for me."

"However you like," Bloch said.

"Folk stories," Ben Luria said, "Quaint. Interesting. *Bubba meissa.* Grandma's tales. Tell me what you knew of my father."

"He was a man determined to build Israel. He wasn't religious. No. But in his heart he would have understood the stories of Isaac Luria."

"Why do you say that?" Yossi asked.

"Because," Bloch insisted, "he was like you."

Bloch drove home to Jerusalem. Alone in his study, he phoned his good friend, the anonymous Chief of Mossad, whose name is never revealed, not mentioned in any government document. Bloch reported that Ben Luria was all right, stable, clear-headed. But he's under stress. He could use a vacation. The Chief of Mossad thanked Bloch for looking in on Ben Luria. Bloch suggested they have a good, long game of chess. The Chief of Mossad declined. "Too busy. No chess right now."

"I thought so," Bloch said. "At least I'll come give you a haircut."

"Yes," the Chief said, "that I have time for. And the need of."

When Ben Luria got home to Safed, Tamar awaited him. They drank wine, talked, and went to bed. She agreed they would get an apartment in Jerusalem big enough for the family. They'd spend more time together. He promised that eventually he'd leave government service to come home to Safed. Tamar didn't believe that. "You'll die in the service," she told him, "an old man, I hope." In the middle of that night, unable to sleep, Ben Luria awoke. He wandered downstairs. Opening the back door, he stood out on the patio, in the clear air. Then, sitting at the kitchen table he wrote on a napkin the words that he kept hearing: "hostile angel…. a terrible fiery death." He wrote a note to his friend, the pilot, Maj. Ilan Hamal:

Dear Ilan,

However this letter reaches you through military mail, wherever you are, as soon as you're back in Israel, please come with me to Safad. Tamar will cook for you. She'll make potions of magical food. You'll be fit to visit with the angels, like Abraham. We haven't seen you in so long. You know what a great cook Tamar is.

Fly right, pal.

Yossi

Ben Luria packed up a few things. He woke Tamar to say good-bye. He left for Jerusalem.

TWENTY-EIGHT

Samia stood on the fire escape of the Hotel Baghdad, eleven flights up, just outside the kitchen window. Hannan slept alone in the bedroom. Curtains covered the closed, locked window. Samia dressed in black slacks, a black shirt, black tennis shoes. With a glass cutter she took from her pocket, Samia scored once around all four sides of the lower window. She applied one suction cup to the glass. With a small rubber mallet, she tapped the scoring around each of the four window sides. The window-glass came out nearly noiselessly. Samia laid it beside her on the fire escape, set the tools on top of it, drew out her pistol, set the silencer to it, parted the curtains.

She entered the kitchen. To her left, beyond the living room, the bedroom door stood open. She walked into the living room, then across the living room to the open bedroom door.

Hannan lay spread-eagled across the large bed. Samia took measure of her clearance space. She must do it in one movement. Taking in one long, quiet breath, letting it all out, she stepped through the opening of the bedroom door, aimed her pistol at exactly where Hannan's head had been, and almost pulled the trigger.

Hannan had rolled across the bed to the other side, jumped to the floor, held in her outstretched arm a Manurhin 7.65 mm. pistol pointed at Samia. Samia raised her silenced pistol to point straight at Hannan.

Both women held fire.

"Who the hell are you?" Hannan demanded through clenched teeth.

"Who the hell are you?!" Samia shouted. "You're no scientist from Paris!"

"You're no nuclear safety engineer from Stanford!" Hannan shouted back.

"Wrong!" Samia said. "I am from Stanford."

Samia moved very slowly to her right, out of the small amount of light that came in from the window. Hannan tracked her with her pistol.

"Don't go one step further!" Hannan ordered.

"We'll both lose this," Samia said.

"Not one step further!" Hannan yelled. Before she got the last syllables out of her mouth she had ducked, dove for the bed, rolled over it landing feet first facing into Samia's face with her pistol rising fast but not quite fast enough. Samia threw her left hand down to deflect Hannan's pistol, crashing hard into Hannan's wrist, sending Hannan's pistol flying.

Hannan's left fist landed on Samia's temple, throwing Samia's head to her left. Hannan, grabbing the pistol barrel in Samia's hand, flung it backwards over her shoulder where it bounced off the closet door.

The two women came to the ground wrestling. Both threw punches, kicks in tight quarters.

Within 90 seconds, Hannan had Samia on the ground in a choke-hold. Down on her left knee, Hannan's knee dug into the small of Samia's back. Samia struggled to grab Hannan or throw her off with her legs, her hips.

"Tell me who you are," Hannan said, "or I'll kill you in one second."

"Tell me who you are!" Samia cried out, "before you kill me. You'll never know who I am!"

Hannan dug her knee deeper into Samia's back, tightened her grip on Samia's neck. Samia piped out: "You're French. I know you're French. A fucking Frenchie will never kill me!"

"Wrong, lady!" Hannan went tighter on Samia's throat.

Hannan had all but closed off Samia's breathing. Samia's eyes closed; her face turned red. She fainted.

Hannan took her knee gradually from Samia's back. With one hand, she reached over to take up her own Manurhin pistol. She walked around the bed, picked up Samia's silenced pistol. She took out the cartridge, put the pistol inside the closet, on an upper shelf, then closed the closet door. Hannan put the cartridge in a dresser drawer, then sat on the bed with her Manurhin pointed at Samia's heart.

When Samia came to on her own, she breathed

small, tight, quick breaths which became gradually smooth.

Hannan stood up from the bed.

"Stand up slowly, hands high in the air," Hannan said. She moved toward the bedroom door. "Take the tie from my robe on the bed, tie it tightly to your right wrist in a square knot, pull it there through the opening in the bedpost, then tie that end to the bedpost in a square knot. Tightly."

Samia did it.

"Sit down on the bed," Hannan said.

Samia sat.

"I want some information from you," Hannan said. "Pull tight on that cord."

Samia pulled on the bathrobe tie. It tightened around her wrist and on the bedpost.

"Give me water," Samia squeaked. "I can hardly speak."

"No water."

"I'll tell you nothing. Shoot me now," Samia said.

"Who are you?" Hannan said.

"You'll kill me anyway. A Frenchie will kill me. I hate you fucking French."

"So. You hate us fucking French, do you? So what does that make you? Iranian or American? CIA? KGB? MI5? Iraqi?

"You'll never know. You'll kill me. You'll get rid of my body. And you'll never know. You'll wonder all your life, who was she? I'm a fortress of resistance."

"I have means," Hannan said. "You're CIA. The Iranians could never pull off someone like you. I know you're not French. So I'll kill you quickly, with all the mercy I would show the CIA, after I get what I want from you. But not by torturing your body."

"What do you want from me?"

"I want to know when Osiraq will complete. I want to know when the new reactor core will ship. I want defense details."

"It's all in the computers. Meshad is dead now. Who knows, maybe you killed him. Get that information yourself."

"You can read those computers," Hannan said. "I can't."

"Ahhhh," Samia said. "You can't read the computers. How sad."

"All right. We'll sit here for a while. You'll tell me."

"You're playing with me. Your government knows when the reactor core will ship. Your government built it. And they rebuilt it. You're asking me questions to warm me up. Your techniques are too transparent."

"What makes you so sure I'm French?"

"Who uses the Manurhin 7.65?" Samia said. "It's a distinctive piece of work."

"You know your stuff, don't you?"

"Just shoot me now. My life isn't worth what you think it is anyway."

"Ok, then, I'll shoot you." Hannan extended her right arm, aiming the Manurhin at Samia. She raised her left hand to give the Manurhin a sturdy grip. "Heart or head?"

"Head," Samia said.

Hannan raised the pistol toward Samia's head, aimed it directly at the spot between Samia's eyes, slightly above.

"Shoot," Samia said, "I'm never going home anyway. Do me the favor. Spare me the torture."

Hannan held the pistol steady.

"For God's sake," Samia said. "Shoot."

"Not yet," Hannan said.

"You'd never let me go," Samia said. "You won. Kill me."

"Who are you?"

"Shoot!"

Hannan kept the pistol aimed at Samia. She went to the closet, retrieved the pistol with the silencer, then took the ammunition clip from the bureau drawer. She loaded the silenced gun. She stood again by the doorway, pointing the silenced pistol at Samia's head. She pulled the trigger.

Nothing.

Samia stared straight at Hannan. Hannan held up her other hand, opened it. It held the ammunition clip.

Samia stared at it.

"Who are you?"

"I am Samia Sa'ad."

"Who are you? You're already a dead woman. Tell me who you are."

Empty now of everything but terror, exhaustion, delirium and resolve, Samia said, "Ani Samia..." She caught herself. "I am Samia Sa'ad," she said.

"You..." Hannan paused. She thought. "You spoke Hebrew. You said, 'Ani.' And you did it by mistake. It's your mother tongue. You are Mossad. Or a traitor. An Israeli traitor."

Samia didn't answer.

"You have failed. You revealed yourself. Now prove to me that you are Mossad."

"Why?"

"If you are Mossad, you will live."

"You need me. For what? For torture. You will never break me."

"No, because you are Mossad. Mossad never break. They are crazy. Prove to me you are Mossad. There is no torture for you. Trust me."

"Trust you? Kill me. You would like to kill a Mossad. Because they are always ahead of you and they will always be ahead of you. What a feather in your cap. Go on, believe I am Mossad. See how Mossad can handle even her own death."

"You are Mossad? Who is your Case Officer?"

"Kill me."

Hannan aimed the pistol again, now at Samia's

heart. "I'll take the risk. I have the gun. Ani Mossad. Gam ken ani Mossad."

"You, too, are Mossad? Don't be ridiculous."

Each woman stared at the other, silent. Not thinking. Silent. Absorbing. Breathing.

"You understood me," Hannah said. "When I just said to you, in Hebrew, 'Gam ani Mossad,' 'I too am Mossad,' you understood me."

"I understood you but I don't believe you."

"My Case Officer is Chaim Gotai. Now do you believe me?"

"I never heard of Chaim Gotai."

"I have no choice. I have to kill you."

"Kill me."

No sound ripped through the room. No bullet was fired.

"You are Mossad. I am Mossad," Hannah said.

The tables turned. Hannah held the gun, but Samia asked the questions.

You prove to me you are Mossad," Samia said.

"How?"

"In the army, where were you?" Samia demanded.

"Golani Brigade," Hannah answered.

"Battalion?" Samia pursued the questioning.

"Barak," Hannah said.

"Where?"

"Galilee, mostly."

"I am not afraid to die," Samia said.

"I know it," Hannah said.

"What is the Hermon Outpost?"

"The Eyes of Israel."

"The Mossad code for Jerusalem?" Samia asked.

"Eliyahu."

"The Mossad code for Tel Aviv?"

"Yofeh," Hannah answered.

"For Safed?"

"Zohar."

"Who is Ariel Solen?"

"Managing Director of Mossad."

"Who is Chief of Mossad?"

"Undisclosed. Not public. No one knows but the PM and the Chief of Staff," Hannah answered.

"But I know. And you know," Samia said.

"Hofi," Hannah answered.

"First name?"

"Yitzak. Yitzak Hofi. There," Hannah said, "I've violated my oath. Satisfied?

"Your Unit?"

"Caesarea."

"Your name?"

"Hannah Ben Eliyahu."

Hannah lowered the pistol.

"You told me you are Mossad," Samia said. "You believe I am Mossad. Take this risk. Let me untie myself. Then, give me the gun."

Hannah shook her head once, in the affirmative.

Samia untied herself, then held out her hand. Hannah handed the gun to her. Samia removed the clip. She took out the first, top bullet.

"This is the bullet that would have killed me. I'll keep it. I'll carry it back to Jerusalem, or however close I get back to Jerusalem."

"You were right about the Manhurin," Hannah said. "I stole it from a French agent. In France. In 1979."

"You…" Samia said.

"I what?" Hannah said.

"You're the woman," Samia said, "with Yossi Ben Luria at Seine-Sur-Mer, *Operation Night Plastique.* 1979. You blew up the first reactor core. There was a woman there. All Yossi told me was that, yes, there was a woman. It was you, wasn't it?"

"You know Yossi?"

"I know him. Yes. And now," Samia said, "the Iraquis know everything about us."

"No. This apartment is bugged, but I've scrambled the bugs. I guarantee you. They hear only a screeching static they wouldn't want to listen to."

"We've been screaming. Yelling."

"They hear only static."

"We are both Mossad. Incredible."

"Both Mossad."

"Then I'll confess to you. I've been here too long," Samia said. "I'm tired. So tired. I'm too tired to live anymore."

Hannah went to the bathroom. Coming back, she offered Samia a warm washcloth and a glass of water.

"Sleep here," Hannah said. "I'll keep an eye on you. Later, we'll figure out what to do. Just sleep."

Curling up on the bed, Samia fell into sleep.

Hannah watched Samia sleep for a while, her fellow Mossad who had become "too tired to live anymore."

Samia awoke after an hour's sleep. Hannah made tea. They talked about Mossad, about life in Israel, about their mutual friend, Yossi Ben Luria, about Arie Solen, about their childhoods in Israeli schools. About their days in the army. They trusted each other.

"I'm sorry," Samia said. "Maybe I've weakened, but I can use someone to trust."

"You're right. You've been here too long," Hannah said. "You've sacrificed too much."

"No," Samia answered. "I've only sacrificed what you would have, what Ben Luria would have, or Solen, or any of us."

"Thank God I didn't kill you," Hannah shook her head.

After a moment's thought, Samia said, "Yes. We came very close. Don't stay here as long as I have. It's brutal. It's inhuman here. You'll lose your soul."

TWENTY-NINE

On Wednesday, April 29, 1981, at *Etzion Air Force Base* in the Sinai desert, Capt. Shai Atari awoke at 0315. A recurrent dream unsettled him. Atari is driving his brother's old Fiat along the coast road heading south, in the opposite direction from where his brother Shaul had disappeared on October 6, 1973, in the Yom Kippur war.

In his dream, Atari slams on the brakes. A man, dressed well, strolls across the road in front of Atari's car. After he passes the car, the man stops. Turning to look back at Atari, the man stands still in the middle of the road. As Atari looks at him, the man bursts into flame. Atari shields his eyes. He gets out of the car. As Atari stands in the street, the car, too, bursts into flame.

Atari jumped up out of bed, went to the bathroom down the hall where he splashed cold water on his face. But he couldn't get himself out of the dream. Right there, in the communal bathroom, the man burned. Right there, the car blazed. Atari wiped his face with a towel, drank some water from the faucet, steadied himself.

Later that morning, Wednesday, April 29, 1981,

at 0730, Capt. Atari was in Lt. Gen. Mitztan's office, requesting a visit with his Rabbi. Mitztan reminded Atari that there was a Rabbi on base. Atari insisted on seeing his own Rabbi.

"I've known him for years," Atari said, "I trust him."

"You're under Top Secret Mission Ready Restrictions," Mitztan said.

"This could be my last mission. Let's not kid ourselves, General. I want to go. I'm ready to go out there and perhaps not come home. You know that. Trust me. Please, sir."

"Who's the Rabbi?" Mitztan asked.

"Avraham Bloch," Capt. Atari said. "He's not a registered Rabbi. He's a teacher. I've studied with him since I was 14."

"Then why did you call him a Rabbi?" Mitztan asked.

"The man is a true Rabbi, more than a Rabbi," Atari pleaded. "He's like the great Jewish teachers of the past, Hillel, Rambam. Trust me, General. Please."

"I'll have an answer for you by this afternoon. You'll have to meet him on base. I can't grant you any base leaves. You're on red alert standby."

"I know, sir. I'm not asking that. I'll be glad to meet him on base."

By the time they got a hold of Avraham Bloch it was late. Bloch drove half the night, arriving at the main gate of *Etzion Air Force Base* at 0545 on April 30,

1981. He presented his identity card, which the Gate Officer checked against the day's list. Another airman searched the car, while another searched Bloch. Bloch drove onto the base, following the route on the map the airmen had given him.

Capt. Atari introduced Avraham Bloch to Lt. Gen. Mitztan in Mitztan's office. Bloch and Mitztan had a brief exchange of pleasantries.

Atari and Bloch went to breakfast in the mess hall. After breakfast, they walked through an unused part of the base. The desert had already reclaimed it. Small sand dunes had built up.

"I had the same dream again," Atari said.

"Tell me."

"You know it. I've told it to you over and over."

"You have to tell it again, Shai," Bloch said, "in precise detail. Don't leave anything out. Each telling of a dream is new."

As they walked, Atari recounted the entire dream. Shaul's car, the road, the village, the man, the flames.

"Did the flames of the man burn out?" Avraham Bloch asked.

"No."

"Did the flames of the car burn out?"

"No."

"Did you catch fire?"

"No," Atari said.

"How far was the sea?"

"Right there. I saw it right there next to me."

"Could you smell the sea?"

"Yes."

"And could you smell the fire?"

"Yes."

"And do you remember this: '*Moses saw that though the bush was on fire it did not burn up.*'

"Yes."

"Perhaps Moses, too, had a dream."

"Do you think my dream isn't important, that it's just a dream?" Atari asked.

"I didn't say that. Was Moses' dream unimportant to Moses? I don't think so. Do you remember what happened to Moses after he saw the burning bush?"

"Of course," Atari said. "He saw the face of God."

"Perhaps Moses also dreamed that he saw God."

"You think he didn't?" Atari asked.

"It's the Bible," Bloch said. "Someone wrote it. It's a book. Maybe whoever wrote it dreamt of an unconsuming fire. If God wrote it, God dreamt of an unconsuming fire. Does it matter? Isn't it our common dream?"

"But Moses lived 3,500 years ago, when dream was reality. I live now. In 1981."

"Time, Shai," Bloch said, "all time is the same time. Time fools us. Moses lives now, in 1981. And you, Rai, you are alive 3500 years ago."

"Why do you say I *am* alive 3,500 years ago?"

"Because you are. Don't let time fool you."

"But, Rabbi...." Atari protested.

"Don't call me 'Rabbi'."

"But Rabbi Bloch," Atari continued, "time is real. Moses *did* live 3,500 years ago. I *do* live now. It's different. They're different times."

"The difference is easy, Shai," Bloch said. "And important. The sameness — of Moses in 1200 BCE and of you, of Shai Atari in 1981 — that's more difficult to understand."

"So, if I'm Moses...." Atari began to ask.

"No. Moses was Moses and you are Shai Atari."

Atari pondered Bloch's contradictions for a moment. Then he asked Block, "Why do I keep having *this* dream? Driving Shaul's car. The man crossing the street."

"Who is the man crossing the street?"

Three Air Force jets roared overhead.

"I don't know."

"I like it out here," Bloch said. "It's so dry. So barren. It gives your mind a light feeling of simplicity. If you were out here too long by yourself you might start hallucinating. I imagine you would. Do you think Moses was hallucinating?"

"I don't know," Atari said. "Who is the man in my dream?"

"Is it your father?"

"No."

"Is it your brother?"

"No."

"Is it me?"

"No."

"Is it God?"

"No."

"Are you God?"

"No. I am who I am and God is what will never be."

"What if God is who He is and you are what will never be?"

Atari laughed. "I give up," he pleaded, "I give up."

They walked on, Atari calming into quiet. Both had sand in their shoes.

"Is it yourself? The man in the dream?" Bloch asked. But then he said, "I'm tired, Shai. May I take a nap somewhere? Don't worry. We'll talk more. Everything will be all right. You won't go up in flames. No wonder you dream about flames here. The heat is amazing. I'm wearing these heavy clothes, slacks, this shirt. Could I change into shorts and a light shirt? I'm dying. It's so hot already."

Avraham Bloch slept, and dreamt: In his dream, Bloch was talking to Col. Yossi Ben Luria. He told Ben Luria about a dream he had. In Bloch's dream within a dream, he told Ben Luria that in his dream, Bloch was the "fire priest" in a primitive tribe. His tribe was still too primitive to know how to ignite fire. Long ago, they had captured flames from a forest fire. In every generation a "fire priest" was born. He tended the fire in a stone vessel, added dry sticks, other fuel, kept it going. When the fire priest slept, his apprentice would tend the fire.

If a fire priest let the flames die, the tribe would sacrifice him, cut up his body, then bury him in a series of graves laid out in a straight line to the east, toward the rising sun.

The fire priest lived in a cave water-cut from the side of rock. A designated tribesman would come to request fire; the fire priest would accompany him to wherever the tribe needed fire. Holding the stone fire-vessel aloft, the fire priest would intone a chant. Then, with ritual movements, dispense fire.

The people would respond with a chant of fire-praise. If the fire were for cooking, the fire-priest would eat with them. If the fire were for warmth, he would sit with them.

His duties complete, the fire priest, wrapped in an animal-skin coat, with his apprentice by his side, would return to his cave. There, he would recite designated chants, then replace the fire vessel in its place.

In the dream, when Bloch finished telling Ben Luria of his dream, Ben Luria held out his right hand. Flames rose up from Ben Luria's palm.

The boom of exploding bombs from practice target ranges woke Avraham Bloch.

Atari and Bloch talked again in the mess hall. Atari

had tea and a pastry, but Bloch ate a big meal of falafel, hummus, pita bread, and a chopped salad. Bloch ate slowly, with deliberation. He would stop eating for a moment, settle back, his hands in his lap, then eat some more. During one of these rests in his eating, he spoke to Atari.

"You've come to the first gate on the way to understanding. You're wrestling with the hostile angel of that gate. You're confronting the anger of that angel in yourself."

"Why is that angel an angel of anger?"

"How does it make you feel, Shai, when I tell you that you have come to the first gate?"

"It pleases me, and it frightens me."

"You tell me, Shai: why is that angel an angel of anger?"

"Guarding every gate is a hostile angel. There must be at least a thousand gates. There must be a thousand levels of anger."

"There are so many passages on the way to understanding they are numberless. Unimaginable. The journey will exhilarate you and make you weary."

"You think I've already begun it?"

"For now, you have to answer this question: do I choose to stand outside of my own suffering, or do I choose to stand within my own suffering. When you've chosen to stand within your own suffering, Shai, then you suffer the suffering not of Shai Atari, but the suffering of God. Your suffering becomes divine suffering. Only then can you bear to live honestly within it."

"How can I possibly know," Capt. Atari asked, "when I've chosen to live within my own suffering? When I'm not just indulging myself in suffering?"

"You'll know. For one thing, you'll encounter the hostile angel at the Gate of Divine Suffering."

"Is that the first gate, where I stand now?"

"You'll know."

"Is the man in my dream, the one who crosses the street in front of me, the one who catches fire, is he the Hostile Angel of the First Gate?"

"Is he?" Avraham Bloch asked.

"Yes he is. For now he is."

"There you go," Bloch laughed. "You're on your way."

Atari smiled, and kept on smiling.

"This happiness that overcomes you now," Bloch said, "don't forget it. It's the Divine Happiness that permeates Divine Suffering."

"And I feel a bit like crying."

"Those are the tears of your wholeness, which you imagine truly exists."

Atari walked Bloch to his car. Bloch drove an old American Ford, a big car for Israel. An automatic shift. As they stood by the side of the car, Atari asked a favor of Bloch.

"Will you bless me, Rabbi Bloch?"

"Don't call me 'Rabbi'! You'll destroy my humility!"

"Will you, Mr. Bloch?"

"When you call me Avraham, then I'll bless you."

"All right," Atari said. "It's not easy for me. Will you bless me, Avraham?"

"What happened when you called me Avraham, just now?" Avraham Bloch said.

"I felt your willingness to bless me. No, I felt my willingness to accept your blessing."

"Exactly. And I do. I give you my blessings." Bloch held his hands up in the traditional form for blessing, thumbs touching, forefingers touching, a gap opened between the second and third fingers, between the thumb and the forefinger. "May your internal flames protect you," Avraham Bloch said.

The two men embraced.

Before Bloch got into his car, Atari stopped him.

"If Moses was Moses, and I'm Shai Atari," Atari said, "then who was Abraham?"

Bloch looked at Atari. "Abraham?" Bloch said. "He was a man who left his home in Mesopotamia, in what we now call Iraq, because it was too near the Garden of Eden. He preferred a more human land of simple milk and honey."

The two laughed together.

Avraham Bloch drove to the gate by which he had entered. The Gate Officer informed him that a certain Lt. Moddan would de-brief him. Bloch satisfied Lt.

Moddan that Capt. Atari had revealed no military information to him. Bloch began the long drive home.

THIRTY

Friday, 0500. May 29, 1981.

"Guys," Maj. Hamal began, "yesterday was a disaster."

No one answered him. All six F-15, all eight F-16 pilots sat without speaking.

"We couldn't kill a flea out there with a 2,000-pound bomb."

All sat silently.

"I'm not blaming you guys. I'm out there with you. I know what it's like."

Hamal paced across the room, first to his right, then back.

"Major...." Capt. David Rose interrupted.

"Yes, David," Hamal called on him.

"Our problem is that we're still scared of these planes."

Hamal turned to focus on Rose. "David," he said, "it doesn't show, but I see it. In each one of us. Those planes are....as Maj. Durham called them, awesome things. Then we've gone and changed them. They are something to be feared. Remember Durham: 'Be safe. Get great.'"

"But," Rose sat forward in his seat, sat up straighter to project clearly what he had to say, "We can't be afraid of them. There's an edge where these planes will give us just what we need, but it won't crack up on us. We have to push ourselves to find that edge and then ride it in to target."

"Well," Hamal said, "yes…."

Atari interrupted him. "Rose is right," Atari said. "I've felt that edge. That's the soul of every plane. But it's doubly true, triply true for this one. It's a finely tuned instrument, very high strung," Atari held up his right hand, his thumb and finger just touching to form a delicate circle, to indicate the fine quality of his aircraft. "When we find that edge Rose is talking about, it's the most incredible plane I've ever flown."

"Exactly." Rose stood up. "I've felt it. I've been there. It's like the plane is skin on my body. I roll where I want."

"We'll all find that edge, David," Hamal said. "We'll get used to it. We'll learn to hold it. Here's our route." Hamal, pulling down a map of the Middle East, took a pointer from the chalk ledge.

"Here we are," Hamal pointed to Etzion. "We fly over Jordan, cross here into Saudi Arabia, cross Saudi Arabia, enter Iraqi airspace here, 343 kilometers from target. I'll have every detail ready tomorrow. Every millimeter of topography. The Saudis will come after us with their MiG 21s. Our F-15s will peel off to deal with them. The F-16s will motor on. Keep schedule.

Timing. When the F-15s have dispatched an enemy aggressor, they'll catch up. The Iraqis will come at us with Phantoms. We have to take them out. We can't have Iraqi Phantoms on our tail at Osiraq. Questions?"

There were no questions, yet.

"I have good news and bad news. The good news: we're green light to go any day. The bad news: we're green light to go any day.

"What if we lose our F-15 cover?" Halevy asked.

"If we lose all six F-15s?" Hamal asked.

"Yes, sir. If we lose all six F-15s. Let's get real."

"Well," Hamal said, "well, well. If we lose all the F-15s, we don't turn tail and run. We ram the bastards with the nose cones of our F-16s."

"We're not suicide bombers," Halevy said. "Value your life above everything. That's Jewish law. Didn't you know that?"

"ok. Seriously. If we lose our F-15s," Hamal said, "we fly hellfire straight for Osiraq, bomb the bastard into soot and cinders, and our mission is done."

"If we lose all F-15s that means me, guys," Avi Gar said.

"Can I have your new stereo?" Nussbaum called out.

"You can kiss my ass," Gar said. "If you lose the F-15s what're you going to do? Lob grenades out the window at the SAMs and the AA? You'll never get close to Osiraq."

"Yes we will," Atari joined in.

"Just how is that, Atari?" Gar said. "Just how you going to do that?"

"Don't worry," Atari said. "It will be done."

"You're crazy, Atari," Gar said. "I'll watch out for you up there. Don't worry."

"Could you see the dome yesterday?" Hamal focused the men back on the briefing. "Do you want the carpenters out there to do anything to the dome?"

"How close is it to what we'll see once we get there?" Halevy asked.

"It's the same. It's what we'll see. We fly low into it, right along the deck, so we'll first see it head on, all of a sudden. When we do see it, it's already there. We'll see the whole thing at once."

"What about timing and the sun?" Davidov asked.

"We make two runs this morning," Hamal said. "This afternoon, two more. The drop will take place at 1730 hours. At last light we're directly in front of the setting sun. It'll be harder for them to see us."

"So at first," Klatzkin said, "we're right into the sun?"

"Watch the sun this afternoon," Hamal said, "watch the glint off the dome. And remember.....we're the Ten Minute Boys. Ten minutes to complete the mission."

"Maj.," Atari said. "We can't go until we're ready. We need practice."

"You'll go when I tell you to go, Atari," Hamal said.

"I'll go when Lt. Gen. Mitztan tells me to go. Mitztan will tell me to go when Gen. Dror tells him to go. Dror will tell Mitztan to go when Begin tells Dror to go. Got it, *Captain* Atari?"

"I know when I can hit that plant and when I can't," Atari said. "I've got two bombs. That's it. Two damn chances, Ilan. Give me the time I need to get good at this. Perfect it."

"We've got the time that we've got, Atari. Let's get out there. Same formations. One by one. Wait for me. I'm waiting for Gar's signal. When the AA is gone, the SAMs are gone, we go. Not until then. I'm tailing you."

"Do you really think that we'll all make it to Osiraq?" Atari asked. "That we'll have eight strike planes? Shouldn't we train for having one strike plane make it through? Maybe two?"

"Capt. Atari," Hamal answered, "Capt. Atari," he repeated. "My dear friend, my fellow pilot, my long time buddy, *haver,* if you, and you alone, are the one single plane to reach Osiraq, do you think you might drop your two bombs right down the chute? Ace in the hole? Good-bye Osiraq? Center of the dome?"

"Yes, sir," Atari answered. "I know I would."

"Thank you, Capt. Atari."

The plane captains each helped their pilots to get into their planes. The pilots climbed aboard their planes, settled into the sixty-six square feet of space where each would negotiate their mission. Hamal's plane captain, Lance Cpl. Etzer Yehuda scolded Hamal:

"Your cockpit's all cluttered, Maj. Hamal. You better clean it up before inspections."

In his cockpit, Hamal had a photograph of his wife, Rachel, and their two kids, Peter and Rebecca. He had also taped up a piece of a note from his friend, Yossi Ben Luria. *"You will be fit to visit with the angels, like Abraham.....Fly right, pal."*

"Have you ever met my family, my friends, Cpl. Yehuda?"

"No, sir, I certainly haven't."

"But I've met your family often, haven't I, Cpl? Been to your house for dinner. Been to your daughter's birthday party."

"Yes, of course."

"If you'd met my family, Cpl., you'd tack their pictures up in your cockpit, too."

Yehuda smiled. "I'm sure I would," he said. "Kidding aside, are they safe here?"

"You mean am I safe with their pictures here? They're not in the way. Thanks for checking."

"Don't forget whose plane this is."

"It's your plane, Plane Captain Cpl. Yehuda. It's all your plane. You keep it clean, you keep it oiled, you probably sleep with it, don't you?"

"You've met my wife?"

"Yes," Hamal laughed.

"If you were married to my wife, would you sleep outside with an airplane?"

"Let me outta here, Yehuda! I'm supposed to go flying right now."

"Bring me back my plane in one whole piece."

Cpl. Yehuda closed the canopy.

In his cockpit, Atari had taped up a paper with a somewhat altered quote from the poet, the Irishman William Butler Yeats:

> *"Many times man lives and dies*
> > *between his two eternities.*
> *A lonely impulse of delight*
> *Drove me to this tumult in the clouds."*

He had also taped up photographs of his mother, his father, and an old, rescued photograph of his mother's first husband, Freiderich Witten.

Halevy had one photograph of his parents, his wife, and his sister, and another of his Grandfather and Grandmother taken at the First Zionist Congress, 1897.

Gar, wing leader of the F-15s, had a photograph of himself, his parents and his wife, taken in the melon fields of his native kibbutz.

Each pilot also carried special artifacts with him, a letter from his wife, a drawing by one of his kids, a watch their parents had given them, a Star of David they'd gotten when they were young, a token from one of their commanders. Halevy carried a toy airplane that his cousin, Samia, had given him for his 11th birthday.

One after the other, the six F-15s rose off the desert airstrip into the slight wind. As they ascended, they formed into two groups of three, forming a "V".

One by one, the eight F-16s powered up and rose into the slight wind. As they ascended, they formed into two divisions of two sections each, rising to fill in the gap left open by the F-15s, but 500 ft. below the F-15s. They headed high, up to 32,000 ft. out into the desert. Two training enemy aggressor jets streamed in from the north. The two leading F-15s, Gar and Kaminsky, hauled out after the intruders. In radio silence they flew by instinct, by knowing where your buddy was.

Gar and Kaminsky split up, each one taking one of the aggressor planes. Gar flew straight toward his target. At just a hundred feet he zipped under the guy, locked onto him from beneath, flipped over behind him, and had him. Gar turned, came up behind the other enemy, who was circling Kaminsky. Kaminsky dove down, leaving the enemy plane facing straight at Gar. Kaminsky came up behind the enemy, flew across his tail, locked on to him, and took him out. Another aggressor sped out of the north. Gar and Kaminsky both headed for him, one on either side, ready to take him out from straight on. As they met up with him, the aggressor locked onto Gar, took him. Kaminsky took advantage of that moment, the aggressor's distraction, and took down the aggressor. Gar, killed, didn't return to base. He noted the kill, returned to the armada.

Turning west, they descended to 3,000 ft. They flew that way straight to mock-up #1 of Osiraq, a life-size replica of the plant. A mile and a half from target, they descended to about 100 ft. The F-16s circled north of the target, then circled around it to come at it from the east, to put the sun behind them, leaving the Osiraq defenders staring into the sunlight to find them.

The F-15s flew in at 100 ft. at 500 mph. They jumped up on the emplacements, fired live away. They hammered away at the anti-aircraft and SAM emplace-ments with cannon and air-to-surface missiles, flying by sight. They circled, then came back for another round. The anti-aircraft guns automatically fired off practice rounds. The F-15s again whizzed by, storm-ing the emplacements. Within 1 minute 32.4 seconds the F-15s had decimated all the mock-up defense em-placements. They roared out to the east, circled to the north, headed back west where they would reconnoi-ter with the F-16s on the way home.

Hamal took his signal from Gar, then signaled his men by tipping his starboard wing down and up and down and up again. The F-16s went for it.

One by one they came in for their drops. They flew radio silence. Hamal came in first. His bomb hit far east of the dome. He pulled out low, to the west. Samy came in second. His bomb overshot the compound, too far for significant damage. Atari came in third. His bomb grazed the edge of the dome, but skimmed off to the west. Nussbaum came in fourth. When he hit the pickle button, his bomb took off to the east of the dome, but his plane rolled suddenly starboard, pulling him too close to the ground. His starboard wing tipped down. He pulled steady to the right. The wing came up just right but the roll had pulled him also askew. He hit the rudders gently, pulled back on the throttle, pulled back on the stick, and he was right in the sky. He flew away from the target ship shape, a little too high, having missed his shot.

Davidov zoomed straight and sweet on the target, altitude perfect, hit the pickle button on command, lifted up away from his bomb, flew out of range, dove under radar, and the bomb smashed right into the east side of the dome. As he flew away Hamal's voice broke silence. "Finally! Partial hit!"

The dome still stood, but crumbled on its eastern side, and listed.

Klatzkin flew shuddering into the target. He had his altitude, but he couldn't steady his wavering. He was off balance somewhere he couldn't pinpoint. He toggled back and forth slightly looking for attitudinal steadiness. He dropped his load, sped off. He had hit just short of Davidov's hit. The east wall of the mock-up shuddered and trembled, but did not collapse.

Halevy came in seventh. He had good air speed, he had good attitude, he was in control. When he got the signal, he hit the pickle button, but soft. He felt it soft. The bomb overshot the dome, but rattled the whole west side of it in its explosion.

Rose came in eighth and last. His stick-hand held steady. His throttle hand shuffled slightly, looking for the right speed. He eased back on the throttle. He saw the dome, he felt the timing, he heard the signal, he hit the switch. His bomb sailed downward, his plane took the upward draft, up and away, he fell into departure route. His bomb fell right where Klatzkin's bomb had hit. The whole east end of the mock reactor collapsed.

While the construction crew jumped in to rebuild the mock reactor, another crew readied one of the other three mock-ups not far away. Two under repair, two ready at all times. The ammunition guys and the bomb-loaders re-loaded the F-15s and the F-16s. The pilots met in the briefing room.

"Better?" Klatzkin asked.

"Better," Hamal said. "Not there yet. But better."

"Not half-way there," Halevy said.

"What happened?" Hamal asked Nussbaum.

"Don't know for sure. I held her. I don't know. Was it bomb weight? Gas tanks? Updraft? It could have been a dozen things."

"Your plane's intact."

"I thought it would be," said Nussbaum.

"Let's eat," Hamal said. "Then we go again. Target range 2. Let's find it and hold it, 'Rose's Edge'."

As they streaked in one after the other to target that afternoon, each Israeli pilot guaged his speed, adjusted his angle of attack, his altitude, sensed his power available, his thrust-power after delivery. One by one they did better, took more measured risks, reached the limits of their aircraft and the pilot skills they had acquired by trying time after time.

Hamal scored one direct hit. Samy came close enough to pose a danger to the structure. Atari overshot. Nussbaum overshot. Davidov scored one direct hit. Halevy scored two. Klatzkin scored one direct hit, one very close overshot. Rose, coming in lower and faster than ever before, had a perfect shot. He let his first bomb go, it hit bullseye on target. The released 2,000 pounds of his first bomb tipped his aircraft slightly starboard. He held his second bomb for a millisecond, coordinating the position in his head, while he also responded to the starboard tip with a tick of his stick portside. The plane leveled back, but the weight of his remaining bomb pulled Rose further than he'd expected. Rose felt it, tipped his stick, but the bomb-weighted wing kept pulling him. He passed the target way off attitude. He released to get rid of his weight. That threw him further starboard than he'd calculated. He was lower than he'd been before. He pulled back gently on the stick for an escape, just the right move, but his starboard wingtip had scraped the ground. The force of that contact with the upward pull of the aircraft spun Rose's plane portward and nose over and within four seconds the craft crashed upside down on to the desert floor exploding instantly into a massive fireball. Sirens raged. Firetrucks and an ambulance surrounded the flames, the firetrucks pouring chemical retardant from three huge hoses. No one – not the firemen, nor the ambulance driver, nor the controllers in the tower, nor one of the Israelis in their escaping aircraft even hoped that Rose might have survived.

When Hamal stood before the group of pilots the next dawn, he didn't know how to begin what he had to say. He hadn't slept all night. At 04:00, Hamal took up his saxaphone, but then left it as he went out into the pre-dawn darkness to walk around the Base. He took a Jeep out to the crash site, stood there for a while, then drove back. In the briefing room, he stood in silence for a long time. He cleared his throat. But still, he could not begin. Dror took up for him.

"The funeral will be tomorrow," Gen. Dror said. "1300."

Hamal interrupted.

"I'll save what I have to say about Rose for tomorrow," he said. "No more flying now. Today and tomorrow we give completely to David Rose. We'll be back the day after."

As the pilots left the briefing room they talked about Rose, about what he meant to them, and about how they had the good fortune to have Rose, an unmarried pilot with no children, in the tailing position, the most dangerous, most vulnerable to attack from enemy aircraft. Capt. Klatzkin spoke up. "Don't worry, it's my position now. David's picture goes with me when we fly."

After the pilots had left, Gen. Dror and Maj. Hamal walked out of the room together.

"It was my plan," Hamal said, "I said the planes could do it."

"I took command," Dror said. "I take the responsibility. The planes can do it. You have two days to grieve for David. Grieve now. All the way down. Then fly again. Train. I'll have all the data on David's crash for you tomorrow."

"Have you ever met David's parents?"

"No."

"They'll take it hard. Of course," Hamal said. "But David's mother especially is not strong."

"I'm sorry," Dror said. "We'll do everything for her. Believe me."

"We'll go with seven planes?" Hamal asked. "Klatzkin trailing?"

"We'll go with eight planes, as planned," Dror said. "I'll find you another plane very soon. In the meantime, you find me another pilot. Unmarried, no kids, if possible. Trailing plane, same as David Rose was. Start training him."

Capt. Baruch Cohen. Wingman to the 2nd Division 2nd Section Leader (Trailing Plane). Born - 1958 - in Tel Aviv. His father and mother were both born in British Palestine, as were his grandparents. His father fought in the 1948 War of Liberation, but his mother did not fight by virtue of severe arthritis which crippled her hands. In 1967, while riding on the #6 bus in Jerusalem, visiting schools in his capacity as Director of Curriculum for the Israeli Ministry of Education, Capt. Cohen's father was killed by a Palestinian suicide bomber. Capt. Cohen is unmarried, and without children.

THIRTY-ONE

A week and a half after David Rose's funeral, the training runs were improving. Each of the guys was hitting the target more directly, more often. They kept talking about "Rose's Edge," and kept finding it. That afternoon, a Friday, Hamal stopped the training early. They all had time to get ready for Friday night Sabbath services. All 14 pilots attended. They came out of their rooms dressed in all whites, walked across the open desert floor lit with a wide light by the late afternoon sun. Everyone had gathered in front of the religious hall, all dressed in white, white slacks, white shirts, white skirts or dresses. The Base cantor sang slowly the song, "Come my Beloved," welcoming the traditional *Sabbath Bride*.

Hamal's Plane Captain, Cpl. Etzer Yehuda, had joined them.

Hamal turned to Atari. "As a child," Hamal whispered, "on kibbutz, I heard this melody every Friday night. It's the sweetest and the most simply joyous song I've ever heard. Every time I would see in my imagination the *Sabbath Bride* herself arrayed in white fly over the treetops. But I really saw her, Atari. I really saw her."

"And now?"

"Now I hear the music. That's enough for now. Anyway, it's all I get."

"Maybe you'll see her again, sometime," Atari said.

"Thanks, but those days are gone."

"Now," Etzer Yehuda said, "Hamal flies over the treetops himself."

"Maybe he's up there looking for the Sabbath Bride of his youth," Atari said.

"She must have been some beauty!" Yehuda said. "The Sabbath Bride herself."

"A spiritual beauty, guys," Hamal protested, "a purely spiritual beauty."

"No physical beauty in the spiritual world?" Yehuda asked.

"Well," Hamal smiled, "OK. Yes. She was fantastic."

"My cousin, Samia," Halevy whispered, "she used to sing that, 'Come, my Beloved,' every Friday night. A wonderful voice."

"Samia Halevy?" Atari asked. "I know her."

"In the Biblical sense?" Halevy asked.

"In the Platonic sense," Atari said. "Don't be mean. We trained together on surveillance. She's Iraqi, no?"

"She's Iraqi," Halevy said, "yes. Came with her parents when she was a kid, 15, 20 years ago."

"Where is she now?" Atari asked.

"Married, Atari, married," Halevy said.

"All the good ones are married," Atari said.

Following the evening service, everyone left the

synagogue for the main mess hall. The cantor made the traditional blessing over the wine and the bread, then the base enjoyed a Sabbath dinner together.

Everyone but essential security personnel had Saturday off, yet, the fourteen pilots and their ground crews continued their practice runs.

The next day, Sunday, May 31, at 0600 the men got the word. No go. Not yet. Gen. Mitztan had delivered the message himself. He gave the men the day off.

"You've got to have some time," Mitztan said, "away from the runs. Away from the target. Time to let it all seep in mentally. You'll get it right. In a day or two, you'll get it right. Do whatever you want today. Drinks are on me."

The pilots headed straight for the Officers' Bar. By 0700 they had begun their breakfast with their favorite drinks. By 0800 they were all out in the early desert sun, sweating out the alcohol. By 1000 they were in the recreation room shooting pool shots and singing old school songs, popular songs in English and Hebrew, national songs, sweet religious songs, love songs.

Capt. Atari got up from where he lay on a couch, raised his beer bottle in his hand for a toast:

"Here's to The Guys," Capt. Atari intoned. "Here's to old Maj. Durham, wherever he is. Here's to us. We're off to hell. Here's to my squadron leader, Maj. Ilan Hamal, a madman if there ever was one. A genius if there ever was one. I will see you in hell, Maj. Hamal.

I hope I will see you again on this God-given earth."

"You sonofabitch," Gar responded. "Don't talk that kind of crap."

Atari, wobbling on his feet, shot back:

"Gar, baby, I love you. When you've watched the planes of your buddies around you explode mid-air from a SAM, flown by the seat of your pants without wings or wheels, when you've brought home more holes than airplane, you can say whatever the hell you want. In the meantime, let me say whatever the hell I want. And may I see you, too, on this God-given earth again."

Atari raised his glass in toast directly to Capt. Gar.

"Look," Halevy tried to sooth Atari, "it's damn bad luck to talk about defeat. We all know what the odds are. Cool it, *haver.*"

Atari had sat back down on the couch. He was crying, drunk crying.

Gar came over to him.

"Hey!" Gar shook Atari by the shoulder. "You've got me up there, flying your cover. Nothing comes close to you."

"Fuck you, Gar!" Atari burst out.

Gar jumped back a step.

Maj. Hamal stepped in between the two men.

"Don't make me be the Major. Not today. I need a day off, too."

Atari looked up at Hamal.

"Hey, buddy!" Atari said. "Hey, Maj. Hamal. Ilan. My buddy. I love you. Don't you know that. I love that bastard, Gar, too. That's why I told him to go fuck himself. Don't love anybody too much. That's what it should say on the side of my plane. Don't love anybody too much. Capt. Halevy sat down next to Atari.

"You love everyone too much," Halevy said. "You can even love a sonofabitch like Gar." Halevy pulled Gar over to them by the arm. "Give Gar a good Israeli embrace. C'mon, Atari."

Atari arose. He and Gar embraced.

"C'mon, Gar," Atari said, "I'm going to whip your ass at pool."

The men gathered around the pool table while Capt. Cohen racked up the balls. Atari, as senior, broke. He practically missed the rack, but knocked one solid ball off to the right. Gar didn't do much better.

Capt. Davidov pulled Maj. Hamal aside.

"Listen," Davidov said. "Should we let him fly?"

"Atari?" Major Hamal asked him.

"Yes. Atari."

"He's just drunk," Hamal said.

"But a pilot has to be able to be drunk, and still be sober. That's what it takes, Major."

"Don't ever fear Atari," Hamal said.

"I fear *for* Atari," Davidov said.

"And you don't fear for me?" Maj. Hamal said.

"If I feared for you," Capt. Davidov said, "I'd have to fear for us all."

"Fear for us all," Hamal said.

"Yes, sir. But now *you* sound like doom."

"I never sound like doom," Hamal said. "I don't believe in doom. I sound like truth."

"Yes, sir."

"Outside," Hamal called out. "Out of this dark and dreary cave. Into the light and blessed heat of the day!"

Atari and Gar stayed at their hopeless game in which neither dropped a ball except by rolling it by hand into a pocket. The rest of the men went squinting into the daylight. They wandered the base, singing, drinking, returning to the Officers' Club for refills. Atari and Gar eventually left the game, laughing hysterically, walked arm-over-each-others-shoulders to the Officers Bar, singing, and found the rest of the guys.

At the bar, Halevy proposed that they gather up wood for a fire, food supplies for dinner, and cook out in the desert over an open fire. The men scattered to gather supplies. At 1545 they all met again at the bar. With backpacks slung over their backs, they headed out into the desert, hiked forty minutes to an area still within base limits. They set down their gear, built a circle for a fire, organized the food, then sat back with beers in hand. By sundown several of the men had taken naps, reawakened. Some had sat around talking. Some had just laid out on a blanket or a sleeping bag, staring out at the desert, thoughts wandering where they will.

Atari organized building the fire. He hadn't exactly sobered, but he'd become used to his level of inebriation. All the men pitched in to get the dinner made: shish-kebobs carted out from the kitchen on ice, pita bread, couscous they reheated, a tub of chopped salad they had kept on ice, ample beer. A couple of the more religious men had stepped aside for evening prayers.

After dinner, the men sat around in what became more or less of a circle. They decided to tell stories for as long as they could hold out. They could make up their stories as much as they wanted, but none could be war stories. Flying stories were all right. Those were the rules. Nussbaum told a long tale about hitch-hiking across America. He started in his native Michigan, hitched out to California, then back to New York. He had, he said, a girl in each state he crossed. He described some of his encounters.

Kaminsky, from the F-15s, told a story about his father trying to keep a horse on his kibbutz. His father couldn't afford to keep the horse, Kaminsky said. So he went to the local Rabbi. The Rabbi told him not to feed the horse so much. A month later Kaminsky's father returned to the Rabbi. '*I did what you told me, Rabbi. It worked great. I fed the horse less and less each day. Soon, I was feeding him nothing. But then, what bad luck I had. He died! Just when I had figured out how I could afford to keep him.*"

"That's an old old folk story!" Klatzkin called out. "From somewhere. I've heard it before!"

"So what!" Kaminsky said. "Maybe you heard it about my father."

Hamal told a story about his daughter, Rebecca. Just after she was born, he said, she began to talk. Then she began to write. She was only 1 month old. She wrote and wrote and wrote. Finally, she finished a whole novel, which she called *Memoirs of a Life in the Womb*. Then she told her father she had finished her writing career. Next, she would be a Justice on the Israeli Supreme Court. "Right now," Hamal said, "she's the only one-year old in law school. She's writing a paper called *A Parent's Legal Obligation to Spoil a Child*." All applauded. "Go, Rebecca," they shouted.

Lt. Gen. Mitztan arrived in a jeep. In the back he carried more cases of beer and enough sleeping bags for everyone.

"Stay out here tonight," he said. "Sleep under the million stars. Watch them all night long. I'm having breakfast shipped out to you at 0430. We'll be back in the bucket at 0700."

The men demanded that Mitztan tell a story before they would let him go. Same rules: no war stories, everything else was ok. Mitztan told about how, as a young man in Beirut, he had worked as a go-fer for a Madame of a very high class establishment. He wove out descriptions of some of the girls, descriptions of some of the visitors, including all the high-level society types and government men, each of whom chose his own girl according to her specialty, spanking, peek-a-boo, wetting-the-bed, playing Emperor, playing Daddy, until he had the guys in hysterics.

Mitztan hopped in his jeep and drove back to the barracks.

The men all slept in the desert that night.

The next morning all the guys were in their planes, curing hangovers with deep draughts of pure oxygen from their flight masks, ready to fly, try again.

THIRTY-TWO

Shimon Peres, ex-Prime Minister, ex-Minister of Defense, came into the Prime Minister's conference room on the morning of May 1, 1981. He carried nothing with him: no briefcase, no folders, no papers. The discussion in the room stopped. Mr. Peres stood next to Prime Minister Begin. Col. Ben Luria got a chair for Mr. Peres.

"I'll stand," Peres said. "What I have to say will take a few minutes. Then I'll leave. You all know that I'm opposed to *Operation Opera*. My opposition is no secret. I base my opposition on two things: the inherent danger of the mission, which could result in terrible losses for us; and international diplomacy. We could lose support worldwide. We could lose U.S. aid. By international law, we'll be in the wrong."

"International law doesn't know...." Uri Hazan interrupted. But the Prime Minister stopped Hazan.

"Let Shimon finish."

"Postpone the operation. Wait for the French election," Peres went on. "Today is May 1. The French election takes place in nine days. On May 10. If Mitterand beats d'Estaing, we can sway him. Mitterrand will stop work on Osiraq. I promise you. I know it. We can't risk losing 14 top pilots and 14 fantastic planes. Wait. I know what I'm talking about."

"If Mitterand doesn't cooperate? You think he'll work with you because he's a Socialist. Not necessarily, Shimon," Arie Solen said.

"If Mitterand wins, but he doesn't cooperate, then we go," Shimon Peres said, "Give me a last chance at diplomacy."

"We've had three years of diplomacy," Arie Solen said.

"Five years," Begin said.

"You're a genius of Mossad, Arie," Shimon Peres said. "I know the military side, but I'm also a diplomat. I can work with the new French government. Why subvert international law when we don't have to? It's a very serious risk."

"May I speak?" Ben Luria asked.

"Let anyone speak," Peres offered.

"We're not violating international law. International law is not a suicide pact. We have a right to what's called 'anticipatory self-defense'."

"I don't care about legal rights," Solen said. "I care about survival."

"Where does this right come from?" Peres asked.

"From 19th Century legal doctrine," Ben Luria said. "We're entitled to strike first when the danger posed against us is, and I quote, 'instant, overwhelming, leaving no choice of means and no moment for deliberation.'"

"No wonder," Peres said, "the Prime Minister chose you for his Aide."

"And....," Ben Luria went on, "if you'll permit me sir...."

"Please," Peres said.

"Five nations attacked us in 1948. *Only* Iraq has never signed a cease fire. Iraq is still at war with us. They call us the 'Zionist entity,' not even Israel. We're in a formal state of war with Iraq."

"He's right on legal doctrine," Solen said.

"International military law class." Ben Luria smiled.

"Let's talk real politics," Peres said. "Our friends won't care about 19th century legal doctrine. We depend on those friendships. Universal condemnation now will sting us badly."

"If d'Estaing wins again...?" Dror asked.

"If Mitterrand loses," Peres said, "we go at once. We hit Osiraq on May 11."

"If Mitterrand does win?" Dror asked.

"If Mitterrand wins," Peres said, "give me a few weeks to negotiate."

"A few weeks!" Dror shot back. "In a few weeks Saddam will have the damn thing."

"Not if Mitterrand stops him," Peres said.

"Shimon," Dror said, "you're playing with big atomic fire. Watch out."

"Shimon," Prime Minister Begin didn't look up at Shimon Peres when he addressed him, but at the group around the table. "You're playing with our survival. Do you risk a nuclear attack on us? A second holocaust?"

"Absolutely not," Peres said. "Sabotage the work at Osiraq. Delay it."

"Let him have it," Dror said. "The pilots....they're my boys. I have to give them every chance. Let Shimon have his negotiations. I don't like it. I hate it. But let him have it."

"Dror!" Solen said. "Don't abandon me. Now! We go now. Anyone who delays us, let him be ready to pay the price for Israel."

"Fourteen pilots! Fourteen families! Take a chance!" Shimon Peres said.

"I'm taking a chance," Dror said. "I'm taking a chance on every one of those pilots."

"Dror," Solen said, "you keep changing sides. Make up your mind."

"My mind is made up, Arie. Don't accuse me. My mind is made up to stop Osiraq. My mind is also made up not to waste the lives of my boys. Send them out there to die. They won't all come back, Arie. Count on it. You go tell their mothers and fathers." Dror had gotten up, shoved his seat back toward the table, walked away, paced at the back of the room.

Solen shot back at Dror: "I'll deliver the message: 'your son died to save Israel'."

"Give me a month," Peres urged them. "One month.

If it doesn't work, I'll stand behind you one hundred percent."

"Give him his month!" Prime Minister Begin shouted, rising. "Give him his month! I hate this waiting. But I hate losing pilots more than I hate waiting. We can delay one month. If," the Prime Minister looked over at Arie Solen, "if Arie can promise us a delay in production at Osiraq."

"I have my personal opinions here," Solen said. "I don't like it."

"You have me as your Commander, Arie. Give me the delay," the Prime Minister said.

"I'll report to you in three days," Solen agreed.

"Tomorrow," the Prime Minister said.

"Tomorrow," Solen said.

"Thank you, Mr. Prime Minister," Shimon Peres said. "Thank you, Arie. I won't let you down."

"You'll always let me down, Shimon," Solen said.

Shimon Peres left the room. Prime Minister Begin adjourned the meeting. When everyone else had left, the Prime Minister spoke to Ben Luria.

"I haven't backed down, Yossi," the Prime Minister said. "Not one millimeter."

"No, sir."

"Do you remember I told you long ago that you would stare into the void every day as we went along?"

"Yes, sir."

"And? Have you found yourself staring into the void?"

"Quite a bit, sir."

"Yes. Can you tolerate one more month?"

"Just about one more month."

"Me too, Yossi."

THIRTY-THREE

On May 6, 1981, at 1527, the main computer system at Osiraq crashed. Ahmed Bhatal, who had taken over for Dr. Yahia El Meshad, ordered an immediate investigation. He authorized the investigators to interrogate everyone with knowledge of Osiraq, including himself.

That evening, Bhatal personally reported on the incident to Mukhabarat Chief, Mohammed Azziz, over dinner in a restaurant in downtown Baghdad. Bhatal said the computer crash was certainly linked with Dr. El Meshad's sudden death. There is a pattern of sabotage. Azziz told Bhatal that Mukhabarat would take over the investigation. Everyone was under suspicion, including himself, Ahmed Bhatal. Bhatal informed Azziz that he, Ahmed Bhatal, had already put himself under suspicion.

"I have already ordered the investigation to include me."

"That could make you look even more suspicious to me," Azziz said.

"I've known you for a long time," Bhatal said, "you've been a son-of-a-bitch ever since I met you."

"That's why Iraq is safe today," Azziz answered.

"Despite your corruption."

"I could have you hung in a minute," Azziz said. "Worse than hung."

"Watch out," Bhatal said, "I could have you hung in half a minute. You haven't done your job. You should have prevented this sabotage before it happened."

"Keep your voice down," Azziz laughed. "If my men heard you they'd kill you before you saw them coming."

Bhatal looked around the busy restaurant. "Maybe these are all your men. Every one of them."

"It so happens," Azziz said, "that there are still citizens in Iraq who are not my men. But they are all my eyes."

"Do all those eyes see who you really are?" Bhatal asked.

"My good friend, I made the mistake of inviting you to some of my private gatherings years ago. But you're a small man, not a great man. Great men live above the rules of society. Small men like you need those rules to make themselves feel comfortable. Great men, like myself, like Saddam, we make our own rules. You can't understand that. You call it corruption. When a small man commits a crime, he must be punished. He wants his punishment. It reassures him. When a great man commits the same act, he expresses the freedom of the whole nation."

"What you do in secret are the acts of a great man?"

"I call myself a great man," Azziz said, "because I

am one. Whatever I do is the act of a great man."

"Not what I saw."

"I'd crush you before you opened your mouth against me. I have the courage to crush you more than you have the courage to speak out against me. There are not many such great men. Stalin was one. Saddam is one."

"And Hitler was one?" Bhatal asked.

"No," Azziz said. "Hitler failed."

The two men stared at each other.

"I'm right, aren't I?" Azziz said.

"You're more cruel than I could ever be. So you're probably right. I wouldn't want your cruelty."

"That's why you'll always be a mere scientist in charge of an important project. Never the power behind that project. Never the one with the vision to construct it. To use it."

"Find out who the saboteurs are." Bhatal pulled out cash from his wallet.

"No," Azziz stopped him. "It's on me. Not on Mukhabarat. On me, personally, Mohammed Azziz. Someday I'll invite you to one of my gatherings again. Perhaps you'll enjoy yourself a little more in the future."

THIRTY-FOUR

They had ransacked Samia's room. They had pried open the jewelry safe.

Samia picked up her copy of *The Thousand and One Nights* from the floor, where it lay face down with its pages twisted. She smoothed out the pages, then placed it on her night table.

She prepared a microfiche message for Yossi Ben Luria and Arie Solen, in code:

"Get out time."

She had written: "I know about the other one," but deleted it.

When her car came to pick her up the next morning, Samia directed Hikmat Sidqui to stop at the kasbah. She had to buy a gift for her mother's birthday. The car, which couldn't get into the tight, crowded streets of the kasbah, stopped at its outskirts. Sidqui accompanied Samia as she walked in. She stopped at a few stalls, looked at tourist trinkets, little copies of the Ishtar Gate, photographs of Saddam Hussein embossed on everything from t-shirts to handbags to cheap jewelry to shopping bags. She would haggle over price for a minute, then walk away.

"Is there something special I can help you with?"

Sidqui asked her. "Something I can help you find? Or someone? Maybe you're looking for someone?"

"Someone?" Samia asked.

They had just stopped at an antique bookstore, *The Mesopotamian Library*.

"This is it," Samia cried. "An old Arabic book. My mother would love that."

They stepped inside the bookstore. It was lit, but dimly. Books flowed from shelves in disarray. The shelves were crowded close together. An Iraqi man stepped out from a room in the back.

"May I help you?" the man asked.

"I'm looking for a gift for my mother in New York," Samia said.

The bookseller peered into the dusky light to see Samia's face as clearly as possible.

"What kind of book would you like? I have no books in English." The bookseller, a thin man with white hair, wore the traditional robe, a white *dishdash*. He continued to look at Samia with his neck bent forward.

"Oh, no," Samia said. "My mother reads Arabic. We're Iraqi. I recently saw a book by an Iraqi author, Ibrahim Kfar. It was about Egyptian mythology. I was reading a section on the Egyptian messenger-god, Ahktut, who carried messages between the heavens and the people."

"I know the book," the bookseller said, "but I don't

have it." He straightened out, turned to a bookshelf. "I have this book here." He pulled a book off the shelf, gave it to Samia.

"It's on Greek mythology, not Egyptian, but a wonderful edition. But that's not the same. It's only about the Greek mythologies."

"No, I want the Egyptian mythology for my mother."

"If you leave me your name and your telephone number," the bookseller said, "I'll find you a copy of the Ibrahim Kfar."

Samia wrote down her name, and the phone number of the Al Rashid hotel.

Squinting in the light as they came out of the bookshop, Samia and Sidqui walked through the kasbah back to their car. When they got in, the driver said that Mohammed Azziz had telephoned to the car phone. He handed a message to Sidqui. Sidqui opened the folded paper, read the message, put it in his pocket, and told the driver to continue on to Osiraq.

At the bookstore, the bookseller, Ibrahim Ibrahim, opened the book on Greek Mythology which Samia had handed back to him. He found the microfiche Samia left between the pages. He slid the microfiche into an envelope, slid the envelope into the purse he carried inside his *dish-dash*. He put on his jacket.

As Ibrahim left the bookshop, he locked the door behind himself.

THIRTY-FIVE

Mohammed Azziz's secretary directed Sidqui to wait in the outer office. Sidqui sat on the couch. Familiar sounds came from behind Azziz's office door. Sidqui waited for a long time, ten minutes, then twenty, then thirty, until, after thirty-five minutes, Azziz called through the closed door:

"Sidqui! I know you're out there. Wait! Sidqui, just wait! Sit still, you squeamish son-of-a-bitch and wait!"

After forty-five minutes of waiting, the door opened. Two 12-year old Iraqi boys old came out, followed by another young man, this one about 17. The 17-year old carried a video camera with him. Then Azziz came out, walking quickly.

"Sit down!" Azziz yelled at Sidqui. "Sit down, you fool. I'll be right back. Do you want a drink? Something to eat? Hassan!" Azziz yelled at his secretary. "Bring Sidqui-the-fool something to eat. Get him a drink. Some tea at least." Azziz left the office, then returned a few minutes later.

"Now," Azziz said, "Mister Sidqui, won't you enter my office."

"You know," Azziz said, having lit a cigar, from behind his cherry-wood desk, "you must try observation. It purifies the soul. To watch, Sidqui. To observe all the passion. Saddam himself....well, to hell with Saddam himself. Their skin, one against the other's, their wildness, their ejaculations so new they frighten them. It's a great art, Sidqui. It's ancient. It goes back all the way to the Babylonian Empire. That's why we're a great people, Sidqui. We have developed the greatest pleasures. Yes? Don't you agree?"

"I suppose, yes," Sidqui said.

"No," Azziz said, "you may not have a cigar, Sidqui. You want one. Of course you want one. They're the best cigars in the world. Another time, Sidqui. Right now I want you to concentrate."

"I don't smoke cigars." Sidqui glanced briefly to his left, to the blood-portrait of Saddam.

"You fucked up on Samia Sa'ad. Do you know that, Sidqui?"

"Somewhat."

"You know they found absolutely nothing in her room."

"Yes."

"Do you still think she's a spy?"

"Yes."

"As do I, Sidqui. But I don't act foolishly on my basest instincts. I search out, I investigate. For you, she's a spy. You are a small man. That's why. For me, Samia Sa'ad is more than a spy. She's a trail."

"She's a spy and I'll get her."

"Somewhere, here in Baghdad, the Iranians have a master-spy. An Illegal Officer who directs all the agents in Baghdad."

"Of course. I know that."

"Perhaps it's even you, Sidqui." Azziz laughed.

"Me?" Sidqui's heart beat four fast beats, then slowed to somewhat faster than normal.

"Don't worry. I won't torture you. Or kill you. Not until I know for sure who you are. That's the way you should work, Sidqui."

"I work on my instincts and I will prove that Sa'ad is a spy."

"Why is your mouth dry when you speak, Sidqui? Are you guilty? Have I hit the nail on the head? Are you the Iranian Illegal Officer in Baghdad? Are you that high up?"

"No. No. No. Nonsense. Foolishness."

"Well, are you the....Israeli Illegal Officer in Baghdad?"

"Never!"

"And might Samia Sa'ad not be Iranian, but Israeli?"

"She's Iranian."

"Don't tell me what you believe, Sidqui." Azziz drew out his words. "Tell me what you know. Do you know she's Iranian?"

"I don't know, I mean, I know, but I can't prove it. Yet."

"Better, Sidqui. Would you like to finish off what the boys didn't do for me?" Azziz laughed.

"Sir?"

"Never mind, Sidqui. The whole point is not to ejaculate oneself. That's the whole point. It's too refined for you, Sidqui. Such levels of knowing....they would drive a simple man like yourself insane."

"They would drive anyone insane."

"And what about the other one, Sidqui, what about Meshad's mistress, what about the Lebanese/Parisian beauty, Hannan Khatib. Have you fucked her yet, yourself, Sidqui? Have you fucked Khatib?"

"I...."

"I've long suspected you of impotence, Sidqui. Are you impotent?"

"Don't....."

"Don't what? Sidqui? Don't push you? To what? What do you think you could do to me? Would you like to prove to me that you're not impotent?"

"Now?"

"When? In eternity? I would like to see your ejaculation. It must be a little trickle of a thing. Those two boys, Sidqui, magnificent. Do you think I would want to see your bestiality after the grace and eternal beauty of those two Babylonian angels? Of course not. Keep your seat, Sidqui. I have some news for you."

"Sir?" Sidqui's heart had almost stopped beating altogether now.

"We'll start with the Lebanese. With Hannan Khatib. I want you to listen to this simple investigative technique. You could learn something."

"Yes, sir."

Azziz picked up the phone on his desk, told Hassan, his secretary, to get him Khaled Soussa, in Beirut, Lebanese Chief of Internal Security. Azziz sat, waiting. After a minute, he spoke to Sidqui.

"The other one, Sidqui, Samia Sa'ad. I had dinner myself with her last night. I trust her, Sidqui. You were wrong about her."

"But, sir....you said...."

"Yes."

"The waiter, Samir al-Wahab....if Samia Sa'ad is innocent, why did he take cyanide when we arrested him."

"Sidqui," Azziz asked, "do you have cyanide?"

"Of course," Sidqui answered him, "I'm Mukhabarat."

"Everyone in Baghdad has cyanide, Sidqui," Azziz said. "Don't you know that? They all fear us, Sidqui. Their fear is our mission. The more cyanide there is, the more successful we are."

"Yes, sir."

"Watch over Samia Sa'ad," Azziz said. Then he spoke into the phone.

"Salaam, Khaled Soussa," Azziz said. "Commander Mohammed Azziz here, in Baghdad. How are you my old friend?" He winked at Sidqui.

"I want you to do something for me. I want you to investigate a Lebanese woman, Hannan Khatib. 28

years old. She was born in Beirut. Her parents still live in Beirut. She left Beirut for the Sorbonne ten years ago, in 1971. She's lived in Paris until recently, probably with regular trips back to Beirut. Now she lives here, in Baghdad. She's supposed to be a scientist. I want to know all about her.....Good, my friend. Thank you. Someday we'll meet in person. You must come to Baghdad. I'll take care of you. Thank you, my friend."

At that very moment, in a room on the second floor of Mossad Headquarters in Jerusalem, three men sat before a bank of electronic telephone equipment with headphones on. Two of them only listened. The third listened, then spoke in Arabic. All three heard:

"Salaam, Khaled Soussa, Commander Mohammed Azziz here, in Baghdad. How are you my old friend?"

The one Mossad agent who did the speaking answered, in Arabic:

"Alekum Salaam, Commander Azziz. What can I do for you?"

The three Israelis then heard:

"I want you to do something for me. I want you to investigate a Lebanese woman, Hannan Khatib. 28 years old. Born in Beirut. Her parents still live in Beirut. She left Beirut for the Sorbonne ten years ago, in 1971. She has lived in Paris until recently, probably with regular trips back to Beirut. Now she lives here, in Baghdad. She is supposed to be a scientist. I want to know all about her.

The Mossad speaker said:

"No problem, my friend. I can do it for you in one day. By tomorrow."

The three Israelis then heard:

"Good, my friend. Thank you."

The Mossad speaker said:

"You're welcome. Anytime. Call me anytime."

The three Israelis then heard:

"Someday we will meet in person. You must come to Baghdad. I'll take care of you. Thank you, my friend."

The Mossad speaker said:

"I'll take you up on your offer. Salaam."

The Mossad speaker hung up his telephone. The other two agents took off their headphones. One of the men stopped the tape recorder, then left the room to report directly to Arie Solen.

THIRTY-SIX

"A ssassinate Azziz," said Samia.

"You'd get caught," Hannan said. "You'd never get away."

"I can get to him. He trusts me. I've got him bamboozled. And....if I got caught....."

"We're not suicide bombers," Hannan said.

"I've been here for a long time," Samia said.

"We're not kamikaze. I want you back in Israel. Alive."

"That's not guaranteed anyway."

"You have lots to go back for."

Samia didn't answer. They kept walking from the auditorium building to the main building at Osiraq.

"I reject the assassination of Azziz," Hannan said.

"Are you the boss?"

"I have a veto, that's all."

"We each work alone," Samia said.

"Not any more. We've discovered each other. That changes it."

"On what grounds do you reject the assassination of Azziz? On the grounds that it's difficult? Do you think I haven't done what's difficult before?"

"No," Hannan said. "On the grounds that it compromises our mission. Right now we need to get specific information."

"Azziz stands in our way. He's watching us so closely now we can't sneeze."

"Look," Hannan said, too loudly, then she lowered her voice. "If we kill Azziz, we don't kill Mukhabarat. They'll be all over us. Even more so."

"Azziz *is* Mukhabarat," Samia said. "Mukhabarat is a shambles without Azziz. They have no organization, no chain of command. He's the Mukhabarat dictator."

Hannan stopped Samia, took her by the arm.

"Don't do it, Samia. Do not do it. Get the intelligence off those computers. I'll get what I need. What Israel needs is intelligence, not sacrificed Mossad bodies. Get home. Get the intelligence and get home."

"Please keep walking. Talk casually."

They walked again, Hannan spoke through clenched teeth.

"Live, Samia. *Choose* to live. Do your job and get out of here."

"We'll see."

"I forbid the assassination of Azziz."

"Are you my superior officer now?" Samia asked.

"No. I'm your friend. Listen to me."

Near the main building they ran into Ahmed Bhatal.

"How was the lecture?" Bhatal asked them.

"Boring," Hannan said. "They never say anything

new. You better speak to our colleague, Samia, here. I had to just take her by the arm and give her a good talking to. She despairs that we can't move ahead without Dr. El Meshad. The computer failure has her down."

"No," Bhatal said, "no despair, Samia. We'll deliver everything and deliver it very soon. All I need is loyalty from everyone. Very soon."

Bhatal opened the door, holding it for the two women to go in. They turned back when Mohammed Azziz's voice called from his car. Bhatal walked over, got in the car, it drove away.

Hannan took Samia with her up to Meshad's old office. Bhatal had left it as it had been, setting up his own office across the hall.

From a stack of five brown notebooks she frequently used, Hannan took out the third one down. She made a gesture rolling one hand over the other, then mouthed the word "rollover." She held up the notebook, pointed to the spine.

From a desk drawer Hannan took out a key to Bhatal's office.

Samia checked the hallway, and the other offices. Two people worked at computers in cubicle rooms. She passed them, went into the small kitchen, drank a glass of juice, then walked back past the two workers. Silently, she slid the key into the lock of Bhatal's office. She looked across the hall at Hannan. Hannan dropped a pile of papers, books, a ruler, a glass. At that moment Samia opened the door, stepped in, and closed the door.

Bhatal's computer was on. Samia left the overhead light off, but the light from the computer screen compromised her. She could be seen from the small window in the office door.

Samia typed in access codes, then searched the data base for what she needed. As she found page after page, she slowly ran the spine of the notebook, with its tiny wheels, across the computer screen. A camera inside photographed the images. A paper clip hit the window. Samia ducked down below the light of the computer screen. In the hallway, someone walked by. They passed. Samia went back to work. The camera could hold 40 pages of computer screen data.

THIRTY-SEVEN

On Thursday, June 4, 1981 at 3:30 in the afternoon, Solen, Dror, and Ben Luria hurried from Solen's office to the Prime Minister's conference room. Dror and Solen each carried a flat briefcase. Ben Luria carried nothing. All three men sweated in the heat, in the rush of their summons to the meeting. When they entered the room everyone else was already there, including Shimon Peres. Peres now sat in the middle of the table. When Dror and Solen had taken their seats, and Ben Luria had taken his place behind the Prime Minister, Prime Minister Begin opened the meeting.

"Let's not waste time. Shimon?"

"I could not do it. He would not budge. He would not cooperate one iota."

"Mitterand?" Dror asked.

"Yes," Peres answered him. "Mitterand. I can't believe it myself. Mitterand, the Socialists..."

"No time for political discussions now, Shimon," the Prime Minister said. "Solen has a report. Or Dror."

"We have all the intelligence we need," Solen said.

Shimon Peres got up to leave, but the Prime Minister waved at him to sit down. Peres sat.

"The French will ship the reactor core out on Sat-

316

urday," Solen said. "*This* Saturday. Two days from now. June 6. It arrives at Osiraq on Sunday, *this* Sunday, at 0700. At 1500 it's ready to go. At 17:20 they turn it on. It stays on for 10 minutes. At 1730 they switch it off. That's our window. It stays off until 1740. Then it goes live forever. Between 1730 and 1740 this Sunday, we have to take it out. That's their exact schedule. That's our exact schedule."

"My God," Yaakov Vulf, Political Advisor to the Prime Minister, said, "this could be madness."

The Prime Minister spoke over him, "Have you got the defense perimeter information?"

"Yes, sir," Solen said. "I got it this morning."

The Prime Minister took a long breath. "Bless that agent," he said. "Bless him for all of eternity. You have 72 hours to go, Dror."

"I'm on, sir," Dror said. "I have 72 hours 14 minutes to go, sir. We'll be airborne."

"Anyone have anything to say?"

"Armageddon is upon us," Rafi Stone said. "May we survive by the light of God."

"What about your agents?" Avraham Shtern, Chairman of the Joint Chiefs of Staff, asked.

"My agents will walk out alive," Solen said. "I have plans in execution. Ben Luria and I are off tonight."

"You're going yourselves?" Shtern asked. "I don't approve."

"You think we're not good anymore?"

"Arie....!" Shtern said.

"You don't have authority over me," Solen said, "and none over Ben Luria as long as he's assigned to me."

"Don't get personal, Arie," Shtern said. "I'm not up for risking the life of our Managing Director of Mossad."

"And Ben Luria?"

"Ben Luria is expendable to me," Shtern said. "If you want to send him, go ahead."

"Only the Prime Minister can order me not to go," Solen said. "Or God. And God doesn't give military orders."

"You go wherever the hell you want," the Prime Minister said. "I'm through with you. I'm not through with you, Dror. And I'm not through with those fourteen boys. I'll see you in the war room on Sunday."

"May I be there?" Rafi Stone asked.

The Prime Minister took a poll of the military chiefs, all of whom agreed to Stone's presence, as long as he not ask any questions or offer any opinions or advice. Stone gave his word.

"Anything else from you, Shimon?" the Prime Minister said.

"I register no objections," Peres said. "Only worries. God speed."

"I want you in the war room with me," the Prime Minister said.

"Because you want me under your control?"

"Yes," the Prime Minister said, "and because you have a great strategic mind, Shimon. I separate my politics from my war."

Solen, Dror, and Ben Luria left together, as they had come. On the way back to Solen's office, Dror split off to attend to the urgencies of his own operation. Solen suggested that they go for a walk in the Old City. It was the last chance they would have before their mission began. Solen took Ben Luria to his favorite falafel stand, on a small rise right at the meeting of the Jewish and the Armenian quarters. Each had a falafel and a coke, which they ate sitting on the remains of an old stone wall. Three young Israeli soldiers in a military jeep kept their customary watch. Dozens of civilians criss-crossed the cobbled streets. Arabs, Jews, Armenians, Christians. Different attire: orthodox black robes, Arab kaffiyeh, tourists in jeans and t-shirts. Many of them stopped for a falafel, most usually a falafel and a coke.

As they sat eating their sloppy and delicious falafel, Solen reminded Ben Luria that the Patriarch Abraham had come from the world's first city, Ur, in Iraq. "How ironic," Solen said, in a low whisper, "that we now go back to Abraham's forsaken homeland to destroy the world's worst weapon. I guess we've come a long way since Abraham."

"Yes," Ben Luria said, "we've come a long way. Abraham had no falafel."

"How do you know?" Solen asked him.

"It's not in the Bible. There's no falafel in the Bible."

The two of them walked around the Old City for a while in the Jewish Quarter. They passed in front of the Wailing Wall, the Western Wall – the shattered remnants of the Temple of Solomon, destroyed by the Romans in 76 CE. As usual, the plaza was crowded. Some of the religious had begun to gather for evening prayers.

"Do you remember," Ben Luria said, "when you were inducted into the army at first, we came here and we stuffed notes into the crevices. Did you do that in your day?"

"Sure did," Solen said. "But you're not religious, Yossi. Did you stuff a note in, a prayer?"

"I just stood there," Ben Luria said, "and thought about it all. Solomon's wall."

"No more wailing now," Solen said.

"No more wailing," Ben Luria agreed. "What odds do you give us on this one?"

"We may well lose some guys," Solen said, "but we can do it. We're fast enough, we're good enough. What odds do you give us, Yossi?"

Ben Luria laughed. "Want to stuff a prayer into the wall?"

"I just want those boys home," Solen said. "I just want that Osiraq damned to oblivion."

"That's it, then," Ben Luria said. "The end of our vacation. Let's get to work."

"I'll meet you at the airport," Solen said.

Ben Luria called his wife, Tamar. He didn't tell her where he was going, only that he had to stay in Jerusalem for a couple of days without a chance to call her. She didn't ask where he might actually be, or go, or why he might not be able to call. Tamar had been in Mossad herself, for two years. He promised that next month, July, he would look for a nice apartment in Jerusalem. He couldn't stand the constant separations.

THIRTY-EIGHT

Hannan mixed in among the Osiraq workers on the lawn outside the administration building. She drank a glass of white wine, then another. She spoke with the French Ambassador, with the French Cultural Attaché, with the French Science Attaché, and with several of the French scientists now working at Osiraq. Over the table of hors d'oeuvres hung a green flag with white letters:

O S I R A Q.

From a raised platform, Heraclium Al Hira, the Project Director of Osiraq, spoke.

"The French nuclear program is named Osiris, after the Egyptian God Osiris – the Lord of Life. Osiris was also the father of the Sun God, Horus-Ra. Now the power of life and the power of the sun, of the unleashed atom, have come home to Mesopotamia, to Iraq, here, at your Osiraq. We welcome our French friends, and we thank the French embassy, the French Ambassador, the French Government, the French Science Attaché for their immense contributions to our program. They have the insight to see that Iraq is the Sun of all of Islam."

Al Hira pointed out the French dignitaries, who

each, in turn, raised a hand to the crowd's applause.

"And," Al Hira continued, "our most magnificent gratitude goes to our Leader, Saddam Hussein, whose wisdom, courage, and vision have given birth to a project on the scale of Osiraq."

Saddam, in tan military uniform, pistol at his side – a pistol he had used not infrequently and at any personal whim – walked to the podium embraced by the shouts of the crowd of just one hundred-twelve people: "Saddam! Saddam! Saddam!"

Hannan turned to the French Cultural Attaché beside her.

"He walks like he owns the world," she said. "He hasn't got a care on earth. He has more power than Osiraq itself."

"You overestimate him," the Attaché said. "You've heard too much of the legend of Saddam and not seen enough of the man."

"But look at him. His noblesse oblige. If it's a legend, it comes straight from him, from who he knows he is."

Saddam stood in the rising adulation, smiling more to himself than to the gathered workers. He raised a hand for quiet, which they immediately gave him – only a moment later to continue receiveiving his words with their own cheers.

"You," he pointed to the crowd in such a way that each person felt personally selected, "you are the lance and the sword that will confront the enemies of Iraq.

You," he paused, "are building today the power and the light that will illuminate the progressive world – not of Iraq, but of all of Arab culture. The time is long gone when conquerors and oppressors rule over you. Today, and forever, Saddam Hussein liberates you. Five hundred years from now, every Iraqi, every Arab living will keep sacred the history of what we do here today.

"Any indignity done to any Iraqi man or woman is an indignity to Saddam Hussein and Saddam Hussein is too great to bear any indignity. I will answer every attack with the hand of Saddam Hussein and so it will be answered with the arm of Iraq. The Zionists who hate Saddam Hussein and so hate Iraq should fear Saddam Hussein. They should fear the name and the face and the fury of Saddam Hussein. For the face of Saddam Hussein is the face of Iraq."

Hannan whispered, amid the crowd's noise, to the French Attaché, "He talks about fury but he speaks with such calm, such poise," she said.

"He enraptures them with nonchalance," the Attaché said.

"He is power," Hannan said.

"You are unleashing the power of the sun. Iraq will harness the power of the sun. With that power, we will build glory."

Unholstering his pistol, looking over the crowd, looking into nowhere, and raising his arm, Saddam fired into the air. He paused. He fired again. Then again. And again. And again.

Heraclium Al Hira came forward to present Saddam with a gold sun-pin. Saddam, gazing right into the crowd that gazed back at him, pulled the trigger once more. Al Hira jumped back. The sixth bullet flew into the air. As if awakening from the mesmerizing distance of some dream, Saddam holstered his pistol. He waived for Al Hira to step forward.

Saddam walked among the crowd, then left the way he had come, walking in his slow, carefree way. As he emerged from the crowd, two bodyguards took their places to the right and left of Saddam, one step behind him.

"It's something," Bhatal said, "to see a man whose photograph you've seen all your life. Now you see him up close."

"And," Hannan said, "how do you feel?"

"He's electrified every village in Iraq," Bhatal said. "I know why."

"Yes," Hannan agreed. "He confronts life with no fear."

"Finally," Bhatal said.

Mohammed Azziz joined the trio of Bhatal, Hannan, and the French Cultural Attaché.

"And now...." Azziz said to Hannan. But an assistant interrupted him.

"Mr. Azziz," the assistant tapped him on the shoulder, "Khaled Soussa, of Beirut, Chief of Lebanese Internal Security, has arrived."

"Yes, yes," Azziz pushed the aide aside, "I know who he is. Where is he?"

"In the lobby."

"Bring him here," Azziz said.

"And now that you have seen Saddam, Hannan, what do you think of Iraq?"

"I think that Iraq," Hannan said, "has her future foretold in the person of Saddam himself."

Azziz's assistant arrived.

"May I present Chief Khaled Soussa of Beirut, Chief of Lebanese Internal Security," the assistant said. Then he introduced the others: "Mohammed Azziz, Chief of Iraqi Internal Security, Mukhabarat, Hannan Khatib, Lebanese scientist working in Iraq, Jacques Luis Lestin, Cultural Attaché to the French embassy in Baghdad." All shook hands around. After a few moments of vague pleasantries, Azziz pulled Khaled Soussa aside. Together they walked toward the open doors of a balcony. On the balcony Azziz spoke more openly.

"*Shoukrane*," Azziz said, "Thank you, my friend, for the information you gave me over the phone. That, of course, was the woman in question herself, Hannan Khatib."

"I'm sorry," Soussa said, "what information?"

"You're a busy man," Azziz answered, "but you must recall. I called you asking for verification of the identity of Hannan Khatib. You very graciously called me back the following day to tell me that her identity was verified."

"No," Soussa said, "when did all this take place?"

"Just last week," Azziz said. "Just last week, my friend. A few days ago. You remember...."

"No," Soussa said. "You have me confused with someone. We've never met, you and I."

"But we have spoken," Azziz said.

"No," Soussa excused himself. "I'm sorry," he said, "but I have to speak with a few people. I've just arrived. I look forward to talking with you later. We must have a lot to talk about."

Left alone on the patio, Azziz thought for just one minute. A hand came to rest on his shoulder. It was Saddam Hussein, alone.

"Many men would kill me," Saddam said. "Of course they would. I've shoved them aside. I've killed their brothers and their uncles. I've trampled on their family names. Because I should be where I am. Do you understand, Azziz?"

"Yes," Azziz spoke. "I understand."

"If I were to depend on men like you, Azziz," Saddam said, "I would be dead. Isn't that true?"

"Yes, my Leader," Azziz answered.

"But you depend on me, to save me. Isn't that ironic? If you were to ever stop depending on me you would be dead, isn't that right, Azziz?"

"Yes."

"Do your job well. Do what I tell you to do. Don't ever question my orders."

Saddam's hand came off of Azziz's shoulder. Azziz turned around, but Saddam was already gone. Azziz rushed into the reception hall to gather two of his assistants, who drove him directly to his office.

When Hannan's cab pulled up at the Hotel Baghdad, Lt. Jazzar opened the cab door for her.

"Your every movement," Jazzar said, "from this moment on, will be known. Be very careful."

"Why are you telling me this?

"I don't want to kill you. You're too beautiful to kill." Jazzar bowed low.

"Irony doesn't suit you," Hannan said. "You're a simple murderer. I'm an innocent woman. I have nothing to fear." She walked past Jazzar into the hotel. Walking straight to the lounge, she took a seat in a booth. When the waiter arrived, she ordered a martini. She sipped at the drink, taking little bites from first one olive, then, having finished that, from the other.

A peddler came into the lounge, a young Iraqi woman overburdened with trinkets, silk scarves, small models of famous landmarks, photographs of Saddam, miniature copies of the complete Koran. Stopping at Hannan's table, she spread out her wares. Sizing up her customer, she concentrated on the scarves. She spread out one scarf after another, floral patterns, geometric patterns, embossed pictures of Baghdad tourist sites, photographs of Saddam Hussein on his white horse, mosque towers. The woman kept up a chatter about the scarves, about Baghdad, about how important it was for a tourist to remember those at home, how buying a gift, even the smallest gift, would bring the loved ones at home to mind, and comfort the tourist, or the traveling business person.

Hannan bought the scarf with the geometric designs. The woman leaned over the table to drape it over Hannan's shoulders, then stood back, admiring it. How beautiful it looked on Hannan, the woman said, how it accented Hannan's own beauty. Hannan took more money from her purse to offer the woman an extra gratuity. The woman bowed in thanks. "Praised be Allah, Praise be to the One God." She took her leave, going from the lounge to the lobby where she stopped some other hotel guests. The concierge, spying her, chased her out.

Hannan went up to her room. She opened her purse, taking out the Air France ticket the scarf-seller had dropped into it. She would leave tonight. Saturday. On her French passport. Air France. She would take nothing with her. Jazzar's men were everywhere. Mukhabarat was surely moving in now. And Samia, what of Samia? For me, Samia cannot exist, Hannan told herself.

In the lobby of the Hotel Baghdad, an argument raged. Three Mukhabarat agents were in the faces of Jazzar's soldiers. Lt. Jazzar himself showed up. He would not turn over his command of this assignment to the Mukhabarat agent in charge, Addis Sophaia. Sophaia convinced Jazzar that two commanders should not argue in front of their men, they should step out onto the street to discuss this calmly, like gentlemen.

Fifteen minutes later, Sophaia reappeared in the hotel lobby. He informed the soldiers under Jazzar's command that Jazzar had ceded authority to him, and that they were dismissed. Sophaia took his two Mukhabarat agents to the elevator, up to the 11th floor, to room 1109. They knocked. No answer. They knocked again. No answer. Sophaia stood sideways to the door, put his face next to the door, then spoke in as audible, yet as quiet a voice as possible, in Hebrew.

"Hannah," Sophaia said in Hebrew, "anachnu Mossad. We're taking you to the airport. I'm putting the room key in the door. I'm unlocking the door. Don't shoot, Hannan."

Sophaia opened the door. Hannah stood facing the three men, pistol aimed straight at them.

"Hannah," Sophaia spoke Hebrew again, "If we are Mossad and you shoot, we'll have to return fire. What a tragedy that would be. If we aren't Mossad, if we are Mukhabarat, or whoever, and you shoot, we'll have to return fire. You have no choice but to go or die."

The four stared at each other. Sophaia stood between the other two men, with his pistol still holstered. The other two pointed their pistols at Hannan. Hannan lowered her gun.

"Throw it on the couch," Sophaia said, still in Hebrew.

Hannah threw her gun on the couch, then walked toward the three men. Sophaia's two assistants each took an arm of Hannah's.

"Bring nothing," Sophaia said.

"No," Hannah said. "Of course not. Either way."

The four walked past Jazzar's men, still lingering in the lobby, waiting for orders. They got into a new, 1981 Mercedes Benz that waited for them. Sophaia got in the front passenger seat, the two men put Hannan in the back seat, between them. Each man still held one of Hannah's arms. As the car drove away, Sophaia spoke again in Hebrew.

"I have two messages for you, Hannah," Sophaia said. "The first one is from Arie Solen. He says, and I quote, 'You are a miracle. You succeeded.' The second message is from Col. Yossi Ben Luria. He says, and I quote, 'See you in Jerusalem.'"

The two agents let go of Hannah's arms. Hannah looked up at Sophaia.

"You are really Mossad. I'm going to Paris tonight, aren't I?" Hannah said.

"You certainly are," Sophaia answered. "And, may I add one more little treat for you: Jazzar is dead."

Hannah smiled.

"The bastard," she said. "And Samia?"

"Who is Samia?" Sophaia said. "I don't know Samia."

THIRTY-NINE

At about the same moment that Hannah Ben Eliyahu stepped aboard the Air France flight for the four hour trip to Paris, Ibrahim Ibrahim entered the Al Rashid Hotel. He presented his papers to the Concierge. Ms. Samia Sa'ad, he told the Concierge, was expecting his delivery. The Concierge insisted on examining the delivery, to the extent of asking Ibrahim to unwrap it completely. When the Concierge saw the contents of the package, a book by Ibrahim Ibrahim, entitled *Timeless Myths of Egypt*, he leafed through the book, then handed it back to Ibrahim. Ibrahim gave the book back to the Concierge, along with the wrapping paper and a cold stare. The Concierge rewrapped the book.

The Concierge rang Samia's room to inform her that her delivery had arrived. Samia directed the Concierge to send Ibrahim to her room, and then not to disturb her, as she and Ibrahim would discuss the book at some length.

Samia and Ibrahim sat at the desk in her room, discussing ancient mythology, passing notes back and forth. In those notes, Ibrahim informed Samia that she must stay at Osiraq on Sunday until 0800 hours. At

0800, he would meet her at the front gate. She should walk through the front gate nonchalantly. The guards will know her, of course, and suspect her, as she'll be on foot. If they chase her, she must run to the car. It will be a very fast car.

Samia asked Ibrahim, through the notes, where they would go. Ibrahim wrote back: "Better not to say right now. Do you trust me? Will you be there?"

"Do I have a choice?" Samia wrote back.

"No," Ibrahim wrote. "You have no choice. But look at my face. See if you trust me. It's better if you do trust me. We can work together then. You won't hesitate."

Samia looked into Ibrahim's face. He smiled at her. His eyes glowed with a certain joy. She didn't write back to him, but nodded her agreement. And all the while they spoke about ancient Mesopotamian and Egyptian mythologies, gods and goddesses.

Ibrahim took all the notepaper with him. At his shop, *The Mesopotamian Library*, in the rear room, Ibrahim slid the notes into the paper shredder, and turned it on. The paper shredder had devoured the paper just as five Mukhabarat agents burst into the front door, just as Ibrahim had slipped into the hiding place behind the rotating bookshelf in the back room. Ibrahim stayed motionless, steadied his breathing, breathed in dust, fought the fear and the claustrophobia and the rage at what they were doing to his shop and the desire to swing open the bookshelves and, with a Kalashnikov blaring and sputtering and spitting, to shout out 'Curse and damn Saddam Hussein and the name of Hussein to seven eternities of hell.'

The five Mukhabarat agents destroyed the shop in search of any sign of betrayal, weapons, papers, illegal books, although the thousands of books made it impossible to search thoroughly. Books lay everywhere. Tables overturned. Signs trashed. A dust storm filled the bookstore. Passersby glanced in but kept walking. Dust billowed out from the front door. Sacred books lay on the floor. Drawers hung open. The Mukhabarat took every penny they found.

In his tiny closet, Ibrahim closed his eyes. *Plunder*, he thought, *utter plunder*. Knowing that he was no longer a bookseller, no longer an underground agent, that he was a full-time soldier again, Ibrahim stayed in his cramped hiding place for over two hours, until the Mukhabarat had left, until he was sure they wouldn't come back. Counting on his underground comrades to get his wife and four children out of Baghdad to safety, Ibrahim set out from the back door of *The Mesopotamian Library* for a place to hide for the night.

FORTY

On Saturday, June 6, Arie Solen and Col. Yossi Ben Luria, bearing British passports, journeyed eastward in several stages. At Ben Gurion airport in Tel Aviv, they boarded the 5:15 a.m. Turkish Air Flight 22. At 7:30 a.m., they landed in Istanbul, at the north-western edge of Turkey. At 9:20 a.m., they left Istanbul aboard Turkish Air Flight 18, heading toward central Turkey, landing in Ankara at 10:20 a.m. At noon, they departed Ankara aboard the four-propeller, sixteen-seat Turkish Air Flight 6, and, at 1:20 p.m., they landed in the southeastern Turkish metropolis of Diyarbakir.

A Mossad agent meeting them in the Diyarbakir airport handed Ben Luria two Turkish transit visas: one in the name of Samia Sa'ad (Halevy), the other in the name of Ibrahim Ibrahim. Then he drove Solen and Ben Luria to an air-pad half an hour away. There, they boarded a helicopter belonging to a Turkish construction company. One hour seventeen minutes later they set down in the distant village of Siirt in the far south-eastern corner of Turkey, 100 kilometers from the Turkish-Iraqi border at Dernakli. They hired a driver to take them to the *Hotel Orpheus*.

Solen and Ben Luria's rooms each had a low wooden platform with a thin mattress covered with a thin sheet. Another thin sheet lay on top of the bed. A 3-drawer wooden dresser stood in the corner. A common bathroom was down the hall. There was a cold-water shower.

Taking their small backpacks with them, Solen and Ben Luria walked around the streets of Siirt. They walked around the mosque with its spire reaching above the town, watching over it. They bought kabobs from a street vendor, chicken for Ben Luria, lamb for Solen. They walked into a neighborhood of mixed stone and mud houses. They walked around the perimeter of the 18th century Ottoman brick fort, which took them an hour. They came back into town where they looked in the window of a rug shop, a clay and ceramic shop, a spice shop, a store with Islamic religious artifacts. They returned to their wooden beds to get as much sleep as they could.

Each locked their door, then shoved two rubber door-stops at opposing angles under the door. Both slept fitfully.

Solen and Ben Luria left the *Hotel Orpheus* at 0530. The Jeep was waiting for them. The driver, a Turk, handed the keys over to Solen. Smiling and nodding, but without speaking, he walked off. Solen got into the driver's seat, attached his one-handed steering-wheel knob to the steering-wheel. Ben Luria unlocked the combination lock on the metal box bolted and welded to the floor of the back seat. Opening the combination lock, disarming the box's alarm, Ben Luria checked the contents: one pistol and shoulder holster each, one combat knife each, one Uzi each, six hand-launched grenades. There was a map, two flashlights, enough food and water for four days. Solen and Ben Luria each took one of the pistols and put it in the shoulder holsters they strapped on. Solen started up the Jeep, turned on the lights. With his right hand on the steering-wheel knob, he drove off toward Route 370 South.

The road was paved. Solen drove without missing a beat, dropping his right hand down to the long shift stick, then grabbing the steering-wheel knob again.

"You like driving, don't you?" Ben Luria said.

"I do," Solen said. "Even on this old road."

"It won't be road much longer. I'll take over then."

"I'm not handicapped, I'm otherly abled."

Ben Luria laughed. "I've never gone off on a mission with a one-armed man before."

"Don't ever do it again," Solen said.

"I should have had the lamb," Ben Luria said.

"The lamb?"

"Last night, the lamb kabobs. They looked juicy. Rich. Better than the chicken."

Solen smiled.

Ben Luria checked his watch. "Thirty-four hours until the boys take off. Twenty-five hours forty-five minutes until Samia and Ibrahim leave Osiraq."

"Fifty-four hours until we're all back in Jerusalem, me, you, Samia, the flyboys, all of us."

"About right," Ben Luria said, "something like that, fifty-four hours."

"No. Exactly. Fifty-four hours. Give or take ten minutes."

"Do you know a guy," Ben Luria asked, "Avraham Bloch?"

Solen glanced over at Ben Luria. He looked back to the bumpy road. Not a car or a truck in sight.

"What about Avraham Bloch?"

"Strange fellow. I was just thinking about him."

"And what other strange things are you thinking about?"

"Nothing," Ben Luria said. "I was thinking about Tamar. That made me think about my family, my friends, Ilan Hamal. That made me think about Avraham Bloch. '…a terrible fiery death.'"

"What?"

"Nothing. Something this guy Avraham Bloch said. About some mystical journey that could end in a 'terrible fiery death.'"

"You think your friend Ilan Hamal will end tomorrow in a 'terrible fiery death?'"

"It's a fear. I shouldn't be listening to crazy mystics."

"And what were you thinking about Tamar?" Solen asked him.

"That she's asleep right now. That I know how she lies in the bed."

"No," Solen said. "She's not asleep. She was Mossad. She knows what you're up to."

"Maybe."

"Not maybe," Solen said, "she's up, she's pacing around, she's keeping herself busy."

They drove on in silence for another 11 kilometers. A canvas-covered truck passed them going north, its lights still on from the night. Then another, a closed truck. These trucks might carry food, gasoline, smuggled munitions, drugs. They could carry anything from anywhere to almost anywhere. They rode on, the Jeep bumping along on the two-lane road.

"I'm just feeling it now," Ben Luria said.

"Yes," Solen said.

"We're in the Field, we're on Mission, we're alone. It's just now hit me."

"Yes."

"It's a great feeling."

"Yes," Solen said.

"Great. Frightening. Exhilarating. Total. You forget any other troubles you might have."

"That's the seduction of it," Solen said.

"With a family," Ben Luria reflected, "it's different."

"Yes."

"We can't fail Samia," Ben Luria said.

"No," Solen said, "we can't fail Samia. Or Ibrahim."

"Even if we have to cross the border into Iraq."

"Yes, of course."

It was full daylight. The road was clearly visible. The landscape spread out on either side of them and before them. Flat stretches of wasteland. Hills rose up here and there.

"Do you like to drive alone?" Ben Luria asked.

"Yes, I love that," Solen said. "But with you, too," he added.

"I didn't mean that. I love to drive alone. That stretch from Tel Aviv to Safed, it's wonderful. Late at night, a clear night...."

"Moving through the silence."

"Yes. Exactly. Moving through the silence."

"You know, Yossi," Solen said, "that Osiraq is named after the Egyptian God Osiris."

"Yes," Yossi said. "I know that."

"And Osiris is named the Lord of Life."

"No, sir, I didn't know that."

"But another one of his names is the Lord of Silence."

"That's quite beautiful," Yossi said.

"And ominous," Solen said.

"Yes," Yossi said, "it is that, too."

Fifty-four kilometers south of Siirt, at Eruh, the road turned from paved to dust. Keeping the windows almost closed, even in the heat, they drove on, Ben Luria at the wheel. Ten kilometers on they stopped for a Turkish army roadblock. They presented their passports to the officer in charge. He conferred with his colleagues for a full 20 minutes. Ben Luria and Solen kept an eye on them as they talked, smoked cigarettes, examined the documents, made jokes. Ben Luria started to get out of the Jeep, but Solen stopped him.

After another five minutes, Ben Luria left the Jeep, walked over to the officer, and asked, in English, was there any problem with the documents? The officer shrugged his shoulders. He held their passports. He said something in Turkish. Ben Luria signaled that he spoke no Turkish. The officer pointed to a special mark on the visa. Ben Luria again gestured, as if to say, 'so'? The officer handed back the documents, then signaled his men at the barrier to allow the Jeep through. As Ben Luria and Solen left the checkpoint, the officer shouted out to them, "Be careful! It's a dangerous road!"

"Bastard," Solen said. "We'll be careful. Let's just get going."

Another 14 kilometers on, the road was blocked again. The Jeep slowed. These were not Turkish soldiers. Half of them wore a variety of military uniforms, the other half wore ragged civilian clothes. All of them carried Kalashnikovs, some of them had side arms. What appeared to be the officer in charge came forward to the driver's side of the Jeep. He took the cigarette from his mouth, blew the smoke away from Ben

Luria's face, then asked them, in Turkish, who they were.

"I don't speak Turkish," Ben Luria said.

"But you do speak English?" the man said.

"Yes, we do speak English."

"Your papers?"

"By what authority?" Ben Luria said.

Solen looked all around, watching the officer and the other soldiers.

"Mine."

"I can't release my papers without proper authority," Ben Luria said.

"All right," the man said, "get out of the Jeep."

Ben Luria and Solen both sat where they were.

The officer gestured to his troops. Several men came forward, opened the Jeep's doors, and dragged Ben Luria and Solen out. They took their pistols, threw them into the Jeep, searched both men, patted them down, searched their pockets. The men looked in the back of the Jeep, lifting up the top of the metal box.

"Hey," Ben Luria shouted, "get your hands off my stuff!"

One of the soldiers came out with an Uzi and a hand grenade, which he held up so that everyone could see.

"Who are you?" the officer asked.

"We're British engineers," Yossi Ben Luria said. "We're scouting out business."

"What kind of business?"

"Engineering business," Ben Luria said.

"Why don't you build this road?" the officer pointed to the dusty trail, laughing. "We could use you."

"If you want to hire us."

The officer shouted out something in Turkish. Eight men came forward with their Kalashnikovs pointed at Solen and Ben Luria. Four men each pushed Solen and Ben Luria off the road toward a shack in the near distance. The officer got into the Jeep and followed them across the hardscrabble plain.

Inside the shack, just four slat-wooden walls with a wood-burning stovepipe stove, a table, a few chairs, and a dirt floor, the soldiers sat Solen and Ben Luria in two chairs. Two soldiers remained inside the shack. Then the officer, getting out of the Jeep, entered.

"So," the officer said, "maybe now you'll tell me who you are?"

"We're construction engineers on a scouting mission," Solen said. "We work for Arcade Construction, London. We have projects going all over Turkey. Ankara, Istanbul."

"Your left arm," the officer said, "you lost that in a construction accident?"

"Yes, in fact I did," Solen said.

"You're sure someone didn't shoot it off with an Uzi?"

"Everyone carries guns around here," Arie said.

"Nothing unusual."

`"No. Nothing unusual. Two Uzis. Hand grenades."

"You never know."

"No, you don't," the officer said. He stood, his hands folded behind his back. He wore a green uniform, but of what country no one could tell. He had no insignia.

"I'm not going to get anywhere with you two, am I?" the officer asked.

"I'm telling you....." Ben Luria began.

"You're telling me that you're engineers from Arcade Construction in London. And I'm the Queen Mother. Do you expect me to give you your Uzis and your hand grenades and escort you down the road, let you go on?"

"No escort. But the rest, yes."

"Of course."

The officer left, taking his soldiers with him. Solen and Ben Luria sat in the room as the heat of the day grew around them. The shack had one window. It was open. Outside, soldiers milled around, doing nothing but carrying their rifles.

After two hours the officer returned. This time alone.

"Are you thirsty?" he asked.

"No," Solen said.

"No," Ben Luria said.

The officer smiled.

"Then you're lying. If you were traveling engineers

from Arcade Construction, London, you would have said 'yes' and taken water from me," the officer said.

Neither Solen nor Ben Luria responded.

"You're disciplined military men. You're from the Turkish Army. You've been sent here with these pistols and these Uzis to look like Israeli spies or something. But you're not. You're regulars. Turkish Army."

"No," Solen said. "You were right. We're Israelis, but we're not spies, we're military. IDF. Israeli Defense Force. Army."

Ben Luria shot a look over at Solen. Solen looked back, steadily.

"You're still lying," the officer said. And he left again.

"Why....?" Ben Luria asked.

"Because they're Kurds," Solen said. "They hate the Turks. They hate the Iraqis even more. And most of all they loathe Saddam Hussein. We're in Kurdistan, Yossi. Only Kurdistan is a country that doesn't exist. The Turks call it Turkey the Kurds call it Kurdistan."

"The Kurds are Muslim, Arie, they're no lovers of Israel."

"The enemy of my enemy is my friend. We're Iraq's enemy. We're Saddam Hussein's enemy. We tell them we're Israelis on our way to help the Kurdish resistance in Iraq. Israeli military advisors. Like we helped the Mujahadeen in Afghanistan. It's half-true."

"If we're not out of here soon we're screwed," Ben Luria said. "And Samia is screwed. And Ibrahim."

"There's a tiny spot....here, Yossi," Solen pointed to the back of the heel of his right shoe. "Pull that..." Solen tugged on it lightly. A knife slipped slightly out. "See? Spy tricks. Basic stuff."

An hour and a half later, as the sun went past 1500, the officer returned.

"Your story now?" the officer said.

"Same one," Solen said, "the truth. We're Israeli soldiers. IDF. Major Solen," he nodded his head. "Captain Ben Luria," Solen gestured toward Ben Luria.

The officer raised his right hand across his body, then with all of his might he backhanded Solen across the face. Solen fell off his chair, but catching himself, he held his seat. Ben Luria jumped up. He grabbed the officer. The officer shook him off.

"Sit down!" the officer commanded. Bruised, sweaty, with adrenaline pumping, Ben Luria hesitated, stood back, then sat.

The officer cradled the back of his right hand with his left hand. "It hurt me," he said, "but I don't mind. The next one will hurt more." He heaved off and let Solen have it again. "How'd you lose your arm?" he demanded, as Solen recovered his chair, wiped the side of his face with his right hand.

"In '67," Solen huffed, out of breath. "The six-day war. In the desert. I'm IDF."

"You're a lying thieving son-of-a-bitch is what you are," the officer said. Then he turned to Ben Luria.

"How'd you like to see your friend here get really hurt?" the officer said. "I mean really hurt. His one good arm, maybe."

"He's telling you the truth," Ben Luria urged him. "I'm from Jerusalem. I'm IDF. We're on our way to Iraq. We're advisers to the northern Kurds."

"You're what!" the officer laughed. He repeated it. "You're advisors to the northern Kurds! What a story. Sit for a while." He left again.

"Take the knife," Solen said.

"You all right?"

"Take the goddamn knife, Yossi."

Ben Luria pulled on the small tab at the back of the sole of Solen's right shoe. The knife came clean. It was 4 inches long, slightly curved upward at the tip. Ben Luria put it up the right-hand sleeve of his shirt just above his wrist.

"They're Kurds all right," Solen said. "They're PKK. Serious bastards. If he comes back alone grab him from behind in a choke-hold. I'll throw the table up to the door. Slip me the knife. I'll give him a couple of jabs to the stomach, just to show him. I'll give you the knife. You hold it to his throat. He's got a pistol under his shirt, tucked into his pants. Did you see it?"

"Yes," Ben Luria said.

"I'll grab the pistol. We leave with him as hostage. Walk straight to the Jeep. I'll walk back-to-back with you, covering the rear with his pistol. Make sure we get our gear. Throw him in the back of the Jeep, face down, keep the knife at the back of his neck, you know where."

By the time the officer returned it was early evening.

"Are you thirsty now?" he asked. "Hungry? Just tell me who you are."

"In my unit," Ben Luria said, "we used to say, 'An Israeli soldier doesn't need food and he doesn't need water."

In one sweep with his one hand Solen grabbed the leg of his chair rose up and swung it at the officer, hitting him hard on the shoulder. The officer slugged out at Solen but Ben Luria had the officer already, from behind, in a choke hold, knife at the officer's throat. Solen grabbed the pistol from the officer's waistband. Ben Luria slipped Solen the knife. Solen jabbed it at the officer's stomach once, twice, a third time. The officer winced each time but didn't cry out. No one yet rushed the door.

"Ready?" Solen said.

"Go!" Ben Luria said.

Solen shoved the table aside, kicked open the door.

They walked out, Ben Luria pushing the officer in front of him. Solen took his position back-to-back with Ben Luria, waving his pistol from left to right to left.

"Tell them," Yossi said into the officer's ear.

The officer yelled out in Turkish.

"I told them to kill you," the officer said, "to kill me too. You Turkish bastards."

The soldiers had their Kalashnikovs, pistols raised. No one took aim or prepared to fire. The trio kept moving: Solen, Ben Luria, the officer. In less than a minute they had reached the Jeep. Solen spun around, opened the driver's door, waved the pistol again at the soldiers. Off to Solen's right a soldier made a move with his Kalashnikov, raised it up a notch. Solen shot him in the chest. The man flew backwards, fell sprawled out, jerking. Ben Luria hesitated for a moment, then moved on.

Ben Luria pushed the seat-back forward with his knee, then shoved the officer face-down on the back seat. There, in the metal box, were the Uzis, the pistols, the grenades, the food, everything. Ben Luria climbed in on top of the officer. He kept the knife to the top point of the officer's spinal chord.

Solen jumped into the driver's seat. He laid the officer's pistol on the passenger seat, took hold of the keys, which were still in the ignition, and the Jeep started up. Solen threw it into gear then swerved away, steering by his steering-wheel knob. They hit the road, heading south. With his left hand, Ben Luria reached into the passenger seat to take the officer's pistol. No one fired even one shot after them.

Two kilometers down the road, Solen stopped the Jeep. Ben Luria got out, bringing the officer with him.

Solen retrieved a pair of plastic handcuffs from his knapsack, cuffed the officer's hands behind him, then put him back in the back seat. Ben Luria climbed in the front. They headed south.

"You were right," Solen said over the rankling of the Jeep, "we're not Israeli IDF, but neither are we Turks. Are we here to help the Iraqi Kurds? In a manner of speaking. Your men need a lot more training. We should have never escaped like this. They should have never left our gear in the Jeep. The keys. The battery hooked up."

"Who are you?" the officer demanded.

"Never mind," Solen said.

"Will you kill me?"

"You're well trained. The way you ask the question," Solen said. "No. We won't kill you. If we don't have to."

A half hour on their headlights caught a man in the middle of the dark road with an assault rifle pointed straight at them. Off the road, to the man's left, stood another man, also with an assault rifle.

"Bandits!" the officer yelled, but in Turkish, so Solen and Ben Luria only understood his tone. "Goddamn bandits. Give me a gun."

"Hit it!" Ben Luria yelled, pointing his pistol out the window, looking for his target.

In one move Solen downshifted to third, floored the gas pedal. He hurled the Jeep straight toward the man in the center of the road. The man froze, and remained in that frozen state and position when the Jeep hit him straight on, throwing him who-the-hell-knows-where. The Jeep jumped slightly to the right. Solen, straightening out, kept going. The other guy turned, ran across the open terrain. Ben Luria fired after him, wide and high. He kept running into that nowhere.

"You guys are fantastic," the officer yelled, laughing.

"You need to train your own guys," Ben Luria yelled over the noise of the Jeep. "Discipline."

"You guys have guts," the officer yelled.

Ben Luria turned around to the officer in the back seat. The officer stared right back at Ben Luria. "Personal discipline," Ben Luria said.

Half an hour on Solen stopped the Jeep again, pulled off onto the hard dirt.

"Here you are," Solen said.

They let the officer out of the Jeep, cut off his handcuffs, set him free.

"Go home," Solen said.

"My pistol?" the officer gestured around the dark landscape.

Ben Luria handed the officer his pistol.

"Good luck," Ben Luria said.

"You are Israelis," the officer said, then disappeared.

As they drove off, Ben Luria said, "We're not all that far now, are we?"

"I don't think so," Solen said. "Are you hungry? Thirsty?"

"Not too."

"I know," Solen said, "funny isn't it? We should eat a little, drink a little. We'll need strength."

"The accommodations in Cizre might be below the elegant standard of the *Hotel Orpheus*, Siirt."

"And I'm exhausted," Solen said.

"Yes," Ben Luria agreed, "I'm exhausted."

"Not one night has gone by," Solen said, "that I haven't lost sleep over Samia. I'm so much in the habit I'll keep losing sleep over her."

"Someday it'll wear off," Ben Luria said.

Solen looked over at Ben Luria. He smiled.

"You're a hell of a fighter, Yossi."

"Thank you." Ben Luria looked down at his hands in his lap, his right thumb rubbing his left hand. "So far so good."

"And I'm a hell of a one-armed bastard, aren't I?" Solen smiled.

"Yes. You are. One hell of a bastard of a one-armed bastard." Ben Luria looked up, laughing.

"I do hope we at least get a bed tonight," Solen laughed.

"After the battle," Ben Luria said, more quietly, "like now, is when I feel the fear. Terror. Anxiety."

"It's good for you. Let it be."

"Anger, too. Rage."

"That, too, Yossi. Let it be."

"Yes, I know," Ben Luria said. "And beyond all that, I feel good. Solid."

"We are solid. So far, solid," Solen said.

The Jeep pulled into Cizre.

— • —

Like a snowy mountain glittering in the sun.
Josephus, Jewish historian and Soldier, 37 - 100 CE

Of the ten measures of wisdom that God has bestowed upon the world, nine of these fall to the lot of Jerusalem; of the ten measures of suffering which God has bestowed upon the world, nine of these fall to the lot of Jerusalem; of the ten measures of beauty that God has bestowed upon the world, nine of these fall to the lot of Jerusalem.
The Talmud

If I forget thee, O Jerusalem, let my right hand forget its skill. If I do not remember thee, let my tongue cling to the roof of my mouth; if I do not exalt Jerusalem above my chief joy. Psalms 137: 5-6

The whole religious complexion of the modern world is due to the absence from Jerusalem of a lunatic asylum.
Thomas Paine, 1737-1809

Pray for the peace of Jerusalem. Psalms 122:6

— • —

FORTY-ONE *JUNE 7, 1981*

Gen. Jonathan Dror, in pajamas, bathrobe, and slippers walks into the kitchen of his house. He opens the refrigerator. Without taking anything, closes it. His wife, Aviva, calls down to him:

"Jonathan. What are you doing?"

"Nothing," he calls back.

A moment later, Aviva comes into the kitchen.

"Come to bed," she says.

"I'm all right," Dror says. He stands under the light by the kitchen table. The single light-bulb illuminates only him.

"Come," Aviva says, "please. You need sleep. I'll help you sleep."

"Sleep? Who can sleep?"

"Menahem Begin," Aviva says. "Menahem sleeps like a baby. Now come."

0450
JERUSALEM

When Prime Minister Menahem Begin gets out of bed, his wife, Alyza, half wakes up.

"I have to go," Begin says, "Sleep. It's early."

"Will you be back?" Alyza asks him, mumbling in her sleep. "I'll wait lunch for you."

"No," Begin says. "I'll be in meetings all day straight. I'll call you this evening about dinner."

"I was just having this funny dream," Alyza says, "about ...."

Begin interrupts her. "Save it," he says. "Remember it and tell me later. I'm sorry. I have to go."

Begin leans down to kiss Alyza on the forehead. She turns over, goes back to sleep.

0514

JERUSALEM

Ibrahim awakes. Nothing surrounds him but the debris which has accumulated under the bridge by the pylon, thrown from passing automobiles, the debris left by thieves or drug addicts or fugitives from the Ba'ath police state who had slept in this hidden spot before him. He smells the rank Tigris river water.

Ibrahim glances around, calms himself, readies himself. He had slept on a large piece of canvas he'd found. Strange to feel rested after such a night's sleep. First, to find tea and something to eat, then wait for Issam Rhamal to find him.

0600
BAGHDAD

Samia leaves the Al Rashid Hotel for the last time. Her day of death or escape. At the café, *The Vizier's Daughter,* she orders the usual, cappuccino and a plain croissant. The city is in motion. Samia leaves everything behind in her room: her clothes, letters from her "parents" and her "fiancé" in New York, her tour books on Baghdad and Iraq, her well-worn Arabic copy of *The Thousand and One Nights.* In her purse, she carries her pistol. A necessary risk. The pistol that awaited her in the hotel-room safe when she had arrived, over two years ago. Into the heel of her left shoe Samia has slipped a hidden knife. A small knob protrudes.

Samia reads the newspaper, *Forward,* eats her croissant, sips her cappuccino, waits for Hikmet Sidqui to arrive with the car. For the last time, Samia will ride beside Hikmet Sidqui, and the odor of his always half-washed body, the constantly nervous look on his face.

"I'm Mossad," she would love to say as they pull off toward Osiraq. Then slide a knife across his jugular.

Patience. He'll know.

Her car arrives. Hikmet Sidqui holds open the car door for Samia, but doesn't greet her with his usual, "Good morning." When he gets into the car from the other side, he doesn't say, "Did you sleep well, Ms. Sa'ad?" As the car pulls away, Samia doesn't look back at her table at *The Vizier's Daughter.*

They pass out of the city onto the highway to Osir-aq. Samia watches out the car window, lowers the window to let in the stream of warm morning desert air.

"Close the window," Sidqui says.

"I'm sorry?"

"I want to talk to you."

Samia presses the button, the window rolls up.

"You are not Samia Sa'ad."

"Who am I?" Samia answers.

Sidqui doesn't answer. He looks straight ahead. Samia nudges open the clasp on her purse. They pass through the security gate at Osiraq, then pull up to the main building.

"I don't know for sure who you are," Sidqui says. "I think I know who you work for. Soon, I'll know who you work for, and who you are. Your days of deceit are over. You'll pay for your treachery in ways you dare not imagine."

"I am who I say I am, Mr. Hiqmat Sidqui," Samia says. "I'm sorry you suspect me. It pains me."

"Who was Samir al-Wahab working for?"

"Who's that?" Samia asked.

"The waiter at *The Vizier's Daughter!*" Sidqui yells. "Don't make up any more stories, Ms. Sa'ad. It's time for the truth."

The driver gets out of the car, walks over to Samia's side, where he stands blocking her door. Samia opens the door to get out. The driver slams it shut.

"You won't escape, Ms. Sa'ad," Sidqui says. "Go to work. As normal. I'll be here to pick you up this afternoon."

"Who do you think I work for," Samia asks, "in your complete confusion?"

"You're an Israeli spy."

"My God, Mr. Sidqui!" Samia laughs. "Not Iranian. Not CIA. But an Israeli spy! A Jewess!"

"Do you know," Sidqui asks, "that your friend Hannan Khatib has escaped to Paris? Last night. We have people in Paris who will take care of her."

"She isn't my friend," Samia says. "She was Dr. El Meshad's friend. They went to Paris all the time. Your imagination has run away with you."

"Give me your purse, Ms. Sa'ad."

"No."

"Your refusal convicts you."

"My refusal absolves me," Samia says, "it proves my loyalty. I have sensitive documents in my purse. You'd have to kill me to get them. Perhaps you are the Israeli spy, Mr. Sidqui. And your driver. Perhaps he's your assistant."

Sidqui motions to his driver, who stands aside. Following his daily routine, Sidqui gets out of the car, walks to the other side, opens and holds the door for Samia. Samia snaps closed the latch on her purse. She gets out of the car.

"Soon you'll pray for your death," Sidqui says. "I'll

be there. To refuse it. It will be my infinite pleasure."
Sidqui smiles at Samia.

"I can't imagine your pleasures, Mr. Sidqui. May Allah reward you for all your desires."

Samia walks in the front door of her building, passing the guard who knows her. The wall clock reads 06:42. Samia smiles. For her, the waiting is almost over.

Samia signs in at the security desk, saying to the security officer, "The waiting is almost over."

"I'm sorry, Ms. Sa'ad?"

"Nothing. How are you this morning?"

"Fine. Just waiting for everyone to arrive so I can have my coffee."

"Yes," Samia says, "We have an early morning today. You'll need your coffee."

0620
JERUSALEM

Prime Minister Menahem Begin, his Political Advisor, Yaakov Vulf, Chairman of the Joint Chiefs of Staff Avraham Shtern, Commander of the Air Force General Jonathan Dror, Commander of the Army General Menasche Slomovic, Naval Admiral Moshe Lavan, Minister-without-portfolio Rafi Stone, and ex-Minister of Defense and leader of the opposition Labor Party, Shimon Peres, gather in the war room in Jerusalem.

A topographical model sits on a large table in the center of the room. It shows the terrain from *Etzion Air Force Base* in the Sinai desert to Osiraq, at Al Tawaitha, thirteen kilometers south of Baghdad. Maps hang on the walls. A giant screen dominates the front wall. Telephones of different colors, black, red, green, abound. Military men and women staff the telephones, the computers.

Gen. Dror takes out the map Yossi Ben Luria had given him, the one Ben Luria sketched late at night at his kitchen table. Dror tacks the map to the side of the topographical model. The room becomes quiet as General Dror speaks.

"They'll leave in nine hours forty-two minutes. At 1600. The Iraqis are installing the reactor core today, Sunday. We're lucky. None of the French scientists will be at Osiraq. We'll have no French casualties. The flight, with evasive maneuvers and without hindrance, will take one hour two minutes. At 1710 the reactor core will be completely installed. At 1720 the Iraqis will turn the reactor on. It will stay on for ten minutes. At 1730 they'll turn it off. The Iraqis are planning to go hot with the reactor for good and forever at 1740. That won't ever happen. Our boys go in at 1732. By 1740 there will be no Osiraq. Does anyone have questions about anything I've had to keep secret? Anything you need to know now?"

"When they do meet resistance?" Gen. Slomovic asks. "Exactly what's the battle plan?"

"If they meet enemy aggressors, the F-15s will fly away to engage them," Dror answers. "The F-16s will steady course, fly on. That's how the F-16s keep on schedule. When the interceptors are destroyed, the F-15s will rejoin the armada. Questions?"

"Do we have absolute on-the-ground timing on the switch-on and switch-off of the plant?" Adm. Lavan asks.

"Yes," Dror says. "We do now. From inside Osiraq itself." He points to one of the red telephones at the front of the room. "The boys in the air are completely radio silent. They have no external communications, no communications among themselves except hand signals, the flashing of lights on their aircraft, and dipping their wings. In all of Israel and the whole world, only that one encoded telephone can contact them." Dror points to a white telephone. "And Hamal and only Hamal accepts or rejects it.

"We're all on highest alert now," Avraham Shtern says. "We'll stay that way for at least a week. But I want to report one unrelated internal development to you. This morning we stopped two suicide bombers from crossing over, headed for Petah Tikva. Every nerve in the whole body of the State of Israel is ready."

"Let me take a minute, before we get too busy," the Prime Minister says. "As we've discussed before, the international ramifications will be tremendous. Everyone will condemn us, including the U.S. I'll handle all of the diplomacy with the diplomats. No one is to make even one diplomatic comment to any reporter. At 1630 we'll notify the U.S. They are the only ones to get notification. They have their AWACs in the air. If they catch our planes on their AWAC radar, they'll launch interception. We have to tell them. But not until 1630. Anything else?"

"They'll urge us to pull back," Peres says.

"Let me handle them," the Prime Minister answers. "I'll tell Reagan that it's a fail-safe mission. The boys will not turn back, even on our command. The Americans won't like it, but they'll buy it."

Dror speaks. "Look, we've all known each other all our lives. Trust that IAF has done everything to make this work. In the hours ahead I appreciate everything we do together here, and what each of you has done with your services. I've listened to everything each one of you has said for the last many months. Believe me, I haven't planned this alone. It wasn't even my idea to begin with. But God willing it'll work. I'm not saying much, really. There's nothing more to say. Is there?"

"No," Shtern says, "there isn't. Do you want coffee, Jonathan? Some fruit?"

0620
SIIRT, TURKEY

"We wait," Solen says.

"How long?" Ben Luria asks. "The border's a hundred kilometers from here."

"We go at 1300."

"Giving us two hours flex time. Not much," Ben Luria says.

"It's all we get," Solen says. "We make it or we don't."

Solen and Ben Luria sit at an open cafe having Turkish coffee and bread. Every citizen of Siirt who passes looks them over. The other men in the café stare. The waiter asks them a question, probably asking where they are from. They shrug. "No Turkish," Solen says. The language barrier surrounds them with a cloud of protection on this day of waiting.

"Can't drink too much coffee," Ben Luria says. "It'll jangle my nerves."

"Yes," Solen says, "Turkish coffee sure will. Strong damn stuff."

0620
OSIRAQ

An in-house messenger hurries through the halls. He gives Samia a copy of a memo. The installation of the core reactor will be delayed by ten minutes

Samia holds the memo in her hands, staring at it. Is this information crucial to Israel? If so, how quickly do they need it? If it's urgent, how to convey it? Samia answers the first two questions by assuming the information is crucial and that Israel needs it now. The most difficult question remains. *How do I convey in-house top secret information to Jerusalem without leaving Osiraq? From inside Osiraq itself. From the heart of Saddam's own heart.*

0700
BAGHDAD

Issam Rhamal takes Ibrahim to a garage off the alley of Boudai Street. Rhamal opens the two combination locks and lifts the garage door. Inside the dark garage, working by the sufficient amount of daylight, Rhamal raises the hood of the lime-green BMW, puts in the spark plugs he carries with him in his pockets, tightens them down precisely with a torque-wrench, hands the keys to Ibrahim.

"I love the garage smell," Rhamal says. "Oily rags, oil and gasoline stained cement floor."

"Of course," Ibrahim says, "you're a mechanic. It's the odor of your life."

"For you?" Rhamal asks.

"For me? The odor of books, maybe. Perhaps the odor of war."

"What's the odor of war?"

"So many," Ibrahim says. "The worst is the odor of the dead. But death itself has no odor."

Rhamal laughs. "I suppose not."

"The car won't give me trouble?"

"The car is perfect." Rhamal pats the hood. "Don't worry."

"Good. I have enough worries. Everything else is imperfect."

Ibrahim gets in the car, starts up the engine, gets a feel for the gas, the clutch, the steering. Then he rolls in reverse out of the garage. Rhamal watches as Ibrahim pulls away out of the alley. After all his labor to make the car run at the top of its mark, Rhamal will wait for the car to come back to him, much abused perhaps, but with his comrade Ibrahim alive.

0714
JERUSALEM:
WAR ROOM

Dror and Begin stand in the middle of the room over a topographic model of the flight pattern terrain: from _Etzion Air force Base_ in the Northern Sinai, over the southern tip of Israel, then over Jordan, Syria, and into Iraq. Hills and valleys. Desert. Steppes. Red flags stuck into the model mark dangerous radar zones. A blue line painted across the landscape precisely traces the planned route. Once the mission begins, plans become hopes.

"Going in," Dror says, "as you can see, they're all

over the place. Coming home, they fly a straight line up in the altitudes."

"Coming home they're in more danger," Rafi Stone says. "Everyone will know they're there. Iraq. Syria. Everybody. After the attack."

"No questions, Rafi," the Prime Minister warns him, "no comments."

"But after the attack everyone will know. Up high the radar will find them."

"We know that, Rafi."

"But...." Stone begins.

"OK, Rafi. I'll give you this, your one question," Dror says, "and my one answer: they use up a lot of gas flying in low. Coming home, they have to fly high to conserve fuel. Fuel's a big problem for us today."

"But..."

"No more comments, Rafi," the Prime Minister dismisses him with a wave of his arm.

"Coming home they're more vulnerable!" Stone protests. "Let them fly high going in."

"Going in they're vulnerable!" Dror explodes at Stone.

"Coming home they're a bunch of expendable pilots?"

"Enough!" Dror shouts again. "Sit down and shut up! Shut up!"

Stone retreats to the rear of the room, where he paces, muttering to himself and to anyone else who will listen about Armageddon. "We are at Armageddon," he says over and over again.

"Now we wait," the Prime Minister says.

"Now we wait," Dror agrees.

"No more staring, but now walking right into the void," the Prime Minister says.

"What?" Dror asks.

"Nothing," the Prime Minister says, "a phrase I have going with Yossi Ben Luria. Together, I told Ben Luria, we'll stare right into the void."

0745
OSIRAQ

Samia walks by Heraclium Al Hira's office. No one is in it. She turns back, walks into the office. Using Al Hira's secure, direct line, Samia calls the Presidential Palace to leave a message from Al Hira for Saddam Hussein. When Saddam's personal secretary puts the call through to Saddam himself, Samia identifies herself, explains to Saddam how she got through to him, what telephone she is calling from, and informs him of the ten-minute delay in starting up Osiraq.

"Why are you calling me, Ms. Sa'ad, rather than Al Hira?"

"Director Al Hira is frantic with delay procedures," she tells him.

"Did Director Al Hira order you to call me?" Saddam asks.

"Yes, Your Excellency. Of course. He trusts me. He knew you would want to know."

"Yes," Saddam said, "I do want to know. You're a very clever woman, Ms. Sa'ad. We'll see how clever you are. Tell Director Al Hira to call me at once. At once, Ms. Sa'ad."

"Of course, Your Excellency."

Samia hangs up. She checks her watch. 0708.

At the Presidential Palace, Saddam tells his Aide to get hold of Mohammed Azziz, to tell Azziz that Samia Sa'ad is a spy who must be eliminated immediately. Saddam leaves instructions with his personal secretary to inform him if Heraclium Al Hira calls.

Saddam returns to a meeting with sixty-five of his senior political party, and military leaders. Standing at a podium, Saddam informs the assembled group that he has uncovered a plot against him.

"The six men involved in this pernicious, treasonous attack on the revolution and my own personal self," Saddam says, "sit in this room. Right now. Among us." Saddam looks around the room at each man individually. "They know who they are. They know they are discovered. At this moment, each one of their hearts beats wildly in his breast, trapped in its terror, never to escape. I say to them: you were fools to dream of success against me. I am Saddam Hussein. I am the people. I am Iraq." He pauses.

"Beginning with the lowest rank," Saddam continues, "I name you, traitors: Sadmah N'alim."

N'alim rises, shouts out his protest. "No!" He rips open the front of his shirt. "I give my heart to Saddam. To Iraq. I......I....with all my heart. Allah hear me!"

Two guards enter the meeting room. They walk down the aisle to N'alim, who has become a quivering, screaming madman. They step over the people in their way. They grab N'alim and drag him out, heaving his body over the row. When they get him to the aisle, he falls to the ground, prostrate, kicking, yelling out to Allah. They drag him out of the room, his feet sliding along the floor.

"I move up the list in rank," Saddam says, "because those at the top should wait, they should have more time to gaze within themselves at their ugly sin. The greatest sin of life is betrayal. To betray those who loved you. Now, sit. Think with your corrupt minds and feel with your beating hearts. Consider the justice that awaits you."

As Saddam reads each name, the protest from each of the accused diminishes. Until Saddam reads the last name, the highest rank, a four-star General. The General, rising, raises his fist in the air, shouts at the top of his lungs:

"I go to a virtuous death with the love of Iraq and the truth of eternal loyalty on my lips. There is no plot. I have sinned against no one. May Allah receive me in grace!"

Saddam stands down from the podium. As the two guards enter to remove the General, Saddam sits in his ornate red chair. He crosses his legs. A smiles grows on his face. He chuckles once. He suppresses further laughter. Then he rises, returns to the podium, waves his arms in the air and shouts out: "You idiots! What do you think of me now?"

The room bursts into applause, thunderous hurrahs, frantic, desperate, devotional chants of "I give my blood for Saddam Hussein! I give my blood for Iraq! I give my blood for Saddam Hussein! I give my soul for Saddam Hussein!"

On the podium, Saddam smiles again. The smile stays on his face. He raises his hands to accept the accolades.

Twelve Guards return into the room carrying the bodies of the six accused men. Each man has been shot once in the back of the head. Blood drips from their wounds. The guards' hands and clothes become bloody as they march around the room. The tile floor becomes sticky and slippery with blood.

While the guards display the bodies, Saddam leaves by a side exit. In his private bathroom, he stares at himself in the mirror. He smiles again.

0801
PARIS

Hannah has a cappuccino and an almond croissant at the *Café Dialogique* on the rue de la Gare. The newspaper, *Le Figaro,* lies on the table in front of her. Unknown to her, the Mossad Head of Station in Paris passes by to have a look at Hannah Ben Eliyahu. Hannah tries to read the newspaper, but too many thoughts distract her: Samia, Osiraq, her family in Ashdod, her friends in Israel, the beginnings of her decompression. A level of constant tension she had ignored while in Baghdad becomes noticeable. She even thinks of a massage she will get in Jerusalem. She can guess at the mission that will soon strike Osiraq. *Will it be today? Tomorrow? Soon. Troops on the ground? Where is Samia?*

0802
JERUSALEM

Avraham Bloch, with a cappuccino and croissant, reads the newspaper, *Ha'aretz*. Soon his wife, Dora, will join him. This morning, a vague anxiety propelled him out the door early. Now he waits for his wife to arrive, preferring company to calm his restlessness.

The usual waiter for a Sunday morning, Hayim Glass, is absent from work. Bloch doesn't believe in the superstition of signs, but he can't help taking Hayim Glass's absence as ominous. The substitute waiter says that Hayim Glass will be in, but later this morning. Bloch waits for his wife and for Hayim Glass to arrive. He doesn't touch his croissant, or his cappuccino, getting cold.

0802
OSIRAQ

Samia walks out the front door of the main building. She carries only her purse. She walks through
the compound unchallenged. She walks past a large
storage shed of corrugated sheet metal. She walks past
the barracks which house the soldiers who guard the
compound. She walks past the building which supplies the compound's daily needs, weapons, and ammunition. She is within fifty yards of the main gate.
She has walked past several people. No one has said
anything to her. She does not see any car on the road
beyond the gate.

As Samia crosses the fifty empty yards, then approaches the main gate, a guard steps out from the
gatehouse.

"May I help you, Ms. Sa'ad?"

"I'm taking some measurements," Samia says.

"You can't leave the perimeter alone," the guard
says. He stands in front of Samia, blocks her way.
Samia reaches into her purse, pulls out a large, spool-
type tape measure.

"I'm taking measurements of the perimeter," Samia
says. "If I make one false move, shoot me."

The guard hesitates. "I have no orders."

"I'm giving you your orders," Samia answers. "Don't

hold up our work. Your punishment would be severe."
She stares him down.

The guard holds his rifle across his chest. Samia
puts the tape measure back in her purse, takes hold
of her pistol. She looks over at the other guard, still
in the gatehouse. The guard blocking her way steps
aside.

"Good," she says. She walks past the guard, through
the narrow opening at the end of the guard-arm, and
off the compound. She walks straight toward the road,
just meters in front of her.

Ibrahim speeds up, then slams on the brakes in
front of Samia, as Samia slides into the opened car
door. As they speed off in the lime-green BMW, zig-
zagging down the road, Ibrahim drops a smoke bomb
out his window. Ibrahim and Samia speed up the road,
running fast through the gears until they hit 80, 90,
110 mph in fourth gear. Ibrahim straightens out the
car, holds it steady, keeps up the speed. The guards let
off rounds of bullets into the smoke, uselessly.

Ibrahim brings the car down to a controllable but
still break-neck speed. They head to catch Route 7,
north to Turkey.

0820
SAFED

Rather than wait for the school bus, Tamar Ben Luria drives Reuven to school and Dina to pre-school. When she gets home, Tamar carries Danny into the house with her, turns on the television, lowers the volume, leaving it on in the background. Even if today were the day, there would be no television news until tomorrow. She keeps the television on.

In the kitchen, Tamar makes coffee with warm milk for herself. She takes a piece of leftover sponge cake from the refrigerator, pours some fresh cream over it, adds strawberries from her garden. Eating her breakfast, she reads through one of her favorite books of poetry, *Love Poems*, by the Israeli poet, Yehuda Amichai:

> "Lovely is the world rising early to evil
> lovely is the world falling asleep to sin and pity
> in the mingling of ourselves, you and I
> lovely is the world."

Tamar sits within arm's reach of the wall phone in the kitchen, yet no phone call comes from Yossi. As none had come last night.

"I know how to wait," Tamar says to Danny, feeding him small spoonfuls of breakfast, and, as if speaking to Yossi, adds, "I know the meaning of an urgent calm. And I know you're all right, Yossi. I know you're in danger, but I just know you're all right."

0820

The two American tourists are among the first this morning to go into Yad Vashem, the Holocaust Memorial in Jerusalem. She is a landscape architect; he is a professional photographer. The American woman remarks to her boyfriend how beautiful the grounds are. They agree that a grim, spare landscape could also be effective, but overdone. The well-tended beauty of the grounds is more effective. It's neither melodramatic nor sentimental. It pays homage to the past as it honors the present. He takes photographs.

They walk along the Path of the Righteous, a tribute to non-Jews who risked or lost their lives during the Holocaust to save Jewish lives.

They come to an actual train car the Nazis had used to transport Jews. The closed car sits on railroad tracks, on a platform built out over a hill, overlooking Jerusalem. He photographs the train car several times, but he isn't satisfied that the pictures will turn out compelling. They'll just look like a railroad car.

"Do you remember the guy we met yesterday at the Dead Sea," he asks, "who said that even without the Holocaust the Jewish State of Israel was inevitable?"

"The historian?" she asks him. "The one we talked to while floating around?"

"Him," he says. "He said that even without the Holocaust, the Jews would have built modern Israel."

376

"That's what he said," she says, "it's a love affair between Jews and Israel."

"But look at this cattle car," he says, "seventy-two of my relatives rode off in these things. Stuffed up into them. No water. No toilets. No air to breath. Unthinkable. Unbelievable. But it happened. Look. It's right there."

"You're going to cry?" she asks him.

"I'm shaky. This cattle car. It's the real thing. Look at it. It could have been me. You. Unbelievable."

"Look at Jerusalem," she says, touching his shoulder, turning him to a view of the city, "it's here and now. Waiting for us."

0820
JERUSALEM
<u>*WAR ROOM*</u>

"We have a phone call from someone inside Osiraq to Hussein," a Mossad Officer tells the Prime Minister. "The tape is dirty. It's from a secure line. We've sent it for cleaning."

"Clean it!" the Prime Minister orders. "I want it as soon as you have it."

"Of course," the Mossad Officer says. "Immediately."

"I'm waiting for it," the Prime Minister says.

"Yes, sir," the Mossad Officer says.

0918
OSIRAQ

After a long, silent ride from Baghdad to Osiraq, Mohammed Azziz speaks.

"Samia Sa'ad is an Iranian spy," Azziz tells Sidqui.

"No," Sidqui says. "She's an Israeli spy."

"You didn't hear me, Sidqui. She is an Iranian spy. When President Saddam just called me, he said that Ms. Sa'ad is an Iranian spy. He said that Ms. Sa'ad called him so the Iranians would intercept the call. Now what do you say, Hikmet?"

"The Iranians are pigs and cowards. They couldn't bug a secure line to save their lives."

"Sidqui!" Azziz yells.

"Yes," Sidqui says, "she is an Iranian spy."

The car pulls up to the main gate and stops. No guard stands duty. No one comes to check their car. Azziz sends Sidqui to check the gatehouse.

Sidqui checks inside, then turns back, standing in the doorway of the gatehouse, and yells out to Azziz:

"The guard is dead! Shot in the head!"

Sidqui steps towards the car to get back in, but the car speeds ahead, breaks the wooden barrier-arm, heads into the compound.

It takes a while for Osiraq to go into full alert, for Heraclium Al Hira to assemble a roll call, to confirm that one of the gatehouse guards is dead, the other gatehouse guard is missing, and Samia Sa'ad is missing. Azziz rounds up a few soldiers, calls in for a helicopter to come meet him, waits an hour for the helicopter's arrival. Just before Azziz leaves, he gives an order to the compound's chief military officer, a Major:

"One bullet through Hikmet Sidqui's head," Azziz orders.

"Yes, sir."

"Immediately."

"Yes, sir."

"Now!"

The Major runs off. Azziz calls after him:

"With your own pistol."

The Major stops, turns around. "Yes, sir," he calls out. "With my own pistol."

"Save me the casing," Azziz yells to him, "I collect mementoes."

"Yes, sir, the casing," the Major calls back, smiling, containing his laughter.

"Perhaps someday I'll have a memento of you." Azziz gets into the helicopter. He orders the helicoper pilot to the Turkish border at Dernakli. He tells the pilot, "She'd never risk the Iranian border now. She'll try to disappear into Turkey."

"Who?" the pilot asks.

"What the hell do you care?" Azziz yells. "Go!"

0930
ETZION AIR FORCE BASE
SINAI DESERT

Atari and Hamal play a game they had invented over their years of war and military operations. 'The Waiting Game.' It has no purpose. Each player puts down one card at a time. The higher card takes the pair. When the deck is exhausted, they reshuffle it, to begin again.

Cohen and Halevy put on work-out clothes to go jogging.

Samy, Davidov, and Nussbaum go off to the gym.

Gar sits in the OC drinking coffee, reading the paper, *Ha'aretz*. Klatzkin sits there also, working on a book of crossword puzzles.

Kaminsky, also in the OC, writes to his wife. "Funny," Kaminsky says, "it's target day, but I can't give a hint of that in this letter. I'm an actor, playing someone who is not myself. I'm someone writing a happy letter to his wife."

"Play that role," Gar says, "be that happy someone. It's better than being a pilot who's just damn waiting."

"I'm going over to look at the model," Gar says.

"If you don't know it by now," Klatzkin says, "forget it."

"I know it better than you do," Gar shoots back.

"Hey!" Klatzkin says, "don't get snappy. Watch

your nerves."

"Watch your own fucking nerves," Gar says. "Up there I'll be watching your ass." Gar walks away.

"He's all right," Kaminsky tries to sooth Klatzkin.

"We're none of us all right yet," Klatzkin says.

"Bullshit," Kaminsky says. "We're all of us all right."

"Sure we are," Klatzkin says, "we're all right now. We're sitting around doing nothing. Waiting."

"Losing your nerve?" Kaminsky asks.

"Hell no," Klatzkin replies. "I was born with nerves cooler than God's."

"Waiting is my time for pumping my guts up," Kaminsky says. "Keep thinking about the gift we've got for Saddam Hussein."

"I hate the goddamn waiting time," Klatzkin says. "I want to fly."

"I love the waiting time," Davidov says, "it's foreplay."

"I can't wait to get up there," Kaminsky says. "It's sheer guts. Jordan, Saudi Arabia, Iraq. Unbelievable. We're making history, guys."

0930
JERUSALEM
<u>WAR ROOM</u>

"Now. Go now," Prime Minister Menahem Begin says. "The whole country on high standby alert. Army,

Air Force, Navy. Police. Every border, every border crossing. All the reserve units."

Men and women at banks of telephones make dozens of calls, issue codes and orders. The Prime Minister himself puts in a call to Teddy Kollock, the Mayor of Jerusalem. He tells Kollock to tighten up Jerusalem and ask no questions. Then he calls Shlomo Labat, the Mayor of Tel Aviv, with the same instructions. Routine guard posts are doubled in the Old City, quadrupled at the Western Wall. Units in the West Bank are enhanced, riot gear is made ready. The Gaza crossing into Israel is closed. Everyone in every corner of Israel feels the sudden movement and takes on the anxiety. Everyone wonders and guesses at the cause, watches the television, keeps the radio on all day in the car, in the office, in the shop, on the tractor. Even, turned low, in the classroom. Every Israeli reads the signs around them, goes about their day making extra phone calls home, to family, friends, discussing the events, arguing about what it all means, waiting for disaster to unfold, not knowing where.

In the West Bank, the Palestinians take the increased patrols for an Israeli build-up against them, preparations for attacks, incursions.

The American Ambassador to Israel, Samuel L. Lewis, reports the intensified action to the White House and receives instructions to keep his eyes open. He calls Yitzhak Shamir, the Israeli Foreign Minister. The Foreign Minister is unavailable until this afternoon. He will return the Ambassador's call. The Ambassador asks for the Under-Secretary to the Foreign Minister. He, too, is unavailable. Ambassador Lewis gets the message. He calls the White House on a hotline, tells the American Secretary of State, Al Haig, that something big is up, but the Israelis won't talk.

Israeli Prime Minister Begin, in the War Room, gets the message that the American Ambassador has alerted the White House.

"Call Reagan," the Prime Minister orders. "Tell him there's a crisis, an attack from Hezbollah in Lebanon, near the border. We're on high alert and will respond to the attacks."

"Yes, sir."

"Ok," the Prime Minister says to an IDF General, "move your units north across the Lebanese border. Tanks and all. Move the tanks."

"The Americans are waiting to hear more from us," an Aide to Foreign Minister Shamir, says. "They want to know if we'll launch air strikes in Lebanon."

"Good," the Prime Minister says. "Let them wait. Let them watch the border with Lebanon."

"Exactly," Shamir agrees, "let them keep themselves busy watching Lebanon."

0945
CENTRAL IRAQ

Sixty kilometers north of Baghdad, Ibrahim and Samia approach an Iraqi army checkpoint.

Samia jumps out of the car, walks to the captain in charge, and introduces herself, holding out her hand.

"Samia Sa'ad," she says. "From his excellency's office."

The captain shakes Samia's hand, but before he can say anything, Samia walks over to the other two soldiers, asks them their names, shakes their hands, says to them:

"You're doing a good job, boys. It's important work. President Saddam himself thanks you."

Samia turns to the captain.

"They're good boys," she says. "And of course you, Captain. Your wife must be proud of you. Look at you, handsome in your uniform."

"I'm not married, ma'am."

"You will be, Captain. Believe me. A handsome man like yourself. Keep up the good work."

"Thank you." The captain salutes Samia.

Ibrahim and Samia head north.

"Did they teach you that in Mossad?" Ibrahim asks.

"I just now made it up," Samia says.

"Just now?"

"Just now." Samia laughs. "I've never done that before."

Ibrahim looks over at Samia with a smile on his face. He shakes his head in disbelief.

"You're something else. If I were a little younger, and not a married man, I'd fall in love with you."

"I could use it," Samia answers him.

Her response puzzles Ibrahim into silence. After an awkward moment, she adds, "My husband divorced me. Four months ago."

"While you were serving your country?"

"Yes."

"Bastard."

"Yes." Samia thinks a moment.

"I'm sorry. You're going home to a terrible emptiness."

"I'm going home, Ibrahim."

"Of course," Ibrahim says.

"I think you know what that means."

"Don't think about it until after you get home."

"No, I don't."

"There'll be more roadblocks. At least one. Perhaps two, three."

"What's the plan, Ibrahim? Where are we going?"

"We head due north to the Turkish border at Dernakli. We get there about 1500. Two Israeli agents will wait for us on the Turkish side with Turkish transit visas."

"What two Israeli agents?"

"I know one," Ibrahim says, "Arie Solen. The other I don't know."

"Solen?"

"He'll be there himself. I insisted. I trust him."

"You know him? Personally?"

"Yes."

"And how do we pass the Iraqi border guards?"

"Bribes. We've bribed them, and we've threatened them with retaliation if they don't cooperate."

"Retaliation from Mossad?"

"Mossad?" Ibrahim exclaims. "No. From us. From the Iraqi resistance. With help from the Kurds."

"What kind of bribes?" Samia asks.

Ibrahim laughs. "We couldn't promise them a place in heaven with a hundred virgins."

"The usual?"

"The usual perversion of Islam. So we promised them money and safety. Protection. Things we can deliver in the north."

"Will you cross the border with me?" Samia asks. "If we get to the border."

After a thoughtful minute, Ibrahim answers her:

"No," he says. "Tonight I'll make my way back to Baghdad."

"You wouldn't accept a hero's life in Israel?"

"How about an honest life in Iraq."

"After Saddam?"

"You sound skeptical, Ms. Sa'ad."

"I'm sorry," Samia says. "Maybe it's possible to topple Saddam."

"You have the typical Israeli skepticism about a

modern Islamic country."

"I'm sorry. It's a prejudice."

"Like the anti-Semitism you think pervades Iraq?"

"It does pervade Iraq. Be honest, Ibrahim."

"I won't cross the border with you, Samia. I am the new Iraq. There are more of us than you imagine."

"And the anti-Semitism?" Samia asks.

"Another perversion of modern Islam."

"What an idealist you are!"

"Who do you think built your Israel, Samia? Idealists."

"No, no," Samia puts her hand on Ibrahim's shoulder as he drives. "I admire you. But I'm not an idealist anymore."

Ibrahim laughs. "Let me achieve my ideal," he says, "a free Iraq. Then I'll become a realist."

Ibrahim swerves the BMW onto an exit from Highway 7, holds to the curve of the exit ramp, then comes to a stop.

"We can't risk the main highway anymore."

"You just decided?" Samia asks.

"Intuition," Ibrahim says.

"You know the roads, Ibrahim. I'm sure you do."

"I know all the roads."

Ibrahim drives furiously along small roads, some paved, some hardpack, some Ibrahim seems to make up himself as they rumble across dirt, up and down hills, over pitted passes. They drive through the middle of villages, and through small collections of mud huts that have been villages since Mesopotamian times. Ibrahim doesn't speak. He concentrates on driving, on the road or the absence of one, on navigation, on reaching the greatest possible speed the car can tolerate.

"Look," Ibrahim says from the depth of his concentration, "there have been times and places in history where Muslims, Jews, and Christians have lived together, sustained each other."

"You've been thinking about that all this time?" Samia asks him.

"No," Ibrahim answers her. "I've been thinking about driving. Getting you across that border. But my head keeps thinking about what you call my idealism."

1000
ETZION AIR FORCE BASE
<u>*SINAI DESERT*</u>

Lt. Gen. Mitznah and Maj. Ilan Hamal meet with the plane captains and ground crew. They brief the crews only as follows: eight F-16s and six F-15s — they name the fourteen pilots — will take off on mission fully loaded at 1600. They'll return at 1830. Any questions?

There were none.

After the meeting, Mitznah and Hamal leave the

briefing room together.

"Do you think the ground crews have guessed what this mission is?" Mitznah asks.

"No one knows this mission because it's unimaginable."

"No one would believe it?"

"No one in his right mind," Ilan answers.

"Surprise is victory," Mitznah says.

"Don't worry, the Iraqis are not waiting for this one."

"Drop one for me."

"Direct hits," Hamal says, "one for me, one for you."

1000
<u>JERUSALEM</u>

Avraham Bloch and his wife, Dora, go shopping for a pair of Italian shoes for Bloch. When they arrive at the store, a sign on the door reads:

GONE ON AN ERRAND AT 10:00 AM. WILL RE-TURN IN HALF AN HOUR. WAJDI HADAD.

"Should we wait?" Dora asks.

"Sure. Look at my shoes. I can't go around like this. I'm a respectable gentleman."

"Yes," Dora smiles at Bloch. He returns her smile. "You are, Avraham, a very respectable gentleman."

Bloch pinches Dora's behind.

"Avraham!" She jumps slightly. "A respectable gentleman. You're so predictable."

"Not with these old shoes I don't have to be a respectable gentleman."

"Then let's get you new shoes! Let's walk around. We'll come back to get some nice shoes, then we'll take Wajdi to lunch."

"Sure." Bloch embraces Dora, pulls her to him, kisses her with a passion she hadn't expected, which she absorbs with her whole body.

As Bloch and Dora walk down the street, looking in shop windows, Bloch says, "Something's going on, Dora."

As soon as Bloch points it out, Dora notices that, yes, there are more police out than usual. Small groups of two or three or four soldiers walk together. More than usual.

"Should we go home?"

"No," Bloch says, "we'll get the shoes, go to lunch. We'll keep our eyes and ears open."

"Let's go home, Avraham," Dora says.

"Are you frightened?" Bloch asks, putting his arm around her.

"A little. I'm not so young anymore."

"It's all right, we'll go home."

"No," Dora counters him, "the hell with it. Let's stay out. I feel better now."

Bloch and Dora walk back to the shoe store. After another five minutes waiting, Wajdi returns.

1000
SAFED

Tamar Ben Luria grabs the ringing phone. It's Meirav Hamal on the line.

"It's a beautiful day in Jerusalem," Meirav says.

"Yes," Tamar says, "here, too, in Safed."

"Just called to say hello," Meirav says.

"Thanks. It's good to hear from you. Everything all right?"

"Perfect. On a day like today. And you?"

"Perfect."

"How's Yossi?"

"Busy," Tamar says. "He's in Jerusalem for a few days. How's Ilan?"

"Oh, Ilan," Meirav says. "He's been gone too."

Meirav says, "Remember that I love you, Tamar."

"You too. I love you, too. Give my love to Jerusalem."

"Anything special today?"

"No. I just took the kids to school. You?"

"Waiting for some friends to arrive. That's all. I'm glad you're all right. I'll talk to you soon. Bye, Tamar."

"Nothing else?"

"You know. Everything. Bye, Tamar."

"Meirav."

"Yes?"

"Everything will be all right, Meirav. Believe me. We'll talk soon. I'll see you soon. Don't worry. ok?"

Meirav hesitates, then answers. "Of course."

Tamar hangs up the phone. Picking up her youngest, Danny, she paces the living room. Danny squiggles to get free. She sets him down. He scrambles across the living room floor.

1100
ETZION AIR FORCE BASE
SINAI DESERT

Bomb-loaders load the F-16s. Gunnery loaders stock up the F-15s air-to-air missiles, their guns, their cannon. Gas jockeys load the tanks — 300 kilos of fuel in the F-16s, 250 kilos in the F-15s. Rumors float around in the buzz of talk that accompanies work. One of the gas jockeys says that, with 300 kilos of fuel and 1800 kilos of bombs loaded, the F-16s will never leave the ground, let alone break the lock-on of a beam rider, out-maneuver a heat seeker, or evade a MiG. Another suggests the F-16s could jettison their bombs to lighten up.

"No way," another one says. "Those bombs have somebody's name on them and those boys'll deliver them in person. I swear. I've never seen anything so secret in my life."

"You're right," another guy says. "If they have to bullet in without wings they will."

"Bets," one guy says, "on how many come home?"

Everyone grows quiet. The guy who said that becomes ashamed. "Come on," the guy says, "battlefield humor. Break the tension. Hey, give me a break. I want them all home."

"I think," another guy says, "we all think they won't all come home. I just smell it. It's a tricky day to say something like that."

"Sorry," the guy who made the comment says, "I'd bet my life if that bet would bring them all back."

As they work around the planes, the guys pat them like they were animals, war-horses, alive. They mutter slogans of courage or blessing. "Get 'em." "Fly high." "Good luck." "Give 'em my best wishes for a good trip to hell." They kiss their fingers and blow those kisses at the fuselages, the cockpits, the engines. When they close the gas-caps, they turn them snug. When they hang the bombs, they check the fittings three times, the alignments, then arm them. They load the F-15s guns, check their movements, their swivels.

When they finish, they hand their logs over to the Plane Captains waiting for them.

1108
JERUSALEM

After leaving the Holocaust Memorial, the two American tourists have an iced tea at a café within sight of the walls of the Old City, the original Jerusalem. They talk with their waitress, who tells them she's an artist. She calls herself, and her group of friends, Israeli Figurative Expressionist painters, then tries to explain what that term means. She tells the American couple where all the good art galleries are in Tel Aviv-Yaffo. When one of her other customers calls for her, she goes back to her work.

As they finish their iced tea, the American woman says to her boyfriend, "We always meet the right people when we travel. And they wind up telling us their life stories."

"I guess we're a good pair," he smiles.

She laughs. "It's you," she says, "people are attracted to you."

"No," he protests. "It's you. Look at how attracted I was to you."

She smiles, blushes, and laughs. "Do you still love me?" she asks.

He laughs lightly. "Yes," he says. "I still love you."

1108
DERNAKLI
IRAQI : TURKISH BORDER

The helicopter carrying Mohammed Azziz and twelve Iraqi soldiers lands near the border with Turkey. Azziz orders the engines shut down. His soldiers can disembark and relax, but they are to stay close and alert. Azziz takes the lay of the land at the border crossing, 200 yards to the north, three Iraqi soldiers stand guard. He counts five Turkish border guards. He radios from the helicopter to the Iraqi Captain of the guards, who drives out to meet Azziz. Azziz tells the Captain of the Guards that they are expecting two renegades who will try to cross the border, an Iranian female spy, and a male Iraqi traitor. He orders the Captain back to his post to put his men on high alert.

1200
ETZION AIR FORCE BASE
SINAI DESERT

Gar and Halevy spar with each other in the gym's boxing ring. They work up the sweat they desire. Desire and sweat feed the waiting.

1200
PARIS

Hannah works on her report, making coded notes while her memory is fresh. The bell-boy brings a salade niçoise with a glass of iced tea to her room. Hannah opens the door, tips the bell-boy, but does not let him in. She rolls the food cart into the room. After eating, Hannah calls her friend, Jeannette Cenci.

"I heard you were back in Paris," Jeannette says.

"Yes, I'm through in Baghdad. The Iraqis don't need me anymore."

"Good," Jeannette says. "Let's have a drink. I'll send a car for you at 7:00."

"Fine," Hannah says. "I'll be waiting."

The car, which will arrive at 7:00 p.m., will take Hannah to Charles DeGaulle airport. There, she'll board an El Al Flight, stepping onto Israeli territory. The flight attendant will announce the flight in Hebrew and English. When she arrives in Tel Aviv, Hannah will tell her Mossad driver to take her first to the home of Samia Sa'ad's mother. After bringing what news she can reveal of Samia, Hannah will go to her own family's house. For Hannah, it will be over.

1236
ETZION AIR FORCE BASE
<u>*SINAI DESERT*</u>

The kitchen staff makes lunch for the eight F-16 and the six F-15 pilots. They prepare a special high protein meal of steak and vegetables. As they work, rumors abound about a special mission.

1236
<u>*JERUSALEM*</u>

Two young IDF soldiers patrol Krachmalna Street. One of them, Sgt. Daniel Leventov, spots a young Palestinian, Farouk Yassin, who looks suspicious, acts nervous, turns to go one way, then another. Yassin wears a light jacket, uncalled for in this heat. The jacket bulges.

Sgt. Leventov fears a suicide bomber. He calls out to Yassin to stop. Yassin takes off running up the street. Leventov fires a warning shot over Yassin's head. Leventov and his partner both yell out in Hebrew, Arabic and English for Yassin to stop. Yassin runs faster. The other pedestrians on Krachmalna Street scatter. Leventov levels his rifle, aims for Yassin's leg, fires once, hits Yassin in the lower back. The bullet pierces Yassin's kidney, penetrates his lower intestines, and passes out his right thigh, just below his groin.

Farouk Yassin's running legs hurl him forward as he leaves the ground; he lands hard, face down on the concrete.

Leventov runs toward Yassin. Leventov's partner radios in to Post Command. A Jerusalem City policeman runs toward Yassin.

A siren wails, then another, then more in an interlacing pattern of clamor.

An American-Jewish tourist couple step out of the doorway they had run into. Having just come from Yad Vashem, the Holocaust Memorial museum, they confront this moment of contemporary Jewish life.

An ambulance arrives with a police photographer aboard who takes a quick round of photographs while the paramedics turn Yassin over, check his pulse, his breathing. Yassin is dead.

The paramedic unzips Yassin's jacket. Inside, he finds six 8 ounce plastic bags of marijuana.

"Why didn't he just stop?" Leventov screams, pacing back and forth, looking at the body, looking away. "Why? Stupid kid. A bunch of stupid dope! What is wrong with these people?" Leventov runs toward the body, kicks at it once, missing it. "You stupid fucking kid!" Leventov yells. "Why didn't you just stop?"

Leventov's partner grabs him, pulls him away from the scene, walks him up and down the block. Leventov keeps complaining: "Stupid kid! I didn't have to kill him. A bunch of marijuana, for God's sake. He died for a bunch of marijuana. Why? Why? Huh? Tell me why!" Leventov grabs his partner by the collar, yells at him: "Tell me why you sonofabitch."

The American tourist tugs at her boyfriend to leave, but he walks closer to the scene. He stares at the body, at Leventov, at the ambulance paramedics, at the police. The American tourist aims his camera at different possible shots, doesn't snap, aims again, doesn't snap, aims again, then takes a few pictures, one of the body, one of Leventov, two or three of bystanders, one of the ambulance, one, a close-up of a paramedic's face. His girlfriend can't bear to watch. She moves away from the scene to wait for him. She watches him as he can't stop take pictures.

1238
JERUSALEM
<u>THE WAR ROOM</u>

Military staff brings lunch into the war room. Sandwiches, cokes, fruit. Prime Minister Begin nibbles a little. Dror eats heartily.

Soldiers, men and women, staffing the telephones and computers, take reports from all over the country, present them to their superiors, who analyze them, then present them to the Security Cabinet. Reports come in from the cities, the villages, the countryside, the kibbutzim, from Gaza and the West Bank, from surveillance over Egypt, Jordan, Lebanon, Syria, Iraq, Iran.

A report comes from Jerusalem of the fatal shooting of a Palestinian youth mistakenly suspected of being a suicide bomber. This news hits the Prime Minister hard. He confers with Shimon Peres, who advises that the Army Chief-of-Staff issue regrets for the tragic incident, that the Prime Minister announce a judicial inquiry, that army tanks move closer into position around the West Bank cities, that the settlements all be warned to heighten security and monitor the situation very closely.

The Prime Minister, agreeing with all that Peres suggests, issues orders.

The Security Cabinet discusses scrapping the Osiraq mission in the expectations of Palestinian riots and terrorist attacks. All agree that it doesn't affect the mission, the mission goes forward.

The Prime Minister tells an Aide to get President Reagan on the phone.

"Mr. Reagan," the Prime Minister begins, "an Israeli soldier has just shot and killed a young Palestinian boy suspected of terrorism. It turns out the Palestinian was a drug dealer, hiding drugs in his jacket. I want to inform you of possible problems. Will you be available in the next few hours?"

"Yes," Reagan answers, "I will be. Good luck with your problems."

"You scared me for a minute," Dror says to the Prime Minister. "I thought you were going to tell Reagan about the mission."

"No," the Prime Minister said, "as we agreed. We don't tell him until we can say our boys are in the air."

1239
WASHINGTON, D.C.

Just after 0600, President Ronald Reagan calls an immediate meeting at the White House of his Secretary of State, Alexander Haig, his Defense Secretary,

Cap Weinberger, the Chairman of the Joint Chiefs of Staff, Gen. David C. Jones, USAF. President Reagan's personal secretary orders the White House kitchen to prepare coffee and a continental breakfast.

1239

Bloch, Dora, and Wajdi Hadad leave the shoe store for lunch at the Café Picasso, two blocks down. The placemats all have Picasso drawings. The plates, cups, and saucers are Picasso-inspired ceramics. Inside, a large photograph of Picasso shows him working in his studio, shirtless and in shorts. Bloch, Dora, and Hadad sit on the patio. Like everyone around them, they talk about the police and military patrols gathering, concentrating in the streets. They speculate, they make jokes of dark humor. They could all blow up any minute. They agree, finally, that only waiting will reveal the cause of the alert.

"Anxious waiting," Hadad says.

They talk family news. They talk about their love of the beauty and the craftsmanship of Italian shoes. Hadad is quite an expert. He'd lived in Rome for many years before returning to his family home in Jerusalem to open the store.

1312
SIIRT
TURKEY

Having checked their gear, strapped on their pistols, and knives, and put the Uzis with them in the front seat, Solen and Ben Luria head out for the Turkish border with Iraq.

"At least the waiting is over," Ben Luria says.

"Not quite," Solen says. "We'll wait again when we get close to the border."

"That's not waiting," Ben Luria says, "that's vigilance."

"True."

The unpaved road from Siirt is desolate. Along the way, trucks pass going in the opposite direction; Solen and Ben Luria pass two trucks going toward Iraq.

"Let's keep going right on to Baghdad," Ben Luria says. "I'll put a bullet between the bastard's eyes myself."

"Hussein?" Solen asks.

"Him and Azziz. The worst of the worst. Right between the eyes. Two Israeli bullets."

Don't forget the mission, Yossi."

"What?"

"The mission. Samia and Ibrahim. Not vengeance."

"Vengeance is mine, saith the Lord," Ben Luria quotes.

"Yes. Victory is all I want," Solen says, "vengeance

can be His."

Small roads lead off to hamlets visible in the distance.

"They look like such nowhere places," Solen says. "Quiet and innocent."

"And who knows what they might really harbor."

"Right."

"Who knows what they already know about us."

"Us?" Solen says. "We're harmless. British engineers."

1314
SAFED

Tamar Ben Luria works in the garden. She spreads mulch around the base of the lemon tree. She plants four new tomato plants, working them around the bottom. She staggers the planting of her tomatoes to have some always ripening. She harvests four zucchini along with their flowers for a pasta dinner. Her mother loves pasta. The kids like it. The structure of ordinary life almost contains her anxiety.

1314
JERUSALEM

Avraham Bloch, his wife, Dora, and Wajdi Hadad, leave the Café Picasso. Bloch and Dora take a stroll.

Hadad starts walking back to his store, but catches up with Bloch and Dora.

"I don't get to see you enough, my good friends," Hadad says. "Let's stroll together for awhile. It's such a lovely day."

1314
JERUSALEM
KING DAVID HOTEL

Having made love, the two American tourists lie together in bed in their room at the King David Hotel.

"We've just made love," she says, "but I'm getting tense already."

"We're not used to this," he says. "We're Americans."

"We think a normal life is normal," she says.

"Try to sleep a little," he says to her.

"How can I sleep," she complains, "I keep seeing that dead kid."

"It's war," he says, "awful mistakes happen in war."

"He was just running a little marijuana," she protests. "Not worth capital punishment."

"Yes," he says, "of course not. But the situation. You can't blame that soldier."

"No," she says, "you can't blame the soldier. Can you blame the kid? The Palestinian kid?"

"For running? Why do we have to blame anyone?

It's horrifying. It's war."

"You're glad the soldier killed him. He's 'the ene-my'," she says.

"Don't be crazy," he says. "Of course I'm not glad. I'm very sad. Very. But there is an enemy here. It's not simple."

"No, it's not simple at all." She turns her back to him, curls up into the arc of his body. He brushes his hand through her hair. She sleeps.

He stares into the room for a long while, at the ceiling. Then, getting up, he begins a letter to a friend in the States:

"I'm a secular Jew," he writes to his friend. "But a Jew. To be a Jew must mean something beyond just a response to anti-Semitism and threat. It must mean something beyond a faith system. What does it mean to me? You can't imagine this place until you've been here. It's better and worse than we in the States think it is. Imagine a place full of true beauty and wonders, then add a constant state of war, actual war, protract-ed, prolonged, vicious war.

"We saw a shooting today. Palestinian kid got killed. I'll tell you the whole story when we get home. I took some photographs. It's bizarre. I'm not a war cor-respondent. I don't photograph catastrophe. But now I do? As I looked through the lens at first I felt like a gawker. But I wasn't. Watching carefully, through the lens, choosing my shots, made me a part of it all, partake in it all, take it all in. It's no cliché, but I killed that kid too, as much as that soldier did. I'm in this war now. That soldier could have been me. That kid, it could have been me too?"

He stops. He turns to watch his girlfriend sleep. She sleeps now on her back, the sheet pulled up to her chin. Still naked, he gets back into bed with her. Still, he doesn't sleep. Getting up, he dresses, takes his camera, goes out for a walk.

1345
TEL AVIV

Meirav Hamal works in her kitchen. She cuts tomato, cucumber, onion from her garden for a lunch salad for herself and her brother, David. The kitchen is bright, full of light from the sliding doors that open onto the garden.

David, at the kitchen table, opens a bottle of white wine.

"If the phone rings before this evening, it's trouble," Meirav says.

"You think?" David asks.

"You know me," Meirav says. "I have an uncanny instinct."

"You do," David agrees, "you're a witch."

"No. Worse," Meirav says, "I'm a fighter pilot's wife."

"You're my sister, too," David says.

"Don't say things like that. You'll make me cry. I'll lose it altogether."

"Lose it then," David says, "that's better."

Meirav, jumping up from the table, yells at David. "Don't do that, David! Don't do that to me!"

David gets up, takes Meirav in his arms, holds her as she cries.

"I can take it," Meirav says, "I can."

"No you can't," David says, letting go of her.

"No, I can't." She smiles at David. "But I do, don't I?"

"Yes, my sweet sister," David says, "you do."

David pours Meirav a glass of white wine. She sips from it.

1345
ETZION AIR FORCE BASE
<u>*SINAI DESERT*</u>

The eight F-16s and the six F-15s sit readied for mission.

The perimeter security and the anti-aircraft around Etzion have been on tight high alert since before dawn. All leave is cancelled, effective at 1400. All entrance to or exit from the base is under direct command of the Base Commander only. All external telephone communication is restricted, under command of the Base Commander only.

Word spreads quickly that all eight F-16 pilots and six F-15 pilots have reported to a special religious service in the chapel.

Rabbi Joseph Cohen blesses the pilots with the ancient, simple credo. He raises his hands, held in the way of the ancient priests, tips of the thumbs touching, tips of the forefingers touching, the second and third fingers spread apart, and he intones:

> *"Yivorechecha adonai v'yishmorecha…..*
> *May the Lord bless you and keep you*
> *May the Lord turn his countenance to shine upon you.*
> *May the Lord protect you, and grant you peace."*

Col. Ilan Hamal stands up before the men.

"I want to read you," Hamal says, "a short statement from Lt. Col. Jonathan Netanyahu, IDF, who, as you all know, was killed in action July 4, 1976, at the raid on Entebbe. Col. Netanyahu wrote:

"The basic assumption in our work is to prepare in the best possible fashion, so that we may stand quietly on the day of judgment, when it comes, in the knowledge that we did everything we could in the time that we had. We are prepared. Now is our time. We will do everything we can in the time that we have, in the spirit of Col. Netanyahu, and so many others."

General Dror's voice comes in from Jerusalem, by telephone, over a set of speakers.

"Your mission is inescapable. The alternative is our destruction. I join Rabbi Cohen in his blessings. I send you strength and hope. We are watching. We know where you are, we are with you all the way there, all the way home. "

Some personnel on the Base walk past the chapel. Some walk out to have a look at the readied planes, surrounded by guards. Some on the base have the leisure of a siesta. Many go on with their daily work.

1416
JERUSALEM

The American photographer walks down Ben Yehuda street, Jerusalem's busiest. He saunters past sidewalk cafés, tourist shops, clothing stores, vegetable stands. All kinds of people fill the streets. Israeli Jews in casual or business dress, religious Jews in their various religious outfits, Arabs in familiar street clothes, some wearing a kaffiyeh, international tourists, families, lots of police, lots of soldiers, lots of young military men and women off-duty, but carrying their rifles.

The photographer keeps a keen watch, takes in the scenes. The more he watches, the more he photographs, the more he understands.

A particular trio attracts the American photographer's eye. It's Avraham and Dora Bloch and Wajdi Hadad. The three of them walk hand in hand down the street. Something in their faces, their eyes, a relaxed yet alert movement of their bodies catches his attention. They embody Jerusalem, modern Jerusalemites.

The photographer raises his camera to photograph the Blochs and Hadad as they walk toward him. He waits, then finds the moment he wants. He snaps the shutter.

An Arab man, a Palestinian from the West Bank town of Jenin, runs toward the American photographer's back, army battle-knife flashing. He lunges at the photographer, yelling "Death to Jews! Avenge Yassin! Allah is Great!" With an overhand thrust he brings his knife down into the photographer's back, straight into his right lung.

Dora screams. Bloch, pulling her to him, surrounds her with his arms. Hadad screams out "No!" in Arabic.

Soldiers, citizens, and police tackle the Palestinian, wrestle him to the ground, pound him with their fists, kick at him with their feet. A policeman, blowing a whistle and shouting, manages to hold back the crowd.

Sirens blare into the afternoon. The crowds scatter. Bloch runs to find a taxi. Hadad tells them to go.

"Will it never end?" Hadad says, embracing Bloch as they each kiss the other's cheeks. In the cab, Dora shakes and sobs. Bloch lays her head in his lap. He strokes her hair.

"No more," Dora cries. "Enough. Why don't they leave us alone?"

"Yes," Bloch tries to soothe her. "Enough of the killing. For them and for us. Enough."

The ambulance medics hustle to load the photographer into the ambulance, then speed off. They know there is little chance of his survival.

Another ambulance arrives to take away the Palestinian assassin. He's badly battered, bleeding from his head, his face, muttering curses and half-conscious prayers with swollen lips, but he'll live. His name is Kaliq Hassan. He is from Hebron.

1416
JERUSALEM
WAR ROOM

"Where the hell are my telephone transmissions," the Prime Minister yells at the Mossad officer in charge of them.

"As soon as we can," the officer begs.

"Now!" the Prime Minister yells. "Before my boys leave the ground. Do you know what those messages mean?"

"No, sir, I don't," the officer says.

"Sit down," the Prime Minister commands the officer. He sits.

"We have a spy inside Osiraq," the Prime Minister says.

"Yes, sir."

"That spy," Begin almost yells at the man, "has called Saddam Husssein on a secure line. Do you know why?"

"Yes, sir, I think I do."

"Because she knows that we would intercept her call to Saddam, that we would hear what she had to say. That was her way of talking to *us*. Not to Saddam."

"Yes, sir. I understand that."

"Now," Begin continues, "Saddam Hussein *knows* our spy called him to send us a message. Saddam Hussein knows that our spy is a spy." Begin yells at the man: "Our spy is dead now! That message is the last thing that she did for Israel. I want that transmission!"

"I understand all that, Mr. Prime Minister. We all do. I'll have it for you as soon as I can, sir. As soon. I promise you. It's not fast work."

"Today it is," the Prime Minister retorts. "Today it is fast work! Now! Someone died to get that information. Don't you think it might be crucial?"

"Yes, sir, do you think I don't know that?" the Mossad officer hurries off.

The Prime Minister spins to face Dror.

"With or without the transcription of that telephone call, we go," Begin continues to yell, but now at Dror.

"Agreed," Dror says. He stares a Begin for a moment. Begins calms himself.

"Have we lost the second casualty of this mission?" Begin asks.

"You mean the spy at Osiraq?"

"Yes."

"I don't know. I hope for the best, even the impossible best."

"Me, too," the Prime Minister says. "We don't have time now for sorrow."

"No," Dror says.

1515
SAFED

Tamar Ben Luria takes Danny in his stroller to do some errands. She takes a portable radio with her, switched on in her purse. Along the way, she and Danny meet several people they know and stop to talk with them. She talks with each one as long as she can. Danny is patient today, even more patient than usual. For a time, he sleeps. He's the hit of their neighborhood. Everyone thinks he's so bright, adorable. "A lot like you," they tell Tamar.

"More like Yossi," she always says.

As she runs into friends they ask about her family.

"Yossi's in Jerusalem," she tells them. "He'll be back in a few days."

One friend she meets in front of a bookstore becomes solicitous. He's a French Jew whose family moved to Safed twenty years ago.

"I'm worried about you," he says. "You look upset."

"No," she says to him, "it's nothing. I'm a little tired."

"Take care of yourself," the Frenchman tells her, "you're young and beautiful and you have a beautiful son. I'll talk to Yossi when he gets home. I'll make sure he takes good care of you!"

"Yossi takes good care of us all."

"Oh?" The Frenchman senses her meaning.

"No, I mean of the family. Of course."

"Of course," the Frenchman says. "He's not a good man, he's a terrific man."

"Thanks," Tamar says. "I just happen to agree."

The Frenchman goes back into the bookstore, the conversation on his mind.

1536
DERNAKLI
IRAQI : TURKISH BORDER

Having shut down its engines when it first arrived, the helicopter starts up again, gets ready for a quick take-off. Its rotary blades whirl, kicking up dust from the barren land where Iraq and Turkey meet. Away from that dust cloud, on the Iraqi side, Azziz takes his men toward the border. Putting his hands to his mouth to project his voice, Azziz shouts past the Iraqi and the Turkish guards, at the two men - Solen and Ben Luria - standing beside a jeep.

"Iran will pay for her murderous sins against us!" Azziz yells. "Your two devils will never cross into your arms."

Solen and Ben Luria don't answer.

A Turkish border guard approaches Solen and Ben Luria, both shouldering uzi's. Solen hands the guard his and Ben Luria's passports. The guard examines them. Then Solen gives the guard two transit visas, one for Samia Sa'ad, an Israeli national, the other for Ibrahim Ibrahim, an Iraqi national.

"Do you speak English?" the border guard asks Solen.

"Yes," Solen answers him. "We both speak English." He has not spoken loud enough over the whirring helicopter blades, so Solen repeats himself, louder. The border guard takes Solen by the arm to lead him further back from the border, where it will be a little quieter. Ben Luria goes with them, but both Solen and Ben Luria keep their eyes on the border crossing.

"What's going on?" the border guard asks.

"We have two legitimate travelers arriving to cross the border," Solen tells him. "These are their visas. I also have the passport of the woman, Samia Sa'ad." Solen retrieves Samia's Israeli passport from his pocket. The border guard examines it. "The other one, Ibrahim Ibrahim, carries his own Iraqi passport."

"What the hell is he doing here?" the border guard points toward Azziz, "with a helicopter, screaming at you?"

"He's a madman Iraqi."

"As far as I'm concerned," the border guard says, "they're all madmen. What do they want?"

"To stop my people from crossing," Solen says.

"I'm not starting a war here," the border guard says. "Get in your jeep and get the hell out of here. Here's your papers. Fast. Get going."

Solen and Ben Luria turn to go, then Solen turns back with his Uzi pointed at the border guard, while Ben Luria turns his Uzi on the other Turkish border guards.

"I'm not leaving. We'll open fire on you. You may kill us. But you'll also die for sure. I promise you. I'm not leaving."

The captain motions for his men to hold back.

"Who are these people you're waiting for?" the captain asks Solen. He looks at the papers again. "Samia Sa'ad and Ibrahim Ibrahim?"

"They're my people," Solen says. "That's all you need to know. The Turkish visas are all legitimate. I have no quarrel with you."

"I'll phone for instructions," the Captain says.

"No. You'll negotiate with me."

"Your people," the captain gestures towards the border.

Solen turns to look over his shoulder. The lime-green BMW pulls up close to the border, behind Azziz and his men. Ibrahim and Samia jump out, Ibrahim with an AK-47, Samia with her pistol.

On the Turkish side, Solen runs to the jeep, throws open the driver's door, uses it for a shield. Ben Luria runs to the guard shack, takes cover behind it, his Uzi turned now on Azziz and his men. The Turkish captain runs toward the border yelling out in Arabic:

"Stop! Everyone stop! You!" he addresses Samia and Ibrahim, "approach the border."

Samia and Ibrahim step past Azziz, toward the border. Azziz and his men follow them with their rifles pointed at Samia and Ibrahim, at the Turkish border guards, at Solen and Ben Luria. Solen, Ben-Luria, and the Turkish border guards keep their weapons trained on Azziz and his men. In the midst of this standoff, Azziz, Samia, Ibrahim, and the Turkish captain meet at the border barrier.

"Give me your passport," the captain demands of Ibrahim.

Ibrahim complies. The captain examines the passport.

"Do you want to start a war with Turkey?" the captain asks Azziz. "You're already at war with Iran. Do you want a northern front with a mighty power against you? Are you mad? Let these people pass. They have legitimate papers."

"They will not pass!" Azziz yells. His men rush forward so that the Iraqis and the Turks are face to face with their weapons pointed at each other.

"Do you want a stupid bloody riot here?" the captain yells. "Get in your helicopter. Go home!"

"I'll take her," Azziz says. "Him," Azziz pushes Ibrahim in the back, "you can have. I don't give a shit."

Ben Luria comes out from behind the guard shack.

"No deal," he says. "No deals made. We are not Iranians, Azziz, we are Israelis. You know that Israelis make no deals."

"You are Israelis?" Azziz yells. He jabs Samia in the back with his knee. "You are Israeli," he yells, "you're a goddamn fucking Jew-bitch Zionist Israeli?" In the quickest of possible motions Samia turns on him as she raises her pistol and fires it point blank into his face. Azziz crumples. The Iraqi soldiers run for cover. Ibrahim and Samia duck under the border-barrier, run for the Jeep, jump into it. Solen and Ben Luria make it to the Jeep. Ben Luria throws the shift into first gear, swerves the Jeep around, heads east-northeast. A few bullets hit the Jeep, harmlessly. The firing stops.

No one in the Jeep speaks. They speed back toward Siirt. After fifteen minutes of hard driving, Ben Luria shouts out to Samia:

"You all right?"

"Yossi?" she yells at him.

"Yes," he yells back. "It's me, Yossi. Are you all right?"

"Yes, Yossi. I am. I'm all right."

"You, Ibrahim?" Yossi yells.

"I'm all right," Ibrahim yells. "But I should be still in Iraq."

Solen turns to face the back seat. "Samia," he says. "I cannot for the life of me believe you are alive, Samia Halevy. You're out. Let me look at you. I cannot believe it. I'll never stop worrying about you. Never. As long as I live." Solen reaches out, takes her hand in his.

"It's me for sure," Samia says. "Samia Halevy. Did they get my last transmission in Jerusalem?" she asks.

"I don't know," Solen says. "I don't know."

"Arie," Ibrahim interrupts. "I am supposed to be in Iraq."

"I know," Solen says. "You're a sight for sore eyes. I can't believe I see you again. What a day, comrade. Ibrahim. Fighter of fighters. I'll get you back to Baghdad. I'll get you wherever you want to go. After you stay with me for a little while at least. In Jerusalem."

Samia leans against the back of the seat. She closes

her eyes. Images pass through her inner vision: Azziz's face as she turned to him. Her table at the café, *The Vizier's Daughter.* Her mother's face. The Jeep tumbles over the roads, bouncing the passengers.

"Is it you, Yossi?" Samia yells over the din.

"It's me, Samia. It's really me."

"Is Hannah home?"

"I don't know," Yossi calls back.

Samia keeps her eyes shut. She hears words in her mind's ear, she sees images in her mind's eye: *It's Yossi Ben Luria. I am Samia Halevy. That's Yossi Ben Luria driving. Yossi. Poor Samir. Poor poor Samir. Mother. I will see you again after all. I see you now. I see your face that I have always seen.* Samia sleeps.

1539
JERUSALEM

At three o'clock, Avraham Bloch falls into a nap on the couch in his study. Despite the heat of the day, Bloch sleeps, dreamless, in undisturbed, imageless and serene inner darkness. After thirty-nine minutes sleep, at 3:39 p.m., a fire erupts in Bloch's dream. Bloch continues to sleep. The fire grows, expands, spreads. It feeds on no other fuel than time. Time is burning. Consumed, unconsumed.

1542
ETZION AIR FORCE BASE
SINAI DESERT

After 38 minutes of pre-takeoff plane checks, Maj. Ilan Hamal's Plane Captain, Cpl. Etzer Yehuda, climbs the ladder up to the cockpit of his F-16.

"Don't scratch my baby up," Yehuda says. "Bring her back clean for me."

"I'll bring her back," Hamal says, "one way or another. When I get home, you can have her. Patch up her bullet holes."

Yehuda leans over further into the cockpit, grabs Hamal's head, pulls it toward him and kisses Hamal on the cheek. "God speed, you lovely bastard, God speed."

Yehuda climbs down the ladder, signals for it to be taken away, signals to the ground crew to begin taxi. The tugs pull the planes out to the runway where they line up one after another, first the F-16s, then the F-15s, Hamal's plane first. Hamal's engine revs, he reads his dials, he settles into his seat. He glances at his position indicator: 30^0 10' 15" North/34^0 8' 22" East. Target: 32^0 12' 30" North/44^0 31' 30" East. He glances at his distance indicator: distance-to-target: 1184.064 kilometers. That includes planned diversions. He glances at his fuel gauges: loaded at 1430 kilos. The fuel/distance gauges give him no readings yet. His air speed: 0.

The tower gives Hamal clearance. At 1555 he moves forward slowly at first, takes the right half of the divided runway for himself, gains momentum, roars up the runway, gains speed, and he's airborne, his afterburner flaming.

Twelve seconds later the second plane, Hamal's wingman, Atari, takes the left half of the runway, powers up, races up the runway, moves into the sky, takes his place just behind, just to the left of Hamal.

Twelve seconds later number three, Nussbaum, off the right side of the runway speeds into flight, takes his position just behind, just to the right of Atari.

Radio silence. But each man knows the other is there, knows exactly where the other one is. When the F-16s have all taken off, the F-15s follow, rise up into a V-formation about one mile above the F-16s.

The armada takes formation with the F-16s at 27,000 feet, at a heading of 095, east and slightly to the south, for deception. They fly at 172 miles per hour for 3 minutes 3.4 seconds over the Sinai, then cross the border into the Israeli Negev desert. They cruise at the same speed over the Negev, just south of Be'er Ada, their last Israeli village.

They settle into their pattern. They settle into their seats. They feel their planes, the air pressures, the balance, the loft. They sense each other. The F-15s check their sightlines to the F-16s. The F-15 pilots watch the air all around, looking for bogies even before they leave Israeli air space.

Later, Atari will tell Hamal his realization, that they are all one, not sixteen. The thought passes through Atari's mind without Atari even hearing it, so tuned in is he to his plane, his companions in the air.

After 6 more minutes, the armada, Hamal first, enters enemy airspace. Jordan. Just north of Dilågha, into heavily radared territory. Hamal dips his starboard wing. Reading his signal, all of the planes form up wing-tip-to-wing-tip into a taut formation that any ground radar will read as a commercial Boeing 747. They should look exactly like the outline of a 747. They drop into commercial airspace, 36,000 feet, they slow to commercial cruising air speed, 400 miles per hour. This 747 look-alike is Hamal's trick, he invented the tactic, configured and tested it on computer, then in the air at Etzion.

1 minute 5.6 seconds into Jordan, Jordanian radar control comes on the radio.

"Jordan control to unidentified seven four seven aircraft. Identify yourself."

"Moroc Air three three six to Jordan control," Hamal responds. "We are Moroccan Air, flight three three six."

"Jordan control to Moroc three three six. Your destination?"

"Moroc three three six to Jordan control, destination Riyadh."

"Jordan control to Moroc three three six. Your point of origin?"

"Moroc three three six. Origin Casablanca."

"Jordan control to Moroc three three six. We have no flight plan for you."

All sixteen pilots listen in. Gar, in the lead F-15, signaling an F-15 high alert, flashes his wing lights once. The F-15 pilots watch the skies, especially to the north, while keeping the formation tight, wing-tip-to-wingtip.

"Moroc three three six. We filed prior to departure."

"Jordan control to Moroc three three six. You are not a scheduled flight. We are scrambling to meet you."

"Moroc three three six. We'll be out of Jordanian air space in just over 23 minutes."

"Jordan control to Moroc three three six. See that you are. We are scrambling to escort you out of Jordanian air space. We are complaining to Morocco. Out."

"Moroc three three six. Roger. Out."

Hamal holds the 747 formation. The F-15s are anxious to fly away and form a barrier. They hold with him. Not having expected a radar detection this early, all the pilots strain to keep themselves from taking diversionary or defensive maneuvers. All hold in with Hamal. For over one minute they fly steady, still looking like a 747 to any radar. Hamal needs only about 2 minutes 4.8 seconds more. He takes that time, long as it may feel. His distance-to-target reads 1006.4 kilometers.

After 2 minutes 4.8 seconds more, Hamal dips his port wing. The group breaks. They increase speed, they dive toward the desert. Out of radar range, according to the Israeli radar guys, the cartographers, the intelligence, they hit the desert. They hold their course-setting of 095 to run fast, they descend quickly to 900 feet. The F-15s ride above them at just 1476 feet. They have to reduce speed to 920 kilometers per hour to run this low, but now they are under radar. It's all desert out ahead of them in Jordan. 172.8 kilometers of desert. 11 minutes 15 seconds.

After 38.4 kilometers of feeling the floor the Jordanian attack aircraft hunt for them high up. Hamal intercepts their radio transmissions telling Jordan control they cannot locate the 747. They search south. The armada maintains course. Hamal wants no fights at this point. Even though no Arab state communicates air intelligence to any other Arab state, still, no fights, no detection. It's Gar's tendency to fly off into a fight, but Gar can almost feel Hamal's command: no fights now, fly tight.

Nothing but desert below them, they rise to skim the peaks of the low north-south mountains, then head back to the desert floor. Their formation continues on, wingman off to the left, everyone in place. Four Jordanian MiGs come after them, the sound of their jets altering the Israeli pilots. But they're gone, lost in their own airspace. Jordanian radar from half a dozen installations hunts for the armada. They all come up soft. No hits.

Hamal is born for this. The flight which animates every bodily nerve fiber, every synapse in his brain. Not a thrill. Seriousness carries it far beyond thrill. As Hamal's craft rises from the desert floor, he accepts with grace his own death. Death is no longer an anxiety of the future, but an act of the present. Any impulse to protect his life invites the error of hesitation, or the error of anticipation, or the error of bravado, or the error of grief. As soon as he takes off, Hamal forfeits his life and all of its commitments. As his plane ascends, that is the moment of his death. If and when he returns, he will connect again with the desire to live, the desire for family, the desire for food and drink, the desire for sleep, for comfort, for happiness, for his country, the desire to be a great pilot, a worthy leader. As he flies he must even abandon the desire to destroy Osiraq. To accomplish his goal, he must relinquish that goal itself to the craft and the discipline and intuition of war, and even to his own death. As the armada flies low over the last desert stretches of Jordan, the foremost to Hamal is the sound of his breath in his mask.

After 37 minutes 21 seconds of flight Hamal's distance-to-target reads 800.48 kilometers. His time-to-target reads 52 minutes 36.2 seconds. They cross over into the air space of the Kingdom of Saudi Arabia.

Below them, a Saudi shepherd gazes up, watches the flash of silver airplanes zoom overhead and past him, surround him, his sheep, his desert, in a roar of sound. As the sound moves gradually off into the distance, his silent desert returns to him.

Saudi Arabia is more dangerous than Jordan. It's a greater distance. And the Saudi radar, the Saudi surface-to-air missiles, and the Saudi air force, with its hot-blooded, arrogant, reckless, glory-seeking Prince-pilots, pose a threat greater than the Jordanians. The armada must stay low, find the right path for 475.2 kilometers. They maintain a 095 heading. They fly over the Jabal 'at Tubaia mountains, which rise 3600 feet. Hamal chooses to go up to that height rather than flying south where they could find an east-west passage through the mountains. They can't waste time and fuel to fly south. They risk the open mountain-tops. They roll over the side of one crest, port wing down starboard wing up, roll over reversing the wings, on to the next ridge, hugging the summit so that any radar might bounce off the mountainside instead of the plane. Hamal's distance-to-target gauge reads 718.08 kilometers. Down to 696 kilometers. Down to 662.4 kilometers. His eyes stay in motion from ridge to crest to gauge to wing to sky to ridge. All his pilots are still with him. Brief refuge lies 345.6 kilometers ahead. Above, a commercial flight heads north, towards Syria. Perhaps it spotted them, perhaps not.

Just past the third highway they cross over, carless as the others, just north of Kh. el Kilwa, Hamal rolls the armada left to the northeast on a 041 heading in preparation to skim the sand when the mountains end. Their new heading turns them more directly toward Iraq, toward Osiraq.

The mountains drop off, the armada drops to the floor. They fly hard, then pop up again over the northwestern leg of the An Nafud mountains, come off that leg, skim the dirt again, then pop up over the northeastern leg of An Nafud. Then down again, they ride the turf. Burning fuel. Wasting it. Hamal glances at his fuel gauge for less than an instant but it doesn't matter now, it will only matter later.

Hamal picks up radio signals that could indicate a radar lock-on but the static is too intense for confirmation and they are too damned low now for radar and there's nowhere to go but straight ahead to target. Did they catch us on the mountain-tops? Refuge ahead. Hamal makes no signal to his armada. He pushes his plane to where he can still maintain sub-sonic speed. Monkey skills and brain power. Instinct and sensitivity. 841.6 kilometers. In formation. Atari on his starboard wing. Samy in command on his left. Gar above him in his sights. Right off the turf. Through this nowhere land.

And then, here comes Ad Wadiy 'an. The key to safety in the Kingdom of Saudi Arabia and all of its princely turf is invisibility. The Ad Wadiy 'an mountains give them 206.4 kilometers of east-northeast mountain passes. They slide into them. Valleys so narrow they fly single file with the F-15s following the F-16s, with their wings brushing dirt. The other key to the passage through the Saudi Kingdom air space is to fly tight between those hills, to just brush the hillsides but never let them turn you, never let them take you, to clean them with your wingtips. Not to crash. No crashes, no detection. No explosions. No flames. Sub-sonic, no sonic booms. The kind of clarity Durham had talked about. The kind they practiced. That breath Hamal and all the others hear in their helmets must keep coming steady and straight, smooth, the body light, no tension. For Hamal, the grace of death-acceptance allows him the freedom of the miniscule motions of his stick. The ability to fly a plane where it should not go.

Hamal becomes as if lost, flying the canyons, but he is not lost by one millimeter. He becomes *as if* lost only because the combination of their speed, the closeness of the canyon walls, the curves of the canyon, make it feel to Hamal as if he has entered another world. Only canyons visible ahead. So another danger here is panic claustrophobia. Which they have all practiced before. Some of the pilots do feel an urge to jet up, get the hell out, but they let that urge pass through them, they accept the confines of the canyons.

Hamal sees nothing behind him, but he knows his guys are all right.

They fly through those canyons for 19 minutes 4.8 seconds. They focus completely. Yet, of course, thoughts pass through them. Thought never stops. But the nature of that thought, the quality of it is bizarre. Thoughts from another world, another level of being, thoughts of men who have nearly left the earth with its normal daily experience.

After those 19 minutes 4.8 seconds, Hamal emerges into strong light. Right over Wadi Hamir. Just where Highway 15 comes to a dead stop at nowhere in the desert. They have flown for 67 minutes 5.6 seconds. Hamal's distance-to-target gauge reads 375.36 kilometers. They have entered Iraq.

They fly now in the declared war zone, in the war between Iraq and Iran. The Iraqis expect attacks from the east, from Iran, not from the west, from Israel. Now they race to burst in on them by surprise. They increase speed up to 1040 kilometers per hour, just below Mach 1.

Hamal fine tunes his heading, adjusts it to 024. They will fly 201.6 kilometers to Lake Razaza, rising once to dive down again to the desert hardscrabble. Once Hamal sees the Lake Razaza water, he will have already accomplished the miraculous. He will have brought fourteen fighter planes across 960 kilometers of enemy airspace. He will then only have to accomplish the utterly stupefying, to destroy Osiraq. If no one else arrives at Osiraq, Hamal will. If only he arrives, he will arrive.

They find the water, they fly at 100 feet over Lake Razaza. They cross it in a flash, in 1 minute 4.8 seconds of blue beneath them.

38.4 kilometers of down and dirty flying and they enter the Valley of Mesopotamia. The home that Abraham abandoned. They return in these machines powered by flame to where Abraham had wandered off, staff in hand.

Heading: 024 direct straight on to target. Distance-to-target: 100.8 kilometers. Gar picks up signals on his radar from due east. Two interceptors at 010. Dead ahead. Gar, Kaminsky, and Keitan accelerate up their F-15s, charging out to meet the oncoming aggressors. Hamal, and the seven other F-16s, and the three remaining F-15s hold the course, moving into an abbreviated V, leaving the trailing F-16s exposed to the rear.

Gar, Kaminsky, and Keitan approach their enemy. The enemy planes look like F-16s. They even look like American F-16s. Just minutes before contact, the enemy aircraft turn, abandoning the battle. In fact they are American F-16s, launched from an aircraft carrier in the Gulf, recalled just in time as the American carrier Commander receives his urgent recall notice direct from Washington. Gar, Kaminsky, and Keitan return to the armada, take their positions, without reporting. The armada has not lost a millisecond.

A voice, violating radio silence, breaks in. Hamal hears:

"Ilan! This is Dror. Code seven two. Breaker Code eight five. Slash Code eight two. Answer me!"

Without hesitation — without asking himself if this is a fraud — for how can Hamal hesitate, right or wrong: "Hamal here."

"Ilan!" Dror says. "The core reactor installation has been delayed ten minutes. Can you delay?"

"Fuel," Hamal says.

"It's yours, Ilan. Call it."

"Ten minute delay," Ilan responds. "Roger. Out."

The radio goes silent. If only they have transmitted this radio contact fast enough to evade detection. All the pilots have heard it. Hamal rolls left, north, just before they approach Saddam Hussein Airport, to a heading of 015. Everyone moves with Hamal. They ascend at a 70-degree angle, they shoot up to 5000 feet, the F-15s race above the F-16s, the F-15s watch everywhere, eyes everywhere for any airplane at all. They level off at 30,000 feet, they enter the pattern of a wide circle, they follow the circle once, twice, three times, four times. Hamal watches his chronometer. He doesn't glance at his fuel gauge. Eight minutes to go. Six minutes to go. Hamal's breath tells him he has remained the way he has to be. It comes calm and smooth, regular. He watches his gauges. His headings. Two minutes to go. He heads west, a heading of 345. Radio silence. Flying by following.

After one minute of westerly flying, Hamal heads down to 3000 feet, 180 heading. Hamal descends down through 2000, 1500, 1000, 500 feet at 024 target heading. Hamal does not watch his fuel gauge. He watches no gauges now. He slows to 120 miles per hour low to the turf while the F-15s zoom out ahead. 1.2 miles ahead of target, Iraqi anti-aircraft guns blaze at them. They each take their assigned targets while they watch for the unexpected. They head in toward the anti-aircraft fire. They rage away, they spend their guts, all their ammunition, they blast the anti-aircraft guns nearly right on top of them, they fly so low that Iraqi soldiers fire at them with pistols, but the F-15 pilots can only watch their targets, they can only keep going, driving forward, toward the SAMs which the Iraqis frantically turn away from the east toward the west, to aim at these jets streaking over them, charging at them. They have to aim right into the sun. Just as planned. They squint. They can't see. The sunlight bounces off the silver planes.

The F-15s must hit the SAMs before the Iraqis fire even one of them. The perimeter of Osiraq has become a horror of machine-gun fire, blaring noise, blasts, body parts flying, men dying, men on fire, men running. Inside the F-15s Gar and all of his pilots execute their close turns in a performance of clarity, precision, trained and skilled execution. One by one they take their targets. The smoke grows thick. They strain to see, although they know their turns. One by one they hit each SAM emplacement as it still swivels, the F-15s missiles getting direct hits or close enough to destroy everything around them.

As fast as the F-15s pull out to the east, the F-16s come into the smoke-filled battlefield. The anti-aircraft is dead. The SAMs are dead. Soldiers in sheer reflex fire AK-47s at the F-16s as they rise, just before target, from the desert floor, to pop up into bomb-release position. AK-47 fire pings off the airplanes. The Iraqis fire off some shoulder-fired missiles but without any accuracy on the ground-hugging incoming aircraft. The Iraqis have no idea these F-16s have no guns. They just have two 4,400 kilo bombs each.

Popping up to 60 feet, just above target, Hamal forges forward. Thumb on his bomb-release, eyes on the prize, the geometry and the angles play in his head. The signal beeps, Hamal pickles his first bomb away, his second bomb away. The bombs fly off at 30^0 angles right down the chute, right down the triangle, gifts for Saddam Hussein. They reach their target, they burst into the dome and the side of Osiraq, they explode like hell. Hits 1 and 2: perfect.

Hamal feels the lift the bomb deployment gives his airplane, and now, 8800 kilos lighter, he can maneuver again as he pulls up fast, steep and away to the west past the corridor the F-15s have secured for him with a ditch they have dug in the sky. Hamal flies past the F-15 barrier, he turns to the north, he glances back at the parade of one F-16 after another, each in turn, all eight of them, at 15 second intervals. They pound Osiraq. They lay waste to the enemy that threatens them. Each plane makes nearly direct hits. Only two bombs miss. The smoke thickens into darkness.

Not just the miraculous, not just the inspired, or the stupefying. The awesome. That which fills Hamal with wonder and awe. Atari hears himself take a very deep breath, let it out. He shivers slightly. He continues to fly: turns into a heading of three zero five. Ascends to an altitude of 4000 feet. Atari falls into line in his wingman slot. Nussbaum falls into Atari's pocket. And they come on streaking into formation. Just above them, the F-15s skirt the limits of altitude, up near 49,000 feet. Their speed increases. Each one pushes his throttle forward slowly. Mach 1. Mach 2. Burn fuel. Fly high.

No one can catch them, no MiG, no enemy aircraft can chase them this high this fast. Radar will detect them. Yes. Let the bastards watch us. In awe and wonder. What we have done with the time that we've had. They form into the three zero five heading which takes them on a direct route straight for home, straight for Etzion, bold in the open skies. If anyone attacks them now, they will have to come high and fast at them, and no one in the world can outmatch the F-15s in the high up, open, fast running, sharp turning skies.

"Catch us if you can. We have done the unthinkable."

Hamal glances at his fuel gauge. The F-15s will make it just fine. The F-16s now have 806.5 miles of flight to landing with a computed fuel supply of 768.3 miles. Nothing to do but fly a bee-line straight along a heading of three zero five. The ten minute delay saved the Middle East from a nuclear holocaust. The destruction of Osiraq saved Israel from its wildest enemy. Hamal made his choices by the instincts of war. Only one thought occurs to him now outside his concentration on flying. If he crashes for lack of fuel it will be inside Israel. The fuel indicator can easily be off by just 60 miles. Keep the breath steady. Keep flying.

The pilots activate their afterburners. They shoot across the sky. At Mach 2, 1440 miles per hour, they have 33 minutes 6 seconds to home — across three enemy countries who all may be alert to them, who all have SAMs which could catch them with heat-seeking lock-ons. Hamal keeps his eyes off the fuel gauges. He believes he has his whole fleet with him, but he doesn't know for sure. He sees a strange apparition in the sky: a great white angel flying before him. He blinks once. Twice. The apparition is gone. The sky is not clear blue any longer, but still light, grayish light. Hamal has plenty of sun left. 23 minutes 4.6 seconds to touchdown. Or much less. Hamal watches the skies for threatening aircraft or missiles.

Gar's F-15 radar picks up the radar blips of a squadron of aircraft below them to the north. If it holds its heading, the Israeli armada will be far to the west by the time the squadron reaches their latitude. He keeps an eye on them.

17 minutes 3.2 seconds. Hamal is half way across

Saudi Arabia. 168 miles to the Jordanian border. Then Hamal will take them south-southwest right through the center of Jordan, 60 miles south of Amman, inside the perimeter of Jordanian air defenses, Jordanian strong radar. Three zero five is the only heading Hamal can take to conserve fuel. According to plan, no matter how risky the plan.

Hamal shoots across the northern edge of Saudi Arabia. If only the Jordanians have not heard of the attack yet. 14 minutes 4.8 seconds to landing. 6 minutes 5.4 seconds to Jordan. Hamal sees the angel again. He doesn't look at it, divert his focus, but there it is. It isn't a cloud. Airy, cloud-like but denser than cloud, white. And large. Huge. It floats, moving forward, ahead, just to the right, at one o'clock. Hamal blinks once. The angel is gone. Nothing. Sky. An hallucination. Strange. Two minutes to Jordan.

Inside Jordanian air space Hamal holds the heading straight on. He watches the skies north of him, even though that's Gar's job. Hamal's job is to fly straight on. Through skies, attacks, fuel shortages, fatigue, hallucinations, or even angels. Or the Mach 2 strain on an aircraft. Hamal and his flight leave behind them their collective sonic boom as they streak toward home.

The eye of Jordanian radar catches them.

"This is Jordan control to unidentified aircraft. Identify yourselves."

"Ilan. I'm Ilan," Hamal says.

"Jordan control to unidentified aircraft. Identify yourselves. I have a number of aircraft. We have scrambled to meet you."

"Catch me," Ilan says.

"Jordan control to unidentified aircraft. Identify yourselves!"

Hamal watches his read-outs, watches the airspace. He is still radio silent, but whispers as if to his F-15s: "watch out for bogies, boys." Below them a squadron of six jets stream past at about 32,000 feet. They veer east. Probably to turn around. They have the armada on radar. But in 1 minute 5.6 seconds the armada will be in Israel. Over the first Israeli village: El Ghor.

The sonic boom roars over El Ghor for over a minute. The residents search the skies, but only see something vaguely, way up.

Now, Hamal glances at his fuel gauges. 102.0 miles to Base. Not enough fuel. Where best to crash in the wide open Negev. Keep the heading: three zero five. Four minutes. Hamal might even glide her home. He descends quickly, followed by the armada.

Hamal breaks radio silence.

"Strike One Leader to Etzion."

"Etzion to Strike One Leader. You are cleared to land at your discretion, runway 2 right."

"Strike One Leader to Etzion. Roger."

As the eight F-16s, then the six F-15s, glide to the runway one at a time, right - left - right - left, the entire base personnel watch the skies from which they descend. Near the hanger where Maj. Ilan Hamal will roll his F-16 in to park, Maj. Hamal's Plane Captain, Maj. Etzer Yehuda, watches Hamal's wheels hit the ground of the tarmac of runway 2. Yehuda pumps his hands in the air.

"Yes!" Yehuda yells, his eyes filled with tears of disbelief. "Yes, you beautiful bastard, you came home to me! Yes!" Yehuda yells, even as he shakes his head from left to right to left to right and then up and down in disbelief he yells, "Yes! Yes! You beautiful bastard," until he breaks down into a full fit of crying, leans his body over, hands on his knees, and cries himself into relief. "Even I didn't believe it, Ilan," Yehuda yells loud. "I thought I had kissed you goodbye."

Yehuda stands up, counts the planes coming in. Two. Three. Four. Five. Six. Seven. Eight. Nine. Ten. Eleven. Twelve. Thirteen. Fourteen. "How can this be? It is a miracle in my own time," Yehuda says, "and I can't believe I witness it."

Yehuda reaches up to the walkie-talkie attached to his collar. Pressing the button, he speaks to his tug-driver. "Go out there and bring me my plane," Yehuda says.

"Yes, sir."

When Hamal docks, the ground crew rolls out the ladder. Yehuda scrambles up to unbuckle Hamal, who has already unsnapped his mask. Once on the ground, embracing each other, jumping, Hamal yells, "Have you called Meirav?"

"The minute you guys hit Israeli air space we called Meirav, we called them all, every wife, child, father, mother and lover. We called them all. You're all home!"

"Are we all in?" Hamal yells over the din.

"By God you are all home," Yehuda yells, then he breaks down in tears again.

Ilan Hamal takes his Plane Captain Etzer Yehuda in his arms and holds him near.

"Then, yes," Hamal says quietly to Yehuda, "we are all home. After one long journey we are all home." Hamal pulls Yehuda closer to him, embraces him tightly.

1152
SAFED

Tamar Ben Luria, sitting alone in her living room, reading, picks up the ringing phone.

"Tamar. It's me. It's Yossi."

"Yossi. My God. Help me, Yossi."

"It's over," Yossi says. "I'm coming home."

"Are you in Israel, Yossi?"

"I can't say."

"Yossi....I can't take any more."

"We're getting older. It gets harder. I'm coming home."

"Please, Yossi," Tamar cradles the phone with both hands, "please come home."

"I'll call you from Tel Aviv. That's all I should say."

"I know, sweetheart, I know. I'll wait for you."

"No. Don't wait. Sleep," Ben Luria says. "Sleep now. The kids?"

"Fine."

"Sleep, sweetheart. It's over. Don't worry."

"I'm sorry….please….don't hang up."

"No. I don't want to. Of course. I won't."

"No. It's ok. You go. Hang up. Call me."

"Yes. I'll call you. From Tel Aviv."

FORTY-TWO

At the private ceremony at *Etzion Air Force Base* on Tuesday, June 23, honoring those involved in Operation Opera, Prime Minister Menahem Begin finishes his opening remarks.

"To me, the gasoline is a miracle. I know. The mechanics and the engineers tell me the boys in the F-16s landed on what seemed like – or was very close to – empty tanks, while the F-15s only had enough gasoline for another twenty or thirty kilometers. Why? Where did it came from? I don't know. But perhaps I am a mystic, or a story teller, but I compare the sufficient gasoline to the one-day's oil that burned in the Temple for eight days and eight nights on Hanukkah. And from now to the end of my life I will call this the Miracle of the Gasoline. It burned fire in your jet engines and it lasted and it brought you home to us.

"This whole mission is a miracle. I once promised Col. Ben Luria that I would try not to lose even one member of his generation in this operation. We lost one, only one Israeli life, in training. That one Israeli life is one life we have all lost, and it is one too many.

Even among all those most at risk. It's unbelievable that we are all here together. Were I to write this as a story, no one would believe it. But, it is not a story. It is history. Generations can read the facts.

"And, of course, there is the miracle of every one of you. Some of you will never reveal the roles you played in Operation Opera, even to those of us in this room with you. Some of you played the role of faithful and trusting husband or wife, a very difficult role. My own wife played that role." Begin nodded toward his wife, Alyza, who sat on the platform. "She knew nothing until it was over. Israel will never forget you, never cease to honor you. We know what you sacrificed, what you were all prepared to sacrifice."

Gen. Dror rising from his seat, approached the Prime Minister. He called out the first name: "Colonel Yossi Ben Luria."

Col. Ben Luria rose, walked to the front, took the medal that the Prime Minister gave him, shook hands with the Prime Minister, shook hands with Gen. Dror.

Dror called the next name: "Samia Halevy."

Samia walked to the front, took her medal from the Prime Minister, shook hands with the Prime Minister, then with Gen. Dror, and returned to her seat.

Dror called the next name: "Hannah Ben Eliyahu."

Hannah repeated the ceremony.

Dror called out, Maj. Ilan Hamal.

Hamal came to the front, received his medal, shook hands with the Prime Minister and with his Commanding Officer, Gen. Dror, and returned to his seat.

No one in the audience stirred. No one coughed, cleared their throat, rustled. No one was in a hurry. Everyone needed the whole time it would take for this ceremony to proceed in its formality, with all emotion contained, restrained.

Dror called out each name in turn: Capt. Reuven Samy; Capt. Shai Atari; Capt. Zev Nussbaum; Capt. Alexander Davidov; Capt. Schmuel Halevy; Capt. Mihael Klatzkin; Capt. David Rose – whose father came to accept his medal - Capt. Baruch Cohen; Maj. Avi Gar; the rest of the F-15 fighter pilots, the men and women who worked in intelligence, communications, high level security positions of secretary, clerk.

The ceremony of medal distribution, calling out each name, presenting each medal, lasted 1 hour 14 minutes. For their own safety, the identity of every medal recipient would remain a State secret.

After the ceremony, *Etzion Air Force base* hosted a dinner to honor the medal recipients. No official or public mention was made of Operation Opera at this dinner.

Col. Yossi Ben Luria and Tamar Ben Luria sat for a while next to Hannah Ben Eliyahu.

"Samia's having a hard time," Tamar said.

"She's retiring from Mossad," Hannah said. "Solen agrees."

"As do I," Ben Luria said.

"Did Begin really promise you he would try not to lose even one member of your generation, Yossi?"

Ben Luria nodded. "Yes, Hannah, he did."

"You were thinking of me, weren't you? And Samia."

"Yes," Ben Luria said. "And Hamal. And Atari. And all of us."

Hannah stared at Ben Luria without speaking. Then she said, "Let's all keep loving each other, Yossi, for as long as we all last."

Ben Luria lifted a glass of wine from the dinner table.

"Don't make me cry, Hannah. I'm really a very sentimental man."

"I know you are," Hannah said, "think I don't know that?"

Ben Luria raised his wine glass. "To our loving each other for as long as we last."

All three drank.

Everyone moved about the dinner tables, exchanging conversations. Yossi and Tamar Ben Luria walked in on a conversation between Ilan and Meirav Hamal and Shai Atari.

"It's confession time. I had a very funny experience," Hamal was saying. "As we flew home that day, I saw, twice, I saw it twice, a huge creamy-colored angel flying up ahead of me. Massive thing. Immense. Its wings were not flying, but laid down on its back.

It moved at about my speed just ahead of me to my right, so it looked like it was moving very slowly. It soared lightly, easily. Especially for its great size. Then, of course, it just disappeared. It reappeared again, then disappeared. What was it? I must have been very stressed by that point. Or exhausted."

"Ilan," Atari said, "this is too much. Too too much. All the way home all I wanted was to see an angel, a very particular angel I have come to believe in. In my own personal journey in life, I know I have to pass by that angel who guards the gate of my own understanding. My own maturity. My own vision. I kept thinking that after the mission, flying home, I would see that angel. I hoped to. But I didn't."

Hamal laughed. "I don't believe in angels, Shai," Hamal said, "but maybe I saw your angel!"

"Yes!" Atari said. "I'm sure you did. That angel is really there. I'll meet with him very soon. I'm ready for him. I know I am. You saw him because he was sending me a message through you. Don't you see, Ilan?"

In his happiness, Atari laughed, and Hamal laughed with him, and Meirav joined in. The three of them laughed out so loud and so long that everyone else watched, but no one asked them the joke.

Dror came by and sat with Hamal and Meirav and Ben Luria. They talked about the Israeli Air Force, about its history, about this moment in its history and how they will be seen generations down the line.

"All the condemnations," Dror complained, "the United States, the UN, the Soviet Union, France, England, everybody. Everybody. The US even voting against us in the UN, passing the resolution of condemnation. We risked everything."

"Don't be hurt by them. It'll pass. They'll never know what we did for them," Ben Luria said. "But we know. Don't worry, Dror, the generations will understand us."

Dror shook his head. "How do you manage to be so young and so wise, Yossi? You don't care. You're satisfied just in yourself. You've always been like that."

"No," Ben Luria answered, "not true. I'm satisfied because of you, Dror, because you know what I've done, and Ilan, and everyone who knows, Meirav, my parents, and all those who've gone before me, Weitzman, Ben Gurion, Netanyahu, all of them, their risks they took, their sacrifices."

"And your kids?" Dror asked.

Ben Luria shrugged his shoulders, held up his hands, gestured with them. "My kids?" he said. "Someday they'll figure it out. Long time from now. And," Ben Luria added, "the Prime Minister. He kept his promise to the guys. He drove right out to Etzion to embrace them each when they got back. That satisfies me."

The music had begun. Israeli popular music. They all danced like they all worked, hard, with joy.

By 1:30 a.m., the guests dispersed. Many strolled around Etzion in the warm summer night. They would meet up with one another, talk, and wander off again in couples or groups. Several wound up at the OC for nightcaps. There, Samia and Hannah talked all night long. Sometimes, other would join them, then walk off again into the ease of the night.

Samia talked about her recurring nightmares. Who could really understand them but Hannah. Hannah, too, was in a Mossad debriefing program, re-adjusting, getting help. Near dawn, the Ben Luria's, Gen. and Aviva Dror, Lt. Gen. Mitznah, Atari and Gar all walked into the OC together.

"The sun's coming up," Atari said. "The ancient Greeks used to say that if you stand on a hilltop and tell the rising sun your nightmare, the nightmare won't come true."

"Let's go watch the sun come up," Gen. Dror said. "We can celebrate. At least this nightmare is over."

Made in United States
North Haven, CT
03 December 2024

60771659R00274